CLOUDLESS

SUMMIT STATE UNIVERSITY

BOOK 1

KATIE B. WRIGHT

For everyone who never felt like they fit in.
Welcome home.

CONTENTS

PROLOGUE

LILA

You never know how important someone is to you until they're dead. Until you're sitting alone in a courtroom full of people, feeling more alone than you thought possible.

Strangers move around with smiles on their faces while they think about what they'll have for lunch, or if their boss is happy with the report they just submitted. They sit in the rows behind me, waiting for their turn with the judge, wondering how long they're going to have to listen to this poor girl talk about her dead parents who died in a car accident.

I'm sure they're thinking about how thankful they are for their traffic violation or their unpaid parking ticket. They're thankful for their ordinary days and ordinary lives.

These strangers will never realize I'm sitting here wondering if I can cry enough tears to bring the dead back to life.

I miss the blissful ignorance that comes with not yet knowing the feeling of your worst day. You don't sit around wondering when that day will happen. Hell, you might think it already has.

I wish I could give them advice. To let them know that if you have to ask yourself if it's happened, *then it hasn't*. Cause when it happens…you'll know.

My breath stalls in my chest as the reality that they're gone hits me like a runaway train. It's like I'm moving along the tracks far too fast without a way to stop. The world blurs by without a care to the panic coursing through my veins.

That's good. That means I got over that moment early today. The all-consuming moment when the loss of them threatens to bring me to my knees.

If I fall, I wonder if I'll ever get back up.

"I know this isn't ideal, Miss Sullivan, but they will force your brother and sister into the system other-wise." Like I could forget I'm all Jasper and Posey have left. Judge Harris' eyes soften as her eyes fall to my clenched hands on top of the table. "The state of Penn-sylvania is very clear on its laws regarding the health and safety of children in this type of situation. Since there are no other relatives in the picture, I'm giving you a six month trial period to prove you are ready to take on this responsibility."

I try my hardest to keep my voice from shaking. "I understand, Your Honor. Thank you for being so under-standing."

She didn't have to give me temporary guardianship of Jasper and Posey. She could have seen my low-paying job, busy school and work schedule, and lack of support as too much to risk. But she didn't.

My frayed nerves have me almost smacking the papers from my lawyer's hands as he shuffles through them for the fifth time since we sat down. It's not his fault my tolerance level is at an all-time low.

Judge Harris adjusts her glasses on her face as she straightens in her seat. "My biggest reservation here is your lack of support. The saying 'it takes a village' holds true in this case especially. You can't do this alone, Miss Sullivan. Raising two seven-year-olds is a tremendous undertaking."

My blunt fingernails dig further into my palm, my mouth suddenly dry as I try to get my tongue to cooperate. "I have plans to get my grandparents more involved."

Her kind eyes soften with relief. "That seems wise." She pauses, as if debating whether she should continue. "I know your relationship with them isn't the best, but I think that is your best option here. I want this to work out for you, Miss Sullivan. It's clear how dedicated you are to Jasper and Posey. I truly think you're their best option here despite still having a year of college left. I just want to make sure we aren't letting emotions impede what is actually best for the twins."

"I agree, Your Honor." Even though the thought of them being taken away from me makes my handful of dry cereal for breakfast churn in my stomach.

She gives a nod of finality as she breaks eye contact to sort through the papers in front of her. "I'm glad that's settled. I'll be assigning Mrs. Evelyn Jones as your caseworker for the next six months. Expect visits from

Mrs. Jones throughout the duration of the trial period." She looks back up at me again. "She is one of our best, Miss Sullivan. I know she will take good care of you."

"Thank you again, Your Honor." The strap of my bag feels foreign in my hand as I stand on shaky legs.

My lawyer's voice fades into a dull murmur as he thanks Judge Harris for her time. I will forever be thankful for my father's lawyer friend, Mr. Porter, who has vowed to help me through all this pro-bono, even though his paper-shuffling habits make me want to pull out my hair.

My parents had every intention of building up their savings after it was reduced to pennies because of my mom's cancer treatments. Moving back to my mom's hometown was supposed to be a new start for all of us. A way to leave behind the shadow that cancer left on our lives.

The shadow of death, however, is far too permanent to be outrun.

My eyes stay unfocused as I numbly follow Mr. Porter through the doors at the back of the courtroom. The smell of caramel candy that seems to cling to him washes over me as he holds the door open.

The door clicking shut behind us opens the dam around my emotions I had no choice but to build while in that room. More stones from my dam fall with every step we take down the hall. The last stone tumbles to the ground as the door to the courthouse closes behind us.

My watery vision blurs the smile on Mr. Porter's face that I wish I had the energy to fake back to him. "That went as well as possible. I'll arrange your first meeting with Mrs. Jones. I've worked with her before, and she is as good as Judge Harris said. If you get everything worked out with your grandparents, I don't see why this case wouldn't work out in your favor." He searches my profile. "I'm so sorry you have to go through this, Lila. When news reached me about your family's return to the area, I was thrilled. Your dad and I were inseparable growing up. I just hate that your dad and I couldn't catch up before…"

Before he died.

I want to tell him it's okay—he can say it. It's not a dirty word. *Death.* It's a natural thing. Expected, even.

He clears his throat to break the awkward silence that has descended like a thick fog around us. "How are the twins holding up? Can Margret and I do anything for you?"

A small smile touches my lips at the mention of his wife. She's the kind of person who's too good for this world. "They're doing okay. Getting Posey ready for ballet this morning was a struggle." My eyes fall to my feet. "Mom was always the one to take her, so—"

He nods as sadness takes over his eyes. "You are incredibly brave, Lila."

I shake my head as I move a pebble around with the edge of my shoe. "I'm just doing what needs to be done."

His warm palm lands on my shoulder that feels so much like the weight of my dad's hand, I nearly fall to my knees. "No one would think less of you, Lila. It's not a requirement for you to take this on."

His hand falls from my shoulder as I take a step back. My sniff betrays the tears I so desperately wish to hide. "I better get going. The receptionist watching Jasper at the dance studio leaves after Posey's class, and I don't want to be late."

The sadness stays in his eyes as he nods. "I should get back to the office. Please call if you need anything. I'll be in touch."

All I can muster is a nod as our feet carry us in opposite directions to our cars. My thoughts are consumed by budgets that only work because my mom prepaid for Posey's ballet lessons through the end of the year.

I wonder how much longer I can keep doing this, and it's only been a week since the car wreck.

What the hell am I going to do when I have to add school into the mix in a few weeks?

I barely feel the impact of my feet against the sidewalk as Judge Harris' words loop through my mind.

It takes a village.

If only my mom would have told me what happened with her parents. Considering my mom hadn't talked to them in over ten years…I don't have high hopes for a joyful reunion. I never imagined Jasper and Posey meeting our grandparents at all, let alone after our parents were dead.

My only memories of my grandparents are of being afraid to touch anything at their house and picking around unrecognizable foods at their fancy dining room table.

But without them, I'm alone.

An extremely familiar burning in my eyes lets me know I've reached my pity party limit of the day. Too bad it's not even lunch yet.

I force myself to focus on the warmth from the summer sun that kisses my cheeks as the canopy of trees sways overhead. The warm breeze, happy bird-song, and crystal blue skies used to represent my favorite time of year. Now, I'm angry at the birds for having the audacity to sing such a happy song.

CHAPTER 1
A LITTLE SUNSHINE
LILA

My backpack feels like a solid weight on my back as I run through the door with a minute to spare. I let out a relieved breath when I realize I won't be late for my first day of classes.

I quickly scan the room before I'm ducking into the last row of seats. I would normally be at least a middle-of-the-room person, if not nearly-a-front-row person, but this semester will have to be different.

My butt has just contacted the seat when the professor takes his place at the podium. His eyes are red, and his tie sits slightly crooked as it falls down his chest.

He moves the projector remote around in front of him as he tries to read the text on the buttons. A relieved breath flows through my lips as my back molds to the seat cushion.

The murmurs of voices swallow the metallic sound of the zipper on my backpack opening. My hands freeze over where my notebook and fresh case of pens should be as I stare at the mound of pink in my bag. With a barely suppressed groan, I shift through the glittery supplies a *certain someone with pigtails* must have left in my bag this morning.

Looks like Posey and I will be having a talk about personal space when we get home. Again.

I collect a fluffy, pink pen, a sparkly coloring book, and an entire case of scented markers on my desk—and still no notebook. The extra weight on my back during my mad dash from the parking lot makes so much more sense now.

A relieved breath leaves my lips as my notebook comes into view at the bottom of the bag. I'm not even mad at the bend in the lower corner or the pink stain on the cover. I'm just thankful I won't be taking notes in the margins of a coloring book.

Unfortunately, my new pack of pens is still MIA. Looks like it's going to be a fluffy, pink pen kinda day.

My breathing slows, and the tension leaves my shoulders as I open the brand new notebook. The untouched paper feels smooth under my fingers as I angle the notebook in the perfect way on my desk.

Bright light flashes through the room as the professor finally clicks the power button for the projector. His voice is as slow as his movements as he says, "I'm Professor Mills. Welcome to Negotiation Strategies." His footsteps echo throughout the quiet room as he takes a stack of papers to the front row. "Take a syllabus and pass the rest back."

I'm practically giddy as my eyes lift to the front of the room. A meticulously laid out plan on a single sheet of paper is exactly what I need to set my life back on track.

I can't keep the smile from my face as two printer-warmed papers land in my hands. A throat clearing next to me has the papers floating to the floor like a leaf from a tree as I nearly jump out of my seat. I can hear the laugh in the stranger's deep voice as he shifts in his seat at the end of the row. "Sorry about that. I didn't mean to scare you."

I lift my eyes from the scattered papers on the floor to find a hulk of a man sitting at the end of my row. A Summit State University hat sits so low over his eyes that I can hardly see them. "Oh, um, it's alright. I just didn't see you there."

His smile shines brightly with the dim lighting of the overhead lights that doesn't quite reach the corners of the room. "I'm not surprised, seeing as you ran in here like your ass was on fire."

I'm thankful for the dim lighting that conceals my blush. The ends of the ribbon holding my ponytail in place fall over my shoulder as I lean forward to get the two papers off the floor. My voice falls to a whisper as I say, "Rough morning."

His seat groans under him as his shoulders shift toward me. "Well, you know what they say about rough mornings?" I shake my head as I dust off the floor crumbs from our papers. "The roughest mornings can turn into the brightest days. All it takes is a little sunshine."

I furrow my brows as I hand him his slightly dented syllabus. "I've never heard that before."

The cockiest smirk I've ever seen pulls at his lips as he takes the paper from my outstretched hand. "Probably because I just made it up."

My ponytail sways behind me as I shake my head. A reluctant smile touches my lips as I say, "You are so full of shit."

He shrugs as he places his paper on the notebook in front of him. "Maybe, but I made you smile."

Heat envelopes my face as my thumb strokes over the face of my mom's watch on my wrist. The cool glass feels smooth against my overheated skin.

I jump as Professor Mills clears his throat next to me. His crossed arms and raised brows have me sinking down into my seat. "Sorry to interrupt your conversation, but some in this room are here to learn."

The creaking of a seat at the end of the row draws the professor's eyes away from my overheated face. "Sorry, Professor Mills. It was my fault. She was just being a good sport and helping me out with the syllabus."

Professor Mills' arms fall to his sides as he lets out a tired breath. "Don't let it happen again, Mr. Stryker."

The professor's footsteps fade as my eyes fall to the man next to me. His smile grows as he takes in my wide eyes. His eyes fall to my lips as I mouth, *thank you.*

With the dip of his chin, his eyes return to the front of the room. His hands dwarf the notebook in front of him as he pulls a pen out of the notebook rings. The click of his pen feels far louder than it should in the quiet space.

The gentle scratching of his pen on paper produces a

calming melody that soothes my racing heart; a melody that not even the glitter from my fluffy, pink pen scratching against my skin can take away.

CHAPTER 2
SHIT LIST
KAM

A sense of calm settles over me as the slam of the door echoes through the hall. The thin blanket of chill bumps and the slight burn of my eyes from the cold air of the hockey rink are a welcome reprieve on this warm Saturday morning.

Wide-eyed seven to nine-year-olds fill the rink. Their eyes are on a constant swivel as they watch my team-mates set up for drills.

Hosting this camp as a team every year is the perfect start to our season. Being surrounded by the innocence of a child, who is here only because of their love for the game, always puts me in the best mindset going into our first practices.

It's also a great way to bond with the new guys on the team.

The front bench groans under my weight as I sit to lace up my skates. The incessant buzzing of a few overhead lights and the stale smell of mold betray the age of Summit Hills' local rink.

Childhood memories flash through my mind as I look around the cavernous space. Saturday mornings with my sister learning to skate, Friday night practices for the local rec league during the summers, and some of the few good memories I had with my dad when he wasn't drunk off his ass.

Nearby whispers draw me from my memories.

"Kam is here!"

"I was hoping he would be here."

"Do you think I can get him to sign my stick?"

I ignore their whispers and give them all a small wave before heading out onto the ice. "Five minutes, guys. You ready to have a good time?"

A chorus of agreement shoots through the line of wide-eyed kids as they double their efforts to lace up.

Raised brows flow through the line of my roommates as my skates take their first bite of ice.

"Cutting it close, aren't ya, Cap?" Dax's cocky grin lets me know just how thrilled he is to not be the one cutting it close on time for once.

The strings of my hoodie sway with my shrug. "Ellie was having car trouble."

Wyatt's usual frown seems magnified under the bright, fluorescent lights. "Is she okay?"

"Yeah, man. She's fine. Something's wrong with her back left tire, though. Keeps going flat no matter what I do. Think you could get your car guy to take a look at it? He did a pretty good job fixing her window last year."

He scratches the dark scruff on his cheek as he nods. "Yeah, sure. I'll take care of it."

Mace shakes his head as a smile pulls at his lips. "It

really pays to know everyone." Wyatt's frown turns into a full-blown scowl as Mace elbows him in the ribs. "Tell us your ways, Ranger. I've never seen someone so quiet know so many people."

He shrugs as his eyes survey our other teammates around us. "Words aren't the only thing that matters."

A muttered, "For fuck's sake," draws my attention from my roommates to my right. Colt's face still holds a few pillow lines as he struggles with the cones in front of the net. His brows crease as his eyes volley between his *friends* around him. "Don't we *pay* people to do this shit?"

I blow out a deep breath. "No cursing in front of the kids, Colt."

Thankfully for him, I don't hear whatever it is he mumbles under his breath.

Dax doesn't even try to contain his chuckle as his eyes fall to the cursing freshman. "Is he the one?"

Mace's head swivels to our roommate with a look of disbelief on his face. "There's no way he's the one."

I nod as I watch the freshman struggle with something we all learned how to do when we first learned to play hockey. "It's him. I was in Coach's office when he showed up last week."

Waves of disappointment radiate from Mace as he crosses his arms. "I don't believe that kid has a dad in the NHL for a second. What did his daddy do? Pay someone to fudge his records? The poor kid can't even set up his own cones."

Wyatt's sigh carries through our group. "I've seen Colt's tapes. He might be an entitled rich boy, but the kid can play."

Mace shifts on his skates as he shrugs. "I mean, it's not like having a dad in the NHL will give him any favors in Coach's eyes." His eyes shift between Wyatt and me as a smirk lifts his lips. "It's not like it helped you two any."

My eye roll can't keep the smile from my face.

Our heads swivel in unison as raised voices pick up from just a few feet away. The little boy's blond hair bounces with every word as he says, "You're just mad Posey didn't want to sit with you at lunch." His little hands tighten around his hockey stick as redness creeps over his cheeks. "You wouldn't be saying those mean things if she would have said yes."

His opponent's scoff has my eyes narrowing. His posse's smiles widen from their places behind him as he crosses his arms. "I wouldn't have even asked Posey if Mrs. Smith didn't make me. Who would want to sit with a new kid, anyway?"

The blond boy's eyes flash with anger as his shoulders rise. It's the slight twitch of his stick that has my feet moving before I fully think it through. "Hey, guys!" The blond's eyes never leave the boy in front of him as he relaxes his grip on his stick. His opponent's eyes flash with recognition as I close the short distance between us. Right away, my eyes fall to the bully's name tag. "Have you done your warmup laps yet, Matt?"

His hair sways around his ears as he shakes his head with wide eyes. "You're Kam Stryker! I was really hoping you would be here! My mom put a marker in my bag so you can sign my stick."

I pat him on the shoulder as I force a smile to my

face. "I'll sign everyone's sticks after we're done today. Why don't you guys get in some warmup laps before we start?"

His smile widens as he turns to look at his posse gathered behind him. "Come on, guys." The blond boy's scowl deepens as he watches the group skate away.

My eyes fall to his name tag as I tilt my head. "What was all that about, Jasper?"

He just shrugs like he didn't just almost deck his teammate over the head with his stick. "He was being a dick."

Well, alrighty then.

I roll my lips to keep my smile from slipping free. "Why was he being a, uh…jerk?"

"He was making fun of Posey, and I didn't like it." The fury in his eyes gives way to a chilling stillness as he looks down at his skates. "I'm the man of the house now, so it's up to me to stand up for her." He looks back up at me with such sadness in his eyes, it nearly takes my breath. "What kind of brother would I be if I let him talk about my sister like that?"

A small smile pulls at the corner of my lips. "I know what you mean. I have a sister, too."

His eyebrows shoot upward as he tilts his head. "You do?"

His hands twist in his shirt sleeves as I nod. "Sure do. She's my twin, so that means we're pretty close."

His eyebrows nearly disappear into his hairline as a genuine smile lights his eyes. "Posey is my twin, too!" He holds up four fingers. "I'm older by four minutes."

My smile grows with his as I lower my voice and

shield the side of my mouth, like I'm telling him the nuclear launch codes and not my birth order. "Well, don't tell anyone, but my sister is a few minutes older than me. She thinks that makes her the big sister and me her little brother."

He scrunches his nose as he stretches as high as he can to poke my bicep. "You're definitely not little."

He giggles as I poke him right back. "Yeah, well, you're not little, either. It takes a really strong person to stand up to a bully." A lightness consumes his eyes as I say, "You stood up to Matt even though he had all his friends standing at his back. You're the tank that charges into battle, Jasper."

He grows four inches in front of me as a splitting smile takes over his face. "I'm a *tank?*"

"You sure are." My poke against his bicep brings another round of giggles to the surface. "Now, go do your warmup laps, Tank."

He holds his head high as he skates away.

My smile falls as I watch Matt and his posse laugh from their spot at the front of the group. Their carefree smiles and easy laughs bring a sudden wave of tension to my jaw.

Well, Matt, welcome to my shit list.

CHAPTER 3
SMOOTH TALKER
LILA

"Come on. Come on." The red light taunts me as I check the clock on my dash for the hundredth time. The numbers tick by without a care in the world as I drum my fingers along my steering wheel.

I am so late.

The tension in my shoulders grows to an uncomfortable level as I beg the light to change colors. I let out a breath of relief and send it a silent *thank you* as it flashes to green.

My tires squeal as I speed through the abandoned intersection. I slow as the needle on my speedometer approaches sixty. "Better to get there late and alive, than not at all," I mumble to myself. Solid advice I wish my parents would have taken.

A sigh of relief escapes my lips as the sprawling building emerges. The black Tahoe in the last row stands out in the empty parking lot. My stomach churns at the inconvenience my poor planning has forced upon this unfortunate soul.

My car sways as I push the gearshift to park and swing my door open. A few stray hairs that escaped my ponytail hours ago fly around my face as the summer breeze washes over my face.

Intense heat rises from the pavement as my sneakers dig into the rough surface of the parking lot. Dark water marks and chipped paint decorate the surface of the community athletics building. A multitude of roof pitches and siding types allude to the many phases of life this building has seen.

The sudden loss of pressure from around my waist and a clatter behind me makes me realize I forgot to take off my apron when I left The Penalty Box. My head swims as I quickly bend to retrieve the battered apron from the ground before continuing up the stairs to the door.

The sting from the sun-warmed door handle against my palm is fleeting as I emerge into the quiet corridor. My sneakers pounding against the laminate floor and the smell of stale air are my only companions as I follow the signs to the rink.

Faded ink and yellowing paper act as my guide through the maze of hallways and locker rooms that seem to stretch on forever.

My grip tightens around my apron and my feet halt as the sound of my brother's laughter floats through the door at the end of the hall. A stuttered breath catches in my throat as a wave of sorrow threatens to drown me.

I can't believe I almost forgot what his laugh sounds like.

My feet carry me through the doorway and into the icy chill of the rink. Bright overhead lights shine like a spotlight on the ice as my brother laughs.

For the first time in weeks, my mother's watch on my wrist, whose weight I cannot seem to outrun, is not at the forefront of my mind.

The sound of Jasper's laughter melds with that of the man following him around the rink. His giggles chase away the chill in the air as I descend the stairs that will take me to the edge of the ice.

Jasper's eyes lift to mine at the sound of my footsteps. "Lulu!" His smile, that I've missed so much, takes over his face. "Did you see how fast I was? It felt like I was flying!"

"Hey, Jellybean! You look great out there!" I clear my throat to hide the watery undertone of my voice. "Change into your sneakers so we can get going."

Pain blooms in my chest as his shoulders fall. "Do we have to go?"

My smile is tight as I say, "I've got to get back to work. I only have a few minutes left of my lunch break."

The smile never returns to his face as he hurries off toward the bench.

The sharp sound of skates against the ice pulls my attention to the man who deserves an apology. My words stall in my open mouth as my eyes catch on his. Their warm depths call to a part of me I don't have the energy to acknowledge.

What beautiful eyes.

The cocky smirk that pulls at his lips looks so familiar, I have to try not to stare as he says, "Your eyes are beautiful, too, Sunshine."

I did not; I repeat—I. Did. Not. Just say that out loud. His smirk grows as flames creep up my neck to consume my cheeks. If the floor could open up and swallow me now, that would be wonderful.

I tilt my head to survey the familiar outline of his jaw and the distinctive tilt of his lips as I try to forget about my slip of the tongue. "Why do you look so familiar?" I shake my head as I push a stray strand of hair out of my eyes. "I'm sorry. My awkwardness normally isn't this bad, and I'm not normally late like this, either." I blow out a deep breath. "Can you just forget I said anything? I don't think I can handle the embarrassment otherwise."

His eyes twinkle, something I didn't know was possible outside of fairy tales and story books, as he shakes his head. "Not a chance. I'm having way too much fun, Sunshine."

A divot forms between my brows as I cross my arms to fight off the chill in the air. "Why do you keep calling me that?"

He shrugs as he leans his elbows against the wall separating me from the ice. "You didn't give me your name in class. Jasper called you Lulu, which I'm pretty sure is a nickname and not your real name. And since Lulu is already taken, I figured I would go with *Sunshine* instead."

The roughest mornings can turn into the brightest days. All it takes is a little sunshine.

I narrow my eyes as my fingers dig into my thin t-shirt in search of warmth. "You're the sunshine guy?"

A loose lock of hair falls onto his brow as he shakes his head. "Nah. You're the sunshine girl, I'm just Kam." Creases form at the edges of his eyes as he tries to contain his smile. "Do I get to know your name?"

"Oh, um, I'm Lila."

His smirk blooms into a full grin. "Lila."

A blush creeps over my cheeks as my gaze falls to my feet. "Um, I'm sorry again for the inconvenience. It won't happen again."

His smile falls as a line forms between his brows. "Getting to play with Jasper was *hardly* an inconvenience."

Kam opens his mouth like he's about to say something else as Jasper chooses this moment to run toward me, his backpack bouncing on his back with every step. "I'm ready, Lulu." He turns toward Kam with a look of awe in his eyes. "Thanks for everything, Kam."

Kam only ruffles his hair and smiles, completely unaffected by the god-status my little brother has placed on his shoulders. "Anytime, Tank. I'll see you at the scrimmage tomorrow?"

Two sets of expectant eyes turn toward me. Jasper clasps his hands in front of him like he's praying. "Can we go, Lulu? Kam invited everyone from camp. I even asked him to get you and Posey some tickets, too."

His eyes light up as I nod. "I think we can work that out." The growing smile on his face falls with my raised finger. "But you have to promise to get your science project done tonight. We were supposed to work on it tomorrow."

Jasper's fist launches into the air as excitement fills his voice. "Yes! I promise I'll get it done when we get home."

Kam's smile returns in full force as his eyes move to mine. "The tickets will be a will call. Just give them Jasper's name." His voice falls to a whisper as Jasper lists off everything he needs to do before the scrimmage tomorrow. "I'll see you tomorrow, Sunshine."

I struggle to swallow as his chocolate eyes hold me captive. "Yeah, um, we'll see you tomorrow."

My ponytail sways around my shoulders as I turn toward the stairs. Kam's voice halts my foot mid-air before I take the first step. "Wait!" His deft fingers pluck the pen from the apron I forgot is in my hands. "Here's my number." Warm fingers pull my hand closer before the pen contacts my skin. "Text me if you have any trouble with the tickets and if you're going to be late picking Jasper up next weekend." His scribbling on my hand falters as he backtracks. "Not that it was a problem or anything. Just so I'll know what to expect and all that." His voice falls to a mumble. "Just shut up, Kam."

I examine the scribbled digits on the back of my hand as he slips the pen back where he found it. A small smile lifts the edges of my lips. "Was that just a clever way to give me your number?"

He bites the edge of his lip as he fights his smirk. "If I was truly clever, I would have figured out a way to get *your* number instead." He loses the battle as his smirk slips free. "This was all I could come up with on the spot."

I shake my head as my own smile slips free. "You're a smooth talker, Kam."

The lightness in his eyes matches the brightness of his smile. "Call me whatever you want, cause I got you to smile again."

Jasper's fingers dig into the hem of my shirt as he

shifts on his feet next to me. "Come on, Lulu. You'll be late for work."

I don't need to glance at my watch to know he's right.

My voice softens as I take a step backward toward the stairs. "Bye, Kam."

"Bye, Sunshine."

CHAPTER 4
MOMENT OF SILENCE

KAM

The Penalty Box's proximity to campus and cheap food are the initial draw for students. The reason we keep coming back, however, is not only because tradition calls for every SSU victory to be celebrated here, but because there's no other place like it in Summit Hills.

The sticky floors and smell of stale beer lingering in the air adds to the charm of the restaurant that's become a rite of passage of sorts. You're not truly an SSU student until you've downed an entire basket of chips and salsa on your own. That's just the way it is.

I originally turned down the guys' offer to grab a bite to eat before we headed home for the evening. That plan went to shit the moment I saw Lila in her Penalty Box t-shirt and learned she was on her lunch break.

Does that sound a bit stalker-ish? Probably. Do I care? Kinda, but not enough to *not* show up for a late lunch.

The spicy smell of wings burns my nose as the rush of air hits my face from opening the front door to the restaurant. I've been here countless times throughout my life. This time should be no different. Except it is, because *she* is here.

I wipe my sweaty palms on my gym shorts as I look for a blonde ponytail and the thin, white ribbon she's been wearing every time I've seen her.

Muscle memory leads me to our usual table in the back corner as my eyes stay on a swivel.

"Well, look who decided to show up." I don't need to stop scanning the room to know Dax has a huge grin on his face from my change of heart.

"I was hungry. Might as well grab a bite before heading home." My unusual lie slips by unnoticed by my friends as I sink down in my seat.

Wyatt's ever-stoic presence looms closer as he whispers, "I'm assuming the parents showed up for Jasper?"

"Sister, actually."

A glance in his direction shows his eyebrows shoot up his forehead. "Sister? That's, uh, unexpected."

I nod as I resume my search around the room. "I know. And get this, you remember the girl I told you about in my negotiations class?"

"Yeah, we remember," Dax answers for the group as all heads turn my way, their interest piqued by the mention of Lila.

"Well, it was her. She's Jasper's sister. And that's not all."

Dax leans closer, his elbows planted firmly on the table, unbothered by the water rings left behind by his glass. "I'm listening."

That's when I spot her. Her ponytail has loosened to

let golden wisps of hair fall around her beautiful face. The dim lighting hides the dark circles and clouded eyes that seem to be her constant companions.

I incline my head in her direction as I straighten in my seat. "That's her."

All my friends crane their necks to watch as she rushes through the crowded space. Dax whistles as Mace mutters, "Damn."

Everyone turns to me with a gleam shining brightly in their eyes.

Dax's face breaks into his usual shit-eating grin as he shoots from his chair. The scrape of the legs on the sticky floor earns glances from patrons around us. He places a hand over his heart as he bows his head. His usual grin falls away to be replaced by solemn eyes. "Let's have a moment of silence for our fallen comrade. Kam was a good man. Stubborn, but good all the same. People will remember his fierce loyalty, but—Hey!"

I interrupt his grand gesture by pulling him down into his seat. The sound of his tailbone hitting the chair is loud enough to hear over all the chatter. I feel zero remorse.

"Don't be dramatic," I seethe, pivoting in my seat so I see her drop off drinks to a table across the room. The excess length of her apron strings float behind her as she disappears through the kitchen door.

Dax only rubs his tailbone and shrugs, completely undeterred by my protest. "I'm just calling it how I see it, Cap. Hell, I hardly recognize you. If your thirty-minute recounting of seeing her in class wasn't enough, the look on your face says it all."

Mace nods in agreement. His mouth full of French

fries obscures his words. "I've never seen you like this, man." He swallows before chewing not nearly enough and turns to our roommates. "When have you ever heard Kam talk about a girl at all, let alone like this?"

Wyatt's green eyes pierce me, but he says nothing.

I'm saved from answering by Kim's long, pink-tipped fingers curling around the back of my seat. Her flirtatious smile hasn't changed since she learned how to use it in elementary school. "What can I get ya, Kam? The usual?"

My eyes never stray to hers as I say, "Yep, and a root beer. Make the food to go. Thanks, Kim."

"Sure thing, Kam." Her fingers drag along the back of my neck before she struts off, clearly walking with a purpose.

Dax blows out an exasperated breath. "Pretty sure that girl's got your wedding planned already, man."

Mace's groan speaks for us all. Thankfully, Kim's distraction shifts the conversation away from my love life, or lack thereof.

I barely contribute to the guys' conversation about tomorrow's scrimmage, spending most of my time watching Lila.

She never stops moving, constantly refilling drinks, delivering orders, and running back to the kitchen to do it all over again. After only a few minutes of watching her, I realize she has almost double the tables of the other servers.

I don't know how she's managing it all, but it's damn impressive to watch.

"Earth to Kam."

I blink rapidly as my roommates come back into

focus, only to find Dax snapping his fingers in my face. "I'm sorry. What were you saying?"

Mace fights his smile as he pushes my to-go bag closer to me. "You ready to go, man?"

I've been so caught up in my head, I didn't even realize Kim brought my to-go order out already.

My movements are slow as I stand. My eyes scan the table in search of any way to delay leaving as I fiddle with my to-go bag.

A blur of red draws my attention to Dax as he walks over to Lila and smiles. Her brows crease as his hands move around him like he's telling the most riveting story.

Mace mumbles, "Oh, shit."

I'm already heading that way, my long strides eating up the distance between me and her in seconds. The other tables are a blur in my peripherals. She's the only thing I can see. Lila and my dumbass best friend who's known for flirting with everyone.

Do I think he will try to "steal" her?

No, of course not.

Do I think he will do everything within his power to push every button I have?

Hell yes I do.

CHAPTER 5
GENDER-FLUID FISH
LILA

Who is this guy, and why the hell is he talking to me about gender-fluid fish?

The wetness from the tray under my arm soaks into my shirt sleeve as I try to control my facial expressions.

"So you see, if they want to ensure there's always a breeding pair left, the most dominant male will need to change from male to female. It's irreversible, too." A dimple on his right cheek makes an appearance as his smile grows along with the volume of his voice. "And that's why clownfish are my favorite saltwater fish." A shadow appears over his shoulder that seems to bring even more deviance to his eyes. He drapes an arm across an unimpressed man's shoulders. "Isn't that cool, Kam?"

Kam?

My head snaps up so fast, pain shoots through my neck. I not-so-subtly rub the sore spot as my eyes fuse to the gorgeous hockey player. Freed from the rink's harsh fluorescent lights, his chocolate eyes convey such striking depth that my breath catches in my chest.

I draw in a quick breath when he speaks my name. "Lila." His voice rumbles between us. "I hope Dax didn't bother you too much." His thunderous eyes fall to his blond friend before softening as they return to me. "He doesn't know the meaning of *personal space*."

I'm already waving away his comment. "I'm used to it."

Set ablaze by my words, his piercing eyes flash to his friend once more.

His friend, Dax, raises his hands in front of him. "Cap, I swear this is my first time talking to her. Besides," he motions toward Kam's phone number still present on the back of my hand, "I see you've already staked *your* claim."

"No!" I race forward before I cause any more trouble with my careless phrasing. "I meant from my siblings. They don't know the meaning of personal space, either." Kam's eyes, now extinguished, return to me. "Hence the fluffy pen and coloring supplies in my bag in class."

A smirk plays on his lips. "I kinda liked the pink pen."

Two new hulking forms join our group. One with scruffy, black hair and stern brows. The other with dark, curly hair and an easy smile.

The one with the easy smile extends his hand for a handshake. "Hey, Lila. I'm Mace." He inclines his head to the other new guy next to him. "And this is Wyatt. He's grumpy, but we love him anyway. What's your favorite breakfast food?"

My mouth opens and closes like the clownfish Dax was telling me about. "Uh, blueberry pancakes, I guess."

Mace's smile never fades, even when Wyatt smacks the back of his head.

Kam's jaw clenches as he shoves his friends toward the front door. "Well, we'll let you get back to work. It was great seeing you again, Lila. I'll see you at the game tomorrow."

My feet stay rooted to the ground as the four guys leave the restaurant. The sensation of eyes burning a hole in the back of my head from the surrounding patrons finally spurs me into motion. I barely feel my feet hit the ground as I hurry through the swinging doors to the kitchen with my empty tray tucked under my arm.

The sound of shoes squeaking on the damp floor and metal spatulas hitting the grill fades to the background as I try to catch my breath.

Posey and Jasper still sit huddled in their usual booth in the corner, completely oblivious to my heart trying to fight its way out of my chest.

What the hell is wrong with me?

"Hey, Lila!" I nearly jump out of my skin as the cook inclines his head toward the plates on the warming table. "Your order's ready."

I give him a thankful smile as I load my tray with shaky hands. The overfilled tray settling on my shoulder pulls a groan from my lips. My back and feet protest my decision to accept an extra section tonight. I was the first to volunteer after a coworker called in sick last minute. I'll never turn down the extra money.

At least that means I won't have time to think about Kam and his chocolate eyes.

LILA'S JOURNAL

Hi, Mom.

You've officially been gone for one month. It seems like a lifetime since that day, but also just minutes.

Posey and Jasper are still sleeping in my room. Jasper has moved to a blanket fort in the corner, but Posey is still in the bed with me. She's here right now, actually.

Jasper still doesn't sleep much. I wish I could ask you how you got him to sleep. I didn't have as much trouble with him tonight, though. Camp must have worn him out.

Oh! How could I forget? Jasper smiled today. And laughed! Can you believe it?! An honest-to-goodness laugh.

Posey's still crying every night in the bath. She thinks I don't know. Maybe I should tell her I cry every morning in the shower, too.

I met someone, Mom. Don't get too excited.

I can't show an interest in him. It's not fair to bring him into all this and to force something new onto the twins. Posey and Jasper need me. I just wanted to let you know, anyway.

His friends are fun, though. Dax told me about his favorite fish and Mace asked what my favorite breakfast is. I mean, what's up with that?

I've already pegged each of them, though. Want to hear what I think so far?

There's Dax. He's the troublemaking, dimpled panty-collector.

There's Wyatt. He's the brooding, dark-eyed panty-killer.

There's Mace. He's the confident, easy-going panty-slayer.

And then there's Kam. Kam is the tempting, chocolate-eyed panty-melter.

You know the type, right?

I don't know how to explain it, but they feel important somehow. Maybe they're supposed to help Jas or something. I wish you could have seen him today, Mom. He looked great on the ice. Dad would have loved watching him skate.

I wish both of you were here, Mom.

Love always,

Lila

CHAPTER 6
WHITE RIBBON
LILA

My reflection stares back at me in the mirror on my closet door. The piles of clothes tossed haphazardly around the room fade from view as I push my statically charged hair from my eyes.

"You look really pretty, Lulu." Posey's feet dangle off the edge of my bed as her eyes take in my outfit once more. "Maybe add a bow or something. That always helps."

My butt sinks into the mattress as I pull my sister into a hug. "Thanks, Ladybug."

Her high pigtails tickle my nose as she shifts to throw her arms around my neck. We're enveloped in the fragrance of her strawberry shampoo as the cheerleader costume—that she insists on wearing to the scrimmage—bunches between us.

She releases me from the hug to grab a thin, white ribbon from my nightstand. With her tongue sticking out of the corner of her mouth, she ties the ribbon around the elastic band that's holding half my hair away from my face. "There. Now you're perfect."

The thumping of little feet against the wooden floor of the hallway is my only warning before Jasper barrels into my room at full speed. "Come on! Come on! We're going to be late!"

The number 23 sits proudly on the front and back of his jersey. This jersey is one of the last gifts from my parents.

The twins' outfits are at least suitable for the game. My scratchy, free SSU t-shirt, given to me during my initial tour of campus over the summer, will have to be enough for me. At least I can wear a long sleeve shirt under it to save myself from the chill of the rink.

"Alright, alright. Let's get going." They burst from my room and reach the front door of our house before I've even gotten up from my bed. I yell after them, "Don't forget your jackets!"

I'm met with groans of protest before Jasper yells back to me, "But it's so hot outside!"

"But it won't be in the rink. Grab us each a toboggan out of the storage bins in the hall closet before you put your shoes on! Oh, and some gloves!"

Did I go a bit overkill with the amount of layers I put them in? *Probably.* But I figure it'll be better for them to shed a few layers than to be cold for the entire game.

You can never be too careful with these things.

Wow. I sound like Mom.

I thought my parents were crazy for buying a house so close to campus, but now I'm thankful for the proximity as we inch along in traffic on our way to the rink.

The unnecessary worry in Jasper's voice brings a smile to my face. "Do you think we'll make it in time to watch them warm up?"

Posey shifts in her booster seat behind me. "Calm your horses, Jas. We're almost there."

I roll my lips to contain my laugh as I let off the brake to roll forward. "Do you mean *hold* your horses, Ladybug?"

I can practically hear her eyes roll. "No. You can't *hold* a horse. They're too big!"

My eyes flash to hers in the rearview mirror. "Right. Of course. What a silly suggestion."

"There it is! There's the rink!" Jasper's seat belt locks tight with a mechanical click as he strains to see through the windshield. "Look how big it is, Lulu!"

The awe in his voice brings a smile to my face as I follow the line of cars into the parking lot. "Pretty cool, huh, Jellybean?"

"The coolest!" His seat belt clicks open as I swing into a parking space that bigger vehicles have clearly passed up, leaving the perfect spot for my tiny Corolla. I can't even be mad about the prints he'll inevitably leave behind as he plasters his face to the window. His voice is so soft I almost miss his mumbled, "Wow."

I clear my throat to keep the emotions at bay. "You guys ready to go?"

Jasper's wide eyes never leave the rink as he says, "So ready!"

Jasper bounces on his toes as we wait in line at will-call. He cranes his neck to catch glimpses into the rink through the crowd passing by. "Where do you think our seats are?"

"I don't know, Jellybean." A quick glance at my watch lets me know we're cutting it close on time. My eyes bore into the back of the lady's head in line ahead of us.

Come on. Come on.

I don't even try to contain my sigh of relief as she moves away with a smile on her face.

The middle-aged woman at the desk never looks away from the stack of tickets in front of her as she says, "Name?"

"Oh, um, Jasper Sullivan."

I shift on my feet as her neatly trimmed nails sift through the tickets with practiced ease. Her words are almost robotic as she hands me our three tickets secured together with a pink rubber band. "Enjoy the game."

The thick paper feels smooth against my chilled fingers as her mumbled, "Name?" to the next customer fades into the chatter of the busy space. *Maybe gloves weren't such a bad idea after all.*

Posey snatches the pink rubber band before I've gotten it fully off the tickets. She secures it around her wrist as we move to the side to examine our tickets. My eyebrows raise as I take in our seat number and section. "This can't be right."

Jasper snatches the tickets from my hand before I can examine them further. "Front row seats? No way! Come on! Let's go!"

His fingers feel warm against mine as he pulls us toward our section. I grasp Posey's hand tightly in mine before she can get lost in the crowd. "Slow down, Jas."

He shakes his head as he leads us through the sea of people. "No way! They're probably already warming up!"

The tight chatter of the hall gives way to distant murmurs as we emerge through the tunnel leading into the rink. My eyes bulge as I struggle to take in the space that's a far cry from the community rink. "Holy shit."

Jasper grins over his shoulder as Posey mutters, "That's a dollar in the swear jar when we get home."

I tilt back my head to look at the gigantic screen hanging over the center of the rink. Photos of the players flash on the screen along with their numbers, positions, and age.

I stumble on the top stair leading down to our seats as Kam appears on the screen. His chocolate eyes stare into my very soul. His posture highlights his intimidating presence as a formidable opponent to any player unlucky enough to face him.

The red number 23 stands out against the white jersey on his chest. As his photo disappears to be replaced by the next player, my eyes focus on the number 23 plastered on my brother's back as he makes his way down the stairs in front of me.

The crowd roars as soon as we find our seats. That's when I see him. I wouldn't need to know what number he is to find him.

He's magnificent, gliding effortlessly across the ice. Someone of his size should not be this graceful balancing on thin blades, but he looks like a dancer out there.

The fifteen minutes of warmups pass by in a blur. My eyes are held captive by the fluidity of his movements. By the sheer beauty that is Kam Stryker.

Jasper presses his face against the glass in front of us as we watch the team do a last lap around the rink.

A few of the players stop around us and wave at the kids from the camp. I've been so focused on Kam I didn't even see the rest of the kids and their parents around us.

Jasper yells, "Hey, Kam!" His arms wave over his head to get his attention.

Kam slides to a stop right in front of my brother and waves. His eyes slice to meet mine. My breath catches in my throat as he mouths, *Hi, Sunshine*. His words disappear into the crowd's roar, but I don't need to hear them. I can *feel* them.

He smiles before racing off after his team. The announcer's voice fades away as he announces the opposing team. His words might as well be another language, since my mind apparently can only focus on all-things Kam.

My heart tries to work its way out of my chest as the lights fall. The crowd's roar vibrates through me from the sheer volume of the electrified space. Spotlights focus on the door where Kam disappeared only moments before. Flashes of red lights pulse in time with the music all around the room.

The announcer starts with the lower classmen, before ending with the captains of the team.

As his name is called last, the hairs on the back of my neck stand up. The brilliant smile on his face has to be visible in the nosebleed section as he takes the ice.

He was born to do this.

I can't take my eyes off him as he goes down the line of his teammates, giving them each a fist bump. He says something to each player along the way. I wish so badly I could hear what he tells them.

Jasper is grinning from ear to ear next to me. "This is *amazing.*"

I can't help but smile back at him. "Yeah, Jellybean. It really is."

I shoot to my feet, along with the rest of the stands, as Kam takes possession of the puck.

A quick glance at the clock shows thirty seconds remaining in the game.

Everyone in the room holds their breath as Kam bobs and weaves through his opponents. His skill is unmatched. If he makes this goal, he'll break the tie and win the game.

His teammates put everything they have left into fighting off the players gunning for Kam. He barely slows as he comes within shooting distance. He takes aim, and the puck flies along the ice so fast, I almost miss it hitting the back of the net.

The stands erupt in cheers, along with the team. I cheer for my classmate as he makes a victory lap around the rink, his stick lifted high in the air as he pumps his arms in victory.

His victory lap bleeds into the last seconds of the game as the scoreboard flashes 4-3.

Jasper jumps into my arms. "They won! They won!"

To my right, Posey jumps up and down in her seat. Her cheerleader skirt flies around her legs as she cheers.

A tap on the glass in front of us interrupts our celebration. I look up and lock eyes with Kam. A grin, matching my own, spreads across his face. He turns from me to look down at my little brother, Jasper's eyes filled with adoration for the hockey player in front of him. Kam's gloved hand points at Jasper before he tosses the game-winning puck over the wall.

I watch as the puck flies in slow motion toward Jasper's waiting hands. Inches from Jasper's outstretched fingers, a meaty hand snatches the puck from the air.

My eyes blaze as they move toward the person giving the puck, meant for my little brother, to a little boy next to him. I grind my teeth to keep from lashing out.

Do not go to jail today, Lila.

I don't have time to go into mama bear mode. An ear-piercing slam on the glass quiets the surrounding stands. I can feel my heartbeat in the tips of my fingers as I turn to find Kam's fist raised to the glass.

Kam's glare cuts a hole through the smug man. I

have no trouble hearing him as he snarls, "Give Jasper the puck. *Now.*"

The man smirks at the terrifying hockey player. "He should have tried harder to catch it. It's Matt's now, fair and square."

Kam's glare goes from a flame to an inferno in the blink of an eye. "Yeah, fuck that."

Three other players gather around Kam's back as he yanks his gloves off. The man's face turns a ghostly white as he assesses the wall of pissed off muscle in front of him.

The smiling, easy-going guys I met at The Penalty Box are long gone. Mace, Wyatt, and Dax stand like sentinels behind their captain.

With a shaky hand and a glare, the man snatches the puck from the boy's clenched fingers and releases it into Jasper's open palm.

Kam's eyes stay trained on him as he skates away backwards. A dangerous edge underlies his words as he says, "Wise choice." His eyes flick to me before he finally turns to leave the ice, his three teammates following him into the dark abyss of the tunnel.

I'm left standing there with my pulse beating wildly in my neck, staring after the captain of the hockey team.

What the hell just happened?

Jasper looks up at me, beaming with his new prize in-hand. "I wonder if he has a swear jar at home, too."

CHAPTER 7
FUTURE BOSS LADY

KAM

My hands shake as I rip off my helmet. "That son of a bitch is lucky there was glass between us."

My friends are silent behind me as my locker door rattles on its hinges. I turn, expecting my anger to be reflected in my friends' eyes, but find grins instead. Even Wyatt has a gleam in his usually stoic eyes.

The creaking of Coach's office door alerts us it's time for his usual end-of-game speech.

His signature three taps on the nearest locker gets everyone's attention. Silence blankets the room as Coach claims his spot near the whiteboard. "You played well tonight, men. You should be proud of yourselves. I know the score was close, but you worked together as a team. That's one of the best start-of-the-season scrimmages we've had here at Summit State."

My ears ring from the echoes of fists banging on lockers in the crowded space. "Enjoy a rest day tomorrow. You've earned it." He raises his voice to be heard over the roar brought on by the news of a rest day. "Be here for practice Tuesday at 4:00 pm."

Coach's all-knowing gaze shifts to me. "Kam, a word."

He vanishes into his office as the room erupts in a collective *ohhhh*.

With a grin, Mace slaps me on the back on his way to his locker. "Good luck with that."

I keep my face blank and my chin high as I step into Coach's office. His sigh speaks louder than any word he could say. A thunk rings through the room as his SSU hat lands in the center of his desk.

The fluorescent overhead lights reflect off his bald head as he takes his seat. My knees touch the front of his desk as I lower myself into the lone chair across from him. Family photos and neat stacks of paper crowd the room, adding to the claustrophobic feeling I get every time I come in here.

He crosses his arms as his sharp eyes bore into me. The chair that's probably older than I am groans under his weight. "Is there something you need to tell me, Kam?"

My face remains neutral under his scrutiny. "No, sir."

He raises one eyebrow. "Really? No *altercation* I need to know about with one of our biggest donors, perhaps?"

My eyes stay steady, never straying from his, as my voice remains firm. "No, sir. Nothing to worry about."

One quick nod is all he gives me before he stands. A clear dismissal for the night. "See that it stays that way."

I give a nod of acknowledgement as I stand. "Yes, sir." I feel his eyes boring a hole into the back of my head as I leave the room.

Chatter flowing from the showers nearly swallows the click of his door shutting behind me. The frosted window in the door shows his shadow moving back to his desk.

Tension never leaves my shoulders as I dig my fingers into the rough fabric of a towel. Echoed voices bounce off the tile walls of the damp room as I make my way into the steam-filled showers.

Wyatt's raised brows drip with shampoo as I pass him to claim my usual shower in the far corner. A quick incline of my head lets him know everything is well.

My impatience to get out of the locker room wins over my desire for a hot shower. The cool water sends a wave of chill bumps cascading down my back as I lather the soap in my hand.

My movements turn automatic as the water warms and images of Matt and his dad's smug smirk flood my mind. I shake the water from my eyes and the images from my mind.

We have a win to celebrate.

Humid air and muffled voices fill the atrium. Faces of friends and strangers alike blur together, along with their offered congratulations and words of encouragement. My eyes stay on a swivel, using my height to my advantage, as I search for a pair of mischievous eyes that remind me so much of my own, and an attitude far too big for her tiny body.

Her scowl and crossed arms fall away to be replaced by a splitting smile as I emerge through the crowd. "'Bout time, little brother. I'm starving." The intensity of the natural red streaks of her chestnut hair, that's only visible in the bright light, move in and out of focus as she closes the distance between us.

The top of her head barely reaches my chin as I pull her into a crushing hug. "I've been your *big* brother since we came out of the womb, Shrimp." The old nickname hits its mark. Her eyes flare as she pushes out of my hug and punches me in the arm. "Hey! That hurt."

It did actually hurt. Growing up with an older brother like me didn't leave her much of a choice in the self-defense department.

Her eyeroll is legendary. "You get much worse than that on the ice, *Goose*." She raises her eyebrows, daring me to challenge her use of my childhood nickname. Her head tilts and her smile falls as my eyes roam around, scanning the surrounding faces. Her voice is quiet as she says, "She didn't show." Ellie's jaw tightens as a hardness shadows her eyes. "Don't give Mom the satisfaction, Kam. She's not worth it."

I nod as I force a smile back to my face. "You ready to head to The Penalty Box? I've got a basket of fries with my name on it."

She nods as the shadows leave her eyes. "Let's get going. Are we meeting the guys there?"

"Sure are. They should be on their way already."

I curse as I emerge into the blinding light of the

evening sun. Pain erupts at the back of my eyes and my bag falls from my shoulder to the nearest bench with a solid thunk. My fingers quickly shift through the bag's contents in search of my sunglasses. A sigh escapes my lips from the cool metal of my sunglasses settling on my face.

The worn fabric of my bag's straps falls from my fingers as Lila comes into view. Waves of long, blonde hair cascade down her back, shining like a beacon in a field of asphalt and dust.

My feet are moving before I give them permission. My sister and my hunger forgotten in favor of my classmate and the open hood of her car.

The delicate strands of the white ribbon in her hair reach for me in the evening breeze. They pull me to her like the tide pulls shells onto a beach.

She turns at the sound of my footsteps. Tears leave streaks of wetness in their wake as they fall silently down her beautiful face. My gut twists as her red-rimmed eyes meet mine. "What's wrong, Sunshine?"

Jasper answers for her as he emerges from the shadow of a nearby tree. "Our car is broken."

Lila's frustrated breath blows a few strands of hair out of her face before they stick to her tears. "It won't start. I don't know if it's the battery or what, but it was fine when we got here. I just, I don't know what to do. Normally I would call my dad, but I—*I can't do that anymore.*" Her voice breaks, defeat ringing clear in her tone. She brings up her shaking hands to cover her face. Her voice is muffled as she rambles, "I'm so embarrassed. I don't know why I'm crying. I think I've hit my limit for today."

I wrap my calloused hands around her delicate wrists and pry her hands away from her face. "There's nothing to be embarrassed about." A warm breeze blows through my damp hair. Tendrils of her blonde waves reach toward me as the scent of mangos fills my lungs. My shoulders lose some of the tension I didn't realize I've been holding as I breathe her in. "I won't leave you here until we get this figured out. Okay?"

Her shoulders sag with relief as her chin wobbles. Dark dots appear on her red SSU shirt as fresh tears drip off her chin onto the cotton. "Really?"

"Really." I reluctantly release her. A chill replaces the warmth from her skin despite the blistering August air. "Let's take a look."

I ruffle Jasper's hair on my way to the driver's side door. "Hey, Tank! Did you have a good time at the game?"

He grins as he takes the place of my shadow and follows me to the car door. "The best time ever!" My eyes fall to the black puck clutched firmly in his little hands before returning to the splitting smile on his face. "You played so good! That goal at the end was awesome! I didn't doubt you for a second." His voice drops to a whisper as he gazes down at the puck in his hands. "I can't believe you gave *me* the puck!"

His genuine praise is in such stark contrast to the meaningless congratulations I just received in the atrium. "Thanks, Tank." I clear my throat to usher away the sudden emotion. "That, uh, that means a lot to me."

The driver's seat squeaks as I push it back as far as it will go. The scalding air trapped in the car hits me in the face as I fold my limbs to fit in her miniature seat.

A rapid clicking noise fills the air as I turn the key. Lila appears next to the driver's side door with red-rimmed eyes. A crease appears between her brows. "What does that mean?"

"It means your car battery is definitely dead." Her eyes shine with oncoming tears once again, so I hurry to say, "But I have some jumper cables in my Tahoe. It's an easy fix."

A huge smile accompanies the wave of relief that takes over her face. "Really? That's great! Thank you so much!"

I have to suppress a groan as I unfold my sore muscles from the cramped space. "It's no problem. Just let me bring my car over real quick, and we'll get you all fixed up."

Jasper's hair sways on top of his head as he scratches his chin like he's a scientist staring at a whiteboard. "Are you going to fix our car, Kam?"

"Sure am, buddy."

He shouts over the top of the car to the passenger side. "I told you he would fix it."

Lila's mini-me materializes out of the shade of the nearest tree that lines the parking lot. The ribbon tied around her pigtails matches Lila's. "Good. I'm tired of sitting out here. It's too hot, even in the shade." Her crystal blue eyes lift to meet mine. Her brows draw together, and her eyes fill with scrutiny as she walks to her brother's side. "Who are you?" She crosses her arms as she glares at me, waiting for my reply.

I can't help but smile at the snark oozing from the very essence of this little spitfire. "I'm Kam. It's nice to meet you, Posey."

Her eyebrows draw together even further. "How do you know my name?"

My smile only grows with her resolve. "Your brother told me about you during hockey camp yesterday."

The fire in her eyes fades to a simmer as she accepts my explanation. Her pigtails bounce as she steps forward, hand extended in front of her for a professional-grade handshake. "It's nice to meet you, Kam."

Future boss lady right here.

My hand swallows hers as I accept her handshake. "It's nice to meet you too, Rosie Posey."

I turn to find a much more composed Lila in front of her car. Still, I soften my voice to keep her tears at bay. "I'll be right back."

She bites her plump bottom lip as she nods.

I stuff my hands in the pockets of my shorts and watch the sun make its final descent of the day as I walk to my Tahoe.

One thing Lila said really stood out to me.

Normally I would call my dad, but I can't do that anymore.

Her statement repeats in my head like an echo bouncing between the buildings in a city. My desire to know her story only grows with every step I take away from her.

CHAPTER 8
HOCKEY PLAYERS DESERVE CHEERLEADERS

KAM

Ellie pushes off the Tahoe's driver door and slides her phone into the back pocket of her jeans as I approach.

The number 23 disappears as she crosses her arms over the jersey she wears to every game. "I would be offended you forgot I existed, had you not also forgotten your hockey gear, too." She waves a hand at my hockey bag, abandoned by her feet.

I grimace. "Sorry, Ellie." The car shakes as I toss my bag on the backseat and slam the door.

My feet move as quickly as they do on the ice as I get in the car. The slam of my own car door cuts off Ellie's sigh. Her mouth works a mile a minute as she makes her way to the passenger door.

Her butt has barely settled in her seat before I'm pulling out of the parking spot. I feel her assessing gaze on the side of my face like the warmth from a bonfire as I drive the few lanes over to Lila's car.

Her brows arch as I pull into the parking spot in front of the vacant car. My heart tries to thump a hole in my chest when I don't see Lila or the twins right away.

The impact of my feet hitting the ground reverberates through my aching knees. I can practically feel the curiosity rolling off my sister in waves as she wordlessly follows me to the back of the Tahoe. The rising trunk door skims the tips of my hair since I can't bother waiting for the damn thing to go all the way up.

Ellie's eyes stay glued to the side of my face, despite the loud pop that rings between us as I open my storage bin. I'll have to remember to thank Dax for always having a dead battery later.

I breathe a sigh of relief, and my heart rate returns to normal, when I spot Lila emerging from the shadow of Posey's tree. The twins follow close behind her. Heat envelopes my face as a shy smile touches Lila's lips.

Her smile falls and her eyes widen as they dart to my sister next to me. A blush starts on her cheeks and creeps down her neck to disappear beneath her red shirt.

In my peripherals, I see Ellie tilt her head to the side as her gaze bounces back and forth between Lila and I. Her signature smile brightens her face as she waves. "Hi, I'm Ellie."

Lila's wide eyes flash to mine for the briefest of moments before she gives a small wave back at my sister. "Uh, I'm Lila."

Ellie's smile grows at the same rate Lila's blush deepens. I busy myself with the jumper cables as my sister throws her arm around a clearly uncomfortable Lila. "I'm glad my *brother* was here to help with your battery situation."

My brows draw down in confusion at the emphasis Ellie puts on *brother*. Lila's shoulders fall with a visible sense of relief at the mention of the word.

The jumper cables slip through my fingers like water and pool in a tangle at my feet as realization dawns.

Wait, was Lila jealous?

A deep sense of satisfaction rushes through my veins at the revelation.

Ellie ignores the relieved look on Lila's face and my obvious fumbling as her attention falls to the twins peeking out from behind Lila. "And who do we have here?"

The redness of Lila's cheeks deepens to scarlet as she tries to compose herself. She wipes her palms on her jeans and steps aside to reveal the twins' matching curious expressions. "Oh, uh, this is my brother and sister, Jasper and Posey."

"It's nice to meet you two." Her full attention shifts to Posey. "I *love* the cheerleader outfit."

A huge smile breaks out on Posey's face. Her skirt billows in the air as she twirls for my sister. "Thank you! Hockey players deserve cheerleaders, too!"

"They sure do, Posey-Pop! It's a good thing all those stinky boys have you cheering for them." She whispers, "I bet you're the only reason they won today." A wink from Ellie makes Posey smile wider.

Flames ignite on my cheeks from the residual heat of Lila's eyes. I clear my throat to dispel the unwanted fire. "Um, let me get the cables all hooked up. It shouldn't take too long."

Jasper bounces on the balls of his feet, a huge smile

set firmly on his face as he helps me gather the cables from the ground. "Oh! Can I help?"

"Wouldn't have it any other way, Tank."

It's official. My sister is in love with Posey and Jasper. Their group hug lasts the duration of time to pack up the jumper cables. The stars in Posey's eyes multiply as she gazes up at Ellie.

Satisfaction fills me as Lila's car continues to rumble in the background. The cool night air is a relief on the back of my neck after contorting the slightly-too-short cables to restart the battery.

Note to self: Get longer jumper cables.

Our footfalls on the asphalt sync as Lila follows me to the back of my Tahoe.

Lila nervously wrings her hands as she comes to a stop next to me. "Thank you for this, Kam. I don't know what I would have done if you weren't here."

I focus on meticulously placing the jumper cables into their bin instead of Lila's proximity. "It's no problem. I'm glad I was here to help." In the empty parking lot, the plastic lid snapping shut echoes like a gunshot.

The rhythmic beeping of the hatch closing in the quiet space mimics my racing heart.

Left with no further distractions, my eyes lift and fuse with hers. The unforgiving overhead lights of the parking lot cast harsh shadows across her face. Her breathtaking beauty shines despite the unflattering light.

To avoid breaking the spell cast between us, I whisper, "Would you like to go to The Penalty Box with us for dinner tonight, Sunshine?"

Her shoulders slump as her gaze falls to the ground. "Oh, um, thank you for the offer, but we've gotta get home." She shrugs as her eyes come back to mine. "We've still got homework to get through before school tomorrow."

I nod as I shift on my feet. "Can I take you out to dinner later this week, then?"

Her hopeful eyes shift to steel determination before they fill with anguish. She lowers her chin and whispers, "This isn't a good idea, Kam."

She looks back up at me, and the force of her gaze nearly knocks the breath from my lungs. My voice is quiet in the darkness. "Why not?"

She shakes her head as a deep crease takes root between her brows. "It's not fair to you. I can't open myself up to a relationship right now." Her eyes plead with me to understand. She glances back to where our siblings still stand near the back of Lila's car. Posey's hands wave around her head as she tells a story too far away for us to hear. "They need me right now, Kam. And I barely have enough headspace to get through the day. Relationships add a layer of complexity I'm not capable of handling right now." She turns her face to hide her unshed tears. "And you deserve better than that."

I know their dad isn't in the picture. I've gathered that much from my conversations with her and everything Jasper said during camp. *Does that mean her mom isn't in the picture, either? Are we at a place in our newfound friendship where I can ask?*

I tilt my head to the side as I study her. Frustration like I've never known before surfaces at the realization that too few puzzle pieces are at my disposal to piece together her story.

With unwavering resolve, I arrive at my conclusion. I can feel my usual smirk bloom as the gears spin in my head. "I guess I'll just see you around, then."

She blinks away tears as a forced smile pulls at her lips. "Yeah, I'll see you in class, Kam."

My eyes never stray from her back as she stiffly makes her way over to her car and ushers the twins into their seats.

My feet move with a mind of their own as I walk toward my driver's side door. A blanket of quietness and calm settles over me as I close myself in my car.

Ellie's eyes are as loud as any words she could say as the Tahoe sways with the closing of her door. Our bubble of silence stays firmly intact as the red car vanishes into the night.

The roar of the engine vibrates through my seat as I start my car. I force hunger back to the forefront of my mind as I carefully pull through Lila's parking spot. "So, did Wyatt say when your car will be done?"

Flashes of the passing overhead lights illuminate Ellie's face as she fully turns in her seat to face me. "Are we really not going to talk about what just happened?"

"Nope." I pop the "p" so she knows just how serious I am.

She lets out a deep sigh as she rights herself in her

seat. "Alrighty, then." I feel her gaze on the side of my face. "Just know, I like her."

Me too, Ellie. Me too.

The dark buildings and empty sidewalks blur by as we drive the few blocks to The Penalty Box. She pulls her phone out of her back pocket and scrolls for the rest of the drive.

That's something I've always loved about our relationship. If one of us isn't ready to talk, there's no pressure from the other. Just support. Always support.

Our usual table is already overflowing with everyone's drinks and appetizers when we arrive.

Dax balances on the back two legs of his chair as he smiles at us. "We thought you two ditched us!"

Ellie claims the empty seat next to my usual place with a smile. "Nah. You guys know how long it takes for this guy to shower." Deep laughs rumble around the table as conversations resume.

I'll have to bring Ellie a tub of Ben & Jerry's later as a *thank you* for not outing me to my teammates.

I glance up to catch Wyatt's piercing gaze. His eyes narrow, obviously not buying Ellie's cover story.

I'll get grilled by the guys when I get home, but for now, I'm left to my own devices to put my plan in place.

Operation Become Lila's Friend is a go.

CHAPTER 9
SENT FROM MY IPHONE
LILA

The roar of voices spills into the hall outside the classroom. I let out a sigh of relief when I see Professor Mills is absent from his desk.

Posey had a wardrobe malfunction this morning that caused us to get a late start. I didn't even know seven-year-olds could have wardrobe malfunctions, but here we are.

Butterflies take flight in my stomach when I spot Kam sitting next to my seat in the back row, scrolling on his phone.

The murmur of surrounding conversations swallows the thunk of my bag hitting the floor as I take my seat next to the aisle.

Kam's eyes light up and his phone lands face down on his desk when he sees me. "Good morning, Sunshine."

His genuine excitement at seeing me warms me from the inside out. "Good morning, Kam."

A piece of printer paper, too far away to read clearly,

but titled and well-filled out, sits neatly on his normally solo notebook. A rush of panic flows through my body as I mentally go through my planner.

Did I forget about an assignment?

I try to conceal my rising panic as I casually incline my head toward the lone piece of paper. "What have you got there?"

An embarrassed smile pulls at Kam's lips as he looks down at the paper. "This is for you, actually."

My brows rise as my panic fades away to be replaced by curiosity. "For me?"

A hesitant laugh escapes his lips as he nods. He absentmindedly plays with the corner of the paper as his brows draw down in contemplation. "I know what you said last night about not wanting a relationship."

I wish so badly I could have taken him up on his offer for dinner. But if I've learned anything over these torturously long weeks, it's that we don't always get what we want.

His eyes turn away from the paper and snare mine. Hope and maybe even a bit of mischievousness shine brightly in his eyes. "But you never said anything about a friend." His long fingers deftly grasp the delicate paper so he can slide it onto my desk. "This is my formal application for the title of your friend."

The single piece of paper settles onto my desk like a butterfly would land on a flower. My eyes scan across the document without actually taking anything in for several moments.

My mind struggles to accept the fact that the captain of the hockey team just handed me a resume, laying out all the reasons I should *allow* him to become my friend.

What the hell is happening?

I lick my suddenly dry lips. "You, uh, want to be my friend?"

"Who wouldn't?" He says it with such conviction, I'm half convinced he's talking about someone else entirely.

Or maybe this is a dream. I dig my fingernails into my thigh and wince at the sharp pain.

Nope, definitely not a dream.

My brows furrow as I lift my eyes to his. "Um, why?"

His voice quiets from his previous confidence as he admits, "You seem like you could use one." His solemn face transforms to hold a cocky smirk as he says, "And I know I'm the best man for the job."

Even though his first sentence cuts me to my core, I feel a smile threatening to appear. "Oh yeah? And why is that?"

Smirk firmly in place, he inclines his head toward the paper sitting on my desk. "That's what that's for."

I sigh as I look back down at the paper, resigned to my fate. "Alright, I'll humor you." A full smile grows on my face as I look at the professional-quality document. "You went all out, didn't you?"

I can hear the smile in his voice when he says, "I don't do things halfway."

I look at him with raised brows, a lightness to my voice I haven't felt in weeks. "Shouldn't that have been one of your perks?"

His smile grows to shine so brightly, he lights up our isolated corner of the room. "I can make a few amendments."

Kamden "Kam" Stryker

484 - 555 - 1823 · Stryker23@email.com · @Stryker23

MISSION STATEMENT

To become the world's greatest friend to Lila (insert last name here). Will provide quality companionship with no expectations or strings attached.

KEY COMPETENCIES & PERKS

Great Listener	Safe SUV	Loyal	Punctual Texter
Extensive Movie Collection	Epic Cereal Maker	Dependable	Handy in a Crowd
Funny *No he's not*	Okay-ish Singer	Great With Kids	Long Arms

FRIENDSHIP EXPERIENCE

Wyatt "Malone Ranger" Malone   **Birth - Present**
Perks: Quality book recommendations and will hardly ever talk to you
Testimonial: *You could do worse.*

Declan "Dax" Hayes   **Freshman Year - Present**
Perks: Sometimes is funny and is good at math
Testimonial:

Kam is a good friend as long as he's not eating my cereal 10/10 would recommend

Mason "Mace" Deveraux   **Highschool - Present**
Perks: Will provide amazing meals
Testimonial: *He's a fucking horrible cook, but I love the asshole.*
My mama loves him, and she doesn't like anybody.

EDUCATION & CERTIFICATIONS

Bachelor of Kinesiology (In Progress)
Human Movement & Sports Science

Lifeguard Certification
Can also teach swimming lessons.

CPR Certification - Children & Adult

Epic Friend
JUST TRUST ME, SUNSHINE.

LIKES & DISLIKES

Likes:	**Dislikes:**
Little White Ribbons	Watermelons
Watching Movies	Hamsters
Being With Friends	Sad Movies
Root Beer	Mustard
Dogs (Big Ones)	Socks
Red Things	Alcohol
Mangos	Mean People
Hockey	Deep Water

I'm not even halfway through reading when a chorus of vibrations fills the room. Laughter trickles through the students as everyone checks their phones.

Kam and I share an intrigued glance as he picks up his phone from his desk. He chuckles as he hands the device to me, his warm fingers barely a whisper against mine.

Laughter I don't even try to contain erupts from me as I read the email pulled up on his phone.

From: j.mills@summitstate.edu
Subject: Classs Canceled

Food poisoningg,
Sent from my iPhone

I hand Kam's phone back to him, careful not to make contact this time, as the rest of the students stand from their seats.

The clear elation in their voices adds to my excitement at the realization I might actually have some free time today. And, by free time, I mean time to do my schoolwork and finish laundry.

Kam chuckles and his chair lets out a startling creak as he straightens next to me. "Poor Professor Mills."

My fingers are careful as I tuck his resume safely into a folder and load it into my backpack before I stand. "Yeah, poor guy. I'm not surprised, though. I've heard he brings sushi for lunch in a brown paper bag and keeps it under his desk." My nose wrinkles as I lead the way out of our aisle. "Who doesn't refrigerate sushi?"

Kam's smile is clear in his voice. "Someone begging for food poisoning."

We walk the rest of the way in silence, surrounded by far too many bodies to have a proper conversation until we exit the building.

As the fresh summer air greets us, students disperse along the many walkways leading around campus. The sunlight provides welcome warmth to my cheeks after being in the air-conditioned building in nothing but a tank top and jean shorts.

A shy smile tilts Kam's lips as the breeze blows a strand of hair over his brow. "Can I walk you to your car?"

I smile down at my feet as I nod. "Yeah, Kam. I'd like that."

Kam sticks right by my side as we walk toward the parking lot. His towering presence provides an odd sense of security on my normally lonely walk.

I've missed the serenity that comes with being comfortable with silence in someone else's presence.

I always enjoy the ever-present chatter that comes with living with two seven-year-olds, but the absence of companionable silence has been felt since my parents' passing.

My mom and I used to sit together and read at least a few times a week. My dad would often sit in the room with us, typing away on his laptop.

We didn't need the complexity of words to enjoy each other's company.

I slow my footsteps to prolong the short walk to the parking lot. An awareness of every breath and scuff of

Kam's shoe against the sidewalk has my heart pounding in my chest.

A surprising sense of loss at the prospect of parting ways with Kam washes over me as my car emerges in the distance.

Silence stretches on as I toss my backpack in the backseat. The gentle close of the door is amplified to that of a slam in the stillness that blankets us.

Roots grow from my feet into the pavement just outside of the open driver's door as my fingers dig into the top rim of the window.

I feel the slight shift of the car under my palm as Kam leans his elbow on the top of the roof behind me.

Gravels crunch under my feet as I turn toward him. It seems like a felony for the shadows of the overhead trees to cover so much of his face.

His relaxed posture is in such striking contrast to my rigid stance, it's almost comical.

With a tilt of his head, the full depth of his chocolate eyes peer into the deepest recesses of my mind. "What's your story, Sunshine?"

My body threatens to buckle under the weight of my grief as I shake my head. "It's not a happy one, Kam."

"Trust me with it, anyway." He continues on like he didn't just shatter another layer of ice that's strangling my heart. His smirk can't hide the seriousness of his eyes. "Look over my resume. I'm serious about my application."

I swallow, my mouth suddenly feeling dry in this August heat. "I will."

"Good." He pushes off the car and straightens. A mock-seriousness forces his smirk to fall. "I expect you to text me any questions that arise during your consideration."

My mimicry of his seriousness fails as a smile breaks through my attempted stern expression. "Of course, sir. It would only be fair."

His smirk resumes its rightful place as he backs away like he can't bear to look away. "I'll see you soon."

I hate the shyness I hear in my voice as I say, "See you soon, Kam."

A tightness pulls at his shoulders as he turns away from me. My eyes never leave his back until he disappears from view.

Scalding heat rushes over my face as soon as I lower myself into my seat. I curse myself for not at least turning on the air conditioner so the car could cool down while I watched him walk away like a stalker.

The car shakes violently as my knee slams into the steering wheel as I hastily twist my body to reach my backpack in the backseat.

I can't wait to forget how I got that bruise.

My zipper makes a groan of protest as I rip it open in search of a certain folder that contains a very important piece of paper.

My hurried motions slow as I open the folder. I pull the paper out of the sleeve with a sort of reverence I would never show a school assignment.

Kam's name sits boldly at the top of the page. Questions flow like a steady stream through my mind as I read through his words.

So, I do the only thing anyone would do in my situation. I pull my phone from my pocket, and I type.

CHAPTER 10

TROUBLE

LILA

MONDAY 11:36 AM

LILA

Sullivan. My last name is Sullivan.

KAM

Hi, Sunshine.

Sullivan like Sully from Monsters Inc.?

LILA

KAM

Top secret. Got it.

My lips are sealed.

LILA

So, no middle name?

KAM

My mom isn't a big fan of middle names, so no.

What's your middle name?

LILA

Do you always send more than one text in a row?

KAM

No.

You didn't answer my question.

LILA

Mae

KAM

Lila Mae Sullivan

I like it.

LILA

That's good, cause there's not really much I can do about it 😜

So, I've got to know the story about watermelons.

And mustard…

And socks…

And hamsters…

KAM

Now who's the one sending more than one text at once? 😏

LILA

Just tell me the stories, Stryker.

KAM

Fineeeeee

Short versions only…

I tripped and fell on a watermelon when I was in 4th grade. We were at a cookout for my hockey team. Broke my arm and got a nasty black eye. I had to sit out for almost half of that season. I've had beef with them ever since.

Mustard is obvious. No one should like mustard.

Socks, well, they just suck. They're hot and restrictive. I wear them inside out, otherwise the seams drive me nuts.

Wyatt had a hamster when we were in 1st grade. Took a chunk out of my finger one night. Never again.

LILA

I would have beef with watermelons, too, if I were you. I won't hold the mustard thing against you. It definitely sucks. I am, however, a huge sock fan. Specifically, any type of fuzzy socks.

KAM

*Adds to Christmas present spreadsheet *

LILA

You have a Christmas present spreadsheet?

KAM

Doesn't everyone?

LILA

What else is on your Christmas present spreadsheet?

KAM

Well, it's set up by category...

MONDAY 6:15 PM

LILA

So, how did you also get a 23 in your phone number?

KAM

Total happy accident.

LILA

Was that a Bob Ross reference?

KAM

Maybe...

LILA

I approve.

MONDAY 9:47 PM

KAM

Did you get your paper done yet?

LILA

Yep! Just hit send on the email, actually! Thanks for your reassurance about Professor Patterson earlier. It makes me feel better knowing you had that class last semester.

KAM

Good! I hoped you would finish soon.

LILA

And why is that?

KAM

Would it be weird if I told you I was just looking forward to continuing our conversation, or would you rather I lied and said I'm just glad you don't have to deal with that project anymore?

LILA

Honesty. Always, honesty.

KAM

Well, in that case, I'm glad you're done, cause I was looking forward to you asking me more questions.

LILA

Well, in that case…How did you convince the guys to help with your resume?

KAM

I told Mace I wouldn't help with the dishes for a month. I just bribed Dax with some chocolate. Wyatt did it with no coercion, but he rolled his eyes and grumbled about it the entire time.

LILA

And why did you feel the need to list that you have a safe SUV?

KAM

I figured if Jasper and Posey were with me, you would want to know they were in a safe vehicle.

LILA

That's...really sweet, Kam.

KAM

Sweet is my middle name 

LILA

You don't have a middle name...

KAM

If I did, I bet it would be Sweet...

LILA

Yeah, or Trouble.

KAM

That's not so bad either...

LILA

TUESDAY 8:31 AM

LILA

Quick, Lucky Charms or Captain Crunch?

KAM

Good morning to you too, Sunshine.

LILA

Morning, Trouble. Don't avoid my question.

KAM

What's your favorite color?

LILA

Light pink...what does that have to do with picking a cereal?

KAM

Nothing. I just wanted to know what your favorite color is.

Lucky Charms. Definitely the Lucky Charms.

WEDNESDAY 9:26 AM

KAM

Don't fall asleep over there.

LILA

If Professor Mills didn't sound so bored, I wouldn't be so bored.

KAM

Have you worked through my resume yet?

LILA

Still working on it.

KAM

The suspense is killing me...

LILA

Just be patient, Trouble.

KAM

Easier said than done.

LILA

I'll distract you with funny animal pictures.

photo of a shark mixed with a horse

It's a shorse!

KAM

Okay, I'm listening…

THURSDAY 2:12 PM

KAM

Did you know that wombat poop is cube shaped?

LILA

Learn something new every day.

KAM

Wombat poop

LILA

That's an ice cube…

KAM

?

LILA

You're right. The ice cube is better.

THURSDAY 3:19 PM

LILA

Did you know, according to Jasper, a shrimp's heart is in its head?

KAM

LOL

Ellie's going to love that one. Everything makes so much sense now.

LILA

You can't leave me hanging like that...

KAM

It all started when Ellie got bit by a shrimp on our trip to the aquarium in first grade...

FRIDAY 9:21 AM

KAM

Professor Mills is in rare form today...

LILA

Am I seeing that right? Did he just pick his nose?

KAM

And eat it?

Yes.

Yes, he did.

Can you distract me with more funny animal pictures?

LILA

I thought you'd never ask...

FRIDAY 10:46 PM

KAM

Hey, Sunshine?

LILA

Yes, Trouble.

KAM

Do I get to see you tomorrow?

LILA

Yeah. I'll see you tomorrow.

KAM

Good.

Goodnight, Sunshine.

Sweet dreams.

LILA

Goodnight, Trouble. Sweet dreams.

CHAPTER 11
FITTING FILTER
LILA

The hallway serves as a makeshift runway. My footsteps echo my thunderous heartbeat as I pace. The cadence of my steps is only interrupted by my shoes switching between the clicking on the hardwood floors and the muffled thud on the two rugs acting like a runner down the hallway.

I maintain a vice-like grip on my phone as I make another lap. Kam's text notification sits uncleared on my lock screen. His name serves as a pillar of strength for the day ahead. A silent battle rages in my mind. My desire to text Kam is losing to my desire to not reveal how much of a mess my life truly is.

His friendship application lies on my nightstand, slightly wrinkled from the hours of use it has received over these past few days.

My fingers itch to feel the now comforting smoothness of the paper. To feel the crinkle in the corner where he bent the paper playing with the edge during our class.

I audibly gulp when a glance at the clock on my phone shows nine minutes until eight. Icy tendrils of dread slide over me as the screen fades. My reflection stares back at me through the inky blackness. The darkness is a fitting filter to my dull image.

The thud of a car door closing outside reverberates like a gong through my bones.

She's early.

The buttery softness of my dress does nothing to calm my shaky hands as I attempt to smooth wrinkles out of the fabric.

Our red front door used to represent my mom's rebellious and artistic nature. Now, however, it flashes in warning at the danger I could find on the other side.

Despite anticipating the soft knock, it still startles me into dropping my phone onto the plush rug under my feet.

I murmur a quiet curse as I scramble to pick it up. My shaky fingers struggle to find purchase on the smooth device against the fibrous rug. The phone slides through my fingers like sand in the wind as another knock sounds at the door.

Vertigo washes over me as I stand too quickly. A sharp clink reverberates through the aching quietness as I bump my phone into a bowl we use to put our keys in on the entryway table.

The cool metal of the doorknob seeps into my sweaty palm. A rush of warm air slides over my face as the door swings open.

The glare on Mrs. Jones' glasses disappears to reveal kind, green eyes.

Shifting the papers she holds, her straight, white

hair gets caught on her jacket's lapels as she offers a handshake. "Miss Sullivan. It's so nice to meet you at last. I'm Evelyn Jones."

I inwardly cringe as my sweaty palm meets her cool one. "Please, call me Lila." I step to the side. "Come in."

I mourn the loss of the calming balm of the morning sun as I plunge the hall into blinding darkness. The click of the door closing feels like the cock of a gun as I watch Mrs. Jones' cunning eye take in our home.

My eyes dart over the immaculate space in search of dust like a hawk searching for a rabbit. The absence of dust doesn't soothe my racing heart or stabilize my shaking legs as I walk behind Mrs. Jones through the entryway.

Suffocating quiet descends like fog around us as we emerge into the open concept dining room, living room, and kitchen combo.

When we moved in five months ago, the open concept space was a pleasant change from the cramped older home I grew up in. Now the cavernous space is too reminiscent of an open field with no cover to protect the gazelle caught in the sights of the waiting lion.

I'm sure at first glance, one in my situation might think Mrs. Jones is the lion. But no. It's my circumstances that haunt me every waking moment. They plague me every second I dare to close my eyes and dream of a way to escape their suffocating presence.

I wake every morning wondering if today is the day the lion finally sinks its teeth into my neck to finish me. Some days I swear I can feel its breath from a taunting graze of its teeth on my flesh.

I blink out of the snare of my mind as Mrs. Jones unloads her arms onto the dining room table. She turns to me with sincere kindness shining in her eyes. "I'd like to begin by saying how sorry I am for your loss, Lila."

I struggle to swallow with an urgent need for water to soothe my parched throat. "Thank you. May I offer you anything to drink before we start?"

A small smile pulls at her lips before she turns to shuffle through the papers on the dining room table. "No, thank you, dear."

My feet carry me to the refrigerator before she's even finished talking. The rush of cool air that hits my face when I open the door thankfully clears my mind of any lingering thoughts of gazelles and lions.

The rough texture of the water cap burns my palm as I struggle to open the lid. Raw skin is a price I will happily pay for the refreshing chill of the water.

The scrape of the chair legs against the floor sends another rush of anxiety cascading through me. We each settle into our seats at the rectangular table as I wipe the condensation from the bottled water onto my dress.

The emptiness of the chairs at either end of the table settles like a weight on my chest. My knuckles turn a ghostly shade of white as I clasp my hands tightly on the table in front of me.

Mrs. Jones eyes me with a tilt of her head. "This is not meant to be a stressful visit, Lila."

I manage a small nod. "Of course. I can't help but to be nervous, though."

Her kind smile slips firmly into place. "That tells me

a great deal about how seriously you are taking this situation."

I sit up straighter in my seat. "This is absolutely the most important thing to me."

"I'm glad to hear that. Let me give you a rundown of how today will go." I nod my head as she glances back down at the papers in front of her. "I would like to start with a tour of the house. Then I would like to meet with Jasper and Posey to see how they are doing with all the changes." She looks up at me. "I may recommend grief counseling for all three of you, but don't be alarmed. That almost always happens in these cases, and it is not a reflection of how well you are doing." I nod my understanding as she continues. "After I talk with Jasper and Posey, I would like to ask you a few questions. That should be the extent of our visit today. Does that sound good to you?"

I actually manage a small smile. My nerves slightly dull to that of a butter knife instead of a steak knife, now that I know what to expect. "That sounds great."

She mimics my smile. "Great. Let's get started."

CHAPTER 12
IN NEED OF DUSTING

The thrum of voices echoing through our house does little to distract me from my phone this morning.

My fingers drum along the couch cushion as I reread the text thread for the third time since I came downstairs. My unanswered good morning text stares back at me like a bad omen.

Why didn't she text me back this morning when she normally texts back right away?

Am I texting too much?

Am I too much?

I decide to save myself the mind-numbing tumbleweed of thoughts and lock my phone. As I lean my head back on the couch cushion to examine our dusty ceiling fan, my phone dings.

Yes, I turned the volume up on my phone so I wouldn't miss a text.

No, I didn't know what my ringtone was before I turned up my volume this morning.

A thrill runs through me at the possibility of seeing

Lila's name staring back at me. I almost drop my phone in my haste to check the notification.

The thrill crashes into a fiery inferno when I find my mother's name instead.

ISOBEL

I need you to call Richard.

That'll be a no from me, thanks.

The last thing I want to do on a Saturday morning is call my dad's former agent and get an earful of why I'm not doing enough to secure my future in the NHL.

I groan as I throw my traitorous phone onto the other couch and resume my inspection of our ceiling fan.

I really need to dust that thing.

I have an hour before we leave. That's plenty of time to dust. And maybe vacuum. My eyes rove over the downstairs living room and entryway. Definitely vacuum.

I wonder if we need to do laundry. Who am I kidding? We always need to do laundry.

I hear footsteps coming from the kitchen before Mace says, "Stop moping around and come help me with breakfast."

"I'm not moping."

He snorts at my response. His voice fades as he walks back into the kitchen. "Yeah. Sure. Whatever you say, Cap."

It's the smell of bacon calling to my grumbling stomach that pulls me from my spot on the couch and into the kitchen.

I point at Wyatt scrolling on his phone at the kitchen counter. "Why isn't he being yelled at for not helping?"

Mace's attention never deviates from the skillet of scrambled eggs in front of him, his apron tied firmly around his waist. "Because *Ranger* did the dishes last night."

Dax chooses this moment to venture into the kitchen, yawning so hard it looks like his jaw might dislocate. His blond hair is a mess from sleep. "What time do we have to be at the rink?" He blinks sleep from his eyes as he settles in his usual seat next to Wyatt.

I raise my voice to be heard over the clacking of me getting the dishes out of the cabinet. "We need to be there by ten-thirty." I turn to level him with a serious glare. "That doesn't mean *leave* at ten-thirty."

He gives me a salute and starts scrolling on his phone.

The click of Mace twisting the stove off acts like an EMP with how quickly everyone puts their phones away.

We line up and fill our plates to the point of over-flowing. As we settle into our usual seats at the kitchen counter, my phone dings again.

The flash of excitement is dull compared to the one earlier in the living room. My mother's name flashing on my phone is reminiscent of a fly at a picnic.

ISOBEL

Richard says he's emailing over with a few documents for you to look at.

My phone glides like my skates on the ice as I push it away from me on the counter until it balances precariously on the edge, much like my sanity.

I feel the weight of three sets of eyes on the side of my face as I push the rapidly cooling scrambled eggs around on my plate.

Another ding rings throughout the room.

This is going to be a long day.

The calming chill of the rink is missing its usual effectiveness this morning. My fingers drum a melody against the sidewall as the kids do their warmup laps.

Colt bolts out onto the ice with damp hair and lipstick stains on his neck. I roll my eyes as every player in the rink sends him a seething glare for being late.

That kid will never make it in the big leagues. Daddy's money may get your dick sucked, but it can't make you likeable.

The weight of my phone in the pocket of my sweats threatens to consume me as I catch another curious glance from Wyatt.

Our normal *no phones on the ice* policy dies a slow death as I check my notifications. Again.

Where are they?

The clock on my screen switches from 10:59 to 11:00. Jasper is officially late.

Right before my screen fades to black, a notification

pops up on my screen. I almost drop my phone as my cold finger struggles to click on it.

I feel the tension in my shoulders relax for the first time all morning as her name stares back at me.

LILA

Good morning, Trouble.

"My sister's been getting that dreamy look on her face every time she checks her phone this week, too."

A strike of pain flares through my neck as I turn too quickly toward Jasper's voice. His hands deftly lace his skates with efficiency normally reserved for more experienced players.

It takes far too long for me to reply. His declaration consumes my thoughts. *I'll file that information away for later.* "Morning, Tank. I was getting worried about you."

He stands, a natural on the thin blades of his skates. "Yeah. Sorry I'm late. We had to deal with the social worker this morning."

I feel my eyebrows practically disappear into my hairline. "Social worker?"

I'm frozen in place as he swings open the door to the ice, completely unfazed by the bomb he just dropped at my feet. "Yeah. She was cool. Lulu was pretty worried about it, though."

My brows descend from my hairline as he's swallowed up into the swarm of boys on the ice. My mind reels with the additional unexpected puzzle piece that's been dropped on my lap like a ton of bricks.

A streak of blonde in the stands catches my attention. My gaze zeros in on the swaying ponytail as she walks down the steep stairs with her mini-me following close behind her. A pink backpack bounces on Posey's back before they take their seats many rows above the throng of parents gathered in the stands.

I'm enraptured, watching Lila's hair flow over her shoulder as she bends to help Posey get settled in the hard plastic seat.

Her gaze finally meets mine with the force of a semi-truck. It's enough to knock any grown man on his ass.

The small smile that lights up her face when she sees me makes me feel like puffing my chest out in celebration.

Yeah, that's right. That smile is for me, fuckers.

"Stop smiling like a lovesick fool at the pretty lady and do your job, *Captain*."

I level a glare on Dax that would have most grown men shitting their pants. The fucker's grin only grows, obviously receiving the reaction he'd been hoping for. He skates away from me before my mouth can catch up to my brain and dignify him with a response.

Questions circle my mind in a never-ending loop as I join the group to begin drills.

Why did Lila and the twins meet with a social worker?

Why does Jasper always talk about being the man of the house?

Why did Lila say she couldn't call her dad about her car battery?

The picture slowly being revealed through the puzzle pieces isn't a pretty one.

I barely take part in the drills for the rest of the day. I'm consumed with thoughts of her. My skin itches with the need to run up the stairs and demand to know what her story is.

By the end of the day, the last puzzle piece clicks into place with a finality that takes my breath.

And it breaks my heart.

CHAPTER 13
MARKER WATERFALL
LILA

Throughout the day, I watch Kam's eyes transform each time he looks up at me. I can see the pity clouding his eyes even from this distance.

He knows.

A hollowness forms in my stomach that threatens to swallow me whole. This is why I didn't want him to know. I can't stand the pity that will undoubtedly replace the warmth I've grown so accustomed to finding in his eyes.

The warmth that has grown into my only reprieve from the icy chill that blankets my life, gone in a matter of moments.

A familiar, feminine voice breaks me out of my spiraling thoughts as the final whistle blows and the kids pour off the ice. "Is this seat taken?"

Posey jumps out of her seat, not even bothering to move her coloring book and open marker case from her lap. The stairs act like a waterfall as markers tumble to the ground and cascade down each step. Posey throws her arms around Kam's sister, unbothered by the runaway markers. "Ellie!"

A genuine smile takes over Ellie's face as she embraces my sister. "Hey there, Posey-Pop!"

Her brown eyes, the same shade as Kam's, flick to mine and narrow as she examines my face. Her smile dims as I confront the painful reality of the loss of Kam's warm gaze. "Hey, Lila. How's everything going?"

She tilts her head as she awaits the reply I struggle to give. My view of her grows blurry as my eyes fill with unshed tears.

"Hi, Sunshine."

I feel warmth on my face as I realize Kam caught me crying *again*. I rub my sweaty palms on my pants as I try to reel in my tears. My gaze stays fixed on my hands in my lap as I hear Kam and Ellie moving around next to me.

Kam's deep voice carries to me like distant music as he whispers to his sister. "Give us a minute. I'll catch up with you later."

There's no hesitation in Ellie's voice. "Hey! Why don't you help me pick up these markers so we can go color together?"

The awe in Posey's voice only grows. "You like to color?"

"Sure do! Can you show me your coloring book?"

Their voices fade into the dull roar of the crowd as they gather the markers further down the stairs.

The row of seats shifts as Kam takes Posey's place next to me. I lift my gaze from my hands to search for my brother. I find him laughing as Dax,

Mace, and even Wyatt chase him around on the ice.

A comfortable silence settles around us while the other kids and their parents pack up.

When we finally have a semblance of privacy, Kam breaks the silence. "Did you know that crows have best friends? They get stressed out when they're separated."

I can't help but smile at his attempt to cheer me up. My voice is so quiet, I'm surprised Kam can hear me. "That's kind of beautiful."

He's silent for a moment before he says, "What can I do to help?" I'm stunned into silence by the unexpected question. I turn so quickly that my ponytail whips violently behind me. Our eyes lock, and I'm met with sheer determination instead of the pity I feared. "Tell me what I can do to help, Lila."

I swallow roughly as I try to formulate words in the tangled mess that's become my mind. "What do you mean?"

He turns toward me in his seat. "I want to help with Jasper and Posey."

My eyebrows draw down in confusion as I take in the sincerity of his eyes. "You want to help?"

His eyes, so open and honest, search mine as he nods. "Yes."

"With Jasper and Posey?"

"Yes. And with you."

"Why?"

"Because that's what friends do. We help each other." He tilts his head. "And I won't let the clouds taking over your eyes keep us apart." A small smile touches the edge of his lips. "Cause, apparently, I'm a crow. I'm a crow that won't let something as simple as clouds come between me and my friends."

"I've not accepted your application yet." Kam's determination never falters with my poor attempt at a joke.

His eyes blaze with molten fire as he says, "You will."

My gaze swivels between my smiling sister, my laughing brother, and the very determined hockey player in front of me.

Kam doesn't say a word as I watch my brother. A free fall of thoughts rush past me as quickly as Jasper skates around the ice.

The only time Jasper and Posey have smiled has been when Kam is here.

The only time I've felt safe since my parents died is when Kam is here.

The only time I feel like I'm not crushed by my life is when Kam's name pops up on my phone.

It's obvious, really.

With a relieved sigh, I admit what I should have days ago. "Alright. I accept."

A lightness takes over his voice that I've never heard before as he relaxes his shoulders and slumps his hulking frame into the small seat. "Really?"

I feel a small smile threaten to appear. My breath catches as our elbows bump on the armrest. He doesn't move, and neither do I. "Yeah, Trouble. Really."

With a quietness that doesn't belong in this bustling space, Kam says, "Will you tell me your story, Sunshine?"

I take a deep breath as I prepare for the overwhelming rush of grief that always accompanies thoughts of my mom and dad.

I run my fingers over the cool metal of my mom's watch as I think back to what I thought would be the worst day of my life. Oh, how I wish that could be true. "My mom received a breast cancer diagnosis two years ago."

Kam's silent, stoic presence calms my racing heart as I tell him my story.

"I watched my mom wither away to become a shell of herself while she fought so hard to stay with us. I never understood the devastation that comes with being so helpless to save the person who means the most to you in the world."

I take in a shaky breath as memories wash over me like a summer rain. "We lived in Chicago then. That's where I grew up. She fought for two years and won."

A smile blooms as I think about my mom ringing that bell after her last treatment. Victory had never felt so sweet.

"After she was cancer free, my parents wanted to move back here to be closer to their childhood friends and distant family. I guess cancer really shows what's important in life. They both grew up here, but moved to Chicago shortly after they got married. We'd only been living here two months when my parents went out for a follow up appointment for my mom. They were running late because my dad couldn't find his shoes."

I huff out a humorless laugh. "Funny how life's simplest choices can lead to such devastating conse-quences."

My voice quiets to almost a whisper as I watch my

fingers glide over the smooth glass of the watch face. "They never made it home."

Kam's hand covers mine, halting my fingers. The gentle squeeze he gives my fingers is such a contrast to the power he displays on the ice. "I'm here for you. You're not alone anymore."

A watery smile is all I can manage as Posey's giggle drifts to us from where she's coloring with Ellie several rows ahead. "Thank you."

A smile lifts his voice as his fingers tighten around mine. "So, I'm going to ask again. What can I do to help?" He holds up a finger to silence my refusal. "I won't stop asking until you give me a job to do. Even something as simple as taking out your trash."

That simple question burns away the weight that's been a constant companion these daunting weeks. My war for independence and self-determination is lost under crushing exhaustion and realization.

I need help.

"Can the twins stay with you tomorrow? It would just be for an hour or two. I have something important I need to take care of."

The smile that takes over Kam's face has the power to light up an entire room. "I would love that."

CHAPTER 14
DISINFECTANT WIPE

LILA

The clattering of dishes and the piercing scrape of a fork against a plate frays my already fragile nerves. My leg bounces so vigorously under the table that my teeth rattle. Condensation drips down the side of the untouched glass of ice water in front of me.

The door to the restaurant swings open as a lightning bolt of dread zings down my spine.

My muscles release a tenth of their tension as a haggard-looking mother comes through the door. Her son pulls her through the crowded room as she balances a sleeping little girl on her hip.

The trio disappears into the crowd to join the equally haggard father as I reread Kam's texts.

KAM

Posey just put Dax in his place. I wish you could have seen her.

Ellie and Posey are officially best friends.

photo of Posey and Ellie coloring

I might have promised Jasper I'd take him to a Flyers game soon.

photo of Jasper watching the Flyers game on the couch with the guys

I scroll through the photos he's sent me in the twenty minutes since I dropped Jasper and Posey off at his townhouse. My heart warms with every swipe as I take in the twins' smiles.

I'm doing this for them.

If the judge thinks they're my best shot at a support system, then that's exactly what I'm going to pursue.

The mental timeline for this visit I spent many sleepless nights working through flows like a slideshow through my mind.

A respectful introduction. Maybe even a handshake.

I offer them a seat at the table I purposefully requested in the quietest part of the restaurant.

We bond over our loss.

They ask how I've been holding up after losing the most crucial people in my life.

The slideshow goes on and on until I get dizzy.

The door to the restaurant opening stings of betrayal as I open the door to a relationship my mom and dad fought so hard to protect us from.

My heart beats a crescendo with every step they take toward me. His dark, tailored suit and her black dress are more fitting for the funeral they didn't bother attending for my parents than a steakhouse on a Sunday afternoon.

Eyes so similar in color to my mom's but so different in sincerity appraise me. Her perfect, white curls don't move an inch as she tilts her head to the side in silent inspection.

Her calculating gaze glides from my simple navy heels, past my white sundress, to settle on my loose curls. With one look, she scrutinizes every failure I've had in her absence over the past ten years. "Hello, Lila."

My eyes beg for permission to look away. I refuse to give it. "Hello, Grandmother."

A gruff voice I so seldom heard, I had forgotten its cadence speaks from behind her. "Lila."

My gaze shifts to be snared by stern, grey eyes. "Hello, Grandfather."

My hands stay locked at my sides as I remain determined to resist the urge to fidget as they glance around the local steakhouse I picked for lunch today.

The slight scrunch of my grandmother's nose is the only sign of her displeasure as her eyes shift back to me. "Shall we sit?"

She pulls the seat out directly across from me before I have time to reply. I don't know why she bothered asking.

Her white tipped nails deftly unclasp her purse as we all get settled at the table. The restraint it takes to not roll my eyes as she pulls a disinfectant wipe from her bag is award worthy.

Awkwardness descends around us as she takes her time wiping down their side of the table. "So, Lila. What did you want to discuss? We were shocked to receive your email last week."

My voice reflects an air of confidence I don't feel. "Well, as you know, my parents passed away a few months ago."

She interrupts, "Yes. A tragedy indeed." Her tone matches what you might expect of someone talking about the weather, not her dead daughter.

"Yes. A tragedy. And I was wondering if—"

"You want money?" This interruption comes from my grandfather. His sudden, harsh tone almost makes me flinch. Almost.

I shake my head as they turn to one another. "No, I—"

My grandfather at least has the decency to lower his voice. "I told you, Victoria. She only wants money."

"No, that's not—"

My grandmother, however, lacks the decency to lower her voice as they continue to talk like I'm not sitting right in front of them. "You're right, Maxwell. It's only ever about money."

"I don't want your damn money!" My eyes spring open at my outburst. I don't need to look around me to know I have many eyes staring me down from the neighboring tables.

The smallest hint of light enters Victoria's eyes with my outburst before she extinguishes it behind her scowl.

I straighten my spine and clear my throat as they both narrow their eyes in my direction. "I'm sorry. What I meant to say is, I did not ask you to meet me today to ask for money."

Victoria scoffs like I'm the one who has been so

rudely interrupting them and not the other way around. "Well then, what did you ask us here for?"

I would fucking tell you if you'd give me a chance.

I take a deep breath to calm my heart and slow my tongue. "I wanted to ask if you wanted to be a part of Jasper and Posey's lives."

Their eyebrows draw down as they share a confused look before Victoria says, "Who is that?"

My mouth falls open as I volley my gaze between the two strangers sitting in front of me. Of all the things I had mentally prepared myself for today, their lack of knowledge about Jasper and Posey wasn't one of them. Of course they wouldn't know they exist. How could they? "My, uh, brother and sister."

For the first time since my grandparents sat down, their eyes light up with interest that sends a beat of apprehension down my spine.

Victoria leans forward ever so slightly in her seat. "How old are they?"

I unconsciously lean away from her as her sudden movement forces a current of her perfume to wash over me. "They're seven."

Maxwell's voice does not reflect the interest barely concealed in his eyes. "Twins, then?"

All I can manage is a quick nod of my head as I watch them exchange a look I can't decipher.

Maxwell stands like a posh robot and digs around in his suit pocket. Victoria's eyes flash with confusion for a moment before she follows her husband's silent sign that this meeting is over.

I sit, frozen in place, as my heartbeat roars in my

ears. My carefully laid out plans crumble around me as I face their rejection.

No.

This can't be happening.

I can't lose them because of these people.

My eyebrows disappear into my hairline as Maxwell hands me a crisp, white card. "We will meet with them. My assistant will call you with the information. Send your phone number to the email listed here." I barely register the fifty-dollar-bill being thrown onto a table we've hardly used as I examine his business card.

In my peripherals, I watch as Victoria smooths the imaginary wrinkles out of her black dress and Maxwell buttons his suit jacket. They're oblivious to the tornado currently wrecking my thoughts.

My neck aches from the whiplash I've endured during these few minutes. "You want to meet them?" I free my gaze from the card in my trembling hand to make eye contact with the only family I have left.

The power they hold in their hands is astonishing.

I don't mean the power they wield with the swipe of a bank card.

No.

I mean the power they hold over two seven-year-olds who mean more to me than anything else in this world.

Maxwell's eyes narrow in annoyance as he's forced to repeat himself. "Yes. We will meet with them. I expect that email by the end of the day."

Without a goodbye, they leave the restaurant as quickly as they came.

What the hell just happened?

The only evidence of them not being a figment of my imagination is the fifty-dollar-bill laying on the table and the crisp, white card in my hand that holds the weight of my entire world.

CHAPTER 15
A PARTRIDGE IN A
PEAR TREE
LILA

The warm glow of the afternoon sun illuminates the row of townhouses. Four vehicles cram the driveway, forcing me to park on the street.

My eyes take stock of the variety of vehicles that belong to the four roommates as I take a moment to catch my breath after the whirlwind meeting.

A black Tahoe that I know belongs to Kam sits closest to me. I don't know enough about the other roommates to decipher who the silver 4runner, the dark green Classic Ford Bronco, and the dark blue Ford F-150 belong to.

Darkness envelops me as I close my eyes and loosen the tension that's taken up permanent residence in my neck. Strands of hair pull tight on the top of my head as I sink into the headrest of my seat. The lingering light invading my eyelids disappears as my fingers dig into my temples. I try my best to massage away the headache that bloomed from clenching my teeth all morning.

I'm still undecided if the meeting went well or not. Even if the path to getting to my desired result wasn't what I had planned, I still got there in the end. That counts for something. Right?

I let out a deep breath as I exit the safety of my car in favor of the unknown that stretches before me. The sparse front porch of the townhouse represents uncharted territory in a life full of uncertainty.

I weave my way between vehicles and underneath side mirrors as I make my way up the driveway. Right as I'm lifting my hand to knock, the sound of revving engines and giggles drifts through the door.

My brows draw down in confusion as the door swings open. Kam's eyes light up to match the afternoon sun as a splitting smile takes over his face. "Hi, Sunshine. I heard a car door close and thought it might be you."

I open my mouth to reply when I hear Dax's muffled groan from further in the house. "That's not fair! I didn't know there was a shortcut there!"

I can hardly hear Posey's reply over deep laughter coming from multiple sources just out of my view. "It's not my fault you suck at this game."

Kam's grin only grows as he steps to the side and waves me into his home. I pass by a lone table in the entryway as my heels click along the hardwood floors.

I follow the laughter past a smiling Kam farther into the house. My eyes take stock of a living room filled with one too many couches, the biggest TV I have ever seen in person, three hockey players, two seven-year-olds, *and a partridge in a pear tree.*

My siblings look like dolls compared to the hulking

hockey players surrounding them. Laughter drowns out Dax's groan as he tilts his head, following the path of the cars on the screen.

I feel Kam's warm presence step up behind me as I watch the chaos unfold on the TV. Four sections divide the screen as cars zoom around a track.

Well, three of the four cars weave through their opponents as they race for the finish line. A lone car's wheels spin in the grass of the side of the track as its driver works tirelessly to redirect itself in the proper direction.

A pink car crosses the finish line as Posey jumps up on the couch. She wiggles around in a happy dance as she balances on the seat cushions. "I won! I won!"

Her head barely reaches Dax's chin as he sulks next to her, his controller abandoned in his lap as his car remains in the grass.

Jasper and Mace cross the finish line in quick succession as the final scores scroll across the screen, showing Posey won by over three-hundred points. A small smile plays on Wyatt's lips as he watches my sister celebrate her victory.

Dax's mouth hangs open as he watches my sister celebrate her win. "You hustled me." His eyes flick to a smiling Mace next to him. "I got hustled by a seven-year-old."

Posey continues her celebration even as a beeping starts from farther in the house. Mace jumps up from his seat and steps over his roommates' legs, creating a maze as they stretch out on the coffee table. His voice booms through the open room. "Lunch is ready!"

His eyes swivel in my direction before he disappears

down a small hallway I assume leads to the kitchen. "Hey, Sullivan!"

I manage a small wave as I struggle to take in the scene in front of me. Kam chuckles as Jasper pops his head up over the back of the couch. His crystal blue eyes lock with mine and flash with disappointment. "You're back already?"

Posey's celebratory dance halts mid-sway as she swings toward me. "No! You can't be back already!"

I quickly bury the flash of pain that comes with the realization they aren't happy to see me in favor of a smile I'm sure doesn't reach my eyes. "You guys ready to go?"

A chorus of protest erupts as five sets of eyes focus on me. The words flow so quickly I hardly keep up.

"They can't go! I deserve a rematch!"

"We can't go! Kam said he would play the winners after lunch."

"I won't go until Ellie gets back. She said she would only be gone a few minutes."

Even Mace pops his head out of the kitchen, a red SSU apron tied around his waist. "They can't go! They've not had lunch yet!"

My mouth opens to protests when I feel Kam's warmth flood into my back as he steps close to whisper, "Stay." The hairs on the back of my neck stand in delight at his proximity.

I look over my shoulder to find Kam relaxed in a way I've not seen before. His hands stay tucked in his pockets while his eyes shine with happiness. A smile never leaves his face as he watches the chaos unfold around him without a care in the world.

Only Wyatt holds his tongue as he leans back on the couch. His all-seeing eyes peer into me until I'm convinced he can see the effects of Kam's attention from across the room.

The front door opening silences the chorus of voices as Ellie's voice rings through the space. "Alright, Posey-Pop! I've got chicken nuggets!" I turn in time to watch her face twist in confusion at the scene she just walked in on. "Uh, is everything okay in here?"

Kam strolls over to his sister and plucks the fast food bag from her hands. "It's perfect. You're right on time. We were just about to sit down and eat." He walks by my frozen form and disappears into the kitchen without another word. The smell of chicken nuggets remains even after he disappears.

My eyes swivel back to Ellie as the rest of the group follows Kam into the kitchen. A muffled debate between Dax and Posey fades as they disappear around the corner.

My heart warms with Ellie's consideration. "You didn't have to go to the trouble of getting her anything else to eat."

She dumps her bag on the lone table in the entryway and kicks her sandals under it with a familiarity that suggests she's done it a hundred times. "It's no problem. We want her to be comfortable here. That includes being happy with what she eats." She pats my shoulder and carries on by me like she didn't just melt another layer of the ice around my heart. "Come on, Lila. Let's go eat."

CHAPTER 16
KETCHUP

KAM

My phone vibrates in my pocket. I reluctantly shift my attention away from Lila, stiffly loading her plate with the chicken enchilada casserole that Mace made this morning.

Dax's fingers fly across his phone screen from his seat across from me. My phone vibrates once again as his blue-grey eyes lift to mine. He smirks like the jackass he is as I pull my phone from my pocket.

THE BENCH WARMERS GROUP CHAT

DAX

I like her

MACE

Me too

WYATT

You hardly know her.

DAX

Don't need to. Did you see the way
Kam shot up like his ass was on fire
when he heard that car door close?

KAM

I'm right here, you know.

DAX

And the way he lit up like a Christmas
tree when she decided to stay for
lunch?

KAM

Still right here.

MACE

Or the way he's not stopped smiling
since he sat down.

Well, until he started reading our texts,
anyway.

Heads turn in my direction from my caseless phone thunking against the wooden table as I turn it face down.

Ellie shoots Dax and Mace an icy glare as their fingers wildly tap on their screens, oblivious to the danger in Ellie's eyes. A shiver runs through me as memories fly through my mind of our childhood that make me thankful her ire isn't directed at me. "No phones at the table, kids."

Their phones disappear into their pockets in a flash. Their eyes stay downcast in remorse as they mumble their apologies.

My eyes gravitate to Lila without my permission. A blush creeps over her cheeks as she realizes the only seat left at the table is next to me. The smirk pulling at my lips falls when the scraps on her plate come into focus.

My brows draw down as my eyes fall to my plate. I'm pretty sure she could add her meager portions to mine, and I wouldn't even notice.

Steam floats above my plate in a mesmerizing dance as Lila settles into her seat next to me. Her quick intake of breath when our knees touch under the table transforms my smirk into a full grin.

I can't help but chuckle as her seat scrapes against the hardwood floor as she fidgets. I hold my breath in anticipation of an accidental contact that never comes. The strength of my disappointment is alarming.

A thunk vibrates through the table as Mace plops a ketchup bottle in front of Posey's face. Lila turns ridged next to me as Posey reaches for the bottle. "Don't squeeze too hard, Ladybug."

I turn in time to watch a silent war play out on Lila's face. She bites her lip as she watches her sister struggle to open the cap of the squeeze bottle. Her hands are clasped so tightly in her lap that her knuckles are turning white from the effort she takes to not reach out and help.

My seat between the two sisters has me volleying my head back and forth between them like I'm at a tennis match.

Posey's brows draw down in adorable concentration as the cap finally pops open. The scene before me transforms into slow motion as she turns the bottle upside down and squeezes.

A fart-like sound erupts from the bottle as ketchup

shoots like a streamer across Posey's plate, onto my plate, and finally, up onto my shirt.

I feel a drop or two of the cool condiment on my chin as it rapidly warms from the temperature of my skin.

My eyes turn to Lila in time to watch her sink down in her seat. Her fingers massage a constant rhythm into her temples as I look down to see my new white shirt painted red.

Posey grimaces as the sound of ketchup dripping from her sticky fingers onto her plate fills the quiet room. Tears rim her eyes as she whispers so silently I almost can't hear her, "Sorry, Kam."

An easy smile transforms my face as I slip the ketchup covered bottle from her tiny fingers. "Hey, it's alright. It's nothing a little wash won't—" My words die on my lips as the slimy bottle slips from my grasp. The deafening thunk of the full bottle landing on the table fills my ears as a stream of red shoots from its top.

The stream flies in slow motion toward Lila's pristine, white dress like it's caught her heat signature.

Lila slowly blinks in confusion as she looks down at her likely ruined dress. A small smile lifts her lips as the rest of our group erupts into laughter around the table.

I watch in fascination as Lila's face transforms until she's barely containing her laughter. It feels like my face might split open from smiling so hard when she finally releases her genuine laugh.

It's a new goal of mine to hear that sound as often as possible.

Dax doubles over to clutch his stomach as his laughter rises above everyone else's. Mace wipes at the corners of his eyes as he says in between fits of laughter, "I am *not* helping clean that up."

Ellie's smile beams as she watches Wyatt's rare laughter trickle through the room.

A quick glance at Posey shows her previous tears of sadness have turned into tears of laughter. A quick poke to her side doubles her laughter as I say, "See, you're not the only one making messes, Rosie Posey!"

A sense of rightness settles over me as I watch the people I care most about sharing in their laughter.

Ellie tears off paper towels as she looks up at me, a smile permanently etched on her face. "Go get cleaned up."

I give her a grateful smile as I slide my chair back. "Thanks, sis."

Lila's still shaking with laughter when I grab her hand and drag her through the living room and up the stairs. Even though her fingers feel far too delicate in my hand, it feels like the most natural thing in the world.

Nervousness hits when I open the door to my room. I only have seconds to wonder if I left any boxers out this morning before the door slides shut behind us.

The sudden stillness of the air closes in around us until all I can hear are our labored breaths as we catch our breath after the much deserved laughter.

Lila's chest rises and falls as her eyes roam over my dresser, open closet door, nightstand, and settle on my queen bed.

Her eyes jump to mine when I clear my throat like she's been caught doing something she shouldn't. I can't help but smirk as a stunning blush creeps over her cheeks.

I continue on like I didn't just catch her checking out my bed. "Sorry about that. I didn't realize how slippery the bottle was going to be."

A smile lights her voice as I disappear into my walk-in closet. "Don't worry about it. It made Posey feel better. That's all that matters." I hear her smile fade before she continues, "Thanks for not making a big deal out of it."

My brows dip as I thumb through my clothes, trying to find something that won't drown her in fabric. "Why would I make a big deal out of it? It's just a little ketchup."

Her shoes click on the floor as she moves around my room. "Yeah, well, most guys wouldn't take a seven-year-old squirting ketchup all over them nearly as well as you did."

"I'm just happy to see her eating something she likes." I select one of my favorite t-shirts I've had since high school and move on to my shorts drawer. "How did that thing you needed to take care of go?"

She blows out a frustrated breath as I settle on a pair of shorts with a drawstring. "It went well. I guess."

I raise my eyebrows as I come out of the closet to find her looking through my movie collection on top of my dresser. "You guess?" She flies back from the dresser like it's burnt her as I chuckle. "You can look at them. It doesn't bother me if you want to snoop."

She crosses her arms and quickly uncrosses them as she realizes she just smudged ketchup all over herself. "I, uh, wasn't snooping."

I hand her a bundle of clothes as I chuckle. "Sure. Whatever you say. These will be huge on you, but they'll do while we put your dress in the washer."

Her fingers brush mine as she takes possession of the bundle. Blushed cheeks have become a constant feature on her face.

Now I need to think about literally anything else other than her stripping out of her clothes in my private space. I gesture over my shoulder to my attached bathroom. "You can, uh, change in there?"

Why the hell did I phrase that like a question?

Lila swallows thickly as she nods. Her eyes never stray from mine as she says, "Yeah, uh, okay."

The constant magnetic pull I feel toward this woman lessens to a bearable level as she closes my bathroom door between us.

I grab my shirt behind my neck and rip it over my head. I'm not a claustrophobic person, but the walls of my room feel like they're closing in around me the longer I stare at my bathroom door.

I close my eyes and take a few deep breaths as I count to twenty in my head. Counting has always been a great way for me to stay focused and calm my nerves before a game. There's no reason it shouldn't work now.

One.

Lila is in my bathroom.

Two.

Lila is mostly naked in my bathroom.

Three.

Lila is putting on my clothes.

Four.

Lila is putting on my clothes in my bathroom.

Five.

Lila is mostly naked, putting on my clothes, in my bathroom.

Holy fucking shit.

My mind isn't any clearer and my heart isn't any calmer by the time I reach twenty. If anything, I've only doubled the images of a naked Lila in my bathroom. Images that really shouldn't be there if I'm just her *friend.*

I groan as I scrub my hand over my face. A deep breath slightly calms my nerves before I open my eyes. My heart doubles its efforts as she cracks open the bathroom door. "Can I, uh, come out now?"

I twist the fabric of my soiled shirt in my hands as I say, "Yeah, you can, um—" *Don't put emphasis on the word come. Don't put emphasis on the word come.* "—come out."

Lila's eyes double as the bathroom door bounces off the doorstop with a solid thunk. A quick glance down shows my bare chest where a clean shirt should be.

I look back up to watch in fascination as her pupils dilate and her breathing grows shallow. I only have a moment to take in how damn good she looks in my clothes.

Her eyes trace a path over my naked chest that I can feel all the way to my toes. I don't recognize the gravel in my voice when I say, "Eyes up here, Sunshine."

CHAPTER 17
NEMO
LILA

My face turns molten. I spin around so quickly that I bump into his dresser. My hip throbs as *Shrek*, *Finding Nemo*, and *The Matrix* fall to the floor and scatter between us as his neatly organized row of DVDs shifts under the sudden movement.

Nemo's beady eyes taunt me from the floor as my mind reels with images of a shirtless Kam.

Oh damn.

Damn.

Damn.

Damn.

What a beautiful man.

What a stunningly beautiful man.

The air that rushes over my face as I bend down to pick up the scattered DVD cases is a welcome relief on my overheated face. "I'm, uh, so sorry. I didn't mean to stare. It's just that, well, you're, um." My fingers fumble against the plastic cases as I take a deep breath to prevent any more embarrassment.

My first attempt to place the DVDs on the dresser misses, and my knuckles make a horrendous clack against the dresser. The throbbing in my hip and knuckles momentarily takes away the sting from the embarrassment. My second attempt at righting the fallen DVDs is a success.

I turn to find Kam's barely contained laughter reddening his face. The embarrassment comes flooding back like a rogue wave.

His grin is present in full force. "I'm what, Sunshine?"

I wave my hand around his entire frame as my face heats to an impossible degree. "You're kinda beautiful." I have to fight not to smack my hand over my mouth to keep it shut. The word *embarrassment* is not a good enough word to fit the stupidity my mouth is spewing.

His grin transforms into an impossibly enormous smile as my face heats even more under the weight of my declaration. "You're kinda beautiful, too."

An unladylike snort tumbles free as I pull at least ten inches of extra fabric away from my abdomen to gain access to some much needed air. "Friends don't lie, Trouble."

His brows pull down as his smile disappears into the ether. "I'm not lying. You've never looked more stunning than you do right now." He takes a predatory step toward me. "Cheeks red from embarrassment." Another step. "Drowning in *my* clothes." Another step. The intensity of his eyes robs the very breath from my lungs as he whispers, "Cloudless eyes."

I don't realize I've been walking backwards until my back bumps into the dresser once again.

The air in the room grows heavy until the magnetism between us grows into a tangible thing. Until his intoxicating scent is the only thing filling my lungs.

His bedroom door swings open and shatters the moment into a million pieces. Kam flies away from me so quickly it makes my head spin.

An amused Dax leans against the door with his arms crossed. His grey eyes light up like a cat who caught the canary as they volley between us. His shit-eating grin grows with his inspection. "Did I interrupt something?"

Kam's long legs carry him past his roommate and through the open door before I've even caught my breath. His shirt being pulled over his head muffles his words as he hurries out the door without looking back. "No. We were getting ready to come back down."

Kam's sudden change feels like being doused in a bucket of cold water. My heart falls to land on the floor by my feet as a sudden twinge of pain threatens to call tears to my eyes.

Dax tilts his head as he swings his gaze from Kam's disappearing form back to me. The rhythmic thumping of Kam's footfalls down the stairs mimics my racing heart.

Dax clears his throat as he straightens. "Jasper and Posey were wondering if they could stay for a rematch. Mace put yours and Kam's food in the microwave to heat up when you go down."

A small smile forms as I push off the dresser. "Thank you, Dax. They can stay for the rematch, but we've got to get going soon. They have a test to study for tomorrow."

He nods as his eyes roam over my face. "Cool. I'll go get the game set up, then. You can throw your dress in the washer downstairs if you want." He turns to leave, but stops at the last moment. "By the way, Kam's a really good guy."

I'm not sure why he feels the need to tell me this, but I'll go with it. "Yeah, I know. I wouldn't have let him watch the twins if I didn't trust him."

He nods as his face turns somber. Even with our limited interactions, I know the look is entirely out of place for the usual goofy hockey player. "I know. I just meant that he'll take care of you. If you'd let him."

He disappears down the hallway. His steps fade until all I can hear are distant voices drifting up the stairs. I grab my sticky dress and straighten my spine after I practically melted into the dresser behind me.

I'm proud of the stability of my legs as I walk down the stairs. I feel Kam's heated gaze for the rest of the rematch and for the duration of our walk to the car. It's not until we disappear down the street that I'm finally freed from the weight of his stare.

I miss it immediately.

LILA'S JOURNAL

Hi, Mom.

I have a few confessions to make.

I saw them today. I'm sorry I did, but I felt like I had no choice. The judge says I need a support system, and with you and Dad gone... They're my only option, Mom. I hope you can forgive me for bringing them into Jasper and Posey's life.

Also, I'm terrified.

I'm scared to let Maxwell and Victoria in again when you fought so hard to keep them out.

I'm horrified I'm doing the wrong thing. Not just with Maxwell and Victoria, but with all of it.

How do you know when to step in and help and when to stay back and let them make their own mistakes?

I fought so hard today to stop myself from taking over when Posey was doing something as simple as putting ketchup on her plate. I know she needs to learn to do it on her own, but I was right there to help her.

You should be the one to be there for her, Mom. You and Dad should be here to help them.

I'm so scared, Mom.

I'm scared of the overwhelming truth that I could love Kamden Stryker if given the chance. He would be so easy to love.

I can't give in to something as simple as a crush. Even if my heart craves his companionship. Even if the potential for something more is monumental.

I have no doubt Kam would take care of me. That's just who he is. He's the team captain for a reason. The thought of opening myself up to someone who has the possibility to destroy me is terrifying.

I saw how easily he could destroy me tonight when he walked away. The ease with which he walked away was in such contrast to the desperation I felt for him to stick by my side and face Dax together.

Does that make me a fool?

That's why Kam will stay in the safety of the friendzone, where his destruction potential is limited to that of my trust and not my heart. That's the only way to protect myself from the inevitable devastation he would leave in his wake when my life proves to be too much for him.

There's just some things in life that are certain.

The sun rises in the east.

A triangle has three sides.

Everyone dies eventually.

You can't turn back time.

The vulnerability that comes with loving someone can be devastating.

Someone as amazing as Kam shouldn't be with someone as damaged as me.

I miss you, Mom.

Love always,

Lila

CHAPTER 18
I MISSED THE PARTY
KAM

Even when I fumbled the winning goal for a championship title my senior year of high school, the disappointment in myself I felt then is nothing compared to what I feel right now.

Missing a goal is an unfortunate reality of playing the game. Going against my character, however, is unacceptable.

My fingers drum an anxious beat along the table in front of me as I wait for Lila. The minutes crawl by at an agonizing pace as the time draws near for class to start.

Memories of dozens of unsent texts flow through my mind from last night. I'm thankful now I didn't send them in favor of the nuance of an in-person conversation.

The thought of Lila not being in my life because of one stupid decision sends fear through me like a bolt of lightning.

At first, her beauty drew me to her like a moth to a flame. Now her heart, her kindness, her determination to step up and be what Posey and Jasper needs is like a balm to my very soul.

When I look at Lila, I'm not struck with the overwhelming sense of love. It's too soon for that, I know. But the sense of familiarity that washes over me every time I look into her eyes holds me captive. The sense that this person is important in ways I can't yet fathom.

It's what haunts my dreams at night.

It's what has me willing to drop to my knees and ask for forgiveness if that's what she deems necessary.

Relief and anxiety flow through me in equal measure as Lila finally appears through the classroom door. Her oversized shirt, messy ponytail, and dark circles under her eyes do nothing to dull her beauty that never ceases to revert me to a twelve-year-old boy watching his first crush on the playground.

A sense of summer and comfort washes over me as her mango scent permeates the surrounding air. She takes her seat next to me just in time for Professor Mills to reach his podium and clear his throat—his usual sign class is about to begin.

Seconds feel like minutes and minutes feel like hours as I wait for class to be over. My actions in my room last night play on a constant loop in my mind as I zone out.

Negotiation Strategies wasn't my first choice, but I can't help but feel thankful it led me to Lila.

My ears perk up at the mention of a group project near the end of class.

Professor Mills' monotone voice carries through the space in a dull current. "You'll get in groups of two to work through a series of contracts. I want you to give me a list of recommended changes for each contract, along with your reasoning. No one sentence reasoning. Do I make myself clear? I want real, thorough responses."

Murmurs circulate the room as other students look for the partner that won't stick them with the most work. My blood pressure rises as a few heads turn in Lila's direction.

Their gazes move on to others when I send them an icy glare.

The seat creaks under me as I turn my body toward Lila. The small smile already gracing her face sends a thrill through me. "Be my partner, Sunshine?"

Her smile only grows as she nods. "Sure, Trouble. Someone's got to keep you in line."

Professor Mills' voice rises above the murmurs as students pair up around us. "Use the rest of the class to discuss your project. You'll find the details of the project in your email inbox and in your student portal for this class. Have a good rest of your day."

The murmurs grow into full conversations as Professor Mills exits the room to disappear into the cave that is his office.

Our classmates gather their things and file out of the room with their partners, clearly not waiting around for the last few minutes of class.

Lila stuffs her notebook in her backpack as I stick my notebook under my arm and stand.

I clear my throat to rid myself of the knot that forms whenever she's near. "So, Lila." I scratch the back of my neck to give myself something to do with my hands. "I actually wanted to apologize for last night."

Her brows draw down in confusion as she slings her backpack over her shoulder. "About what?"

I decide to spit it out before my nerves take over. "You trusted me with the care of your siblings and with our friendship, and I almost ruined it. I respect your decision to just be friends, Lila. I don't want you to think I don't. Our friendship is far too important to me to risk in the way I did last night."

The slight tension in her shoulders leaves her frame with her next breath. "Thank you, Kam. Our friendship is important to me, too."

I leave the weight that had become a parasite since I left her in my room last night behind as I follow her out of the aisle. Tendrils of escaped hair reach for me in the wind as she moves toward the door. I follow helplessly in their wake.

She raises her voice to be heard over the waves of students in the hall as we walk together. "Thank you for watching the twins yesterday. That's all they talked about when we got home."

I laugh as I think back to the rematch Posey won yesterday and how butthurt Dax was for the rest of the night. "I'm glad they had a good time. They're welcome anytime."

I hold the door open for Lila as the warm breeze washes over my face. I curse under my breath as I realize I forgot my sunglasses at home. Memories of the last time I direly needed my sunglasses spring to the forefront of my mind like a welcome friend. I laugh under my breath as I ask, "Have you had any more trouble with your car battery?"

Her small laugh is almost as warm as the summer

sun. "Thankfully, no. I'm still not sure what caused it to die that day."

Seconds of comfortable silence stretch between us as we walk along the crowded sidewalk.

I speak before I've given myself permission. "I value your trust. I know it's not easily given." Quietly, I add, "I was very disappointed in myself yesterday. That's why I left the room so quickly."

The noise around us fades until we're cocooned in our own bubble. She peeks over at me as we walk. The sight of her crystal blue eyes burdened by clouds again breaks my heart.

Her voice is gentle when she says, "What's really going on, Kam?"

My throat grows tight as my mind rejects the idea of speaking the very thing I've worked so hard to heal from. "I don't want to be like him."

Her presence never wavers as we walk. "Like who?"

The melodic beat of our footfalls on the sidewalk calms my racing heart. "My dad." I blow out a breath that was intended for calming, but comes out shaky. "He wasn't a good man, Lila. The media talks about the great Brock Stryker, NHL starting center. Record setting career high for goals. Multimillion dollar contracts."

I shake my head as I say, "What I saw when I looked at him was different. I saw a man who made my mom cry every time he went to an away game because he couldn't keep his dick in his pants. I saw a man who would almost drink himself to death and gamble away his fortune every time he lost a game. I saw a man who wanted that same life for me." Students pass as we walk. I wonder what they see when they look at me.

Her eyes hold no judgement when she looks at me. "You're not your dad, Kam."

I nod as I'm forced to look away from her pure eyes for fear I might crumble under the weight. "I know. I've worked very hard not to be. When I went against your wishes last night and talked and acted in a way that went beyond friendship, I saw remnants of him." My voice quiets to a whisper. "That terrified me."

She pulls me to a stop as her delicate fingers weave through mine. The warmth of her palm soothes a fracture in my heart that I thought had healed long ago.

My voice is shaky as I admit something I've never said to another soul. "I thought I would be free of him when he died. I thought his harsh words couldn't haunt me, but his legacy always will." A humorless laugh escapes me as I shake my head. "That's so selfish to say when you hurt so badly from what happened with your parents."

Her fingers tighten around mine as her eyes blaze with determination. "Just because your experience with the death of a parent differs from mine, doesn't mean you're not entitled to your feelings, Kam. It's okay to admit your dad was a dick." Her smile threatens to dull the intensity of the sun.

The intensity of the laugh that breaks free almost startles me. "You're right. My dad *was* a dick."

Her eyes light up as she steps so close, there are only inches between us. "Say it again, Trouble."

"My dad was a dick."

She takes another step so the tips of our shoes are almost touching. "Louder!"

I tilt my head back and yell so loudly that birds fly from the trees on either side of the sidewalk. "My dad was a DICK!"

My sister's voice breaks the moment. "Sounds like I missed the party." Lila drops my hand. I instantly miss the contact.

Air floods between us as she steps toward my sister with a smile on her face. "Hey, Ellie. I wanted to thank you again for getting Posey some nuggets yesterday. She's always been such a picky eater."

"It's no problem. I was happy to do it." Her eyes turn mischievous as she looks between us. "Now, tell me why you were screaming about our dick of a dad for all of campus to hear."

"I was just telling Lila how his legacy doesn't match up with reality."

She nods as her eyes search mine. "Ah. I see." She turns her full attention to Lila. "Want to grab a coffee? I was just heading to the cafe."

Lila glances at her watch before she nods. "Sure. I've got an hour before my shift starts."

I watch in fascination as the girls link arms like they've known each other their entire lives. "Sorry, Goose. No boys allowed."

A laugh erupts from Lila as the clouds disappear from her eyes for a moment. "Goose?"

A seriousness takes over Ellie's voice. "Have you ever been chased by a goose, L?"

Lila's eyes light up as their voices fade the farther they get from me. "No, I haven't."

The sheer joy emanating from Ellie is palpable. "Well, Kam has." She glances over her shoulder as she drags Lila toward the cafe. The mischievous smirk on her face makes me fear for whatever she's about to say to Lila in my absence. "He has a scar in the shape of a bite mark on his ass to prove it."

My groan is followed by a small laugh. My feet are rooted to the ground as I watch them walk down the sidewalk. Ellie's ponytail and the tendrils of Lila's escaped hair blow in the wind.

Their laughter lingers in the air like the sweetest of fragrances as I watch them disappear into the crowd.

My chest feels lighter as I continue on the path to my Tahoe. A smile lingers on my face the entire way. I opened up and talked to Lila about things I've hardly admitted to myself. And it felt damn good.

CHAPTER 19
MONICA AND RACHEL
LILA

A constant thrum of voices and too loud of music assaults my ears as soon as I open the door to the cafe. The line stretches just feet from the door as most of the morning classes on campus finish up for the day.

The thrum of voices and gentle music falls to the background as I mentally count through the change in my pocket. My rumbling stomach protests when I realize a snack is out of the question. I'll just have to eat some fries or something while I'm waiting for my orders to be ready at work.

The smell of coffee and baked goods permeates the air as we get in line. Ellie's inquisitive eyes roam over my face as she tilts her head. Her silent inspection sends chills down my spine as her chocolate eyes take me in.

The similarity between her and Kam is normally subtle. Except, however, the color of their eyes.

We inch forward in the line as she breaks the silence between us. "What are your intentions with my brother?"

My mouth opens and closes like a fish out of water as her question floors me. That is not at all what I expected her to say. "I, uh, my intentions?"

She's unfazed by my stammer as she continues to inch forward in the line. "Yes. I want to know what you want from my brother."

I break eye contact to look down at my sandals as the weight of the similarity of her eyes to Kam's becomes too much to bear. My voice displays the uncertainty I'm trying so hard to hide. "I, um, we're friends. Just friends."

Her voice is kind as she says, "I didn't ask what you are. I asked what you want, L. There's a difference."

I swallow thickly to regain a modem of my composure. "I…I don't know."

Her eyes take on a mischievous light. "Yes, you do. You just don't want to admit it to yourself."

She leaves me standing behind her with my mouth gaping open as she steps forward to place her order. As she orders, her voice is a jumble of unidentifiable sounds. My mind swarms with unease as my eyes frantically roam the room, in search of an exit route to this conversation.

Ellie's words finally come into focus as she gently taps my shoulder. Her kind smile doesn't calm my fight-or-flight instincts that are screaming for me to flee this conversation I'm nowhere near ready to face. "What do you want to drink? It's my treat."

I'm shaking my head before she's even done speaking. "Oh, no. That's okay. I can just get my own."

A megawatt smile takes over her face as the poor cashier rolls his eyes, more than ready to move onto the next customer. "No way. I insist. If you don't choose, I'll be forced to pick something for you, and I don't think you want that. I've been told I have a horrible taste in drinks."

The weight of the line behind us bears down on me enough to cause me to cave to her demands. "Okay, uh, I'll take a small iced honey lavender latte, please."

Her ponytail almost hits me in the face when she turns from me to the cashier, who most definitely does not get paid enough to deal with college students all day. "Great! It'll just be the cotton candy frappe and the iced honey lavender latte, then. Oh, wait!" The cashier almost drops the cup he's writing on when she lunges toward him. "I also want a cake pop. A pink one." She turns to look at me over her shoulder as she raises her brows. "Want a cake pop?"

"Um, no thanks."

She raises a brow as my stomach lets out a monstrous growl. A victorious smile touches her lips as she pulls her card out of the wallet attached to her phone case. "Two cake pops then, please. Desserts are always better before a meal, if you ask me."

She takes her receipt, and we step over to the crowded pickup counter. Her hip digs into the counter with the coffee-cozies and the straws as she crosses her arms. "You didn't answer my question."

"Yes, I did. I said, I don't know what I want."

She pokes me in the arm so forcefully, I know I'll be sporting a bruise in the morning. "That's not a proper answer, and you know it."

My arm throbs as I try my best to rub away the pain.

"I really don't know what I want. I do know what's best, though. Friendship is best."

"Monica and Rachel. Order up."

Her smile turns sinister as she goes to the pickup counter. "Is friendship what's best, or is it just what's the least complicated?"

My brows rise as she sits the two drinks clearly labeled *Monica* and *Rachel* down next to me on the counter. "Um, those aren't ours. I didn't hear our names called, either."

She plops two straws out of the holder and hands me one. "Why use your real name when you can be someone new every time you get a drink?"

She rips open her straw wrapper and uses the free end to blow the wrapper into the trash. Her moan of delight when she takes her first drink has heads swiveling our way. "Oh my goodness. That is so good." A shiver rolls through her body as the sugary drink enters her bloodstream.

As soon as my straw wrapper enters the garbage can, she grabs my hand and pulls me toward the door. "Come on. Let's sit outside. It's too pretty today to be stuck in here."

My plastic cup immediately begins sweating with the first hit of the summer sun. Ellie doesn't release my hand until we are firmly planted on a bench in the shade of a maple tree.

The shadows on the sidewalk dance from the swaying branches overhead as I take my first sip of my drink. The liquid leaves a cool trail through my chest as it settles happily in my stomach.

Birds sing a happy song in the branches of the

surrounding trees as the chaos of the cafe melts away into a distant dream. I wipe the condensation from my cup onto the hem of my shirt. My voice is quiet as I admit, "I like him. It's just…"

Her body turns toward me. "It's just what?"

"It's just not fair to him. He deserves someone who can give as much as she gets. That's just not me." My voice fades into nothingness as I whisper, "It can't be."

She's quiet for so long, I begin to believe she's not going to say anything. With a sigh, she finally says, "He doesn't talk to anyone about our dad."

A humorless laugh escapes me as I run my finger over the rim of my plastic cup. "He must talk to someone about it."

Her voice is serious as she shakes her head. "No. He doesn't. He's never talked to me about it or his friends. I mean, I lived it with him, so I know a lot of what happened. Wyatt knows a lot too, since he was there for most of it. Dax and Mace know some things, but nothing like what I overheard him telling you today." She blows out another breath as her voice grows quiet. "You're special to him, L."

My fingers drift from the rim of my cup to the face of my watch. "He's special to me, too. I won't take advantage of that."

She nods her head slowly. "I know. He wouldn't trust you with his heart if you didn't deserve it."

I scoff. "He hasn't trusted me with his heart."

A smile lifts her voice. "Maybe not yet, but he's on his way."

My mind grasps for a way to change the subject. "So, what's going on between you and Wyatt?"

Her eyes grow into saucers. Her back straightens so fast, she almost drops her drink. "What makes you say that? Nothing is going on between us. We're just friends. Always have been, always will be."

A laugh erupts from me as she rambles. "Friends don't look at each other like that, Ellie."

She hangs her head in shame as she groans. "It's just a little crush, okay? I keep hoping I'll outgrow it or something, but have you seen the man?" My laugh only grows as she shifts her weight on the bench. "It's fine. I'm fine. It'll go away someday. It has to." Her eyes grow wide and pleading. "Right? I mean, I can't crush on my brother's best friend. We grew up together, for crying out loud! He saw what I looked like when I had braces and before I learned how to fix my eyebrows!"

I clutch at my stomach as I laugh so hard it's almost silent. She swats me on the arm as she gives in to her laughter. "Hey! It's not funny!"

I wipe the tears from the corners of my eyes. "It kind of is, though. I mean, it's one of my favorite book tropes."

Her eyes light up. "You like to read?"

I nod as I wipe my tear on the hem of my shirt. "Love it. I used to read a lot more before, well, before. Now it's hard to find the time."

She taps her finger against her chin. "So, what would your tropes be, then?" She ticks a list off on her fingers as she thinks. "Definitely strangers to friends to lovers. College hockey romance for sure. Oh!" She snaps her fingers. I can practically see the hearts in her eyes. "He falls first! That's such a good one!"

My face heats with her insinuation. "He has not!"

A mischievous glint fills her eyes as she pats my leg like I'm a child needing comfort. "You just keep believing that, honey." She takes a gulp of her drink that is worthy of the world's worst brain freeze.

Alrighty then. Time to change the subject. "Why are you calling me 'L'?"

She rolls her eyes like it's the silliest question. "Friends have nicknames for each other. Obviously. And I'm not about to start calling you Sunshine."

Friends.

What a nice thought.

By the time my hour is up and it's time for me to go to work, we've talked about our favorite books and exchanged phone numbers.

A sense of friendship, which I didn't think was possible to develop so quickly, has replaced the heaviness that marked the beginning of our conversation.

As we rise to leave, her words are barely audible beneath the pressure of the hug she gives me no choice but to partake in. "I like you, L."

Tears spring to my eyes as a sense of belonging washes over me. "Yeah, E. I like you, too."

CHAPTER 20
UNDERWEAR MODEL

KAM

The email stares back at me from my screen like a snake ready to strike.

Mace wrinkles his nose as he reads over my shoulder. "Are you sure this is English?"

I close my eyes and massage my temples to block out the string of emails with potential contracts I received from my dad's former agent this morning. "I really don't know, man. I was hoping taking negotiation strategies this year would really help when it came time for Richard to send me this shit."

Potential contracts and offers have been coming in like college brochures I received relentlessly my senior year of high school. I recline back in my chair at the dining room table to gain some distance from the mounting responsibilities that will inevitably come with signing with the NHL.

I groan as Dax's nosey ass appears over my shoulder. He gulps down his post-workout electrolyte drink as he scans my screen. "Underwear model? You've got to take that one, man. It comes with a lifetime supply of your choice of underwear."

His arm brushes the tips of my hair on top of my head as he leans closer to the screen with squinted eyes. "Oh, never mind. You have to sign an exclusivity contract with them to get the lifetime supply. Totally not worth it."

He saunters off toward the stairs, whistling the tune to the newest Taylor Swift song. I run my fingers through my hair and pause when they come away damp. I groan as I realize exactly what's coating my fingers. "You sweated on me, you fucker!"

Dax's laugh booms down the stairs as Mace snickers. "He totally did that on purpose."

I wipe my damp fingers on the neighboring seat cushion. That decision has nothing to do with it being Dax's usual seat. Nope. Nothing at all.

The soft thunk of my laptop lid closing feels like I'm closing the door to my casket as I choose once again to ignore the problem in hopes it will disappear. It hasn't worked out yet. I'm not sure why I think this time will be any different.

Isn't that the definition of insanity? Doing the same thing over and over again and expecting different results definitely fits the bill.

A soft knock on the front door sends my heartbeat into overdrive. The legs of my chair squeak against the hardwood floors as I stand.

The scene that greets me on the other side of the door has a laugh threatening to break free. Posey's face is twisted in disgust as she holds a lock of hair covered in pink gum in between pinched fingers.

Jasper's voice turns watery when he sees my face. "You gotta help, Kam. I swear, I didn't mean to. It just fell out."

Lila's flushed face is dripping with desperation as she blows a lock of hair out of her tired eyes. "Know any tricks for how to get gum out of someone's hair?"

My eyes swivel between the group as Mace appears over my shoulder. I scratch the back of my neck as Posey makes a gagging sound. "Get this out of my hair before I throw up."

The remorse in Jasper's eyes morphs into anger. "It's not gross!" He throws his arms up in the air in exasperation. "We shared a womb, for Pete's sake!"

Lila's eyes crinkle in the corners as she tries desperately to hold in her laugh.

I wave them into the house as I take a backpack from Lila's arms that's covered in glitter and has a cartoon character on it with eyes far too large for its body. Her own backpack falls from her shoulder and onto the floor by the entryway table as she grabs Posey's hands. "No! Don't pick at it. You'll only make it worse."

Posey rolls her eyes so violently, I'm shocked it doesn't hurt. "How else am I supposed to get it out?"

Mace's laugh bursts free as he turns toward the kitchen. "I'll get the peanut butter."

Lila's eyebrows rise as she places her body between the twins, who are currently glaring at each other. "Peanut butter?"

Mace's voice grows closer as he emerges from the kitchen with a half-empty jar of peanut butter. "Yep! We'll just slather some of this on there and it'll pull right off." He pulls a dining room chair out and motions for Posey to come over. She sticks her tongue out at Jasper as she heads in Mace's direction.

He reaches a finger into the jar to gather a solid helping of peanut butter. "My sisters were constantly getting gum in each other's hair." He massages it into the strands of Posey's hair as he talks. "My mama got tired of taking them to the hair salon every time it would happen, so she started trying her own at home remedies." He laughs as he dips back into the jar for another helping. "This was before Google, ya know?"

The scoffs that come from Posey and Jasper has Lila and I both laughing. The twins share a look of bewilderment as Jasper says, "You were born before Google was invented?" He tilts his head to the side as he looks at Mace like you would expect a farmer to look at cattle at an auction. "How old are you, anyway?"

Mace tilts his head back and laughs. "I'm only twenty-one, buddy! Don't look at me like I lived in the Stone Age!"

Posey whispers under her breath, "You practically did if you didn't even have Google when you were born."

Mace nudges her with his shoulder as he continues to turn her light blonde hair brown with the peanut butter. "Hey! I heard that!"

She shrugs her tiny shoulders. "I won't apologize if it's the truth."

Lila massages her temples as she mumbles, "Sweet mercy." She peeks at me from in between her fingers. "Regretting meeting here instead of the library yet?"

I'm shaking my head before she's done talking. "No

way. You can't bring the twins to the library, and we've got to work on our group project sometime." I shrug. "It just makes sense."

Lila waves a hand between Posey and Jasper, who are bickering about the best flavor of gum. "You may regret that by the end of the day."

"Not a chance, Sunshine. Not a chance."

CHAPTER 21
COOKING IS MY LOVE LANGUAGE

LILA

My eyes grow dry from staring at my laptop screen for the past two hours. My attention span wanes and my mind drifts from the ever present set of distractions that come in the form of two very cute seven-year-olds and three over-sized hockey players.

Dax's voice carries from the living room into the dining room where Kam and I have been holed up for the past two hours. "Okay, Rosie Posey. You've got three problems left." He clears his throat as he reads, "Amy has fourteen apples. She gives her friend Jack six of her apples. How many apples does she have left?"

"Ummm. She has eight apples left!"

I hear the smack of a high five as Dax says, "Heck yeah, she does!"

The nudge of a shoulder has me blinking back to reality to find Kam's warm eyes fixed on mine, his signature smirk firmly in place. "Come back to me, Sunshine."

"Sorry, I zoned out for a bit." Blissful relief flows

through me as I close my eyes and massage away the blooming headache that seems to be my constant companion. "I think I've reached my limit of reading over contracts for today. I stayed up way too late last night working on another project."

Kam leans back in his seat as he stretches his arms over his head. His shirt rides up to reveal tantalizing inches of toned skin that has my tired mind flashing with memories of what he looks like without a shirt on. I shake my head to clear the memories as Kam's shirt slides back into place.

The tendons in his neck bulge with his yawn. "Yeah, I'm going cross-eyed. My future agent sent over some contracts for me to read before you got here. I'm pretty sure my brain was fried before you walked through the door."

A horrible cracking sound fills the air as I straighten out my neck. I cringe as I rub away the weird feeling. "You're getting contracts already?"

He blows out a breath. "Yeah. I've been putting all this off for as long as I can. I don't have the mad skills you do with contracts."

My brows furrow as I lean my elbows on the table. "Isn't that what agents are for? Aren't they supposed to be there so you don't have to know what a good contact looks like?"

He nods his head as he plays with a loose string on the sleeve of his t-shirt. "Yeah, but my dad got screwed over big time by his first agent. In my mind, Richard, my dad's agent when he died, wasn't much better. I always told myself I would learn the skills for myself so I didn't get in the same position." A sheepish laugh escapes him as he gestures to the mess we've made of the dining room table. "I guess it's proving to be harder than I thought."

I tilt my head to the side as I take him in. "Why sign with him, then? It sounds to me like you'd be better off with someone else."

His brows furrow as he thinks. "Well, everyone always just assumed I'd sign with him when the time came. I technically can't sign as long as I'm still playing college hockey. He's only allowed to give me *advice* in the meantime."

"Who's everyone?"

He pulls on the string on his t-shirt so hard the seam unravels. I'm not even sure he's realized what he's doing. "Umm, my mom. I guess. She's always talked like it's a done deal." He abandons the poor string to scratch the back of his neck. "I never really thought there were any other options, I guess."

Mace pops his head out of the kitchen right as the familiar smell of baked potatoes hits my nose. "Dinner's ready!"

A smile lifts the corner of my lips as I take in his signature SSU apron. "You know you don't have to cook for us all the time, Mace."

He places his hand over his heart like he's in pain. "You wound me, Sullivan. Cooking is my love language."

I stand from my seat and hold my hands up in surrender. "I got it. I got it. Cook away. I was just letting you know you deserve to be cooked for every now and then, too."

As soon as I'm within arm's reach, he wraps me in a

crushing hug. He rests his chin on the top of my head as he squeezes me. "You're a peach, Sullivan."

I take a moment to return his hug. His very firm chest muffles my voice. "Well, uh, you're an apple, Mace."

He squeezes the air out of me as his laugh reverberates through his chest and into my ear. "You're not from the south, are you?"

I shake my head as he releases me from his vice-like grip. I run my fingers through my hair to smooth the strands his scruff assaulted. "Nope. Chicago, actually."

He pats me on the head as he walks by. "It shows. It really shows."

I scrunch my brows up as I look at Kam to explain what the hell just happened.

His laugh grows as he takes in my confused expression. "Don't look at me. I've lived in Pennsylvania all my life. I know nothing about being in the south."

I help Kam get the dishes out to set the table while Dax, Posey, and Jasper round the corner. Dax's voice is adamant as his hands wave around him in circular motions. "It's important that you visualize the circle. Okay, so Adam has a pizza that is split into twelve slices. Barbra comes along and takes three." He mumbles under his breath, "Which is totally rude, by the way." His voice picks up as he walks through the kitchen. "How many slices of pizza does Adam have left?"

I exchange an amused look with Kam as we laugh. "Are you sure he doesn't mind helping them with homework? We can just do it when we get home."

He hands me a stack of plates from a shelf far too

high for a normal person. "I promise. He's actually wanted to be a teacher. This is good practice for him."

My eyebrows raise. "Dax wants to be a teacher? I thought he would play for the NHL or something."

Dax's head lifts when I make it to the table. "I do. I'll play for a few years, then go teach somewhere and become a coach. I can't waste the opportunity to make all that money."

I pass the plates out around the table as Wyatt appears in the doorway. Water droplets drip from his hair to leave dark-grey dots on the shoulders of his t-shirt. He groans as he inhales. "That smells amazing." Jasper's giggles float through the air as Wyatt ruffles the thick strands of his hair on his way through the kitchen.

As he pulls his seat out, the sleeve of his shirt rides up to reveal the beginning of a tattoo. Great, now my mind is reeling with all the places Kam might have a tattoo.

Mace places an enormous plate piled high with baked potatoes in the middle of the table. "Hey, Ranger. How was your workout?"

Wyatt shrugs as he grabs a plate. "It was fine." I pretend not to see the pink lollipop sticking out of his pocket that will no doubt end up in Posey's backpack later.

My breath catches as Mace sits a plate of chicken nuggets down in front of Posey. A serving of ketchup is already on the plate in the shape of a heart. My eyes water as I clear my throat of the emotion that's currently suffocating me. "Mace. Thank you so much. You didn't have to go through all that trouble."

His eyes shine as he gazes down at my sister. "It's no trouble at all. A few of my sisters are picky eaters. I just figured it would be nice to have some nuggets in the freezer."

I look away from the scene in front of me before my tears betray me. The smile I hear in Posey's voice brings a watery smile to my face. "Thanks, Mace!"

"Anytime, little Sullivan."

Kam's eyes snag mine from beside me as tears gather in the corners of my eyes. He grasps my hand under the table and gives me a comforting squeeze. He whispers, "Do you guys want to come to the beach with us on Saturday after the last hockey camp?" His eyes flick toward the twins. "I meant to ask before we came in here, in case you had something else going on. I didn't want to get their hopes up. It'll be all of us, a few others from the team, a few other friends and girl-friends."

My eyes drift to Jasper and Posey's laughing faces before they return to a smiling Kam. "Yeah, Trouble. We'd love to."

CHAPTER 22
MAILBOX CONVERSATIONS
KAM

I turn the knob on my dashboard so my music fades into the background as I pull onto her street. The varying shades of tan and gray houses blur by as I scan the mailboxes for number 2722.

Her red car sits alone in the driveway of a two story gray house in a cul-de-sac at the end of the street. Empty flowerpots frame the fire engine red door. The mailbox lid is open, and the trash can sits at the top of the driveway. My car door slamming behind me echoes through the quiet street. A horrible squeaking sound fills the air as I close the empty mailbox.

I take two steps up the driveway before the squeaking sound fills the air once again. The rusty hinges protest as I slam the lid back into place. I cross my arms as I have a stare-down with a mailbox in the front yard of the girl I've got a crush on.

Like an opponent on the ice taunting me, the lid slowly falls back open. I level it with a glare. "You just declared war."

Great, now I'm talking to mailboxes.

A crease forms between my brows as the envelope in the mailbox catches my attention. The red words *Passed Due* might as well be a glowing neon sign in the dimly lit hole.

I can hardly feel my feet moving along the pavement as I walk up the driveway.

Before I get the chance to knock, the door flies open to reveal a smiling Jasper clad in bright red swim trunks and a white t-shirt. His tight grip on my hand forces the frown from my face as he yanks me inside. "Hey, Tank. Are you guys ready to head to the beach?"

"Lulu and Posey are still getting ready. They should be done soon. Do you want to see my room?"

I shut the door and twist the lock as my laugh grows. His grip on my hand tightens as he pulls me through the house. "Sure, Tank. I'd love to see your room."

My eyes are on a constant swivel as he drags me through the living room and down a slender hallway. Family photos lining the hall show a history of the Sullivan family. A young Lila sits between a man and a woman in the first photo. I would assume the image was of Posey if I didn't know better.

The family grows as I continue down the hall. Two babies lay cuddled together in the middle of a blanket.

Lila smiles as she holds two crying toddlers in her arms, her blue teeth proudly on display. A birthday cake with blue and white icing sits partially eaten in the background.

Lila's voice travels to us from a room at the end of

the hall. "Jasper! I told you not to answer the door unless I told you it was okay."

Her hair billows around her shoulders as she steps into the hall. The strap of her white dress falls down her shoulder as I trace the outline of a pink bathing suit underneath. Her pink tipped toes sink into the light green rugs as she walks.

Jasper groans as he comes to a stop in front of his sister. "I knew it would be Kam. You told me he was on his way."

As she crosses her arms, her dress rides up to reveal a few extra inches of her thigh. I force my eyes away from her to examine more of her family photos as she argues with Jasper.

A slightly younger Jasper and Posey stare back at me. They each hold signs in front of them displaying stats for their first day of kindergarten.

My name is Posey Anne Sullivan!
First Day of Kindergarten at Monroe Elementary
I am 42 inches tall.
I am 5 years old.
My favorite color is pink.
My favorite food is chicken nuggets.
I want to be a Princess when I grow up.

My name is Jasper James Sullivan!
First Day of Kindergarten at Monroe Elementary
I am 45 inches tall.
I am 5 years old.
My favorite color is red.
My favorite food is popcorn.

I want to be a Hockey Player when I grow up.

The rising panic in Lila's voice has me snapping my head in her direction. She's squatted down in front of Jasper. Her fingers dig tightly into his shoulders. "Promise me you won't answer the door like that again, Jasper."

His eyes turn glassy as he nods his head. His voice is barely a whisper. "I promise, Lulu. I'm sorry."

She pulls him into a tight hug as her voice softens. "It's okay, Jellybean." Her eyes lift to mine as she draws slow circles on his back. "It's okay." She forces the worry from her eyes and a fake smile onto her face as she pulls back from her brother. "Why don't you go see if Posey is ready to go?"

His smile returns as he nods. His bare feet thump against the ground as he runs to the room Lila appeared from earlier.

Lila's smile falls as he disappears around the corner. She closes her eyes and lets out a deep breath before she stands. "Sorry about that. I'm just so afraid it's going to be a stranger or the social worker that's at the door. I don't think she would be happy about him answering the door unsupervised."

My instincts are screaming for me to pull her in for a hug. I stick my hands in the pockets of my swim trunks instead. "It's okay. I'm glad it was me this time."

"You and me both." Her hair sways around her shoulders as she turns away from me. "Just let me grab our bags and we'll be ready to go. We just need to grab the twins' booster seats out of my car before we go."

I scratch the back of my neck. "Oh, about that."

She stops in the doorway of what I assume is her bedroom as she turns to me. "Yeah?"

"I, uh, went ahead and got them some booster seats and installed them this morning." Her eyebrows raise as I hurry to continue. "I hope you don't mind. I looked up their ages and guessed at their weights so I could get the best ones."

A smile takes over her face. She moves so fast she's almost a blur as she wraps her arms around my neck for a tight hug. My shoulder muffles her voice. "Thank you, Kam."

She fits so perfectly in my arms, it nearly takes my breath away. I tighten my arms around her as I take in her mango scent. "You're welcome."

She pulls free from my arms and gives me a beaming smile as she turns to go back toward her room. I feel the loss of her in my arms immediately. "I'm just gonna grab my stuff."

I nod as her warmth from our hug slowly seeps away from me. "Sure. Do you need any help?"

Her voice fades as she rounds the corner to what I assume is her bedroom. "No, thanks. I've got it."

My legs strain with the force it takes for me to not follow her into her room. My curiosity is overwhelming me to the point I don't see Jasper and Posey come out of the room at the end of the hall until they're right in front of me.

Posey's voice pulls my focus from Lila's door as she throws herself at me for a hug. "Hey, Kam!"

I laugh as I pick her up off the ground and spin her around. "Hey, Rosie Posey. Are you ready to have a good time at the beach?"

Her giggles float through the air like clouds. "Yes! I'm bringing my sandcastle supplies and everything!"

I stabilize her on her feet before I let her go. "I guess we'll be building an epic sandcastle today, then! Should it be medieval or fantasy inspired?"

She scoffs. "Fantasy, obviously."

I hold my fist out for a fist bump she gladly gives. "Right on, Rosie Posey."

A thunk at the end of the hall has all our eyes turning to find Lila struggling to get through the door with a huge tote on her shoulder and a cooler wedged under her arm.

My feet carry me to her before I have time to blink. "Are you going to let me help before you hurt yourself?"

She shakes out her fingers as I take the cooler and the tote bag from her possession. "I can carry it on my own."

"I know you can, but you don't have to." I adjust the pink tote on my shoulder as I grab the cooler by the handle. A vibration courses through the ground as the cooler falls to the floor. I look from the handle still in my hand to the cooler on the ground as a chorus of laughs erupts from the siblings behind me.

Lila's voice is unburdened by her previous worry. "I forgot to mention the broken handle, didn't I?"

A smile takes over as I look over my shoulder. "Oh, you are so getting dunked in the water for that, Sunshine."

Her laughter turns into a wicked smile. "You'll have to catch me first, Trouble."

CHAPTER 23
BITCH TENDENCIES
LILA

The beach used to be my mom's favorite place in the world. I can feel her here just as clearly as I can feel the salty breeze blowing over my sun-warmed face.

I can hear her laugh drifting through the wind as clearly as I can hear the crashing waves in the distance.

The warm sand shifting between my toes feels like a *hello* from a long-lost friend as I take my first steps onto the sand without my mom. For the first time, memories of her don't threaten to drown me in grief, but instead fill my heart with happiness for the time I had with her.

My pink-tipped toes disappear into the sand as Posey and Jasper's laugh drifts toward the water. Sand flies into the air behind them as they run through the crowd toward our friends.

I don't know when I started calling them friends, but watching the way they embrace my brother and sister with fierce hugs, I can't think of any others more deserving of the title.

"They make everything better, don't they?" I can

hear the smile in Kam's voice. His eyes are alight with happiness as he watches Dax spin Posey around in the air. Sand flies off her feet as her giggles float to us in the wind.

Kam's eyes grow serious and his voice grows so quiet it's almost swallowed up by the wind as Jasper follows Mace and Wyatt toward the water. "It's scary to care about them so much. Jasper fell on the ice this morning at camp and almost gave me a heart attack."

I smile as Ellie drags Posey down onto her beach towel and envelopes her in a tight hug. "It's definitely scary, but loving them is worth it."

He nods as his eyes never stray from my brother in the water. "Is he a strong swimmer? I think I'll go join them. Looks like they're getting ready to play football. I'm sure they could use one more."

I laugh as he takes off toward the group of hockey players currently throwing a football to my brother. "Hey, Trouble!"

His body tilts toward me, but his eyes never leave the water. "Yeah, Sunshine?"

"You might want to drop off the bags first!"

He glances down with a look of surprise as he realizes his arms are full of beach supplies. "Oh, yeah. Probably a good idea."

He dumps the supplies at Ellie's feet and takes off toward the water without a backwards glance.

Ellie laughs from her place on her towel in the shade as I approach. Her bright red one-piece stands out against the pale sand. "What's his problem?"

I battle the corners of my towel as it blows in the wind, laying it out next to hers under the umbrella. "I think he's worried about Jasper being out in the water."

Her eyes soften as she watches our brothers laugh together. "Ah. I see. Kam's always worried about everyone else."

I smile as she braids Posey's hair out of her face. "And you're not?" My fingers twitch as I fight to keep them in my lap. "You don't have to braid her hair. I can do it."

Her eyes shine with a mischievousness I'm growing to love as she ignores what I said. "Only certain people make my list, L. And once you've made the list, you're stuck on it for life."

Posey twists to look at Ellie over her shoulder. "Am I on your list, Ellie?"

Ellie's fingers weave deftly through Posey's hair, despite the wind. "You sure are, Posey-Pop!" Her voice grows quiet as she turns toward me. "All three of you are."

"Oh. Hi, Lila. I wasn't expecting to see you here." Kim's voice makes me turn to find her walking from the parking lot. She's surrounded by a few other girls from work and one I've never seen before.

I fight the eye roll that's begging to be set free as I take in her barely there bikini and a full set of jewelry. "Hi, Kim. I wasn't expecting to see you here, either."

I fight a growing smile as the corners of her fake smile dim and her eyebrows pinch together. The movement is so slight, I almost don't notice. "Well, I *always* come to the annual beach day. They do this every year before their first regular season game, you know." Her smile brightens. "I never miss it."

The rubber band snaps into place in Posey's hair as Ellie turns to our new guests with a smile firmly in place. "Funny how you never fail to miss it, even though you're never invited."

Kim's face transforms from Barbie to bitch in record time. "The only reason you're even invited at all is because your brother is the captain."

Ellie's smile grows as she tilts her head to the side. Her hands slide over Posey's ears before she says, "That's funny. I'll have to tell him you said so when I go over to their townhouse for dinner this week. I'm sure he'd love to be reminded of your bitch tendencies."

The girl I don't recognize from work is the only one that doesn't scoff at Ellie's remark. The rest of the group practically has steam coming out of their ears. If they're not careful, they'll melt their full faces of makeup off.

Ellie turns back to my sister in an obvious dismissal. "Alright, Posey-Pop! Are you ready to build that sandcastle?"

Kim either didn't take the hint or simply wants to get the last word in; it's hard to tell. Her eyes blaze as she stares a hole in the back of Ellie's head. "Come on, girls. They obviously can't tell when someone is trying to be nice."

Ellie rolls her eyes as she helps Posey empty her bucket of all the sandcastle supplies that used to be mine when I was little. "Watch them settle in the sun. I hope their skin turns to leather."

A laugh that has been waiting to burst free finally pushes through my last restraints. "Have they always been like this? They are absolutely the worst thing about working at The Penalty Box."

She lines the supplies up in a neat row as she gives me a humorless laugh. "No. They were actually my *friends* in elementary school."

My eyebrows disappear into my hairline as I search her face for any sign that was a joke. "You used to be friends with them? I have a hard time believing that. You don't fit in with them at all."

She smiles at me as Posey flattens a spot in the sand for the castle. "That might be the nicest thing you've ever said to me."

Curiosity runs rampant through me as I fail to imagine Ellie in their friend group. "So, what happened?"

She blows out a breath. "They turned into mean girls when hormones started happening. I chose to 'become one of the guys' instead." Air quotes accompany her eye roll. "I like it better this way. The guys are always honest and there's no drama. You've just got to watch yourself and make sure you don't ask a question you don't want to know the answer to."

I hand the empty bucket out to Posey. "Hey, Jellybean. Why don't you go get some water so we can harden the sand up a bit?"

Sand coats every square inch of her legs as she stands and runs toward the water with the pink bucket. I smile as her braid floats in the wind behind her. I laugh as I run my fingers along the shadow of the umbrella on the sand. The cool sand transitions to warmth as my fingers move over the shadow. "I can imagine. It's kinda like that with kids, too. They'll say whatever they're thinking if it will hurt your feelings or not."

She groans. "I made the mistake of asking Kam if he thought my dress looked nice for a date one night. Let's just say I've never worn that dress again."

I laugh as the image of a fuming Ellie fills my mind. "I bet you didn't ask him again."

Her answer is immediate. "Of course I do. Who else will be that brutally honest with me?"

My laughter dies as I think back to the few friends I've had in my life. "To be honest, I've never really had a lot of friends, especially after we moved here. What few friends I had, I left behind in Chicago. My mom was always my best friend, anyway. And Posey and Jasper after they came along."

"Well..." Ellie pulls two cans of lemonade out of a cooler next to her. As she hands one to me, the icy chill of the metal seeps into my overheated skin. The wind swallows the sound of our tabs snapping open. She holds her can out to me with a warm smile on her face. "Here's to new friends. May they last a lifetime and always be your perfect alibi."

A smile takes over my face as I clink our cans together. "To new friends."

CHAPTER 24
MY GIRLS
KAM

Waves pull at my legs as the water races toward the shore. A smile touches my lips as Posey races toward the water. She dunks a pink bucket into the crashing waves and tiptoes back up the beach. She leaves blotches of wet sand in her wake as she weaves through the sparse crowd that separates her from our sisters.

I only allow my eyes to return to the water when she disappears into the shadow of the umbrella.

"I've got eyes on the girls, Kam. Don't worry about it."

I spare a quick glance at Wyatt as the football lands in his waiting hands with a wet slap. I don't even try to conceal the worry in my voice. "I can't help it. I'm the one that invited them here. It's up to me to look out for them."

He sends the ball flying toward our other teammates as his eyes return to my girls on the beach.

Yeah, that's right.

My girls.

Wyatt's voice is a calming balm on my raging nerves. "Not everything rests on your shoulders. Mace and Dax are watching out for Jasper, and I'm watching the girls. Just try to have a good time. You've got to share the burden now and then, man."

I sigh as the ball lands in his hands once again. He passes it to me as I smirk. "Easier said than done." The ball spirals through the air as streams of water fly off it. The ball lands with a wet thunk in Colt's hands fifteen yards away. His laugh carries over the water as his fellow freshmen push each other into a coming wave.

Wyatt nudges me in the arm as another wave crashes into my legs. "Uh, Kam?"

My eyes snap to him as the strange undertone of his voice registers. His finger pointing in the girls' direction has my stomach dropping. What I see, however, practically turns my world upside down. "Fuck."

Amusement colors Wyatt's voice. "You're screwed, man."

Lila's bare legs shine in the summer sun as she strips her white dress over her head to reveal a striking pink one-piece swimsuit. My mouth waters as I follow her fingers as she straightens the straps on her shoulders.

A wet slap resounds through the air as the football smacks me in the face. I don't even feel the impact, as I'm rendered powerless against the waves against my legs and the sheer beauty of Lila Sullivan.

Her golden hair blows in the breeze and falls in waves down her back. I'm captivated by the motion as she throws her head back and laughs at something Ellie says. I'm jealous of the wind as it swallows up the sound before I get a chance to hear it.

The elongated column of her neck begs for my lips as I trace the length of her profile with careful eyes.

Her rays of sunshine reach me all the way in the water. All I want to do is bask in her light for as long as she'll let me.

If only she could see herself through my eyes.

A wave of guilt washes over me as I yet again catch myself thinking about Lila as more than a friend. She's made her wishes very clear, and I intended to respect that.

My muscles turn to stone as Colt lets out an appreciative whistle in Lila's direction. "Who the hell is that?"

My voice is pure gravel as my full attention zeroes in on him. "*She* is not your concern."

His eyes light up with a challenge as he lazily tilts his head in my direction. "Is *she* yours, Kam?"

She will be.

My teeth grind together as I work to maintain my composure. "No." An image of Colt with his filthy hands on Lila flashing through my mind makes me see red. "She's off limits, Colt."

A grin takes over his face. "Says who?"

"We do." Wyatt's voice is pure steel as my roommates crowd around my back.

My blood boils as it speeds through my veins.

Colt's grin turns sinister. "Seems like that's a decision she should make for herself. Don't you think, *Captain?*"

Dax's hand lands on my shoulder as I practically vibrate with rage. Colt doesn't deserve her. No one does. She is too pure for this world. Too good to be corrupted by his hands.

Dax's voice dips to almost a growl as his fingers dig into my damp skin. "This isn't a hill you want to die on, Colt." His voice drops to a whisper. "Settle it on the ice, Kam. Not here. *Little eyes* are watching."

I look down to find Jasper's big blue eyes staring up at me from his position between my roommates. His eyes volley between me and Colt. Clarity enters my mind as I take a deep breath.

At first glance, Lila may seem weakened by grief and struck down by her circumstances. But when I look at Lila, I see strength.

Strength to step up and fight for her brother and sister when no one else could.

Strength to tell me no so she could do her best for them.

Strength to laugh through her grief and live despite it all.

I've seen glimpses of her fire, and I can't wait to watch her set it loose.

My faith in Lila dims the uncontrollable rage, trying to take hold inside me. Memories of my dad losing control flash through my mind as I fight to maintain a hold on my emotions, despite the blazing challenge still present on Colt's face.

I am not my father.

My determination is no match for the strong current fighting my legs as I walk in Colt's direction. My voice stays steady as a new determination floods my veins. "You're right. It's a decision she should make." His eyes betray his fear he tries so desperately to hide. "But make no mistake." Inches separate us now. "She will turn your sorry ass down, because that woman knows her worth." My voice drops to a dangerous level. "And you're not good enough."

His smirk is a desperate attempt to show strength he doesn't possess. "And you are?"

I shake my head slowly. "No. That doesn't mean I won't try to be." A smirk lifts my lips. "Oh, and Colt?" His eyebrows raise as he fights not to fidget. "You might want to rinse the lipstick off your neck before you go. Wouldn't want her seeing your true colors so soon."

The darkness now present in his eyes is no match for the certainty ringing through me as water fills the space between us. My smirk grows into a full grin. "I look forward to watching you fail, Colt."

My eyes never leave his as I back away toward the wall of muscle that is my roommates.

Jasper's voice rises over the rage still boiling through me. "I'm glad you're the man of the house now, Kam. It's a really hard job."

A genuine smile takes over my face as my eyes soften on the little boy, who now takes up much of my heart. "You three aren't alone anymore, Tank."

And you never will be again.

Mace's hand lands on my shoulder as I focus on the feel of the sand between my toes. His voice betrays the anger he tries to hide from showing in his eyes. "I hope you didn't make things worse with Colt. I've only known him for a few weeks, but I can already tell he holds onto a grudge like they're going out of style."

"Lila can handle him."

His eyes lighten as a smile breaks out on his face. "Oh, I know she can. I'm just worried about you having to watch it."

My muscles tighten as Colt makes his way out of the water with a smirk on his face and determination in his eyes. He rubs at the lipstick on the side of his neck as he walks.

My hands clench into fists at my side as I will my feet to stay where they are.

You've got this, Sunshine. Let them see your beautiful flames.

CHAPTER 25
RED ISN'T YOUR COLOR

LILA

The sun warms my back as I tap on the bottom of the bucket to release the sand. A smile blooms on my face as I slowly raise the bucket to reveal a perfect imprint of a castle.

Ellie's hand waves over the crumbing mess she's made on her side. "How do you get them to come out so perfect when mine looks like this?"

Posey laughs as she stands. White streaks of sunscreen run down her back to mix with the inch of sand now coating her legs. "You aren't using enough water. I'll go get us some more."

I nod as I stretch my legs out in front of me to ease the stiffness from sitting too long in one position. "Tell Jasper it's time for more sunscreen."

Ellie's smile falls as her eyes focus on the direction of the water. "Here comes trouble."

The look on her face lets me know it isn't the good kind of trouble I now associate with her brother.

I use my hand to shade my eyes as I look in that

direction. My brows furrow as I zero in on the only person coming our way.

The sun gleams off his tanned skin as his curly, blond hair bounces with every step he takes toward us. His face transforms into a cocky smirk as his eyes trace over Kim and her friends as they lounge on their towels. Their giggles float through the air as I fight the urge to not roll my eyes.

His eyes turn away from them to zero in on me. I never look away from the predatory look in his eyes as I whisper, "Don't you dare leave me."

Ellie's voice lowers to match mine. "Wouldn't dream of it."

The arrogance rolling off of him reaches me before he does. His stark white teeth are blinding in the summer sun as he smiles down at us. "Ladies."

His eyes rake over me as I fight to not grab my dress for an added layer of protection against his slimy gaze.

Ellie's annoyance bleeds into her tone as she straightens her spine next to me. "What do you want, Colt?"

His eyes roam down my body as he answers her. "I'm not here for you, Ellie. Don't get your panties into a twist."

His stomach muscles bunch as he tries to act like he's not flexing on purpose. I draw my knees to my chest to cut off his view. His eyes bounce back up to mine as he smiles like a Cheshire cat.

Ellie huffs out a humorless laugh. "Then why are you here?"

His eyes brighten as his gaze rakes over my legs clutched tightly to my chest. "I was wondering if the new girl wanted to go for a walk. We can go down to the pier."

Ellie opens her mouth, but I cut her off before she has time to speak. "The *new girl* has a name."

His eyes flare with lust as he takes a small step closer to us. "Are you going to tell me what it is, or am I going to have to guess?"

The audacity of this man. No, boy. He's definitely a boy.

My eyebrows raise as I lower my legs back out in front of me.

I will not cower.

I tilt my head in a challenge as I channel my inner-Ellie that I've always been too scared to set free. I guess that makes it my inner Lila. "No. I'm not playing your game."

His eyes blaze with a molten fire I have no desire to entertain. "And why not?"

"Fuck boys don't get to know my name."

A smirk blooms on his face as he enjoys the challenge I now represent. "And what makes you think I'm a fuck boy?"

I rise from my towel with a newfound power that feels like it belongs within my veins. Power that has been set free because of the support of my new friends. "There's a few, actually." I dust the sand off my hands as I walk closer to him. "First, I wasn't the only girl you stared at on your way up the beach."

The flames in his eyes turn from flames of lust to flames of anger as I take another step in his direction. My voice is steady. "Second, you frowned at my sister as she walked by on her way to the water." Now his eyebrows draw down in confusion as his smile completely melts away. "And third," a smile grows on my face as I stand right in front of him, "you couldn't even bother to wipe the lipstick off your neck before you came to talk to me. *Red really isn't your color.*"

His eyes turn into a fiery inferno of pure anger as I step around him. His hand shoots out and grabs my wrist in a punishing grip. "You can't just walk away from me."

I wrench my wrist from his grasp. "Watch me."

I step around him to find a seething Kam only a few feet away, with the twins and a wall of muscle at his back. His chest rises and falls as his eyes bounce between the blooming redness around my wrist and the *boy* at my back.

Wyatt's voice is barely a rumble in the wind as he whispers, "On the ice, Cap."

Rivulets of water drip down Kam's bare chest as I stop inches in front of him. My voice is barely a whisper as I watch the current of emotions rush through Kam's eyes. "Take me to the water, Trouble."

His jaw ticks as his knuckles turn white from how tightly he's clenching his fists. My hand shakes as I uncurl his fingers. His rough calluses against my smooth skin feel like heaven. He vibrates with anger as his warmth seeps into my palm.

His breathing slows as his eyes lock onto mine. The tension in his jaw lessens as he bends down and tosses me over his shoulder, and jogs toward the water.

The wind blows through my hair as my laughter bursts free. I close my eyes and enjoy the safety that comes with being with Kam. It feels like I'm flying as he tosses me into the water.

The warm water surrounds me in a quiet cocoon before my head breaks through the surface. I wipe the water from my eyes as I take in Kam's smiling face. There's no trace of his anger in his voice as he wades into the water. "That was for the cooler."

The waves swallow my legs as I back away from him. "That's not fair. I didn't even get a chance to get away."

A brief glance up the beach relaxes what's left of my nerves when I find our friends surrounding Jasper and Posey. Their laughing faces warm my heart as they sit around the sandcastle with no Colt in sight.

A predatory gleam shines brightly in Kam's eyes as I inch away from him. The predatory look Colt gave me on the beach felt slimy and unwelcome. Kam's gaze feels like a caress that soothes my racing heart.

He lunges for me right as I dive into the water behind me. The weightlessness I feel as I'm submerged in the water lasts only seconds before a strong arm clamps around my waist.

The firmness of Kam's chest presses into my back as he pulls me from the water. His scruff tickles my cheek as he bends his head to whisper in my ear. "That was too easy."

My smile grows as the sound of our labored breaths drift through the air. "Maybe I wanted to get caught."

Kam's chuckle vibrates through me. "Oh, Sunshine. I'm counting on it."

CHAPTER 26
EVERYTHING

KAM

The flames flicker in the fire pit as the smoke reaches toward the stars. Posey's hair tickles my neck as she shifts in her sleep on my shoulder. Her deep exhale makes me smile as she burrows further into me.

The light from the fire dances across Lila's smiling face next to me. "I think they're worn out."

My laugh is quiet so I don't wake Posey. "Playing in the water all day will do that. I'm pretty worn out, too."

Ellie smiles as she runs her fingers through a sleeping Jasper's hair as he lies on a towel next to her. "They wore me out, that's for sure. My legs will be sore tomorrow from all the running through the water."

Dax's legs move closer to the fire as he stretches out on a towel across from me. "They gave us a better workout than Coach."

Mace groans next to him. "For the love of all things hockey, never mention that to him or he'll have us skating suicides." A shiver runs through him that I'm sure has nothing to do with the chill in the air, and everything to do with vomiting his favorite Italian food after the last time we had to skate suicides.

A rare smile takes over Wyatt's face as his eyes scan over our group.

Dax's booming laugh causes Posey to stir on my shoulder. "It's not my fault you have a weak stomach."

I rub slow circles on Posey's back as I shift her onto a towel next to me. Pins and needles race through my arms as I shake the feeling back into them.

Her nose scrunches as she turns her back to the fire and settles onto her side.

Lila's eyes soften as she takes in her sister's peaceful sleeping form. Her voice is soft as she looks around the fire. "I could never thank you guys enough for all you've done for us."

Ellie nudges Lila's shoulder as smiles flow through our group. "You're one of us now. We take care of our own."

Lila's eyes mirror the fire's reflection as she turns to study my face. Her voice is barely a whisper. "Yeah. I'm beginning to see that."

Conversation flows to the upcoming game around us as our eyes stay locked together. As I lean closer, a bubble of solitude forms around us. "Take a walk with me, Sunshine."

The start of a smile appears before it vanishes to be replaced by a furrowed brow. Her eyes move between her siblings as she shakes her head. "I can't leave them."

Ellie gently grabs Lila's hand as a no-nonsense look

takes over her face. "They'll be fine here with us. Go on."

They share a silent look before Lila's eyes return to mine. "Okay."

I raise my eyebrows as a smile takes over my face. "Yeah?"

Her smile returns as she nods. "Yeah. You've got thirty minutes, Trouble."

My head spins as I stand too quickly after a day in the sun. I extend my hand to her, palm up, as a smile becomes a permanent fixture on my face. "We better make them count, then."

Her hand slides into mine like it belongs there as I pull her to her feet.

We're quiet as the warmth from the fire fades to be replaced by the chill in the night air.

The sand hardens beneath our feet as the sound of the waves grows closer. Flashes of green and purple light the pier on the horizon as the Ferris wheel spins.

The vastness of the dark ocean spreading before us makes me feel like I'm stranded in the expanse of space. It almost feels like we're the only two people left in the world.

The minutes fly by as the pier looms closer. I'm already mourning the loss of our solitude. "We should probably head back."

Tendrils of her hair reach for me in the wind. Her voice barely rises above the roar of the waves. "Yeah. You're probably right."

I follow her bare footprints as she turns back toward the way we came. We drift toward the water's edge until Lila's silhouette breaks the streak of moonlight reflecting off the surface.

The first wave washes over her feet and bubbles on its way back to its rightful place.

"Tell me something I don't know about you."

Her hair glows in the moonlight as she looks over her shoulder with a smile on her face. "What do you want to know?"

"Everything."

Her smile dances in her eyes. "That's a tall order, Trouble."

I mimic her smile as a wave comes within inches of my feet. "I'll settle for one thing then. At least for now."

"I don't really know what to tell you. I'm not very interesting."

Her eyes are free of clouds as I follow her into the water. I might just follow her anywhere if she keeps looking at me like this. "That's pretty subjective. And you, Sunshine, happen to be my new favorite subject." The warm water rushes over my feet as I close in on her.

The water rises on our legs as she backs away from me. Her voice is so quiet, it almost disappears into the darkness. "I ran track in high school."

I shake my head as my eyes roam over her face. "Not good enough."

Her smile falls as the surrounding air turns serious. "What do you mean?"

"If I'm settling for one thing, you better make it good."

She tilts her head as she thinks. "I, uh, I like to read."

I shake my head again as the water pulls on my legs as I pull on her walls. I beg them to fall and let me in. "Try again. You can do better than that."

"I'm, uh, a business major."

The solitude we've found in the water fuels my resolve. "Still not good enough."

I can barely hear her voice over the rushing waves. "I don't know what more you want from me."

"I want something real. I want something that no one else knows." My voice falls to a whisper. "Something that's just for me."

A war plays out on her face as her eyes search mine. The sound of the rushing waves and indecision fills the space between us.

Her eyelashes flutter against her cheeks as she closes her eyes and takes a deep breath. Apprehension is written all over her face as her eyes open and connect with mine. "I can't imagine our future without you in it, Kam."

Her words nearly steal the breath from my lungs. "You don't have to."

She shakes her head as the clouds move back to her eyes. "You don't know that."

"You're right. There are very few certainties in life, but know this, Lila Mae Sullivan." Steel determination rings through my voice as I close the distance between us. "I'm not going anywhere. I'm here. With you. For you. Beside you. Whatever you need. I want to be that for you." My voice falls to a whisper. "As long as you'll let me."

The string of friendship we've woven between us pulls taut as she searches my face. I beg her with my eyes to cut the string and set me free so we can weave a new thread. A thread that seems so full of possibilities.

Laughter drifts to us from the shore. Lila's eyes flick behind me before she takes a step back. The night air takes her place as she moves away from me. "Looks like your thirty minutes are up, Trouble."

I know I'll find our friends packing up if I glance over my shoulder, so I choose to stay in our bubble a bit longer. I grab Lila's hand as she tries to walk back to shore. The clouds in her eyes move in and out of focus as she gazes up at me.

The cool chill of her skin seeps into my palm. "Come to my game tomorrow night."

Her eyes flick back and forth between mine. I see the exact moment she gives herself permission. She can't hide the trepidation in her voice. "Okay."

I mourn the loss of her hand as soon as I let it go. The waves wash around my legs as I watch her walk away.

I know one thing for certain.

Thirty minutes will never be enough.

CHAPTER 27
SEMANTICS
LILA

My eyes volley between the jersey on my bed, the note in my hand, and my crush's sister as I try to calm my racing heart. "He gave you this?"

The number 23 on the back of the jersey grows smaller as the name "Stryker" written across the top grows larger. The significance of wearing Kam's last name on my back to tonight's game feels monumental.

Ellie groans from her place on the edge of my bed. "For the hundredth time, yes. He wants you to wear it. Open the note and read it for yourself."

I trace the edges of the paper in my hand like I would a bomb. Logically, I know I won't be the only girl wearing Kam's name on my back tonight, but I'll be the only one he *asked* to wear it.

That means something, right? It has to.

I turn my back to Ellie to gain a semblance of privacy as my shaky fingers unfold the notebook paper. My eyes roam over the neat handwriting twice before I actually read any of the words.

> *Wear my jersey tonight, Sunshine. It'll look better on you than me.*

How can twelve little words hold so much meaning?

I exhale a shaky breath as I refold the paper and slide it into the back pocket of my jeans.

I turn back around and come face to face with a grinning Ellie. Her excitement is palpable as her smile turns blinding. "So, will you wear it?"

My eyes trace the bold letters on the back of the jersey once more before they return to her. I nod my head with a hesitant smile. "Yeah. I'll wear it."

Her answering squeal startles me into almost tripping over the toy cars at my feet. "Yay! We need to get started then."

I back away from her as she roams her calculating eyes over my form. "Get started on what, exactly?"

Her nose wrinkles as her eyes lock onto the messy bun on the top of my head. "We have a lot of work to do, L. We need all the time we can get."

An hour later, I hardly recognize the woman staring back at me in the mirror. Soft, blonde waves cascade down my back and blend with the thin, red ribbon tying my hair out of my face.

Dark lashes stand out against my freckled cheeks.

My blue eyes glow from the bronze eyeshadow I almost didn't allow Ellie to apply because of how scary it looked in the pan.

The number 23 sitting proudly in the middle of my chest feels like a statement I'm not sure I'm ready to make, but the sense of rightness that it creates settles my erratic heart.

Posey's soft voice pulls my attention from my reflection. I didn't even hear her enter the room. "You look beautiful, Lulu."

Ellie envelopes my sister in a crushing hug from behind as they both stare at me with hearts in their eyes. "Doesn't she, though?"

I smile as I take in Posey's cheerleading costume and high pigtails that are tightly secured with matching red ribbon. "Thanks, Ladybug."

The pounding of little feet in the hall reaches us before Jasper does. "Come on! We're going to be late!"

Ellie's smile turns sinister as her eyes gleam. "I guess we better get going, then."

If only I had her confidence.

The roar in the stadium sets fire to my already-fried nerves.

Ellie's voice is muffled by the crowd and the handful of popcorn she just stuffed in her mouth. "Why do you look like you're about to throw up?"

"I do not." I push the sleeves of my black, long

sleeve shirt to my elbows and fan my face with the game day program Jasper insisted we take from the lady who scanned our tickets.

Ellie huffs out a laugh as she stuffs another handful of popcorn in her mouth. "You're turning green, L."

"I don't know, okay. It just feels like everyone is looking at me and they all know Kam gave me this jersey and they think I'm not worthy to wear it and that I'm just an imposter and I—"

Ellie's calming hand on my arm silences my raging thoughts I didn't realize were tumbling out of my mouth. "Woah there. Take a deep breath in." I follow her lead as she takes a deep breath in through her nose. "That's it. Now let it out." We breathe out through our mouths as the chill in the air finally cools my heated cheeks.

We breathe like that for several seconds until my heart returns to its usual rhythm. She waits until my coloring returns to normal before she begins her speech. "First, no one knows anything about what's going on with you and my brother. Even if they did, it's none of their business."

I groan as I lean back in my seat. "I know. You're right."

She holds up her hand to silence me once more. "I wasn't finished. Second, if my brother chooses to love you, that makes you worthy of that love."

My spine straightens to an impossible level as I almost levitate out of my seat. "No one said anything about *love!*"

She dismisses me with a wave of her hand before

she continues. "Semantics. And third, you're not an imposter."

I raise my eyebrows as my spine relaxes a fraction of its tension. "You're not going to give me a reason *why* I'm not an imposter?"

She stuffs another handful of popcorn into her mouth. "Nope. I can't give you all the answers to life's problems."

I roll my eyes at the girl who is quickly becoming my best friend. "What would I do without you?"

She shrugs her shoulders as her eyes roam up and down my polished form. "Look like a hot mess. Still hot, just a mess." A look of concentration takes over her face as she digs around in her bag of popcorn. "Have you heard from your grandparents anymore?"

I sigh as I think back to the phone call I shared with Victoria a few days ago. "Yeah. They want to watch the twins for a few hours after the game tonight. They think it'll help them 'bond'." Air quotes accompany my eye roll.

Her eyebrows go up and a stray popcorn kernel falls to her lap as her hand stalls halfway to her face. "And how do you feel about that?"

I shrug as I turn my attention to the ice. My eyes immediately lock onto Kam as he skates laps around the rink. "It's terrifying, but that's what the judge told me to do. I don't see any other option."

She nods as her eyes flood with sympathy. "You should come to The Penalty Box tonight after you drop them off. It'll help keep your mind off things. You deserve a night off every now and then."

I blow out a thankful breath. "That would be great."

She picks the stray popcorn kernel off her lap and tosses it over my head at Jasper before turning back to me like nothing happened. Jasper's head swivels around, looking for the culprit as Ellie hides her popcorn bag under her arm. "And you're sure you don't have a long-lost aunt or something you can contact instead?"

"Not that I know of, unfortunately."

Her eyes light up and I can practically see the light bulb above her head switch on. "You can do an at-home ancestry genetic test and try to find relatives that way! This girl in my economics class found out she had a half-brother by doing one of those. Let's just say her mom was not very happy when she found out."

"I thought about that already. That's not guaranteed to show any results or that the relatives I find would be interested in meeting us." Her eyes flare as I steal a piece of popcorn. "Plus, they take weeks to get back. I need to build a relationship *now*."

Her expression falls as she resumes digging in her popcorn bag. "Ah. That's a bummer. I hate to say it, but I think you're just going to have to give your grandparents a chance."

My resigned sigh gets lost in the voices surrounding us. "I know. I'm just going to make the best of it. People can change, right?"

She rolls her eyes as she looks over at the empty seat next to her. "I'm beginning to doubt that."

Sympathy constricts my heart. I would give anything to have my mom sitting next to me, but Ellie and Kam's mom can't bother showing up. "Does she ever come to his games?"

I watch as Ellie stows away her sorrow. The action is so seamless and practiced, I'm not sure she realizes it even happened. "She only tries when it's convenient." She shrugs like that's not the saddest thing in the world. "You get used to it after a while."

I clench my teeth as my fingers dig into the armrest between us. "Yeah, but you shouldn't have to."

Her eyes follow her brother on the ice as a small smile lifts the corners of her lips. "That's why we always show up for each other. Kam and I. We have to be there for each other if no one else will."

My heart aches as I watch my brother and sister share a box of Skittles next to me. Every time Jasper pulls out a red one, he hands it to Posey because he knows it's her favorite. It doesn't matter that it's his favorite, too.

I can't help but smile. "That's what family does."

Her eyes turn away from her brother to search my face. "You're family now too, L. I hope you know that."

I'm starting to.

CHAPTER 28
PROUDEST SISTER MOMENT

LILA

An electrifying current flows through the air as the lights dim. My ears ring as the emcee's voice booms through the pulsing arena. A sea of red and white flashes by the glass in front of me as the players take the ice.

Goosebumps flow across my skin as the cheering faces around me flash red and white from the spotlights moving around the space.

My heart beats like a relentless drum in my chest as Kam's name is called last. His smile beams throughout the rink as he moves through the line of his teammates. Their grins double as he hands out his usual fist bumps. The team stand unified on the frozen stage before me.

A grin breaks out on Kam's face as he bumps fists with an opposing player with a 'C' on his chest. The look they share is that of old friends instead of what I might expect from rival captains.

I raise my voice to be heard over the rumble of voices around us. "Does Kam know the other captain?"

A small smile graces Ellie's face as she watches the teams retreat to their benches. "That's Knox. We all went to the same high school. They grew up playing together."

I hold my breath as the lights return to normal and the players gather in the center of the rink for the puck drop.

The puck falling to the ice and landing on the dividing line transforms the ice into a battlefield. A practiced dance unfolds as the two teams work to secure the black bullet as it flies through their ranks.

Kam takes possession of the puck and flies toward their goal like he's unburdened by something as minuscule as gravity. All SSU players slow and come to a standstill at the halfway point of the rink as Kam sends the puck flying toward Colt, who is now isolated from the rest of the team.

Confusion flashes across Colt's face as the stands fall silent. As soon as the puck contacts Colt's stick, he's surrounded by players from the opposing team. His legs fly out from under him as the puck flies through the air to land on the other side of the rink.

A collective gasp rings throughout the cavernous space as Colt disappears in the throng of players. Fists fly as sticks are abandoned at their feet.

I crane my neck as I stand to get a better vantage point. All SSU players stand idly around the center of the ice. Hard expressions take over all their faces as their coach's face turns bright red.

The boos and cheers that erupt from the stands dull the shrill sound of the ref's whistle as the fight continues.

The screaming fans around me fade to the recesses of my mind as Kam's eyes connect with mine.

A smirk transforms his face as he mouths, *Hi, Sunshine.*

Ellie whistles next to me as I hold eye contact with her brother. "This might be my proudest sister moment."

My voice is almost swallowed up by the crowd. Vibrations flow through my feet from the stands as everyone around me gets to their feet. "What do you mean?"

A bloodied Colt is dragged out of the throng of players. Streaks of blood stain the ice as the refs clear the rink.

A team of staff carrying red bags flood the ice and surround him as he scrubs his face with bloodied hands. Streaks of red shine in his blond curls as he waves the team medics away.

Ellie's eyes light up as she waves a hand over the ice. "I know you're new to hockey and all, but that kind of shit doesn't happen. Your team doesn't just sit there while you get your ass handed to you like that."

Frustration replaces my confusion as I search her face. "You're going to have to spell it out for me, E."

A shit-eating grin takes over her face. "What I'm trying to say is that was Kam's way of getting back at Colt for what happened at the beach." The giddiness rolls off her in waves as she grabs my hand. "*And* he did it in a way that wouldn't get him in trouble." She mimes wiping away a tear from the corner of her eye. "Hence, my proudest sister moment."

My heart stutters at the thought of Kam getting in trouble for me. "Why would he have gotten into trouble?"

She shrugs like it's the most obvious thing in the world. "It's frowned upon to fight with your own team on the ice. Fighting with the other team is basically expected."

Colt retreats slowly to the bench as the staff clears the blood from the ice. "So, you're saying Kam orchestrated that fight? For me?"

She nods her head so adamantly, I'm not sure how it doesn't fall off. "Yes, and yes."

I'm speechless.

Utterly speechless.

"Why would he do that?"

I don't realize I said that out loud until she answers me. "Because he's crazy about you, L. Isn't it obvious?"

My mind reels with snapshots of these past weeks.

Of everything Kam has done for me and the twins.

Of how lost I would be without him. Not just because of how much he helps with the twins, but because I now consider him my friend.

Of how heartbroken I would be if he called someone else 'Sunshine'.

Of how devastated I would be if he was looking at anyone else the way he's looking at me right now. Surrounded by his teammates, but with his full attention on me.

It takes a village.

But Judge Harris never said my village needed to share my blood.

My voice is watery as I admit something that terrifies me. "I've been an idiot, E." My watery eyes lock onto hers with a sense of pleading that's palpable. "I've been such a fool."

Her eyes turn soft as she envelopes me in a hug that muffles her voice. "It's okay, L. We're all stupid sometimes."

She smooths my hair as she pulls away from me. I rub my nose with my shirt sleeve as I search her eyes, which are so similar to her brother's. "What am I going to do? I've turned him away. I told him I just wanted to be friends."

Her brows dip before determination lights her eyes. Her shoulders square and her back straightens like she's preparing for battle. "You tell him. He's not going to try again unless you lay it out for him. Girls can take the lead, too. Find your inner strength and use it, L."

"My inner strength?" I pull my bottom lip between my teeth as nerves take hold.

Her hand tightens around mine. "Yes! Find it and use it! You're an independent woman who doesn't need a man, but you *want* one. And you want *that one*." I follow her finger as Kam skates around on the ice to get in position. "So go get him. It's time for you to take what you want, L."

My palms start to sweat from nerves and how tightly she's holding my hands. "Right now?"

She looks around like we could magically press pause on the game. "Um, maybe wait until after the game?"

I nod my head as my eyes return to the ice. "Probably a good idea."

Cheers erupt around us as the whistle blows and the game resumes. My thoughts move as quickly as the players on the ice as everyone takes their seats.

My inner strength.

It can't be that hard to find. Right?

CHAPTER 29
GOOD LUCK CHARM
KAM

I dodge the passing servers and congratulatory pats on the back as my eyes scan the dim restaurant.

I pass over all the familiar smiling faces in search of one that I'm positive is the cause of me playing the best game of my college career tonight.

A sinking pit of disappointment opens up in my stomach when I don't spot her. I reluctantly sink down into the seat next to my sister. The conversations around me turn into a jumbled mess of noise as I force my focus onto the abandoned straw wrapper in front of me.

The wrinkled paper crinkles easily in my hands before it tears in half.

"There's no need to take it out on the wrapper, Goose. She'll be here soon."

I sit up straighter in my seat as all my senses zero in on my ever observant sister. "She, uh, she will?"

"Yep." She pops the 'p' as she chews on her straw. She doesn't even try to hide the smirk that appears at my obvious excitement at her news. Her eyes gleam as she looks over my shoulder at the entrance of the restaurant.

"Hey, Trouble."

A bolt of lightning flows through me at the sound of her voice.

The tension flows from my muscles like water from freshly melted snow as I turn and take her in. "Hi, Sunshine." I quirk a brow as I tilt my head at the tension visible on her face. "What's wrong?"

She waves away my concern. "Just a little headache." A smile brightens her tired eyes as she takes the empty seat next to me. Her attention swivels around the table as she greets everyone else. "Hey, guys. You all played great tonight." Her eyes snare mine once again as her grin turns into a beaming smile. "Two goals are pretty impressive."

Dax scoffs from his seat across the table. "Nah. A hat trick would have been impressive."

The quick flash of a smile is the only indication of Wyatt's pride in my performance tonight. "A hat trick would have been nice, but pair two goals with four assists, and you're on track for Best Playmaker."

Lila's brows furrow in confusion as she settles into her seat. "What's a hat trick? And what's Best Playmaker?"

Mace wipes salsa off his chin with one hand and reaches for the basket of chips in front of him with the other. "A hat trick is when a single player scores three goals in one game. And Best Playmaker is given to the player with the most assists that season. We'll turn you into a hockey pro eventually, Sullivan."

The conversation moves on around us as I lean closer to Lila. "Where are the twins?"

A flash of anxiety zings across her face before she buries it under a neutral expression. She can't hide the worry from her eyes, though. "I just dropped them off at my grandparents' house."

My eyebrows rise. "How do you feel about that?"

Her shrug doesn't convince me. "I'm dealing with it."

I open my mouth to respond, but am cut off by our server with a pad and pen in her hand. "Are you guys ready to order?"

A smile blooms on Lila's face as she turns to greet her coworker. "Hey, Sammy. How's your shift going?"

I nearly stop breathing when I see my name written across her back. Obviously, I knew it was there. I gave her the jersey, for Pete's sake. Seeing it, though? That's an entirely different ball game.

My eyes trace the block letters as my breathing turns shallow. I force my eyes away from my name, only to discover a red bow in her hair.

I need to get out of here before I do something stupid.

Something I can't take back.

Like kiss the hell out of her.

The legs of my chair squeak against the floor as I rush to stand.

I have to stop looking at her.

My fingers glide along the smooth fabric as I wipe my suddenly sweaty palms on my pants. My thoughts feel like a runaway train as I search for an excuse to get out of here. I have to fight not to let out a relieved breath as the tips of my fingers connect with my wallet in my pocket. "I, uh, I forgot my wallet in the car. I'll be right back."

My throat constricts to a painful level as I struggle to swallow. My friends share confused glances as an amused smirk blooms on my sister's face.

The other tables become a blur as my legs carry me through the restaurant and out the front door. I'm thankful for the first signs of fall as the cool night air washes over my face.

My fingers dig into my still-damp hair as the chilled air fills my lungs.

Breathe. Just breathe.

I sync my breathing to the numbers as I count to twenty.

One.

She has my name on her back.

Two.

I want to kiss her.

Three.

I can't kiss her.

Four.

Damn it. I can't kiss her.

"Kam?"

I close my eyes and take one more deep breath to prepare for coming face to face with my greatest temptation.

The reflection of the streetlamps in the parking lot shine brightly in her eyes as she searches my face. "Are you okay?"

The level of pain in my voice is surprising as I grit my teeth. "No. I'm not okay."

Her eyes flash with concern as she takes a step toward me. "What's wrong? What can I do to help?"

I take a step away from her to maintain the distance I have no choice but to put between us. "I need you to go back inside."

Her concern is replaced by hurt that I immediately regret putting there. Her voice is small and timid in the abandoned parking lot. "Why?"

I hope she can see the desperation on my face as I beg her with my eyes to listen to me. "I'm just feeling a bit off. It's nothing you need to worry about."

Her eyes narrow. "I saw the outline of your wallet in your pants, Kam. I know you didn't forget it in your car." Her eyes and voice soften. "Be honest with me."

I spread my arms out to my sides with my palms up as I lay myself bare before her. "Because I'm not strong enough to stay away from you when you have my name written on your back. I'm just not." My voice falls to a whisper as realization and something that looks suspiciously like relief dawns in her eyes. "I'm just not strong enough."

A fire erupts in her eyes as she takes a defiant step toward me. "Maybe you don't have to be."

I nearly groan with the sudden rush of hope that I can't allow to take root in my chest. I shake my head as I take a retreating step away from her. "Don't tease me, Sunshine. My heart can't take it."

The fire in her eyes morphs into a raging storm as she closes the distance between us. I clench my hands at my sides to keep myself from reaching for her. "I'm not teasing, Trouble."

I stand like a statue, ready to cut my hopes down by the roots, if necessary. "I need you to say what you mean."

A small smile pulls at her lips as she skims her fingers down my arm and intertwines our fingers with a steady hand. "I want you, Kam." Her smile grows as my heart warms in my chest. "As more than friends." Her eyes turn mischievous as her smile turns into a grin. "Did you start a fight for me tonight, Trouble?"

My heart races with the memory of the satisfying crush of Colt's nose. "No." Her eyes flash with confusion and a hint of disappointment before I continue. "But I orchestrated one."

The disappointment lifts from her eyes like a storm cloud being burned away by the sun. "Why did you do that?"

My grip tightens on her hand as flashes of the redness around her wrist fly through my mind. "Because no one gets to lay a hand on you and not answer for it." I let out a shaky breath as I use our joined hands to close the last few inches between us. "If you don't want me to kiss you, I need you to walk away, Lila. My restraint is on its last leg."

Her cloudless eyes roam over my face. "Then kiss me already."

I let out a groan of relief as my lips *finally* connect with hers. Her mango scent becomes a part of my soul as I breathe her in.

Relief flows through me with such intensity my

fingertips tingle as I grasp the sides of her face with a gentleness I'm not sure how I possess.

The softness of her lips molding to mine feels like coming home as I pour weeks of built up frustration into one kiss.

With every sharp intake of breath I feel her take, bricks from my walls crumble to the ground to lay at her feet. Like an offering to a goddess, the crumbled stones piece together to offer shelter for her heart that I hope to one day possess.

Our lips move in a long overdue dance as I wind my arm around her waist. Her front molds to my chest like she was made just for me.

I pull away from her lips and glide my fingers through her hair as I search her eyes for any sign of regret. I let out a relieved breath when I don't find any.

A smirk forms on my face as I grasp the end of the silky ribbon in her hair and pull until the tension releases. Her hair falls freely around her face as I tuck the ribbon in my pocket. "This is my new good luck charm."

Her eyebrows crinkle with confusion as she watches the ribbon disappear into my pocket. "You can't just take my ribbon."

An uncontainable smile spreads across my face. "It's either the ribbon or you, Sunshine. Take your pick."

She rolls her eyes, but the smile on her face betrays her true feelings. "Fine. You can have my ribbon." Her eyes shine with mischief. "Do I get something else in return?"

My smirk can't be contained when she's looking at me like this. "What do you want?"

Her fingers dig into my back like she thinks I'll run away. She couldn't be more wrong. "A date."

"You're supposed to wait for *me* to ask *you*."

She just shrugs. "I'm trying this new thing where I just take what I want. How am I doing so far?"

I pull her in for another kiss as I whisper against her lips, "It looks good on you. It really does."

CHAPTER 30

THE BENCH WARMERS GROUP CHAT

KAM

THE BENCH WARMERS GROUP CHAT

DAX

So, Cap, why were you grinning like a hyena when you came back in from getting your wallet last night?

MACE

Isn't it obvious?

DAX

Obviously not…

MACE

Cap got kissed last night.

DAX

And you know this, how?

MACE

Again, obvious…

DAX

...

MACE

If Sullivan's blushing cheeks weren't enough of a tell, Cap's death grip on her hand for the rest of dinner should have been a dead giveaway.

DAX

THEY WERE HOLDING HANDS?!

MACE

I worry about you sometimes, Dax. I really do.

WYATT

We can't help you if you can't see what's right in front of your face, Dax. It's a wonder you manage to cross the street on your own.

DAX

HEY!

KAM

I was not grinning like a hyena...

MACE

You totally were.

DAX

Yes, you definitely were!

WYATT

...

KAM

Fuck off.

DAX

I need details, Cap! You can't leave us hanging like this!

KAM

There's nothing to tell. We kissed. It was mind blowing. We're going on a date tomorrow night.

DAX

NOTHING TO TELL?! Bullshit! That's a lot to tell, man! Why didn't you say anything last night? We've only been waiting for this for an eternity!

MACE

You're going on a date?! Where are you going to eat?

KAM

Yes, we are going on a date. And it has not been an eternity...

MACE

WHERE ARE YOU EATING?! I NEED TO KNOW. If you need restaurant recommendations, I've got you!

KAM

About that...Wyatt...I need to borrow your truck.

WYATT

👍

DAX

WHY DO YOU NEED TO BORROW HIS TRUCK?! WE NEED ANSWERS, CAP!

KAM

And, Mace? I need your dad's phone number and your spaghetti sauce recipe.

MACE

I'll send over his contact info AFTER YOU TELL ME WHAT THE HELL YOU PLAN ON DOING WITH MY RECIPE!

KAM

Like I would risk telling you and your big mouth.

MACE

I am offended.

WYATT

He has a point though…

MACE

DO NOT TAKE HIS SIDE!

DAX

KAM

You gossip more than my sister…

MACE

That's not fair! Ellie doesn't have any friends to gossip with. Plus, I have four sisters, Cap. FOUR! The amount of gossip that would flow through our house on a nightly basis was impressive. Check your email for the recipe.

WYATT

At least Ellie has a personality…

MACE

Low blow, man. Low blow.

DAX

So, let me get this straight…You're borrowing Wyatt's truck, Mace is providing a recipe, and you're getting Mace's dad's help? Everyone else has a task…

KAM

…

DAX

This is me asking for a task, Cap.

KAM

Um…

DAX

…

KAM

Can I borrow some parmesan cheese?

DAX

CHEESE?! IS THAT ALL I'M GOOD FOR?!

MACE

If the shoe fits…

DAX

Stay out of this, Mace!

WYATT

KAM

Parmesan cheese is an essential part of any spaghetti dinner. Everyone knows this…

DAX

I'LL GET THE BEST DAMN PARMESAN CHEESE IN PENNSYLVANIA!

MACE

That's the spirit!

DAX

Where do I buy parmesan cheese?

WYATT

You're kidding, right?

MACE

Please tell me you're kidding…We can't be friends anymore if you aren't kidding, Dax.

DAX

Of course I'm kidding!

WYATT

You just Googled it, didn't you?

DAX

MACE

We are no longer friends. I expect full custody of the others in our divorce.

KAM

Mace, do you have a simplified version of this recipe?

MACE

WHAT'S WRONG WITH MY RECIPE?!

KAM

Nothing…It's just that I have no idea what half this stuff is!

MACE

Oh, yeah? Like what?

KAM

What the hell is pancetta and why does it need to be diced? Can't I just get some ground beef?

MACE

I'm learning a lot about you guys today…

KAM

And what's the difference between extra virgin olive oil and olive oil?

DAX

What makes it a virgin or not, Mace? These are the real questions in life.

MACE

I officially hate all of you.

WYATT

From what I can tell from SouthernLiving.com, it's mostly a way for large companies to charge more for the same product.

DAX

A scam if I've ever seen one. That's for sure.

MACE

NO. Just no.

KAM

You either send me a simplified version, or I'm turning to Google.

MACE

STOP! I'll do it. Don't threaten me like that, Cap. And you call yourself my friend. You should be ashamed of yourself.

KAM

What does "a palm full of basil" mean?

MACE

Do I just need to come home early?

KAM

I mean, I wouldn't say no...

MACE

You're all idiots. Every single one of you.

DAX

Yeah, but we're your idiots!

WYATT

Do you want me to wash my truck?

KAM

You washed it three days ago...

WYATT

That doesn't answer my question.

KAM

No, Wyatt, I don't want you to wash your truck.

WYATT

KAM

Where's the cooler?

MACE

Where it always is...

KAM

...

WYATT

In the storage room under the stairs.

MACE

It's official. Cap's lost his mind.

KAM

?

MACE

YOU PUT THE COOLER THERE DUFFUS!

WYATT

What's a "duffus", doofus?

MACE

DAX

Do we get to watch the twins while you're on your date?

KAM

No. They're staying with Lila's grandparents.

DAX

BOOOOO!

KAM

Mace, your recipe says to cover the bottom of the pan with garlic…

MACE

And?

KAM

Which pan should I use? There's three and they're all very different sizes.

MACE

Use the one with the dent in the upper left corner.

KAM

It's a round pan. A circle doesn't have corners…And you guys think I'm the one who's lost his mind.

MACE

Put the handle in your left hand. The dent should be on the upper left.

KAM

AH! I see it.

DAX

KAM

Why can't you have actual measurements for this recipe like a normal person? "Cover the bottom of the pan with garlic" and "a palm full of basil" can mean very different things depending on what pan and whose palm you use. Just saying.

MACE

THAT'S MY MAMA'S RECIPE!

KAM

My bad, why can't your mama have measurements for this recipe like a normal person?

MACE

That's it, I'm turning my phone on do not disturb.

DAX

But what will your idiots do without you?

MACE

Not my problem.

KAM

It will be if I set our kitchen on fire...

WYATT

Maybe one of us should go home?

DAX

I'll be home in twenty minutes...

WYATT

I meant Mace or I...you know...the adults...

DAX

MACE

Idiots helping idiots. God help us.

CHAPTER 31
PATIENCE
LILA

The tips of my fingers tingle as butterflies take flight in my belly because of the man standing in front of me. I'm proud of my composure as my eyes roam over the shiny, black truck in my driveway. "Did you get a new truck while I wasn't looking, Trouble?"

His smile shines brightly with the evening sun as he runs his fingers through his hair. I wonder how many times he's done that today since the normally styled waves stick in every direction. "Wyatt was nice enough to let us borrow his truck for the night."

My eyebrows practically disappear into my hairline. "And why exactly do we need his truck?"

His smile transforms into his usual smirk as his voice quiets to a whisper. "You'll see."

I raise a brow in question as I push the sleeves of my sweater up my arms. "Does it have anything to do with why you told me to dress warm?"

His eyes linger on me as he examines me from head to toe. "Maybe." A quick glance at his watch has his feet moving quickly in my direction. "We need to get going if we're going to make it in time."

He opens the passenger door and extends a hand that I don't hesitate to take. "I'm guessing you're not going to tell me why we're in a rush?"

"Nope." He pops the 'p' before he closes the door in my face. I don't miss the gentle caress of his fingers against my palm.

I breathe in the new car smell as my eyes roam over the massive truck. A lone white scuff on the dashboard the size of my pinky nail stands out against the dark gray interior.

A red handled glass breaker and seatbelt cutter combo sits in the tray that I would fill with junk before I even left the car dealership.

The vast gray expanse of the backseat is only interrupted by a red cloth cooler that's covered in half peeled stickers and dark scuff marks. I assume the handle was white at one point.

I face forward in my seat as I rub my growing headache from my temples.

The driver's door opens to surround me in the familiar sounds of my neighborhood before the truck bounces as Kam effortlessly folds himself in the driver's seat. His eyes rake over me as they flash with concern. "You okay, Sunshine?"

"Yeah. My shift last night just took a lot out of me. How long has Wyatt had this thing, anyway?"

He shrugs as he slams the driver's door, the click of his seat belt snapping in place reverberates through the quiet space. His eyes flick to my fastened seat belt as he twists the key to start the engine. "I don't know. Maybe two or three years." He checks the mirrors before pulling away from my driveway.

My eyes nearly bug out of my head. "Two or three *years?* There's no way he's had this thing for more than a month! It still smells brand new!"

His eyes light up with laughter. "I know, right! You should see his bedroom. Ranger's got a bit of OCD." A scowl transforms his face in seconds. "Uh, on second thought, maybe you shouldn't see his bedroom."

My voice turns teasing as he fidgets in his seat. "I have no desire to see Wyatt's bedroom, Trouble."

A relieved breath escapes his lips like he actually thought that was a possibility. "Good. That's good."

His long-sleeved, black shirt is rolled up to his elbows, giving me the perfect view of his forearms as he drives with only his right hand.

I wonder if men know how many women love that sort of thing? Do you think they do it on purpose?

I'm transfixed by every muscle strain as he takes every curve out of my neighborhood with confidence.

The fingers of his free hand drum along the top of the window frame as his diligent eyes scan the road.

His impossibly long legs look normal compared to the large floorboard of Wyatt's truck. Dark jeans mold to his legs like they were crafted just for him as he deftly operates the pedals.

The blur of my neighborhood through the driver's side window acts as a backdrop as I trace the outline of his profile with careful eyes.

A crease forms between his eyebrows as he turns toward me. "You okay over there?"

A rogue wave of heat travels over my face and

down my neck as I realize I've been caught ogling him. "Oh, uh, yeah. I'm fine. Totally fine. Really." My fingers fumble with the air vent in front of me as I redirect some much needed air on my overheated face.

His laugh pulls a smile from my lips. "Just making sure. You look a little flushed."

Surprise halts my response as he takes a left turn away from downtown instead of the expected right. "We're not going to town?"

He shakes his head as an unusual smile blooms on his face. If I didn't know any better, I would say Kamden Stryker is nervous. "Definitely not going downtown."

I settle back into my seat and cross my legs. "Now I'm really curious."

His nervous smile turns into his usual smirk. "Patience, Sunshine. Patience."

Thirty minutes later, Kam pulls off the two-lane road we've been on for the past ten minutes. Dust billows behind us as the tires sink into the dirt road.

The tiredness brought on by the smooth movements around the curves of the road vanishes as my head swivels around us. The trees grow dense on either side of the truck as we bump along the dirt road. "Is this where you take people to kill them?"

Genuine humor lights his eyes as his booming laugh

fills the cabin of the truck. "It wouldn't be smart to tell you, now would it?"

I mimic his smile as he navigates the winding turns like a pro. "You're not giving me much confidence in my situational awareness."

His voice has a lightness I'm not sure I've heard from him before. "You don't need any if you're with me."

My head falls back against the headrest as the road turns into a steep incline. "Wyatt is going to hate what this is probably doing to his truck."

His eyes turn mischievous as the sound of rocks hitting the bottom of the truck fills the space. "We'll run it through the carwash after we get done. It'll be good as new." As we near the crest of the hill, he whispers, "Close your eyes, Sunshine."

I comply without hesitation. "I hope you realize how much trust it takes for me to go along with this."

I can hear the smile in his voice as I willingly plunge myself into darkness. "It'll be worth it."

The truck rocks back and forth on the uneven ground before I feel us level out and finally come to a stop.

The engine shuts off and plunges us into silence as he says with a gentle voice, "We're here, but don't open your eyes."

His door opening and closing rocks the truck as he leaves me alone, surrounded by the darkness of my own making.

A cool breeze washes over me as he opens my door. The sounds of birds in the surrounding trees is like a balm to my overstimulated soul.

I jump as Kam's warm hand envelopes mine. His chuckle vibrates through me as his fingers tighten around mine. "Sorry. Probably should have warned you."

My foot slides along the floor mat until I find the drop off that might as well be fifty feet. "This is way more terrifying than it should be."

Strong hands wrap around my waist and pluck me from the car like I weigh nothing. An involuntary squeak sneaks from my lips as I become airborne.

My feet land on solid ground as his fingers intertwine with mine as his laughter flows through the air. "Just take slow steps. Yes, just like that."

He guides me over the uneven terrain as I cling to him. "Don't let me fall."

"Never." I can hear the hint of a smile in his voice as he brings me to a stop. His breath tickles my ear as he bends down to whisper, "Open your eyes."

I suck in a quick breath as I open my eyes to a vast expanse of rolling hills. The thick trees are bathed in various shades of pinks and oranges from the setting sun.

Patches of grass and scattered barns dot the horizon as small black shapes move along the open fields. I struggle to catch my breath as the beauty of the land around us overwhelms me. "Oh, Kam. This is beautiful."

"Yeah. It really is."

The strange undertone of his voice has me looking his way to find him with his eyes on me instead of the view in front of us. "Don't look at me. You'll miss the sunset."

A grin takes over his face. "I don't need to look at the sunset when I have something more breathtaking standing right in front of me." His smile only grows with my confusion. "You're not just my sun*shine*. You're my sun*set*."

My voice is barely a whisper. "And why is that?"

"Because you're my favorite time of day." His voice is quiet as he admits, "Sunset used to be my favorite time of day. Now my favorite is anytime I'm with you."

The vulnerability shining bright in his eyes pours new life into me.

He clears his throat as he uses his thumb to point to the back of the truck that's facing the view. "Want to see the rest of your surprise?"

My eyebrows rise as my eyes roam over the covering over the back of the truck. "There's more?"

The sunset reflecting in his eyes adds to his beauty. "So much more."

CHAPTER 32
SECRET PLACE

KAM

I hold my breath as I fold the cargo cover back to reveal a mound of mismatched blankets and pillows that definitely took a tumble during our drive.

My eyes scan her face as her eyes widen before flicking to me. The disbelief in her voice and the grin on her face pulls a reluctant smile from me. "Did you take the comforters off everyone's beds?"

I rub the back of my neck as my eyes scan over the mess I've made in the back of Wyatt's truck. "Maybe?"

Her eyebrows raise in question as she tries and fails to hide the humor from her eyes. "Was that a question?"

I shrug as I force my already pushed up shirt sleeves even farther up my arms. "Would you believe me if I said we didn't have any other blankets in the house? I didn't have time to go buy any before I came and picked you up." My voice lowers to a whisper. "A problem that will be dealt with soon, I assure you."

Her laughter is so beautiful, it competes with the

sunset behind us. "You're really sweet. Did you know that?"

"It, uh, it's nothing really. I just didn't want to take you on a normal date. You deserve more than that." What I won't admit is it's become a personal goal of mine to give her the best first date she's ever been on.

I stand as still as a statue as she goes up on her tiptoes to plant a quick kiss on my cheek before she turns back to the truck. "It's perfect, Trouble." I fight my natural instincts to rub the spot that's still warm from her kiss. She rubs her hands together and gets a mischievous gleam in her eyes. "So, where do we start?"

We take a few minutes to sort through the tangled mess of blankets. Before I know it, we're all spread out in the back of the truck. There are so many layers of blankets and pillows under us that I can't even feel the unforgiving, hard surface of the truck bed.

We bask in the purple light from the first sign of twilight as we laugh at our efforts to smooth the blankets under us. My fingers snag in a loose thread on Dax's comforter before I finally give up. "I think that's just going to have to be good enough."

My heart nearly skips a beat as she chooses the blanket from my bed to settle under. "A few lumps and bumps never hurt anyone."

As the sun disappears behind the distant hills, so does the warmth it normally brings. Leaves in the nearby trees sway in the light breeze that now carries a biting chill.

A wave of pride washes through me as she burrows

further under my blanket. "Now you see why I wanted you to dress warm."

Her eyes light up with her smile as tendrils of hair around her face blow in the wind. "Good call, Trouble." Her eyes roam over the distant landscape that's now shrouded in shadows. "How did you find this place, anyway?"

My eyes trace her profile as I settle into a more comfortable position. "Well, Mace's dad is a park ranger. I've heard him talk about this place a few times. I called him last night to make sure I knew where it was. The road is easy to miss if you don't know what to look for."

She lets out a deep breath that takes some of the tension in her shoulders with it. "Well, it's stunning. You'll have to thank him for giving away his secret place."

"I will. He was excited we were coming up here. He said we might get lucky and get a visitor or two."

A smile pulls at my lips as her eyes flash with equal parts excitement and confusion. "I don't know if I should be worried or excited about that."

I shrug as my smile turns into a grin. "Guess you'll just have to wait and see." She searches my face as she opens her mouth to ask another question I know she's dying to know the answer to. I ask a question of my own before she gets the chance. "Are you ready for dinner?"

She sits up as straight as the lumpy blankets and pillows will allow. "There's dinner?"

My feet get caught in various blankets thanks to my

sneakers as I try to exit the truck bed with a laugh. "You didn't think I'd let you starve, did you?"

She quirks a brow. "I'm not making any assumptions."

Relief flows through me when I land on solid ground. *Thankful* isn't a good enough word for what I'm feeling, knowing I didn't just face plant in the dirt on our first date. "Well, always assume this. I will always take care of you. That includes making sure you're warm and fed."

She gives me a mock solute on my way to the back-seat of the truck. "Sir, yes, sir."

My chuckle follows me into the back of the car as I secure the still-warm cooler under my arm. The truck sways as I slam the door to the backseat. "Maybe I should be the one calling you 'Trouble'?"

The cooler lands with a heavy thunk in the truck bed before I climb up to settle back in my place. This time, I leave my sneakers on the ground so I don't have another near-embarrassment experience next time I try to get out.

The sound of the zipper of the cooler opening accompanies the crickets, who now sing their nightly song from the tall grass on the side of the dirt road.

Her voice is full of amazement as she takes in the full cooler in front of her. "What's all this?"

I strain my neck to look into the cooler to make sure the Tupperware containers haven't spilled during our drive. A relieved breath flows through me as I realize not only are the lids still on, but the silverware I packed is still neatly wrapped in their paper towels. "I, uh, I made you spaghetti."

Her eyebrows fly up and her eyes grow impossibly wide as her gaze shoots toward me. "You made all this?"

I run my fingers through my hair. "Well, I used pasta from a box. Mace wanted me to make homemade pasta, but I wanted us to actually be able to eat the meal once we got here. And I didn't make the cheese, obviously. Dax was in charge of that, so it's hard telling what he got. But the sauce, yeah. I made the sauce."

Her arms wrap tightly around my neck before I realize what's happening. The smell of mangos washes over me. Her voice is quiet and watery as she squeezes me in a death grip. "Thank you, Kam." She pulls back to reveal the tears rimming her eyes. "This is perfect."

I catch a stray tear with my thumb as it trails down her cheek. "Why are you crying?"

She laughs as my arms finally catch up with my brain and wind around her waist. "Because you're perfect, and that scares the hell out of me."

My fingers glide through the silky strands of hair around her face as my voice falls to a whisper. "I'm not perfect."

She makes a disbelieving noise as the cool night air fills the space between us. "You seem pretty perfect to me. Why would you want *me*, Kam? This isn't a way for me to get you to say I'm perfect, too. I'm not. Look at my life. I'm practically a single mom to two seven-year-olds. What college hockey star in his right mind would want to dive headfirst into that?"

A smile pulls at my lips despite a piece of my heart breaking every time a fresh tear rolls down her face. My arms tighten around her so our chests are nearly touching. The need to dispel the space she's put between us grows with every breath I take. "I guess I'm not in my right mind, then. I want it all, Sunshine. Every messy, beautiful piece."

She shakes her head like that's the stupidest thing she's ever heard. Her voice holds a sadness that tears me up inside. "Why? How could you possibly want that?"

"Because I want you." Determination shines brightly in my eyes and through my voice. "And I want those two seven-year-olds, too. I've decided I want you in my life. No, I *need* you in my life. And I will do that in any way I can." I search her eyes as I pull her closer. "Will you let me do that?"

Her eyes shutter closed before they open once again. Fresh tears stream down her face that I don't bother wiping away. I need them to fall to my chest and brand me like I've been needing her to do for all these weeks.

Her eyes flicker back and forth between mine before a calmness takes control of her. She sags against my chest and lets out a deep breath. "Okay. But only if you're sure."

"I've never been more sure of anything." I push a few stray strands of hair out of her face. "Now that we've got that settled. Are you ready to eat?"

She wipes a few lingering tears from her cheeks as a smile breaks through her darkness. "I was born ready."

CHAPTER 33
JUST THE WIND

LILA

A chill runs down my spine as the bushes on my side of the truck rustle. We've been up here long enough for me to know it's not from the gentle breeze that's blowing through my hair.

My spine turns ramrod straight as my eyes swivel around in the darkness. "Did you hear that?"

The darkness cloaks the trees in a moonlit silhouette as I inch toward the safety Kam provides. I was thankful for the dim lamp Kam brought when my only thought was stargazing. Now I wish for a police grade spotlight to illuminate the trees.

I shiver as Kam chuckles next to me. "It's just the wind. Nothing to worry about."

I clench my teeth as the sound happens again. "You are so full of shit, Kamden Stryker. That is *not* the wind." I whimper as the sound moves farther to my right. An involuntary squeak escapes my lips as I plaster my side to Kam's.

His answering chuckle vibrates through me as he

slips his arms around my waist. His soft voice against my ear sends another round of chills down my spine for an entirely different reason. "Yeah, you're right. I don't think that's the wind."

My mind briefly flashes to our empty Tupperware containers sitting abandoned by our feet as my voice falls to a strained whisper. "Do you think our food attracted some bears or something?"

The secure pressure of his arms at my waist offers only momentary relief from my anxiety before a shuffling sound coming from the tree line threatens my sanity.

The reflection of two eyes staring right at me from the trees sends a bolt of panic through me. I squirm backwards until my butt is nestled firmly on Kam's lap. His hand slips over my mouth to contain the scream that's begging to be set free as the eyes disappear into the dense trees.

His breath tickles my ear as he makes shushing sounds as the eyes multiply around us. "It's okay." Faint silhouettes of tall creatures move through the trees as our single lamp illuminates the edge of the dark void.

His hand muffles my words as I tuck my legs to my chest. "Nothing about this is okay."

A smile lifts his voice that I find wholly inappropriate for our current situation. "Just trust me."

Even with his hand over my mouth and arms around my waist, I turn on his lap to get a good look at his eyes. The humor I find in them relieves some of the anxiety in mine.

His chuckle vibrates through me as he whispers,

"Don't look at me like that. You're going to like our visitors. I promise." I want to ask how he can promise such a thing when he inclines his head toward the tree line. "Just wait."

I roll my eyes as I reluctantly focus my attention back on the tree line. My ears ring as I fight my body's natural instinct to tuck tail and run the hell away from the scary creatures in the woods.

I nearly jump out of my skin as the click of Kam turning the lamp off reverberates through me. The accusatory glare I shoot over my shoulder is lost to the darkness that envelopes us like ink.

The shuffling sounds grow more numerous now that the blanket of darkness stretches through the small clearing.

My breath catches in my chest as I all but stop breathing as a massive creature steps through the curtain of trees.

Moonlight reflects off the wide back of the creature as it lets out a chirping sound that doesn't fit with the size of the beast before me.

Answering chirps sound throughout the trees as footfalls grow closer. The giant creature's head swivels until it's looking straight into my soul. My eyes adjust to the darkness to reveal intelligent eyes reflecting back at me.

Its head tilts to the side as it inspects us with an ear twitch that is surprisingly cute on such a large animal.

Kam's hand falls away from my mouth as the beautiful creature blinks at me. My whispered voice holds a sense of awe I feel all the way to my toes. "What is it?"

I can hear the satisfaction in Kam's voice as he whispers, *"She* is an elk."

She shuffles on her feet as she lets out a sad sounding whine. Her head moves so she can look over her shoulder back to the tree line. My heart melts as a calf with faded white spots scurries from the trees to join her.

Their noses touch in greeting as more silhouettes emerge from the trees until we're surrounded. Chirps and mews fill the air as they carry on a conversation we're not meant to understand.

I relax back into Kam's arms as we watch them in silence. His rhythmic breathing would lull me to sleep if I wasn't so fascinated by our visitors.

They move around in the darkness on sure feet as they munch on the long grasses that seem short against their long legs.

They're unbothered by the chill in the air or the way the crickets halt their song when they approach.

A sense of loss fills me as they slowly disappear back into the trees to carry on with their nightly routine without us.

The last mom sends her calf into the woods before looking over her shoulder. When my eyes connect with the gentle creature, all I feel is gratitude for her, allowing me a small glimpse into her life.

The darkness of the woods embraces her like a long-lost friend as she disappears from view.

I turn in Kam's lap until we're face to face. The memory of the moonlight reflecting in his eyes will stay with me for a lifetime. "Thank you."

He pulls my legs until I'm straddling him. Our

chests brush with every breath we take. "We just got lucky. Mace's dad said there wasn't a guarantee we would see them."

I shake my head as I weave my fingers through his hair. "Not just for that, but for never giving up on me." A gentle laugh escapes my lips to float in the scarce inches between us. "I didn't exactly make things easy on you."

The beauty of his smile rivals that of the stars. "You were worth the wait."

The moon is our only witness as his lips connect with mine. The warmth of his lips chases away the chill of the night as he deepens the kiss. My gasp fuels his desire as his tongue runs over my lips in request of entry I gladly give.

He groans into my mouth, and his barely there scruff bites at my cheeks as my front molds to his.

Hands roam up my back to find purchase in my hair as a howl starts in the distance and glides over the hills. A shiver travels down my spine as an answering call sounds from the surrounding trees.

Our mouths break apart as our labored breaths fill the air between us. Concern clouds my voice as my arms fall from his hair to his shoulders. "What was *that?*"

His brows draw down in concern as he tries to catch his breath. "Probably a coyote." My arms tighten around his neck as the howls pick up in the distance. "Don't worry. I'll protect you."

There's no doubt in my mind he means it.

CHAPTER 34
PERPETUITY

KAM

Lila's eyes scan my laptop screen as I run my thumb over a notch on the edge of the dining room table.

A crease forms between her brows as her eyes turn to me. "And this came from a professional agent?"

I grimace as my chair shifts under my weight. "That bad, huh?"

She's nodding her head before I finish my sentence. "You could say that."

I raise a brow. "Alright. What would you change about the contract, then?"

She blows out a breath before turning her attention back to my laptop. "Well, for starters, the agent fee is way too high. Eight percent? More like three to five percent, max."

A sinking feeling settles in my stomach as reality sets in. My elbows dig into the hard wooden table as I lean closer to her. "Go on."

She tucks her hair behind her ears as she straightens in her seat. "He's also wanting to sign you for five years. I wouldn't sign for longer than two. One year would be ideal. There's also a line here that was a huge red flag." Her eyes move quickly over the screen before victory takes light in her eyes. "Ah! Found it. 'The agency retains the exclusive right to license and monetize the client's image, likeness, and name in perpetuity.'" She turns her attention back to me with a grimace of her own. "That basically means only the agency can make money from your image and name. You wouldn't legally be able to do it on your own."

I scrunch my nose as my eyes fly over the screen without actually seeing anything. "Well, that sucks."

"That's not all."

I roll my eyes. "Of course not."

I watch her eyes as she reads, "'All disputes shall be settled exclusively through binding arbitration from an arbiter of our choosing, with no right to pursue legal action in a court of law.'" Her eyes flick to mine.

The words flying through my mind hold no meaning. "You might as well be speaking Spanish right now."

I can see the apology in her eyes and hear it in her voice. "That's their way of having you sign away your right to sue them."

I rub the tension from my temples as I let out a defeated breath. "So, what you're basically saying is, my future agent is trying to screw me and taking our negotiations class hasn't helped me at all?"

A mischievous lightness fills her eyes as a small smile lifts her lips. "I wouldn't say that."

Somehow, she brings a smile to my face. I grab the edge of her seat and pull it closer to mine. "Of course.

How could I forget? Without that class, I wouldn't have met you."

"Get a room! Some of us are trying to be productive here!" Dax's voice echoes through the house to compete with the sound of revving engines coming from the living room.

Our smiles grow as Posey's muffled voice filters through the air. "Don't even try to use them as an excuse when I win later."

I push a strand of stray hair behind Lila's ear as I laugh. "Have you told the twins about us yet?"

The lightness in her eyes dims as she pulls away from me. "I don't want to confuse them."

"Confuse who?" A red popsicle muffles Jasper's voice as he comes around the corner from the kitchen. He tilts his head as his eyes volley between our two very close seats at the table. "Is this about you and Kam?"

Lila's eyebrows raise as she wipes her palms on her jeans. "Uh, I uh."

"Cause if it is, we already know." He licks a melted stream of red syrup from the side of his hand like he didn't just explode his sister's world.

"You, uh, you know *what*, exactly?"

His shrug almost forces a laugh from my lips. "That you're together. You know, like a real couple." My laugh breaks free as Lila tries to pick her jaw up off the floor. "It's a good thing. Just so you know. You smile more now."

My laughter dies as my heart warms. My eyes roam over Lila's face as she fights the tears threatening to break free. She clears her throat before dabbing at the corner of her eyes. "That's good. Really good."

Dax's voice breaks the spell between us. "Yo, Jas! It's your turn!"

Lila's body turns to jelly as her brother disappears into the living room without a backwards glance. "Well, that happened."

My fingers glide over her back as I let out the full force of my laugh. "At least we've got that out of the way."

Mace pops his head out from the kitchen with a gleam in his eyes that I know from experience can mean one of two things. One, dinner is ready. I don't smell anything cooking, so that can't be it. Or two, he has a wild idea. "Hey, guys! Did you submit that group project you were working on?"

I reluctantly nod my head. "Yeah. Lila was just helping me go over the contract Richard sent over this morning."

He rubs his hands together as he fully emerges from the kitchen. "I have a great idea." I fight a groan since past experience means this could either be fun or end in a hospital visit. "Hear me out, Cap. The rink is empty tonight, right?"

I raise a questioning brow as I nod my head. "Yeah, it's empty."

His eyes turn to Lila as he nearly splits his face in half with his smile. "Get your skates, Sullivan. We're going ice skating."

She unconsciously leans toward me as Mace's enthusiasm grows into a tidal wave that threatens everyone in its path. "Uh, I've never been ice skating before."

I add my shock to Mace's as he gets a determined look in his eyes. "That gets fixed tonight." His long legs carry him from the dining room to the stairs in record time as he belts orders. "Get ready everyone! We're going skating! Call your sister, Cap! We need an even number of people!"

A hesitant laugh breaks free from Lila as she stands. "Should I be worried?"

I nod my head without a second thought. "Definitely."

CHAPTER 35
YOU MAKE IT SO EASY
LILA

I fidget with the zipper on my jacket as Kam kneels before me. The chilly air cools my overheated skin as I take deep breaths. "Are you sure about this?"

His confident smirk calms my nerves as he ties the laces of my skates so tight it's bruising. "I won't let you fall, Sunshine. I promise."

I roll my eyes as he pulls a smile from my lips. "You can't promise that."

His smirk turns into a full-on grin as he stands. "Watch me."

I take his extended hand as I stand on shaky legs. "How am I supposed to walk in these things?"

Jasper walks by unimpeded by the blades on his feet. "You don't walk, Lulu. You skate." His skates connect with the ice as he mumbles, "Obviously."

Kam doesn't fight his grin as he steadies me. "He's right, you know."

My light smack on his shoulder adds fuel to his grin. "Don't make fun of me."

Happiness dances in his eyes as he threads an arm around my waist for added stability. "Oh, but you make it so easy."

I take an uneasy step as my knees threaten to buckle under the weight they've had no problem holding for years. "How do you make this look so easy? I'm not even on the ice yet, and I feel like my knees are about to crumble."

My eyes are so focused on my feet that I feel more than see Kam's shrug. "Practice. I've been skating since I could walk."

I take deep breaths to settle my raging heart as I reach the boundary that separates me from my laughing friends and siblings. I stand on the edge of the ice like I would a cliff as the six-inch drop to the ice looms before me like a daunting leap of faith I'm not prepared to take.

Kam's quiet words flow through me. "Take the step. I'm right here. I won't let you fall."

I take the leap of faith and raise my foot as I grab Kam's hand in a death grip. My blade touches the ice with a feather-light kiss as I stand stranded between the edge of safety and the edge of uncertainty.

My foot slides with the first hint of pressure as my stomach threatens to spill its contents. I grit my teeth and transfer my weight to my front foot.

Ice and a blade will not beat me. Not today.

My legs wobble as I plant both feet solidly on the ice. "I'm doing it!"

Kam chuckles behind me as my momentum propels me forward. "Heck yeah!"

A relieved breath leaves my lips prematurely. My

feet slowly spread under me as panic takes hold of my voice. "Um, how do I stop?"

I dig into Kam with both hands as he pulls me to a stop. His laughter booms through the rink as I fight for balance. "One thing at a time."

Mace looks like he's floating as he flies by us with a grin on his face. "Looking good, Sullivan!" His voice falls to a level to prevent little ears from overhearing. "Glad we finally popped your ice skating cherry!"

Kam's muscles tighten under my hands as a growl rumbles through his chest. His eyes turn dark as he clenches his teeth. "Not funny, Mace!"

My face heats. Not from Mace's comment or the wink he sends my way as he speeds off, but from the look on Kam's face as his eyes stay locked on his friend.

I tighten my hold on Kam's arm until he dials back the fire in his eyes. "Hey, it's alright." I shrug as his eyes search my face. "I thought it was funny."

Kam grumbles, "He should know better than to say something like that at all, let alone to you."

I raise a brow as I fight a smile. "Oh, yeah? And what makes me different from everyone else?"

His voice falls to a deadly level as he grabs my waist. "Because you're *mine*."

I lose the fight on my smile as butterflies take flight in my belly. "Oh, really? I don't recall you asking."

"You didn't ask her to be your girlfriend? What's wrong with you? I taught you better than that, Goose." The exacerbation rings through Ellie's voice as she slips her skates onto her feet at the edge of the rink.

Kam's eyes blaze as they stay locked on mine. "Stay out of this, Shrimp."

Dax's whistle echoes through the empty stands as he skates over to us. "You didn't lock her down? What's wrong with you, Cap?" His dimple appears as a smirk blooms on his face. "Go ahead then, ask her."

Wyatt rolls his eyes as he circles us. "You guys are ridiculous."

A smile blooms on Mace's face as he stabilizes Posey before she takes off around the rink again. "You love us anyway, Ranger."

My eyes are drawn back to Kam by the weight of his stare. His eyes hold a hint of apology. For his friends' antics or this situation, I'm not sure. "Did I really not ask you last night?" I shake my head as determination fills his eyes. "Be my girlfriend, Sunshine."

I raise a brow as a smile takes over my face. "Was that a question?"

A smirk pulls at his lips as his hand tightens on my hip. "No."

Silence descends around us as everyone stops to watch a moment I'm sure will stick with me forever. "Well, in that case, I would love to."

Cheers from our friends take the place of the silence as Kam's lips connect with mine. He breaks the kiss as smiles bloom on our faces. His voice is a whisper against my lips. "I'm sorry. We should have left the hill last night as a couple. That was my intention when I planned everything. I just got distracted by our visitors."

Ellie's voice infiltrates our bubble as she throws an arm over my shoulder. "I, for one, am glad you forgot.

This way, we all get to bear witness to the beginning of your story." She fakes wiping a tear from the corner of her eye. "It's beautiful, really."

Wyatt grabs a handful of the back of her sweatshirt and drags her away from us. "Alright, Ellie. Give the new couple some space."

A pout forms on her face even though she doesn't even try to fight his grip. "Ah, come on! I was just having a little fun."

Their banter fades to the other side of the rink as my eyes gravitate back to Kam. "It's alright, Trouble. It all worked out in the end."

Regret takes over his face as he looks down at our skates. "That just wasn't how I wanted it to happen."

I poke him in the chest to get his attention. "Hey! No pouting!" My lips pull into a mischievous smile. "My new *boyfriend* is supposed to be teaching me to skate!"

His eyes light up as his smirk returns. "I can't keep my new *girlfriend* waiting, then."

Dax makes a gagging sound from across the rink. "You guys are so cute. It makes me sick."

CHAPTER 36
ALWAYS
KAM

My phone screen fades to black to reveal a deep groove between my eyebrows reflected on the dark screen. My fingers drum an erratic beat on my desk that mimics my heartbeat as I glance at the door once again.

Come on, Sunshine. Where are you?

I unlock my phone to reread my unanswered good morning text as Professor Mills takes his place at the podium. "Morning, everyone. I hope you all successfully submitted your group projects last night with no issues."

I lean back in my seat as his voice fades into a distant hum. Worry strangles my heart like a vice as the worst possible scenarios race through my mind.

Did something happen to the twins?

Did she get in a car accident?

Did CO_2 fill their house while they were sleeping?

Sweat beads on my brow as I try to convince myself I'm being an idiot.

I'm sure she's just running late. There's nothing to worry about.

Except I can't shake this overwhelming feeling that something is just...*wrong*.

I abandon my seat and my heart by my feet as my phone shows an incoming call from Lila's number. Surprisingly, I remember to grab my notebook before I race from the classroom without a backwards glance.

My fingers fumble against my screen in my haste to answer her call. The classroom doors closing behind me cut off Professor Mills' words to be replaced by the welcome silence of the hallway.

I let out a sigh of relief as my back molds to the wall just outside the doors. "You had me worried, Sunshine. I thought something happened to you."

"Kam?"

My back straightens as surprise flashes through me. "Jasper?" I'm thankful for my long legs as they carry me toward the parking lot at top speed. "What's wrong? Where's Lila?"

The worry coating his voice has my legs pumping faster. "She's sick."

I fight to keep my voice calm as the overwhelming need to just *be there* takes hold. "What do you mean, she's sick? What's wrong with her?"

"Her forehead is really hot, and she won't wake up."

Worry like I've never known before rushes through me like hot lava as I burst through the doors and into the sunshine. "Don't hang up, Jasper. I'm on my way, okay?" My fingers fumble in my pocket as I search for my keys, not wanting to waste time fumbling with the button on the door handle to unlock my car. "How long has she been like this?"

I hear the uncertainty in his voice that I wish so badly I could take away. "I don't know. She said she had a headache last night before she went to bed. Her alarm woke us up this morning, and when she didn't turn it off right away like normal, I got worried."

My voice portrays a sense of calm I certainly don't feel as the parking lot comes into view. "It's okay, Tank. Everything's going to be alright." *Please don't let me be lying to him.*

"Okay." The tears threatening his voice almost make me crumble.

I can't hold back the sigh of relief as I lock eyes on my Tahoe. "I'm getting in my car right now, Tank." The sound of my door slamming shut doesn't register as I struggle with my seatbelt.

Music blasts through the speakers as soon as I press the button to start the engine. I slam my palm down on the knob with more force than necessary. My hand is surprisingly steady as I switch the call to speakerphone. The phone lands in the cupholder with a solid thunk as I try to control my breathing. "You still with me, Tank?"

"Yeah, I'm here."

I flick my emergency lights on and clench my teeth as I back out of the parking spot. "Good. I'm leaving campus now. I'll be there in three minutes. Go to the living room window and watch for me to pull up. Do *not* open the door until I get there."

"Okay." His voice quiets as he pulls away from the phone. "I'm going to go watch for Kam."

I curse under my breath as I realize I forgot about one very important person. "How's Posey doing?"

The echo of his footsteps reaches my ears as I speed through a green light. "She's okay. Just worried about Lulu."

"I know, Tank. I can see your street. Are you by the living room window?"

I hear a rustling on his end that I would bet is the living room curtains. "Yeah, I'm here."

"Good. Go ahead and unlock the door for me."

Lila's red car comes into view at the end of the street as I hear Jasper unlock the door. "It's open."

I pull in her driveway at an angle, not even taking the time to straighten the tires. Thankfully, I still have enough brain cells to remember to put the car in park and turn it off. I end the call and slip my phone in my pocket as I slam the car door behind me.

Jasper's blue eyes peek around the curtain with the phone still to his ear. My sneakers dig into the pavement as I pump my legs. The doorknob is warm against my palm from the morning sun despite the chill in the air as I twist the metal with a crushing force.

Birdsong and the sound of distant cars fades as I close the door behind me. As soon as the latch clicks shut, Jasper's arms are around my waist as he buries his face against my stomach. "Thank you for answering my call."

Without a second thought, I bend down and scoop him into my arms. "Always, Tank."

I move toward her room with him clutching my neck. My breath stalls in my chest as his fingers dig into the hair at the nape of my neck as I enter her room.

Posey's sad eyes meet mine as she looks over her shoulder from her spot on the bed next to her sister. The worry melts from her shoulders as her eyes light up. "Hi, Kam."

I force a smile onto my face as I sit Jasper on his feet at the foot of the bed. "Hey, Rosie Posey."

My breath stutters in my chest as I take in Lila's sweat soaked brow and pale skin. I inch toward her as I count her breaths. The relief that floods my chest is immediate when I realize her breathing is normal.

A soft yellow rug provides cushioning for my knees as I kneel next to her. My voice is soft as I place the back of my hand against her forehead. "Hi, Sunshine." A crease forms between her brows as she tilts her head closer to me. "I'm here now. You're going to be okay."

I run through the possibilities in my mind as I take her pulse. She was fine when we left the rink last night, so this came on fast, whatever *it* is. Her pulse is normal, which is a great sign.

I perform the skin turgor test on the back of her hand to check for dehydration. Her skin takes a second and a half to return to normal.

Did I see her drink any water last night?

No. I don't think I did.

"Damn it, Lila."

I jump as Posey's voice registers. "That's a dollar for the swear jar, Kam."

A reluctant smile forms on my face despite the worry still coursing through my veins. I force myself to move away from Lila, even though that's the last thing in the world I want to do. "Okay, I've got a job for you guys. Are you ready?"

Their eyes light up as they nod their heads.

"I need you guys to go get ready for school while I make a few phone calls. Can you do that real fast for me?"

Their hesitant eyes roam over their sister before they fly from the room as I pull my phone from my pocket and dial my sister's number.

Her cheery voice sounds from the other end after two rings. "Hey, little brother."

"Ellie, I need your help."

Without a pause, she replies. "What do you need?"

CHAPTER 37
DREAMING OF CHOCOLATE EYES

LILA

I dream of a secret place filled with beautiful sunsets and large, gentle creatures.

I dream of a hockey rink filled with red and white and a warmth that takes my breath away despite the icy chill in the air.

I dream of chocolate eyes that make me feel safe and whole.

Voices filter through my mind on distant waves as dreams fade in and out of focus. I yearn to move closer to the gentle voice that speaks of sunshine, but no matter how hard I try, that voice is always just out of reach.

A bee sting on my arm pulls me from my dream as the voice grows closer. "And you're sure that's all we need to do?"

I want to call out to the owner of that voice and beg them to stay forever. But I don't get the chance. I'm yanked back into the darkness to dream about a house full of laughter and revving engines.

"I think she's waking up."

Warmth connects with my hand as fingers intertwine with mine. "Come on, Sunshine. Open your eyes."

My eyes refuse to follow his command as more voices grow closer. "Is she going to wake up?"

Fingers tighten against mine. "Yeah, Tank. She's going to be okay. Her body just needs to rest."

Little warm fingers find my other hand. "You can wake up now, Lulu. I even cleaned my room, so you would be extra happy when you woke up."

"Alright, Tank. Dax and Wyatt are here to help with your homework. Why don't you go help them get set up in the dining room?"

"Will you let me know when she wakes up?"

"Of course I will."

Footsteps fade as I fight against my stubborn eyelids.

Warmth runs over my forehead. "Wake up."

My throat is scratchy and the sudden need to pee hits me so hard I nearly levitate off the bed.

I win the battle and open my blurry eyes to a familiar ceiling. Chocolate eyes come into view as I groan, "What happened?"

Relief floods Kam's face as his fingers tighten in mine. "You haven't been taking very good care of yourself, Sunshine."

My brows furrow as I try and fail to sit up. "What do you mean?"

"He means you've been so focused on taking care of everyone else that you forgot to drink water, you silly fucker." Ellie's tight eyes connect with mine from the doorway as she folds her arms over her chest. "You scared us half to death, L. What were you thinking?"

"I, uh, I guess I wasn't."

Kam tugs on my hand to get my attention. "All that matters now is that you're doing better, and this will *not* happen again. Isn't that right?"

Tears fill my eyes as the gravity of the situation falls on my chest at full force. "I didn't mean to, guys. I swear. I've just been so preoccupied lately."

Tears rim Ellie's eyes as she steps into my room. "Well, that changes *today*. Kam already ordered three different water bottles for you to pick from. No more excuses."

A tired smile pulls at my lips before panic slides down my spine like ice. "What time is it?"

Kam glances down at his phone. "It's almost seven."

My eyes nearly bug out of my skull. *"PM?"*

His nod has me struggling to swing my legs out of bed. Firm hands push me back into the mattress as a no-nonsense look takes over his face. "And where do you think you're going?"

I huff out an annoyed breath as I stop fighting against him. "I need to get ready. The social worker will be here any minute. We have a meeting scheduled for tonight at seven. I've already missed taking the twins to school today. I don't think missing a meeting would look good on my record."

Kam crosses his arms as he settles back in the seat next to my bed that was not there when I went to sleep last night. "First, the twins made it to school. They were about an hour late, but they made it." My eyebrows fly up in disbelief. "Second, I've already called the social worker. Posey told me about the meeting tonight. We rescheduled it for next week. Mrs. Jones said for me to tell you she hopes you feel better. She thinks you have the flu, by the way."

I try to keep the skepticism from my eyes. "Just like that?" I lick my dry lips." But—But what about dinner?"

The bed dips as Ellie sits on the edge across from her brother. "Mace just dropped off chicken parmesan." Her eyes light up with excitement. "And get this! Posey ate an entire plate full of it!"

My mouth drops to the floor. "What? How did you manage that?"

She shrugs like it's not a battle I've fought every day for the past few years. "She asked for it. Said Mace's cooking isn't gross."

"What about their homework? They have a math test tomorrow."

A smile lights Kam's eyes as he leans his elbows on his knees. "Dax and Wyatt are taking care of it. Don't worry."

I blow out a relieved breath that takes all the tension in my shoulders with it. "Thank you guys so much. I really don't know what I would do without all of you."

Ellie squeezes my shoulder as she stands. "You'll

never have to find out." A smile pulls at her lips. "I'm going to go put the leftovers in the fridge and let the twins know you're awake. They've been worried sick, so prepare for lots of cuddles."

My eyes roam over Kam's exhausted face as she leaves the room. "How did you know I was sick?"

He slips his hands in mine as a crease forms between his brows. "Jasper called me this morning when he couldn't wake you. He nearly scared me half to death." His eyes turn pleading. "*Never* do this to me again."

I nod as I tighten my fingers around his. "I'll do better." My arm feels like lead as I try to lift it to his messy curls. A sharp pull on my arm halts my movements. I look down and follow the clear tube attached to my arm to an IV set up next to my bed. "How in the world did you get an IV set up without taking me to the hospital?"

A blush crawls up his cheeks as he rubs his thumb over the back of my hand. "Coach's wife is a nurse. She came right over when I called this morning."

"Lulu! You're awake!" A splitting smile blooms on my face as my brother and sister race into the room. Jasper's voice still holds a hint of fear I will regret putting there for the rest of my life. "We were so worried when you wouldn't wake up."

They crawl onto my bed with a gentleness I've never seen from them before as I pull them close. "I'm sorry I worried you. I'm going to take much better care of myself from now on."

My eyes find Kam's as they settle against my chest like they did when they were only a few months old, and Mom and Dad would put on a movie for us all to watch.

The smile on his face can't hide the dark circles under his eyes that weren't there last night.

I'm realizing that if I want to take care of the people I care about, I need to take care of myself first.

I mouth *thank you* to Kam as I snuggle back into the blankets. His answering wink ignites butterflies in my belly that I'm not sure will ever go away when I'm around this man.

I'm not sure I want them to.

CHAPTER 38

THE BEAUTIES AND THE BEASTS GROUP CHAT

KAM

THE BEAUTIES AND THE BEASTS GROUP CHAT

Ellie has added you and four others to the group.

DAX

Yo! New group chat for the win!

MACE

I did not consent to being added to this group chat.

Ellie has removed Mace from the group.

Wyatt has added Mace to the group.

MACE

THAT WAS A JOKE

ELLIE

A bad one 😕

LILA

Aww! Thanks for adding me, E!

KAM

How much water have you had to drink today, Sunshine? And why hasn't it been enough?

LILA

photo of empty water bottle

KAM

Refill the bottle, Sunshine.

ELLIE

So, I brought us all here today to discuss something very important.

DAX

The debate between pancakes and waffles?

MACE

Waffles. Obviously.

ELLIE

Our Halloween costumes...

DAX

Come on, Ellie. Pick one.

LILA

Pancakes have my vote.

KAM

Pancakes for sure.

WYATT

Waffles

ELLIE

Fine. Waffles are my pick. Can we move on now?

DAX

NO WE CANNOT MOVE ON! Pancakes are my favorite. Thanks for asking. But this means we have a tragedy on our hands.

ELLIE

Do I even want to know what you mean by that?

DAX

It means we need a tie breaker! We have three votes for waffles and three votes for pancakes.

LILA

The twins both vote for pancakes…

DAX

YES! Screw all you waffle loving suckers!

ELLIE

Moving on…What do we want our Halloween costumes to be? A group costume would be so fun!

DAX

Can't I just reuse my costume from last year?

WYATT

You can't go as the color red for three years in a row, Dax.

DAX

And why not? We could each be a different crayon color. I've already got it all worked out.

Kam - Blue | Lila - Yellow | Jasper - Green| Posey - Pink | Ellie - Orange | Wyatt - Black | Me - Red | Mace - Green

WYATT

Why am I black?

DAX

It would match the dark cloud you've always got hanging over your head.

WYATT

MACE

Or we could all go as different fruits!

Kam - Apple | Lila - Peach | Jasper - Lime | Posey - Lemon | Ellie - Strawberry | Wyatt - Pear | Dax - Pineapple | Me - Banana

DAX

I can NOT be a pineapple…

MACE

And why not?

DAX

I am not explaining that to him. I refuse.

MACE

Explain what?

KAM

Not it. Someone else explain it to him.

WYATT

Nope. Not me.

LILA

Absolutely not.

ELLIE

Oh, for goodness sake. I'll dm you, Mace.

MACE

Pineapples aren't an option. Got it.

DAX

Oh! I've got it! We could all be different insects!

Kam - Dung Beetle | Lila - Honey Bee | Jasper - Cricket | Posey - Ladybug | Ellie - Stink Bug | Wyatt - Praying Mantis | Me - Firefly | Mace - Spider

KAM

A dung beetle…Really? And you know spiders aren't insects, right? They're arachnids.

DAX

WHAT

ELLIE

I AM NOT DRESSING UP AS A STINK BUG

DAX

SHAPES

KAM

Is that a suggestion, or are you just saying random words?

MACE

We could all be different types of pasta!

Kam - Penne | Lila - Rigatoni | Jasper - Ziti | Posey - Macaroni | Ellie - Fusilli | Wyatt - Rotini | Dax - Farfalle | Me - Shells

WYATT

How does one become a type of pasta?

ELLIE

You would make such a cute Rotini, Ranger!

LILA

Aww! You really would, though!

WYATT

And I was just starting to like you, Sullivan...

KAM

There's eight of us, right? We could each be a different planet...

Me - Jupiter | Lila - Saturn | Jasper - Mercury | Posey - Venus | Ellie - Earth | Wyatt - Mars | Dax - Neptune | Mace - Uranus

ELLIE

And how exactly does someone dress as a planet, little brother?

KAM

Not my problem. You're the one asking for suggestions.

DAX

I WANT TO BE URANUS

MACE

I'm still offended by Pluto no longer being a planet btw.

WYATT

Pluto is technically considered a dwarf planet now.

LILA

It's actually called a dwarf planet??
That's kind of cute, tbh.

MACE

That makes me slightly less mad.

KAM

Happy now, Dax?

Me - Jupiter | Lila - Saturn | Jasper - Mercury | Posey - Venus | Ellie - Earth | Wyatt - Mars | Dax - Uranus | Mace - Neptune

DAX

Yes. Yes, I am.

LILA

What about everyone being a different season or type of weather?

Kam - Snow | Me - Summer | Jasper - Fall | Posey - Spring | Ellie - Rainbow | Wyatt - Storm Cloud | Dax - Tornado | Mace - Winter

KAM

That has my vote!

MACE

Shut up, Cap. Of course you're going to pick your girl's idea.

KAM

ELLIE

I'VE GOT IT

KAM

Do I need to be scared?

DAX

I feel like we should be afraid...

MACE

The suspense is killing me...

ELLIE

You guys are gonna love this...

CHAPTER 39
CUMIN
KAM

A deep crease forms between Wyatt's brows as he looks down at the painted sweatshirt that fits snugly against his chest. "I can't believe I let you guys talk me into this."

My grin breaks free as he crosses his arms. "Ah, come on, Ranger. It's not that bad."

His deadpan look makes me lose the battle I've been fighting against my laugh since he walked downstairs. "I have an ice cream cone on my head, Cap. A fucking ice cream cone."

I hold my finger up to halt his complaints. "A *foam* ice cream cone *headband*."

He raises his brows as his scowl deepens. "Is that supposed to make it sound better?"

Dax struts into the kitchen like you would down a runway. His mint green shirt glowing under the fluorescent kitchen lights highlights the badly painted chocolate chips on his chest. "I, for one, am feeling great about our costume choice."

Mace follows closely behind with a grin on his face as he adjusts the headband on his head. Brightly colored sprinkles are scattered across his chocolate brown sweatshirt. "Me too!"

Wyatt rolls his eyes as he fidgets with the headband on his head. "You're just happy we're dressed as food, Mace."

Mace shrugs without a care in the world. "We could have been spices. Be glad I didn't make you walk around all night with 'Cumin' written on your chest."

Wyatt tilts his head in thought before he nods his head. "You're right. That makes me feel better about walking around as a six-foot-four chocolate chip cookie dough ice cream scoop with a cone on my head."

Mace smacks him on the back on his way to the fridge. "That's what I'm here for, buddy."

The snap of Dax opening a bottle of water fills the kitchen. "You're just worried about this ruining the dark and mysterious aura you've got going on. It's hard to look like you're mad at the world when you have an ice cream cone on your head."

Wyatt rolls his eyes as he straightens the headband for the third time in as many minutes. "No, what I'm worried about is this thing cutting off the circulation to my brain. How do girls wear these things all the time?"

I lean back against the counter as a headache blooms behind my eyes. "Well, they're not made for your gigantic head, Ranger."

"Oh. My. God." I turn in time to watch my sister's face transform with utter delight as her eyes roam over our small group. "You guys look adorable." She digs in the back pocket of her jeans without moving her eyes away from us. "I've got to take a picture."

Dax pulls us all into a tight hug as he grins from ear to ear. "Heck yeah! We need to document this moment. We can print out the picture and hang it in Coach's office!"

A huff leaves Wyatt's lips as he reluctantly poses. "There's no chance Coach wants to stare at your face all day, Dax."

I can hear the eye roll in Dax's voice. "I'll let him be the judge of that, thank you very much."

The sprinkles drawn on Ellie's rainbow colored sweatshirt dance as she adjusts her position in front of us. "Everyone say 'ice cream'!"

Even Wyatt echoes the sentiment under Ellie's command as she clicks away on her phone.

Dax releases his death grip as Ellie flicks through the many photos she just took of us with a smile on her face. He races over to her like a giddy child. "Let me see them!" His eyes light up as he points at her screen. "I like that one! You even got Ranger to smile!"

My heart takes flight as the familiar sound of the front door opening brightens my smile. The pitter-patter of little feet on the hardwood makes a rush of warmth flow through me that has nothing to do with the thick sweatshirt I have on.

Jasper's ice cream cone headband slides around on top of his head as he rounds the corner at full speed. "Kam!"

He runs into my open arms with a thunk. The Neapolitan colored paint on his shirt crinkles as he squeezes me. "Tank!" His headband lands on the floor at our feet with a light thunk as he wiggles out of my arms to run to the fridge with a grin on his face. "Mace! Can I have a popsicle?"

Posey launches herself into my arms as soon as I let go of her brother. "Hi, Kam!"

The flush of her cheeks matches her strawberry pink shirt. "Hey there, Rosie Posey!"

Her feet have barely touched the ground before she's running to my sister. They collide in a hug so tight their matching sprinkles form an undefined blob. "Posey-Pop!"

My ray of sunshine appears in the doorway with a smile so bright she lights up the entire room. Her eyes lock on mine as my heart stutters in my chest.

I move through the room with an efficiency that's only rivaled by my time on the ice. My arms automatically find their way around her waist as I breathe her in like I haven't seen her in days instead of hours. My voice falls to a whisper. "You're the cutest scoop of lemon ice cream I've ever seen, Sunshine."

Her smile transforms into a grin as she winds her arms around my neck. Her chest molds to mine as I feel every breath she takes. She leans in for what I think is a kiss before she deviates, so her lips brush against my ear to whisper, "Yeah, well, cookies and cream has always been my favorite."

She pulls back to send me a wink that shoots straight to my dick before she walks away to hug my sister like she didn't just leave a bomb at my feet. The innocent look on her face doesn't match the words coming from her mouth.

I never thought I would be grateful to be dressed as a cookies and cream ice cream scoop, but here I am.

Ellie claps her hands like our first grade teacher used to do to get everyone's attention. I welcome the distraction from the heat currently coursing through my body from a simple wink. "Alright guys! I've got our evening planned out!"

A grin breaks out on my face as I mumble, "Of course you do."

Her eyes snap to mine with laser accuracy as her smile turns sinister. "That'll be all the commentary we need from you tonight, Goose." Her smile turns soft as she glances around our group. "As I was saying before I was so rudely interrupted. We will leave for trick-or-treating in approximately…" She glances at her phone screen with a look of concentration reserved only for my sister. "…seven minutes. When we get back, we will go straight into a movie marathon I've planned around the twins' bedtime. If anyone needs a bathroom break before we leave, now would be the time." Her eyes swivel to Dax. "I'm looking at you, Hayes."

He rolls his eyes as he reluctantly heads toward the bathroom. "I peed in a bottle *one time*…"

Lila's eyes connect with mine as his voice fades into the distance. Her brows lift in a silent question as I mouth, *I'll tell you later*.

Lila nods before looking around the room. A gentle smile blooms on her face as she clears her throat to quieten the room. "I wanted to let everyone know that Jasper and Posey have a birthday coming up. They wanted to invite you all to their party next weekend."

A chorus of excitement flows through the room as voices overlap.

"Of course we'll be there!"

"Wouldn't miss it for the world, Posey-Pop!"

"Can I make your cake?"

"Did you wait till I left the room to invite everyone on purpose, Sullivan?" The grin on Dax's face betrays the stern tone of his voice.

A lightness enters Lila's eyes that's a far cry from the clouds I've gotten so used to seeing. She mimes zipping her lips and tossing the key over her shoulder as a smile takes over her face. "I'll never tell."

CHAPTER 40
THAT'S NOT LOVE
LILA

I envy the cocoon of soft blankets and peaceful dreams I left the twins in upstairs. My palms grow sweaty and my spine turns rigid as the naïve girl on the screen ventures further into the never ending cave.

I know one thing for certain: I would make a horrible scary movie protagonist. At the first sign of a ghost in my house or a creepy creature in a dark cave, I would *nope* out of there so quickly the movie would end before it even began.

The sound of her friends' voices fades behind her as the darkness envelopes her like a pool of ink. My heart beats a relentless rhythm in my chest as my fingers dig into the thick blanket covering my legs, as if it alone is what keeps me from following her into the darkness.

A silent, white blur flashes behind her as my mind fights my body's need to run from a fictional situation that poses no real danger other than to my blood pressure.

The colorless creature stalks her from the shadows

as she ventures further from the safety of her friends. Every breath the creature takes, I can feel against the back of my neck like I'm stranded alongside the girl who takes far too many risks with her life for my taste.

The clicking of the creature's talons against the ceiling, *yes, the freaking ceiling,* feels like nails on a chalkboard. The girl's steps falter as the unnerving sound finally reaches her ears.

Her eyes search the cave floor, completely unaware of the danger that lurks just above her head. Her gulp feels like my own as she slowly looks up to the ceiling of the cave to find the creature that will haunt my dreams for weeks. A scream builds in her chest as the creature descends.

The screen flashes to the horrified look on her friends' faces as her screams echo through the cave they never should have been in.

A chill runs down my spine as a commotion sounds from the kitchen behind me. I levitate off my seat and land firmly in Kam's lap as a scream escapes my lips that rivals the actress on the screen.

My fingers dig into the hair at the nape of his neck as I bury my face in the warm safety of his neck. Tremors wrack my body as he clutches me to his chest.

His chuckle vibrates through me as my eyelids glow from the overhead light being turned on. I hadn't even realized I closed my eyes.

Mace's voice holds a lightness I'm not sure I'll ever feel again. "I guess you were right, Ranger."

I pry my face away from Kam's neck and blink away the sting from the bright lights. Wyatt stretches his arms as he unfolds himself from his spot on the couch. "I told you to stack those bags of candy better than that. I'm surprised it took them this long to fall."

Ellie rubs the sleep from her eyes as she stretches her arms over her head. "I guess this is a good time for a snack break. Anyone want anything?"

Dax shoots from his spot on the couch with a grin on his face. "I'll make some popcorn."

In unison, Kam, Wyatt, and Ellie all say, "No!"

Dax rolls his eyes as he crosses his arms over his chest. "I won't burn it this time."

I relax my grip on Kam's neck as their voices fade into the kitchen. "Sorry for my death grip. You might have lost a few hairs."

His laugh vibrates against me as he rubs small circles against my lower back. "I'm happy for the sacrifice of a few hairs if it gets you in my lap like this."

My leggings glide against his jeans as I wiggle into a more comfortable position. I halt my movements when I feel a very firm bulge against my thigh. We both turn rigid as heat envelopes my face.

Careful of the growing bulge, I fix my eyes on the ceiling as I try to maneuver off his lap. The blanket holds my feet hostage as I try to free myself from Kam's hold and this embarrassing situation. "I, um, I'm sorry. I, uh, I'll just, uh—"

His firm hands circle my waist as he lifts me like I weigh nothing to sit me firmly on my feet in front of him.

I don't take the time to look at his expression before I bolt from the room. I don't have a destination in mind as I race through the back door. My bare feet connect with the rough wood of the deck as the chill in the air cools my heated face.

My fingers dig into the railing as I count my shallow breaths. The full moon illuminates the smoke from a distant bonfire that lingers in the air as I try to fixate on anything besides the heat coursing through my body.

"Sunshine?" My breath stalls in my chest at the pain in his voice. "Are you okay?" I let out a stuttered breath as his heat seeps into my back. His voice falls to a whisper that not even the bats flying above our heads can hear. "Talk to me." My eyes flutter closed as he moves the hair from my neck to rest over my shoulder without touching my skin. His breath tickles my neck like a feather-light kiss. "Did I make you uncomfortable?"

I shake my head as I open my eyes to the vacant yard before me. "No. You didn't make me uncomfortable."

The skin of my neck begs for his touch he has yet to give. "Then what is it?"

"I don't know."

I feel his exhale against my neck as I dig my fingers deeper into the wood of the railing. "Can I tell you something that terrifies me?"

The vulnerability in his voice finally gives me the courage to turn and face him. His chocolate eyes glow in the moonlight. "Always."

His eyes search mine as he pushes a stray hair from my face. I yearn for the warmth that ghosts over my skin from the proximity of his fingers. "When my body reacts to you like it did in there, all I feel is shame."

My brows crease with confusion. "What? Why?"

His eyes turn pleading as he takes a deep breath. "I spent so long denying myself your touch that now I don't know how to take it. I spent so long convincing myself to be your friend that now I don't know how to be anything but. Even though I want to be more, Sunshine. So much more. I just don't know how."

A small smile breaks through my confusion as I lace my fingers with his. "Can I tell you a secret?" He nods as a reluctant smile blooms on his face. "I ran out of there because I don't know what I'm doing. I've never had a serious boyfriend before. I've never *wanted* someone the way I want you. I have no idea how to handle all these new feelings, and what I'm supposed to do about them. But I know I don't feel any shame about the way I feel about you, and I don't want you to feel any shame about the way you feel about me, either."

He lets out a deep breath as his shoulders relax. "That's easier said than done."

A small laugh escapes into the night air as I grip his fingers tighter. "I know, but we can figure it out together." I shrug as a full smile pulls at my lips. "Plus, we don't have to do it like everyone else."

His fingers weave through the hair at the nape of my neck as he finally touches my skin of his own volition. "I think I'm terrified of being like him."

"Your dad?"

He nods his head as a crease forms between his brows. "I saw the way he treated my mom, Lila. I saw the way he let his desires dominate their relationship and control my mom. I saw how it ultimately tore them apart. How could you do that to someone you love?"

My hands firmly clench his sweatshirt, channeling

the strength I aim to convey through my voice. "You don't. That's not love, Kam. Your needs and wants are no less valid than mine. It doesn't matter if they're physical or emotional. The difference between you and your dad is that you value my needs and wants, too."

His smile transforms his face as he tightens his grip on my hair. He's so close that his words flow against my lips. "How did you get so wise?"

My lips brush against his as I say, "Being the guardian of two seven-year-olds as a twenty-one-year-old will do that to you."

Relief that feels like the first drink of ice water on a warm summer day flows through me as his lips connect with mine. And suddenly, all is right in the world.

CHAPTER 41
DECISIONS

KAM

Sweat drips down my cheek as my eyes follow the streak of black along the icy backdrop. The distant roar of the crowd fades into the recesses of my mind as my legs scream for a break I don't have time to give.

I feel the rapid rhythm of my heart beating in my fingertips as Dax transfers the puck to me.

The familiar thunk of the puck hitting my stick has tension coiling in my legs as I propel myself toward our goal with one thought in mind.

For a single moment, my eyes connect with the goalie. His piercing eyes stay locked on the puck by my feet. With a nearly indistinguishable tilt of his hips, he fills my favorite corner of the net. He doesn't realize the power that's coursing through my veins brings a determination that cannot be broken.

This one's for you, Sunshine.

I flick my eyes to the right as I swivel my hips like I'm sending the puck in that direction, right where he expects me to. A slight smirk lifts his lips as he celebrates a premature victory. I twist to the left at the last moment with a smirk of my own. My breath stalls in my chest as I send the puck soaring through the air toward our goal.

Silence blankets the rink as everyone collectively holds their breath as they await the puck's fate.

The goalie's brows furrow as he switches positions too late. The puck soars into the top left corner of the net as vibrations from the stands course through my legs.

My teammates swarm me as the last seconds tick down on the clock. The emcee's voice reverberates through my chest. "He's done it! Kamden Stryker has secured the first hat trick of the season!"

The pull of her stare from the stands is unmistakable amidst the surrounding chaos. I don't free my smile until my eyes connect with hers. Everything else fades away as her smile blooms. I barely notice my friends jostle me around on the ice as I place my hand over my heart before using it to blow a kiss to my ray of Sunshine.

Satisfaction flows through me like a raging river as a blush creeps over her cheeks. Her smile grows as the crowd erupts in a deafening roar. All eyes turn to her as I openly claim her as mine.

The thrill of a hat trick is no match for knowing my girl is in the stands, cheering me on with my name on her back.

I don't pull my eyes away from her even as shouts go through my teammates.

"Is that Cap's girl?"

"Way to go, Cap!"

"Lila's on the jumbotron!"

She ducks her head with a shy smile as I'm pulled in all different directions. I allow myself to be pulled away by my teammates even though the last thing I want to do is take my eyes off her.

But the quicker I get the interviews done and make it to the locker room, the quicker I get to see her. That's all the motivation I need to kick everyone into high gear and get this shit done.

Students spill out of the front door of The Penalty Box like an overstuffed pizza roll. The sea of people part, and cheers move through the crowd as soon as I'm spotted.

Their *congratulations* mean nothing to me compared to my need to get inside and find my girl. This need to hold her and bathe myself in her mango scent is overwhelming.

There were too many layers separating us at the rink. Layers of glass. Layers of people. Now that she's so close, I can't get to her fast enough.

My eyes relentlessly search for her in the crowd of meaningless faces. A flash of a red bow that matches the one tied around my wrist pulls my attention.

A sense of rightness settles in my chest as she comes fully into view. My name sits proudly on her back like a beacon for all to see. A beacon that proudly shouts, *This woman is mine!* My fingers itch to trace my name and feel the warmth of her skin.

She's not the only one in this restaurant who's sporting my name on her back, but she's the only one who deserves it.

The only one whose presence is now as necessary as breathing.

Her laugh cuts through the elated voices around us as I close in on her. My smile rings clear in my voice. "Hi, Sunshine."

She graces me with a beaming smile as she throws her arms around my neck. That smile that's reserved just for me never fails to send a wave of butterflies through my stomach. "Ah, you're here! You played such a good game!"

I secure my arms around her waist and let her mango scent override the smell of stale beer and nachos that is an ever-present staple of The Penalty Box. "It's all thanks to my good luck charm." The bow around my wrist is a statement as powerful as the kiss I blew to her on the ice tonight.

Her eyes practically sparkle as she leans back to look at me. "Nah. That's all you, Trouble."

A sudden elbow to the ribs turns my attention away from Lila to find a teasing smile on Ellie's face. "I see how it is! You get a girlfriend, and the rest of us just disappear into the background to live our lives as side characters."

One arm stays firmly around Lila's waist as I pull Ellie into a side hug. "There, happy now, Shrimp?"

She rolls her eyes in mock annoyance as she grabs

Lila's hand. "It'll do, Goose." Her eyes turn pleading as they fall on Lila. "Come on, I've got to go to pee."

The strength it takes to unlock my arm from Lila's waist is immeasurable. "Hurry back."

The smile shining brightly in her eyes holds me captive as my sister drags her into the crowd. "I'll be back before you know it."

The hole they made in the crowd seals behind them as I take my usual seat at our table. Dax's eyes narrow as he examines me with a tilt of his head. "You know, you started playing the best games of your life after Sullivan came around." His eyes swivel to Mace next to him as a smirk takes over his face. "Maybe it's time we settled down, Mace. Seems like that's the best way to level up our game."

A sultry voice that sends chills, and not the good kind, down my spine reaches my ears. "Great game tonight, Kam."

I reluctantly turn to find Kim's low cut top directly in my eyeline. I somehow fully hide my cringe as I realize it's my jersey she's wearing. "Uh, thanks, Kim."

Her eyes crinkle as the fakest smile I've ever seen sprouts on her face. The overpowering stench of her perfume washes over me as she leans a fraction of an inch closer. "Are you going to the party at the Football House tonight?"

My ass cheek hugs the edge of my seat as I try to move out of her orbit. "No. You know we don't party like that."

I've had a strict no alcohol rule since I turned twenty-one. I refuse to end up like my father.

How she pouts her lips with all the filler in them, I'll

never know. "Aww, come on, Kam." Her pink-tipped nails brush down my shoulder, and I recoil from her touch like I've been burned. "It'll be soooo much fun."

I open my mouth to reply, but don't get a chance. A familiar hand slips under hers to replace the chill of her touch with a warmth that seeps into my bones. "He said no, Kim." Lila's eyes blaze with a fire that sets my heart ablaze.

Kim's boney fingers dig into her hips as she lets out a huff of annoyance. "Kam's a big boy. He can make his own decisions."

A smirk blooms on Lila's face as her ass lands in my lap, right where she belongs. "He already did." My arm immediately finds its place around her waist, a possession as certain as the name written across her back.

My eyes lock with Lila's as laughter erupts from the surrounding tables. I don't bother looking away to confirm that Kim has stormed off to find her posse that will help her self-esteem recover.

The heat of her body seeps through my layers of clothes as I pull her closer. I hardly recognize my voice with the amount of pride flowing through it. "That was the sexiest thing I have ever seen." Judging by the look in her eyes, I know she can feel the evidence of that growing in my pants.

It's not just that she stood up to Kim for me, it's that we felt like a unit. An unbreakable force that can withstand the test of time and nature.

Lila's fingers weave into the hair at the nape of my neck as some of the fire fades from her eyes. "You're mine, Kamden Stryker."

My heart fights to crawl out of my chest to fall at her

feet. Her words sink into me like aloe on the burns left behind by those that came before her.

A slow clap starts up around us as Dax's voice shines with approval. "That was even better than Kam's hat trick."

Ellie's face stretches in an impossibly large smile as she vibrates in her seat. "I couldn't be prouder of you, L. I can't wait to tell Posey. She will flip her lid."

The absence of the twins is felt around the table, but we all know how big of a deal it is for them to have their first overnight visit with their grandparents. My voice is a feather-light kiss against Lila's cheek as I whisper, "Do you have any plans tonight?" Her smile turns shy as she shakes her head. "I have an idea."

"Should I be worried?"

My shrug shifts her in my lap. "I guess you'll just have to wait and see."

CHAPTER 42
NO PEEKING
LILA

I remember how excited my mom was when she found this huge couch. Her words ring through my mind like I heard them only yesterday.

"Now that is a proper movie watching couch!"

Now, this giant couch feels miniature compared to the giant hockey player sitting on it next to me. The glow from the lamp in the corner of the room showcases Kam's profile like a work of art as he unwraps the box on the coffee table.

I don't even try to hide the skepticism from my voice as a smile takes over my face. "Are you sure about this?"

His grin only makes my smile grow. "Not even a little bit. This was one of my other ideas for our first date."

He waves his hand around to overcome the glue-like static that has permanently attached a stray piece of plastic to the side of his hand. I don't even try to contain my laugh as a paint tube falls to the floor. "You know this will only end in disaster, right?"

His eyes shine as they connect with mine. "Oh, definitely. In fact, I'm counting on it." He raises his brows as his hand stalls mid-air. "You're not even going to try to help me? I see how it is. Laugh at the guy who's losing a fight to a piece of plastic."

I roll my eyes in mock annoyance as my laugh grows. "I'm having way too much fun to interrupt," I wave my hand in his general direction, "whatever it is you're doing. It's clearly working so well."

The mischievous look that takes over his face reminds me so much of his sister. "Just remember, you asked for this."

His speed on the ice makes an appearance as he grabs a handful of discarded plastic and dumps it over my head. It rains down on me like fresh snow as my jaw falls to the floor. "You did *not* just do that, Kamden Stryker!"

His eyes hold no remorse as his laugh breaks free. "Has anyone ever told you how cute you are when you're mad?"

I huff out a laugh and groan combo as a piece of plastic sticks to my face like I've walked through a spider web. He doubles over with laughter as I try to blow another piece free from its prison in my hair.

The plastic taunts me as it flutters with my breath. In the low light, the movement produces a cascade of shimmering, iridescent sparkles. Our laughter fades as we watch the show. It's amazing how something so simple can be so beautiful.

The awe in his voice draws my eyes to his. "I didn't

know it was possible for you to be more stunning." I fight to keep my eyes from falling away from him. A smirk blooms on his face as he tilts his head to the side. "You don't take compliments well, do you?"

I shake my head as I scrunch my nose. "It's never really been my strong suit."

"Don't worry, you'll get used to it." Thankfully, his eyes move away from the blush that's taking over my face to the now plastic-free canvases on the table in front of us. "Alright, where do we start?"

I shrug as I look over all the painting supplies he just happened to have in his car. "I don't know. You're the one carrying around all the supplies."

Now it's his turn to blush. "Well, I, uh, wanted to have a backup plan for our first date in case it rained or something and we couldn't go to our secret place."

My eyebrows disappear into my hairline as I stare at this conundrum of a man in front of me. "You mean to tell me you've had this stuff in your Tahoe all this time?"

He shrugs as he rubs the back of his neck. "It's not a big deal. I just wanted to make sure everything went okay."

An *oof* slips from his lips as I crash into him. He sits as still as a statue as I throw my arms around his neck in a crushing hug. I muffle my voice as I bury my face in his warm neck. "That is so sweet, Trouble."

After a few seconds, his arms tighten around my back to mold me to his chest. "You deserve that and more. I hope you know that."

I hope the wobble in my voice isn't as obvious to

him as it is to me. "I may need you to keep reminding me."

His smile sends butterflies scattering through my belly. "It would be my pleasure."

My smile doesn't match the mock aggravation in my voice as I try to use my body to hide my canvas. "Stop peeking! It's against the rules!"

His firm fingers dig into my side in an attempt to tickle me away from my spot at the dining table. "We agreed to not look at each other's paintings until we were done. Well, I'm done, so I'm going to look."

My breathing comes in short bursts as I try to fight off his tickle assault. "Well, I'm *not* done! So, no peeking!"

The legs of the chair squeak against the floor with my jerky movements. I'm not a fool. I know he could move me if he wanted to. I'm still in my seat because he deems it so. That doesn't mean I'm not going to fight like hell to stay here, anyway.

Our laughter dies and our movements halt as his warm fingers contact the bare skin of my stomach. The only sound blanketing the still room is our labored breaths and my heartbeat echoing in my ears.

Chills follow the path of his fingers as he traces the tiny gap that opened between my leggings and t-shirt during his assault. I fight my natural instincts to arch my back to encourage his exploration.

The gravel in his voice sends a shiver down my spine. "Do you want me to stop?" All I can manage is a shake of my head as his fingers stall their exploration. "I need your words, Sunshine."

I struggle to swallow as I try to find my voice. "No. I don't want you to stop."

Without hesitation, his fingers slip farther up my stomach. His skin feels like the softest silk against mine despite the hard earned calluses that decorate his hand.

A shaky breath escapes my lips as he traces the edge of my leggings with a featherlight touch. His gentle touch turns to steel as both hands circle my waist. Cool air washes over my back as I'm lifted out of my warm seat. Empty paint tubes fall to the ground with a clatter as he places me on the table in front of him with impressive strength.

My legs open for him on instinct as he captures my mouth in a kiss that pulls the air from my lungs. We swallow each other's gasps as relief flows through me at having his lips on mine.

I can feel the warmth of his hands through the fabric as they glide against the hem of my shirt. His groan flows into me like life-giving water as his skin meets mine.

My legs close around his waist to trap him against me. His hardness rubs against the apex of my legs as a groan of frustration leaves my lips. The need for relieving pressure grows with every stroke of his fingers against my over-sensitive skin. And yet, his fingers haven't ventured any farther than the waistband of my leggings.

His lips break from mine as his harsh breaths flow

over my face. I open my eyes to find his full of hesitation. His words come out in a rush as we try to catch our breath. "I need to tell you something."

He follows the movement of my tongue against my lips as I try to wet them. "What is it?"

A blush creeps over his face. "I've never done this before. I mean, I've kissed other girls before you, and, uh," his nose wrinkles, "done a few other things, but, um, I've never gone all the way." He searches my face as he takes a tiny step back from me. My legs fall away as I clench my hands in my lap. "I just thought we should talk about that, you know, before things went any further."

Surprise and relief flow through me in equal measure as a small smile lifts my lips. "So, you're a virgin?"

He nods his head slowly. "Yes. I'm a virgin." His words flow from him like water from a dam break. "It's okay if you're not. There's no expectations for you to be a virgin or to *not* be a virgin. There's also no expectations at all, really. I just thought you should know before things went any further. I just, um, wanted to talk about it to see where your head's at, and—"

My hand closing over his mouth is like putting a stopper in a wine bottle. Shock registers in his eyes as a smile blooms on my face. "Hey, stop fretting. I've never done this, either."

My smile only grows as his mouth moves against my hand. "You haven't?"

I shake my head as I free his mouth. "No. I haven't. I'm glad you brought it up. I've been kinda freaking out about it."

His groan is filled with relief as he basically falls into my vacated seat. "Me too. I didn't want to make anything weird, but I also didn't want to just ignore it, either."

"You made the right call, Trouble." His leg doesn't move an inch as I nudge him with my foot. "I have to admit, I'm kind of surprised. I definitely didn't expect the captain of the hockey team to be a virgin. Aren't hockey players known for having a parade of girls at their beck and call?"

A smile blooms on his face as he moves his chair closer so he's nestled between my legs. "Well, you might have noticed that me, Dax, Mace, and Wyatt are all a little different from the other guys on our team. I guess that's why we all became friends." He shrugs, and I can practically see the memories flashing behind his eyes. "Don't get me wrong, not everyone is a virgin. That's not what I'm talking about. We're just each different in our own way."

"I like different, Trouble." Questions fly through my mind as I tilt my head. "I assume there's a reason you've never had sex with anyone."

A coldness falls over his eyes that I wish I could burn away. "I saw how much sex controlled my dad's life. He couldn't have a good time and celebrate a win without it. It didn't matter if my mom was there or not. I guess I just never wanted to open myself up to the temptation." A humorless laugh leaves his lips. "My dad obviously had an addictive personality. Whether it was alcohol, gambling, sex, whatever it may be, he couldn't control it. Hell, even hockey was an addiction for him. That scares the shit out of me." The ice melts from his eyes as the warmth returns. "But I'm realizing, after all this time, that I'm really not like him."

"You're really not, Kam."

The warmth of his breathtaking smile seeps into my chest as a lightness takes over his face. "I know. Cause when I think about celebrating a game, the only person I see is you. The thought of anyone else makes me want to run as fast as I can in the opposite direction. That alone shows how different I am from him." He inclines his head toward me as his eyes roam over my body with a gentle caress. "What about you? Why haven't you been with anyone?"

My hands gliding along the smooth fabric of my leggings soothes a part of me that always gets defensive when thinking about sex. "I never found someone worthy of giving that piece of myself." I shake my head as a humorless laugh escapes my lips. "It's funny, I would always get made fun of for being a virgin, but girls who weren't were called a whore or a slut. It's like the world can't make up its mind."

The rhythmic vibration of my phone against the dining table sends a bolt of dread down my spine. Victoria's name stares at me from my phone screen as my heart tries to beat out of my chest.

My eyes connect with Kam's to find my worry reflected back at me as I answer her call. "Hello?"

"Lila. Come to my house right away."

CHAPTER 43
THE BRIDGE BETWEEN US
KAM

My fingers dig into the leather of my steering wheel as I fight to watch the road instead of the woman next to me. Waves of anxiety roll off of Lila as I count the minutes that seem to last an eternity.

Her leg bounces an unrelenting rhythm as she chews on the nail of her index finger. We've barely spoken a word since she ended the call with her grandmother. The silence stretches between us like a chasm I don't have a way to cross, as the dark road stretches endlessly before us.

The city streets transform into neighborhoods with ever-expansive houses the further we move through the darkness. Spotlights illuminate the ornate fountains and pristine landscaping of the mansions as I turn onto the street Lila points out.

Cars that are worth more than our townhouse fill the driveways of the sleepy street. My heartbeat pounds through my temples as I turn into the driveway of the last house on the left. Iron gates sit open at the end of the driveway, despite the clock reading nearly midnight.

The hinge bounces violently as Lila throws her door open before I've put the car in park. She slams the door behind her without a care for her grandparents' sleeping neighbors. Her blonde waves stream behind her as she flies to the front porch.

My sneakers give me the traction I need to catch up to her just in time for the front door to fly open. Tears stream down Posey's face as she lunges for her sister.

Lila's eyes frantically move over her sister, despite the calmness present in her voice. "What's wrong, Ladybug? What happened?" My spine straightens as sobs pour from Posey like a raging river.

Tiny fingers grasp the hem of my shorts in a death grip. As I squat down to his level, Jasper's red-rimmed eyes turn to me with heartbreaking relief. "Thanks for coming, Kam."

Without hesitation, I lift him into my arms and secure him tightly against my chest. "We'll always come when you call." My eyes fall to my girls as he tightens his hold around my neck. "What's going on, Tank?"

At the sound of my voice, Posey's eyes lift to mine before he has time to answer. She's running toward me with open arms within seconds. I meet her halfway and lift her sweaty little body with one arm. She buries her face in my neck as her tears soak into my skin.

Her body wracks with every shaky breath she takes. As soon as she's secure in my arms, I carry her and her brother to my Tahoe without looking back. I don't give a shit what happened. They're not going back in that house. At least not tonight.

I waste no time securing them in the booster seats that have been in my car for weeks at this point. "It's alright, guys. We'll get you home soon."

Lila's faint voice drifts to me through the chilly autumn air as her grandmother appears in the doorway. I clench my teeth as I realize I can't hear what they're saying because of the distance.

My eyes connect with Jasper's as I click Posey's seatbelt into place with one hand, while my other remains firmly secured in her clenched hands. I try to pull my hand away, but stall my movements as her fingers tighten around mine.

Thankfully, her old tears drying on her face fail to be replaced by new ones. Jasper's eyes shine with a determination reserved only for a brother's love. A different type of determination shines through my voice as I straighten to my full height. "I need you to tell me what happened, Tank. I can't fix it if I don't know what happened."

His eyes flick to the illuminated front porch where his grandmother hands Lila a duffle bag. I grit my teeth at the waver in his voice. "Posey had a nightmare. She got scared when she couldn't find me. They made us sleep in separate rooms."

My eyes soften as they fall to the little girl huddled in her seat in front of me, still clutching my hand tightly to her chest like you would a stuffed animal. "Are you alright now, Rosie Posey?" Her bottom lip wobbles as she nods her head. "Good. You'll be home in your own bed soon." I lift our joined hands. "I'm going to need my hand back so I can drive us home, but Jasper's going to hold your hand the entire way there. Okay?"

Cool air replaces the warmth of her hand as she releases her grip. Their hands link to dangle over the space between their two seats like a bridge.

I close their door as Lila's steps sound from behind me. Her lips are set in a tight line as the front door to her grandparents' house closes with a soft click.

I raise my brows at her in a silent question. She drops the duffle bag by our feet with a soft thunk as she walks straight into my arms. A deep breath falls from her lips as the tension leaves her shoulders. The tension might have left her shoulders, but it sure hasn't left her voice. "I don't know what I expected to find when we got here, but that wasn't it."

I rest my chin on the top of her head as I rub small circles on her lower back. "I know. Jasper said Posey had a nightmare and freaked out when she couldn't find him."

Her voice is muffled against my chest. "I thought they had been doing better. They've been sleeping in their own beds for a few weeks now."

I shift her in my arms as I try to fight off the frigid chill with my body heat. "It's a new place. It makes sense they would have a hard time adjusting."

She nods against my chest as she tightens her arms around my waist. "I know. I just hate it for them."

My lips connect with her forehead in a much-needed kiss. If only I could just convince myself the kiss is for her instead of me. "Come on. Let's get them home."

As soon as we're settled in our seats, my hand finds hers in the darkness. The contact and the security of the twins' safety in the backseat calm the relentless pounding of my heart to a calming rhythm in my chest.

Two statements repeat in a constant loop in my mind for the rest of the drive.

They're here. They're safe.

The last of the tension I didn't know I have been carrying melts as I cut the engine in their driveway. My head thunks against my headrest as my neck screams from the constant strain of the past thirty minutes.

A quick look in my rearview mirror shows two peacefully sleeping seven-year-olds with their hands still clenched tightly together.

Lila's eyes flick to mine before we wordlessly venture out of the solitude of the car and into the darkness of the night.

The cool chill of the autumn breeze lifts Posey's hair to tickle my nose as I carry her into the house. She feels like a bag of flour in my arms as she lay limply on my shoulder.

Lila's light footfalls echo behind me as I shift Posey in my arms to open the front door. She still sleeps peacefully on my shoulder despite the floorboards creaking under my feet.

Posey's curls fan out around her shoulders as I lay her in the middle of Lila's bed. She wrinkles her nose before turning to her side to burrow further under the blankets.

I straighten slowly to prolong my time here as Lila lays Jasper on the other side of the mattress. A piece of me longs to stand guard at Lila's door tonight to fight off any lingering snapshots of Posey's nightmare that dare to threaten her sleep.

The twins reach for each other in the dark. The way they huddle together in the middle of the bed reminds me of what they might have looked like before they entered this world. I know logically they're fraternal twins, but it's obvious they still find comfort in their proximity. I hope this space resembles the safety they must have felt while they were being carried by their mother.

Tears rim Lila's eyes as she watches over her brother and sister like a sentry. Her voice wavers as she whispers, "How is it possible for me to take care of something so precious and fragile?"

My fingers weave into the hair at her nape as I pull her into my side. Our eyes never leave the bed as I hold her. "I couldn't think of anyone more worthy."

I'm not ashamed of the time I take to gather the will to leave. I'm quickly realizing that no amount of time with them will ever be enough.

Lila's soft kiss against my lips feels like more than a goodnight. Maybe when I finally lay down in my bed tonight, I'll have enough brain power to think about what it means. For now though, I just drink her in like she's the only thing in the world keeping me alive.

It feels like I'm leaving a piece of my heart behind as I close the door behind me and venture into the night.

I only have one thought as I glance in my rearview mirror to back out of her driveway.

That view looks awfully damn empty without the twins in the backseat.

CHAPTER 44
IT'LL ALL MAKE SENSE SOON
LILA

KAM

So…I probably should have asked if this was okay before I did it.

No, scratch that. I definitely should have asked if it was okay before I did it…

My heartbeat echoes in my ears as I walk through the full parking lot of The Penalty Box. The stale beer smell feels like a permanent coating on my skin after my shift this evening.

Thirty minutes ago, the only thought on my mind was making it through my shift, picking up the twins from Ellie's, and showering off this grime that feels like it's embedded in my pores. Now, unease slithers down my spine to settle near my aching feet like lead.

My fingers hover over the phone keyboard like I've pressed pause on life. I almost drop my phone as the device vibrates in my hands with an incoming text.

KAM

If you want us to take it down, just say
the word.

Take it down? What the hell does that mean?

LILA

What do you mean? Is everything
okay?

The bubbles come and go on the screen as he types. With every disappearance of the bubbles, my anxiety doubles.

KAM

Everything's fine! Just...don't freak out
when you see the backyard...

LILA

The backyard? What happened to the
backyard?

KAM

Just come to your house instead of
going to Ellie's. It'll all make sense
soon.

LILA

Okay...I'm leaving now.

KAM

Drive safe, Sunshine.

The sunset bathes the familiar cars that line the street in a wash of warm pinks and oranges. Silence descends like a comforting cocoon as I cut the engine and rest my head against the headrest.

I fight a battle in my mind between curiosity and apprehension as I eye the gate to the backyard. Curiosity wins despite the relentless pounding of my heart against my ribs.

The chill of the autumn air burns my lungs compared to the heat I had blasting on my face in the car. My door slamming behind me reverberates through my bones as the sound of deep, distant laughter drifts on the gentle breeze.

Kam's familiar laugh calms my racing heart as I dig my fingers into the rough wood of the gate. The shrill squeak of its hinges feels like nails on a chalkboard compared to the melody of voices just around the corner.

My breath stalls in my chest and my feet ground to a halt in the dirt as my friends come into view.

My eyes never stray to the wooden fence lining the property line or to the swaying trees at the back of the yard that hide my neighbor's house from view. They don't linger on the firepit that my dad never got to use, or the row of empty flowerpots against the back of the house.

Instead, I blink slowly as I try to process the smiling faces surrounding a swing set that was definitely not in my backyard when I left my house this morning.

I open and close my mouth like a fish as Dax sends an elbow into Kam's ribs to alert him to my arrival. His smile falls and a crease forms between his brows as his eyes roam over my face.

Swing set isn't a good enough term for the structure standing before me. A slide juts from the side of a white cottage that sits proudly on stilts. A freaking staircase leads to a landing that connects the cottage to another slide big enough for two. As if a literal staircase wasn't enough, you can also climb a rock wall to get to the cottage. Three swings hang between the primary structure and a set of monkey bars that beg to strip the skin from my palms.

How the hell did they build all this while I was at work?

Kam rubs the back of his neck as he inches toward me. "I, uh, I'm sorry I didn't ask before we installed it. I just heard Jasper and Posey talking about wanting one. I figured it would be the perfect birthday present for them. Everyone pitched in." The worry clouding his eyes grows sharper with every step he takes toward me. "If you don't want it in your backyard, we can take it down and put it in ours or something."

My eyes slide from his to the hockey players behind him. They make the swing set look miniature as they gather the tools that litter the yard. I hate the apprehension I see on their faces as they await my reaction.

"Say something, Sunshine." I haven't even realized I haven't said anything. Kam's eyes turn stormy as he follows a silent tear as it falls down my cheek.

The waver in my voice must ring clear, judging by the shifting of our friends on their feet. "You did all this for them?" He nods his head slowly, like he's afraid to spook a wild animal. His eyes follow another tear as the crease between his brows turns into a canyon. "Thank you, Kam."

His brows fly up as he takes his turn opening and closing his mouth like a fish. "You're, uh, not mad?"

I shake my head as I launch myself into his arms. His *oof* ruffles the baby hairs around my face as I tighten my arms around his neck. "Of course I'm not mad! Look at what you've done for them! That is so sweet, Trouble. Thank you!"

I block out the voices of our friends behind him as he tightens his arms around me. He muffles his voice as he buries his face in my hair. The warmth from his chest radiates through me to fight off the chill in the air. "I would do anything for you three. Anything."

I burrow into the warmth of his chest as those distant voices grow closer. The smile in Dax's voice accompanies the crunch of footsteps in the grass. "I told you she wouldn't be mad, Cap. You were worrying about nothing."

A giddy smile takes over Mace's face as he bounces on the balls of his feet. "Can we call Ellie so she can bring the twins over to see their gift? I don't know how much longer I can wait."

Four sets of expectant eyes turn to me. Even Wyatt's eyes hold a lightness that he deserves to feel more often. I nod as my smile grows. "Yeah, you can call Ellie."

The world blurs around me as Kam and I are enveloped in a group hug. A grumble leaves Wyatt as Dax's voice thunders in my ear, "Family hug!"

Family. What an excellent word.

CHAPTER 45
CHOCOLATE SNOB
KAM

I wipe my palms on my pants as the sound of car doors closing reaches the backyard. Lila's eyes sparkle with the reflection of the first embers of a bonfire as a smile takes over her face. "Don't be nervous. They're going to love it."

Sparks fly into the air as Wyatt drops another log on the fire with a thunk. "Don't worry, Cap. It's a great birthday present."

The significance of his words isn't lost on me like they are the others. The two of us spent many birthdays together on the ice, with our only gifts being harsh words from our fathers.

When I got old enough to realize that's not the norm, I vowed that if I ever had kids, they would never know the pain of feeling like a game meant more than their happiness.

I know the twins aren't mine, but they sure as hell feel like they're supposed to be.

I hear the moment they see their gift. Their sharp

intakes of breath cascade through the yard as their footsteps come to a sudden halt. I look up in time to watch the awe transform their faces to what I imagine they would look like on Christmas morning. The sight of their smiles and wide eyes burrows its way into my heart, where it will live for the rest of my life.

They bounce on the balls of their feet as they take in every feature of the structure I spent way too long picking out.

The excitement that radiates from them in waves compels me to move closer so I might bask in their joy. The warmth from the fire fades from my back as Lila's fingers dig into my sweatshirt to replace the warmth she's no longer getting from the fire.

My smile grows with every step I take toward them. "Happy birthday, guys!"

Confusion pulls at Posey's brows as Jasper vibrates next to her. "Our birthday isn't until tomorrow."

Ellie laughs as she comes around the side of the house with an arm full of grocery bags. "We wanted you to have your present early, Posey-Pop!" The plastic bags crinkle as she drops them by her feet. Her smile never wavers, even as she rubs the redness from the bags digging into her arms. "What are you waiting for? Go check out your new gift while we get the s'mores ready!"

Twilight descends around us as they race toward their gift. They leave a trail of laughter in their wake as I add motion detection lights for the backyard to my to-do list.

Mace points an accusatory finger at my sister as he races to catch up with the twins. "You better have gotten the good stuff, Ellie. No more of this cheap, barely considered chocolate."

Ellie rolls her eyes even though Mace has already turned his back to her. "Of course I did. You've made me a chocolate snob, Mace. I'll never forgive you for it."

Mace's laughter mixes with the giggles flowing from the twins as they explore their new domain. "I can live with that!"

The last time I saw Lila bathed in firelight, all I wanted to do was kiss her. To claim her as mine for all the world to see.

Now, as I watch the light dance over her face, the reality that I can just reach over and kiss her anytime I want hits me like a freight train. And I've never been one to waste an opportunity.

Jasper and Posey's giggles mixing with the laughter of our friends drifts through the wind. The gentle sway of the swings and an occasional scuff of a shoe against the slide fades into the background as my eyes trace the outline of Lila's lips.

I anchor my hand at the back of her neck as a surprised gasp leaves her lips with the contact of my heated skin. Her soft lips mold to mine as I fight the groan threatening to rise in my throat.

My need to deepen the kiss is overwritten by the awareness of our audience. The chill in the air isn't the cause of the chill bumps that flow over my skin as I end the kiss far too soon.

The back of my throat burns as I suck in a deep lungful of cool air.

Her eyes roam over my face as embers from the fire ascend into the darkness to be swallowed by the stars. "What was that for?"

Her hair falls through my fingers like silk as I release her neck. "I just wanted to kiss my girl." I raise my brows as a smirk pulls at my lips. "That alright with you?"

She mirrors my smile as she drifts closer on the blanket we've claimed next to the fire. "It's perfect."

The warmth from her cheek seeps through my clothes as she settles her cheek on my shoulder to watch the flames dance to their own beat in front of us.

The cracks in a log near the bottom of the pile glow red and orange with the flames that infiltrate its core. An unexpected sense of camaraderie fills me as I watch the log grow weaker until it finally releases its hold and gives in to the crushing weight of the logs above it.

When this semester started, the weight of my father's legacy felt as consuming as the weight of the logs. The expectations forced upon me since before I could walk felt like flames dancing in my core.

Now, with the intensity of Lila's light and the strength of her heart, she dims the burn of my father's legacy. She lessens the toll of the expectations that have always seemed so crushing, despite my constant fight against them.

For the first time since I slipped a pair of ice skates on my feet, I feel like I can take my first full breath. Like my lungs aren't fighting against the crushing force of the circumstances thrust upon me. Like the only thing expected of me at this moment is to be here with these people. With *my* people.

The burn and the toll are still there, but they don't seem as important now. Especially not compared to the girl resting her cheek on my shoulder, and the two little kids playing on their swing set.

CHAPTER 46
RIGHT THING

KAM

There's glitter on me. I can practically see it floating in the air as I settle in my seat. I'm not sure I'll ever be free from it again.

Shrill giggles and fake personalities assault me from all sides as I realize I really don't belong here. There's only one person who could convince me to sit in this waiting room, and there's five minutes until her class is over and I can get the hell out of this place.

Classical music drifts through the air as little girls in ballerina outfits swarm the room like bees would their hive.

Jasper's leg brushes mine as he tries to avoid the snotty toddler in the seat next to him. Maybe if her mom wasn't glued to her phone, the poor kid wouldn't have snot stains all over her shirt.

Loud chewing draws my attention to the blonde coming to a stop in front of me. Her eyes roam over my body as a massive, pink bubble blocks half her face, only to pop all over her lips. Her hand lands on her hip as she pushes her chest toward me. My eyes never stray from her face, even though her low cut top is directly in my eyeline. "Hi, there! Can I help you? I'm pretty sure I would have remembered seeing *your* face around here."

I have to fight to keep a neutral expression on my face since she apparently never learned to chew with her mouth closed. "No thanks. We're all good here."

She inches toward me until the tip of her shoe touches the tip of my sneakers. A predatory gleam shines in her eyes as she extends a hand for a handshake I have no intention of giving. "Well, I'm Molly. Are you here for something specific? I'd love to show you around the studio."

I clear my throat to disguise the movement of me tucking my feet under the seat where they'll be safe. Her hand stays suspended in the air as I use Jasper as my scapegoat. "That's alright. We're just waiting for Posey to get out of class. Isn't that right, Tank?"

He nods his head. "Yep! She'll be done soon. Then we're going to our birthday party!"

Molly shuffles even closer to me without a single mention of Jasper's birthday. What kind of monster do you have to be to not even wish a kid a happy birthday? "So you're the reason Lila hasn't needed me to watch Jasper while Posey's been in class?" Her aggravation at losing an easy twenty-bucks slips from her eyes as she says, "Are you Lila's brother or something?"

"Kam!" Posey pushes right past Molly to launch herself into my arms.

My laugh breaks free as Molly's face turns a satisfying shade of red. "Happy birthday, Rosie Posey!"

"And who do we have here?" A tall, wiry woman in her mid-twenties stops just behind Molly. Her auburn hair is pulled back in a severe bun that rests at the nape of her neck.

Taking advantage of the space between us, I stand from my seat. Their eyes widen to a comical level as they take in my full height. I can barely hide the smile from my face as they try to hide their interest. My eyes turn to Molly. "Thank you for the offer of a tour, but we've got to get going."

The wiry woman steps around Molly with an outstretched hand that I intend to avoid like the plague. "Wait just a second. You can't just take one of my students without me knowing who you are."

I raise my brows. "My name is Kam Stryker. Lila added me to Posey's checkout list a few weeks ago."

Posey's fingers dig into the hem of my sweatshirt. "Kam is our friend, Miss Emma."

Normally, I would be all for her making sure Posey was leaving with the right person, but the look in Emma's eyes betrays her true intentions. My seat groans under my weight as I sit back down. "We don't mind waiting while you check your records."

Emma's eyes never leave mine as she waves over her shoulder at Molly. "Go check the records, Molly. I'll keep Kam company while he waits."

I take Posey's dance bag from where she dropped it by her feet and place it in the empty seat next to me. Her nose scrunches as she follows my movements. I keep a friendly smile on my face. "I'm sure the process would be quicker if you helped Molly look through your records."

My eye twitches as she waves away my concern. "It's alright. She's capable of looking through the files herself." A flirty smile pulls at her lips that makes my dick shrivel in my pants. "So, Kam, you play for Summit University, right?"

I nod my head as I cross my arms. "That's right."

"Well, I hardly ever miss a game. Maybe we could catch dinner after your next one? I know this great place—"

My voice is as sharp as my eyes as I cut her off. "No, thank you. I prefer celebrating a win with my girlfriend."

Posey and Jasper's voices overlap as they both say, "And with us, too!"

A smile pulls at my lips as I look down at them. "Of course!"

Her brows crease as she opens her mouth for a reply that I'm sure to hate as Molly appears over her shoulder with a file folder. My muscles don't relax despite the relief that flows through me with her appearance.

"What is your date of birth and phone number, Kam?" Molly's eyes move over the paper as I rattle off the answers to her questions. With a sigh, she says, "That matches your information on file. You're free to take Posey with you."

"If you'll excuse us, we have a birthday party to get to." I would normally say it was nice meeting someone after our first introductions, but in this case, I would be lying.

Posey's dance bag is light on my shoulder compared to the weight of that conversation as we leave the dance studio.

I'm thankful for the cool air that helps cool my aggravation with every step we take away from the building.

The twins don't utter a word as we file into my Tahoe. Jasper's sharp eyes connect with mine in the rearview mirror. "I don't think I like Molly and Miss Emma anymore, Kam."

My smirk blooms as I back out of the parking spot. "That's alright, Tank. I don't like them, either."

He tilts his head, and I can practically see the gears turning in his head. "My teacher at school says it's not nice to say you don't like someone."

Well, shit.

My mind screams, *abort! I'm not prepared for this! This is adult stuff and I'm not ready to be the adult in the room.*

It's not like I have a good example to look back on for things like this. My mom and dad let us figure out everything for ourselves. That resulted in me never feeling like I knew how to handle situations on my own.

What would Lila say?

Then it clicks. "Well, did I say anything mean to Miss Emma and Molly?"

He straightens in his seat. "No."

My voice rings with certainty I'm not sure I feel. "Well, that means I was still being nice, right?"

A smile takes over his face that is nearly blinding in the rearview mirror. "Right!"

I relax into my seat, feeling like I just won the lottery. I replay my words over in my head, just hoping I've said the right thing as another thought pops into my head. "But you can always tell me or Lila when you don't like someone, okay?"

A surprising flash of hope enters his eyes. "I can?"

His blue eyes search mine in the mirror as we approach their house. "Of course you can, Tank."

He nods as his eyes move to look out the window. His shoulders deflate and a calmness takes over his face.

Please let that be the right thing to say.

CHAPTER 47
HAPPY OR SAD
LILA

I groan as I straighten from my position on the floor. "I know I brought them in the house. It's not like a package of paper plates can just get up and walk away." Items shift and fall in the cabinet as I close the door. *That's a later problem.*

Ellie's head disappears into the cabinet across from me, where she digs through our pots and pans. "How would you know?"

A crease forms between my brows as my footsteps stall in the middle of the kitchen. "Ummm, because I've never seen one get up and walk around. Have you?"

She blows a strand of loose hair out of her face as she pops her head out of the cabinet. "No, but that means nothing. They could move around behind our backs for all we know."

Rubber squeaks against the hardwood as hurried footsteps sound from the hall. "Found them!" Dax's rosy cheeks expand and contract as he leans against the counter to catch his breath. "They were in the bathroom for some reason. Do you need me for anything else, or can I get back to the grill?"

A smile takes over my face as he relinquishes the bag of paper plates into my custody. "Thank you! I have no idea how they ended up in there." The plastic stretches under my fingers as I move through the kitchen. "You can go on out. Kam and the twins should be here any minute."

A wave of voices flows through the open door before finally disappearing into a distant hum as Dax closes the backdoor behind him.

A satisfying crunch comes from Ellie as she pops a chip in her mouth. "Do you think he realizes the guys volunteered him to help with the search just so they could get him away from the grill?"

I watch through the kitchen window as Dax comes to a stop next to Mace and Wyatt. "I doubt it."

Blurs of various colors run by the window as Jasper and Posey's friends play with a ball they found behind one of the flowerpots.

Parents twice my age occupy the tables the guys set up around the yard this morning. The vast age difference just further adds to the feeling of being an imposter in my own home.

Their judgmental eyes roam around the yard that should have two other people in it. Two very important people.

Ellie's voice pulls me from thoughts of what could have been. "Are you expecting anyone else?"

I clear my throat as I unwrap the plates and set them at the front of the line for dinner. "Just my grandparents, I think. There was one kid in their class who got the stomach flu. Thankfully, the parents have enough sense to not bring them, anyway."

Her eyebrows raise, and she pauses with a chip halfway to her mouth. "That's a thing? Parents will bring kids knowing they're sick?"

I nod my head as I stand back to look at everything laid out on the counter. "Oh, yeah. Isn't that stupid?"

With the sound of the doorbell, a stone settles in my stomach. My heartbeat thumps with a painful beat in my chest as my eyes connect with Ellie's.

I take deep, soothing breaths as my socks glide along the floor. The cool metal of the doorknob meets my palm far too soon as I shake the tension from my shoulders.

My smile, which felt so easy before, now feels like a chore as I open the door. "Good evening. I'm glad you could make it."

Victoria's lips twist into an ugly snarl as she peers behind me with calculating eyes. "Yes, well, are you going to invite us in?"

I stare at them in stunned silence for approximately two seconds before my brain comes back online and I move out of the doorway. A cloud of perfume fills my lungs as they walk by. My lungs beg for a chance to cough that I refuse to indulge as I follow behind them like a lost puppy.

Their dress shoes click against the floor as they follow the voices through the house. Victoria's dress is so stiff and constricting that the fabric doesn't move as she walks.

I narrowly prevent myself from falling into Maxwell's back when they stop abruptly in the kitchen.

I peer around his shoulder to find Ellie in a stare-off with Victoria. Ellie's legs dangle from her spot on the kitchen counter as she clutches a bag of salt and vinegar chips to her chest like you would a baby.

Ellie gives them a little wave with her crumbly fingers as she speaks around the chip she just stuffed in her mouth. "Hi, I'm Ellie." Her bare feet thunk against the floor as she slides from the counter. Her hand glides along her jeans as she wipes the chip crumbs on the fabric before extending her hand for a handshake. "It's nice to meet you."

The two strangers in my kitchen eye Ellie's hand like it's a snake. Victoria's nose scrunches for the second time in as many minutes. "It's nice to meet you, Ellie." It seems Victoria is the only one capable of speaking today. Her crystal blue eyes turn to me as she dismisses Ellie. "Where are the twins? We would like to give them their presents before we have to leave."

Ellie's eyebrows disappear into her hairline as her eyes turn to me. She mouths, *What the hell?*

I shrug as I turn my full attention to my grandmother. "They'll be here soon. Kam and Jasper went to pick Posey up from her ballet class." I tilt my head to the side. "And what do you mean, *leave?* You won't be staying?"

Maxwell clasps his hands at the small of his back as he looks around my kitchen. "No, we have a business dinner to attend this evening." Ah, he speaks.

"Oh, um." *Am I happy about this or sad? Happy, definitely happy.* "That's too bad. I'm sure Jasper and Posey will be disappointed that you can't stay."

They will be disappointed, right? That seems like a question I should know the answer to.

The familiar creak of the front door reaches us in the kitchen as the sound of two sets of feet running on hardwood grows closer. An easy smile blooms on my face as their voices rise. "Lulu!"

Jasper nearly trips Posey in his haste to get to me. His eyes are wide as he pulls on the hem of my shirt. "Guess what happened!"

I raise my brows as I sink to my knees in front of him. "What happened?"

His chest rises and falls in quick succession as he tries to catch his breath. Posey's excited voice fills my ears as she wiggles next to Jasper so they're both standing in front of me. "Molly asked Kam on a date!"

My eyebrows raise even further as I fight the laugh threatening to break free. "Oh, she did?"

They nod their heads in tandem as heavy footsteps grow closer. "She did not! Don't exaggerate, you two." His eyes shine as bright as his smile as he comes around the corner to stand in the crowded kitchen. "She wanted to take me on a tour of the studio. That's not a date. Miss Emma is the one who asked me on a date." His brow raises as he sends a smirk barreling toward me at full force. "I politely declined, by the way."

Victoria's voice doesn't hold an ounce of the humor the rest of us are trying to keep from our faces. "Ah, so you're *the* football player."

Kam's features relax into an effortless smile as his eyes zero in on my grandparents. "Um, hockey player, actually." He extends a hand that I'm surprised Maxwell takes. "It's a pleasure to meet you two."

Maxwell angles his head to where he is looking down his nose at the hockey player who has at least five inches on him. "You're the one who picked up our granddaughter from ballet?"

Kam nods his head as his smile grows. "Yep! Today was my first time, actually."

Kam's smile falls as Maxwell turns his attention to me. I don't miss the way he wipes the hand Kam just shook on his jacket. "I find it very interesting you would allow someone outside this family to wield that power."

I scrunch my brows as I take a step in front of Kam. The need to physically block him and the two kids at his side from danger is overwhelming. "I, uh, I don't know what you mean. I don't see a problem with that. Kam is great with the kids."

Maxwell focuses his icy stare over my shoulder as Kam's hand settles on my hip. Victoria's head tilts ever so slightly before her eyes flick to mine.

Kam's fingers dig into my shirt as he pulls me back to his side. He seems to grow another four inches right before my eyes.

Victoria tilts her head back as she eyes Kam. "He might be great with the kids in public, but you don't know what he's like when he's *alone* with them."

Kam jerks back like her words are bullets. His face falls as he rubs at a wound in his chest that's not visible to the naked eye.

My blood boils just under my skin as I grind my teeth to keep my mouth shut. I hear Ellie's footsteps move toward us from her place in the back of the room. I know if I had the will to look away from my grandparents, I would see fire in her eyes that matches my own.

Her steps come to a sudden halt as Kam steps in front of her to stop her advance. Thankfully, we can't hear the words she grumbles under her breath.

I take a deep breath to calm the fire within me before I clear my throat. "I trust Kam to be around the kids. That's all I'm going to say about your accusation." I force a smile onto my face as I turn to my siblings, who are cowering behind me. "Now, who's ready for some hot dogs?"

Their weary eyes glance over my shoulder before looking at Kam next to me. Whatever they see on his face must give them the courage they need to nod.

A relieved breath leaves my lips. "Great!" I turn to a red-faced Ellie. "Can you let everyone know it's time for dinner? *Take the twins with you.* I'm sure they would love to see their friends."

Her nod is choppy and her movements are rigid as she leaves the kitchen with a last glance at her brother. The twins follow silently in her shadow.

I fasten my smile tightly to my face as I turn to my grandparents. "It's a shame you can't stay for dinner. You can give the twins their gift another time. Maybe when things aren't as hectic."

A hard edge shines in their eyes as they exchange a look that they both seem to understand. Maxwell is the one who breaks the silence. He clears his throat as he straightens his jacket. "The gift can wait. Have a pleasant evening."

The loose hairs that escaped my ponytail blow in the

breeze they create as they leave the room. Kam and I don't move until the front door clicks shut behind them.

I slowly lift my eyes to find devastation on his face. I allow the fire to shine through my voice as I pull on the collar of his shirt until we're eye level. "Don't you dare waste a second of your time worrying about the nasty things that come out of their mouths. They're not worth the heartache."

His voice cracks as he grabs the fabric of the back of my sweatshirt. "They gutted me, Sunshine. They cut me deeper than I thought possible with simple words."

A breath stutters out of me as our foreheads meet. "Don't give them the satisfaction of bleeding, Trouble."

When his eyes meet mine, and I see the pain written in his irises, I know without a doubt that Kamden Stryker can be trusted.

With my brother and sister.

With our safety.

And with my heart.

LILA'S JOURNAL

Hi, Mom

I know I talked to you yesterday, but today was a big day.

The twins turned eight today. I wish you could have been there to see them playing with all the friends you were so worried about them making when we moved here.

Posey's getting into makeup now. I have no idea what I'm going to do with all the makeup she got today, or all the signed hockey gear Jasper now has scattered around his room.

Posey's ballet recital is coming up. She's so excited to get on stage and "shake it like I mean it!" Her words, not mine. Well, if we're being honest, they're probably Ellie's words.

I wish you could have seen the cake Mace made for the birthday party. It was half makeup, and half hockey themed.

Oh, I forgot to tell you, Kam fixed the mailbox lid while he was putting together the twins' swing set yesterday. I didn't even know about it until I checked the mail this morning. That crazy man.

The countdown is officially on for the court date. When Judge Harris told me six months, I thought that day would never come. It's hard to believe it's been that long since you've been gone.

Anyway, I'm going to get to bed. Keeping up

with twelve second graders and four overgrown hockey players is exhausting.

Love you, Mom.

Lila

CHAPTER 48
SOMETHING YOU MIGHT REGRET

LILA

My fresh sheets and the warm light of my room envelopes me like a cocoon as the smell of laundry detergent surrounds me. The clock on my nightstand ticks on without a care for my anxiety as the dark screen of my phone taunts me from its place on my nightstand.

I force my eyes away from the device to trace the familiar pattern of my bedroom ceiling. No matter how hard I try to think about literally anything else, my thoughts always return to one thing. Well, one person, if I'm being specific. The hockey player who's supposed to video call me in—yet another glance at the clock I'm trying to ignore—two minutes.

The sudden vibration of my phone against the table startles my heart into a gallop in my chest. My satin pajamas are almost my undoing as I nearly fall off the bed in my haste to reach my phone.

I sound like I just ran a marathon as I finally answer the video call request. Kam's smile transforms his face as he comes into focus on my screen. I can't help but mimic his smile as I settle back on my pillow. "Hi, Trouble."

Amusement accompanies his smile as he adjusts the phone in his hand. "Hi, Sunshine. Did you just run a lap around the house?"

I watch as my reflection in the bottom of my screen turns pink with the blush that takes over my cheeks. "No. I almost fell off my bed, though." My breathing slows as I catch my breath. "Great game tonight, by the way!"

Now it's his turn to blush. "Thanks. Were you able to go over to Ellie's to watch the live stream?"

The sound of my hair moving against my pillow as I nod my head is loud in my ear. "Yep. The twins and I made it just in time for the puck drop." I roll to my side to ease the burn in my arm from holding my phone in the air. "Speaking of the twins, you'll never guess what Posey did today."

His previous amusement returns in full force. "Does it involve her saying something she shouldn't have?"

My pillow shifts under me as I shrug. "Depends on how you look at it, I guess."

He settles his arm behind his head as the bright white hotel pillows practically glow behind him. "Well, go on then. The suspense is killing me here."

I blow out a breath as I shake my head. "She defended your honor at school today."

His eyebrows fly up as he opens and closes his mouth. "She—what?"

I nod as a laugh breaks free. "You heard me right. Apparently, one boy in her class is a Raiser's fan. He was talking all about how they would beat you guys tonight, since they would have the home team advantage." I bite my lip as I try to rein in my laugh. "Posey did *not* take it too well."

He doubles over in laughter as the phone blurs before landing face down on his sheets. A shuffling sound comes through the speakers as he picks up his phone. His red cheeks contrast against the white sheets behind him. The color difference makes him look like the cutest tomato I've ever seen as he wipes tears from the corners of his eyes. "What did she say to him? I would have paid big money to be a fly on the wall in that classroom."

My desire to not have to go through the bedtime routine again if the twins wake up is the only thing keeping my laughter in check. "If I recall correctly, her exact words were, 'Not knowing enough about something isn't a reason to lie about it.' I can't remember what else her teacher said when she called me today, since the two of us could barely contain our laughter."

Kam settles back against his pillow as our laughter dies down. "Remind me to buy her some ice cream when we get home. It's the least I can do since she defended our honor so well."

A small smile pulls at my lips. "I'm sure she would love that. Speaking of you getting home, what time will you guys be leaving tomorrow?"

"We should head out first thing in the morning. I might even be back in time to grab some lunch with you before your shift."

"That sounds great!" I roll onto my back. "Oh, before I forget, can you watch Jasper and Posey next

Tuesday night? Ellie and I want to start a book club. We think that'll force us to take the time to read, since we won't make it a priority otherwise."

He raises his brows as a smile pulls at his lips. "I left town for two nights, and you guys have started a new book club? Of course I'll watch the twins. Do you need a place to meet? You can always use the townhouse."

"Thanks for the offer, but I think we're going to have it here since I have a lot of parking. I'm not expecting many people to show up. Ellie has someone she wants to invite from one of her classes. So, it may only be the three of us, but I'm not sure yet. Who knows who will show up if Ellie is in charge of inviting people."

He nods since he knows his sister better than anyone. "Knowing her, she'd bring a rabbit she found in the backyard or a stray cat." His eyes flick away from the screen as what sounds like banging on a door reaches my ears. "I've got to go. The guys want to get some pizza before the restaurant downstairs closes. And by the way, you look damn good laid out on a bed with your hair all fanned out like a goddess."

A flirty smile pulls at my lips as I extend my arm so more of my body fills the screen instead of just my face. "You think so?"

He traces the outline of my lace strap with heated eyes. "You're my greatest temptation."

Liquid heat flows through my body to settle between my legs as I whisper, "I wish you were here."

He swallows before blowing out a deep breath that doesn't seem to have the calming effect he requires. "Me too. But my will is strong enough to make sure the first time I see you naked isn't over a video call. What's growing between us is more precious than that." He takes another deep breath. "So, I'm going to end this call so my dick can calm down enough for me to walk again. I refuse to answer the door with a raging hard on."

A laugh bubbles free before I can catch it, despite the emotions floating through my chest. "You're truly one of a kind, aren't you, Trouble?"

"As long as I get to call you mine."

The banging on his door starts again. This time, Dax's voice accompanies the harsh rhythm. "Come on, Cap! I'm starving out here!"

Kam rolls his eyes as he raises his voice. "I'm coming! Don't get your panties in a twist!"

Laughter accompanies Dax's muffled voice. "I don't need to know about the state of your dick, Cap. That's between you and Sullivan."

Kam closes his eyes as he shakes his head. "I'm going to kill him."

I don't even try to contain my laughter. "Don't do something you might regret, Trouble. Dax is a great defenseman."

The background blurs behind him as he stands from the bed. "You're right. That would be a mess to deal with this late in the season." A softness takes over his eyes as he examines my face. "Goodnight, Sunshine."

"Goodnight, Trouble."

As my phone screen fades to black, I relax back into my bed, which has never felt as empty as it does right now.

CHAPTER 49
ONE MORE
KAM

The smell of hairspray hangs in the air as I search the theater for familiar faces. It's moments like this that make me appreciate my height as I peer over everyone's heads to get a better view of the room.

A nervous energy flows through the space as kids run around in costumes. Parents with exhausted faces chase after them as I try not to step on anyone.

Three tall figures in the distance standing above the crowd act as my landmark in the over-crowded space. I clutch the overpriced flowers to my chest as I weave through the aisles to get to my friends.

A blanket of darkness descends as I reach our row of seats just in time. I ensure the aisle seat remains empty for Lila. Wyatt's brows raise as we lower into our seats. "Cutting it close, aren't you?"

Jasper's face lights up as he pokes his head around Wyatt. "Kam! I thought you got lost." The multitude of toy cars lining Wyatt's legs shift as he tries to keep Jasper from tumbling out of his seat.

I lower my voice as classical music takes the place of voices around us. "Nah, I couldn't miss Posey's performance. Traffic was just a lot worse than I was expecting."

Dax's voice filters through the darkness. "This place is packed. Who would have thought a ballet recital could rival our crowd size?"

There's no way this is a stadium full of people. However, I have to admit I'm shocked at the turnout. "Have you seen Lila? I know she was having an issue with Posey's costume."

Mace's voice is the one that rises above the music. "We got it worked out. Nothing a safety pin couldn't fix. She should be back out soon." His voice falls to a whisper. "Should we have saved some seats for the grandparents?"

I shake my head as I fold myself into the tiny seat. "Nope. Lila said they aren't coming."

He raises his brows. "I figured they would be here. Especially since the court date is coming up."

I shrug as Miss Emma's voice drowns out the music from her place on center stage. "Thank you all for coming to our Annual Fall Recital. All my students have worked very hard these past few months to bring you our take of Swan Lake." A practiced smile pulls at her lips as she looks around the crowd. "I hope you enjoy the show."

I swivel in my seat to look for any signs of Lila as applause follows Miss Emma from the stage. A streak of blonde catches my attention despite the low lighting.

A smile blooms on my face as Lila pushes the spring-loaded theater seat down before settling into it with a huff. "I never want to see another ripped seam again."

A quiet laugh tumbles from my lips as I push the hair from her face. "But you conquered that ripped seam."

She raises her brows as a smile touches her lips. "It's not like I could let it win." Her eyes grow soft as they fall to the flowers sitting in my lap. "You got Posey flowers?"

I'm thankful for the darkness that hides my blush. "Well, yeah. She couldn't be the only one without flowers."

The gentle kiss she plants on my cheek is more than worth the money I forked up for the flowers. How someone could live with themselves after charging almost one hundred dollars for twelve roses, I'll never know. I definitely won't be using that florist for her next recital.

My ears ring with the increase in the music's volume as the kids in white spin on stage.

A stray hair around Lila's face tickles my cheek as I lean closer to whisper, "When is Posey's group supposed to dance?"

Her mango scent washes over me as she turns slightly. "She should be next."

The music fades as the dancers take their final poses on the stage. Sweat coats my palms as I try not to crush the bundle of roses in my arms.

I take deep, even breaths as a nervousness takes over that's more severe than anything I feel before a game. I can control my performance and live with the mistakes I make. I just don't think I can watch Posey mess up her dance, knowing the embarrassment that she would feel and look back on for the rest of her life.

A line of pink files onto the stage with a practiced efficiency. My eyes move past the boys and girls until my eyes land on Posey in the middle of the group.

Her gaze sweeps across the rows of seats before settling on ours. The wattage of her smile grows with every seat she sees that's filled with people who love her. Warmth blooms in my chest as she sends us a little wave before taking her starting position with her classmates.

The pounding of my pulse nearly overrides the music I've grown so used to hearing her practice with in my living room these past few weeks.

I anticipate each movement and step in my mind as they follow the music. Her happiness shines as brightly as the lights that illuminate her smile as she dances. Lila's fingers find my leg in the darkness as she digs her fingers into the fabric. I sit up straighter in my seat as *the* spin draws near.

I lost count of the times Posey fell in my living room as she tried to master a spin that always seemed just out of reach.

My breath stalls in my chest as I intertwine my fingers with Lila's. Posey's feet are sure under her and her ankle is stable as she raises her arms above her head and spins.

I count every turn.

One.

Two.

Come on, Posey. You can do this.

Three.

Come on. One more.

Four!

Our group releases a collective breath as I fight to stay in my seat. Our shouts of celebration, however, flow freely through the theater as Posey's smile doubles in size.

My heart pounds in my chest as the music fades. I have no idea if our row is the only one standing. I don't look around at anyone else as Posey exits the stage with a triumphant smile. To be honest, I don't really care what anyone thinks about our group.

My only focus is clapping and cheering loud enough for Posey to hear me.

CHAPTER 50
GRABBY TERRORS
LILA

My palms tingle with anticipation as we walk up the driveway to the craftsman style house. My steps are careful as I ascend the stairs of the front porch that's overflowing with burgundy mums. The last thing I want to do is meet Kam's mom after I've just face planted in front of her house.

The late November air is cool against my face despite the midday sun. The skin on my arm burns from my frequent scratching along the itchy fabric of my sweater dress.

Maybe I should have worn the thinner yellow dress instead.

It's too late to worry about that now.

Ellie's quick elbow to the ribs nearly makes me jump out of my skin from the sudden contact. "Hey, don't worry about it. You'll be fine."

Her words don't carry the calming effect she hopes they do. It's not the words she says that freak me out, it's the words she doesn't. If I were bringing Kam to my house, to meet my parents, I would have said, "Don't worry! They're going to love you!"

She must not be confident enough in our Thanksgiving lunch to utter those words to me.

The comforting weight of Kam's hand settles into mine as he intertwines our fingers. His gentle squeeze speaks louder than words ever could. With one touch, he says, "I won't leave you to face her alone."

I've seen Kam's face fall every time his mom's name pops up on his phone. I've seen the tension leave Ellie's shoulders every time a hockey game starts and the seat next to her remains empty.

I have some expectations for how lunch will go today. I just hope I can make it through the day without making a fool of myself in front of the person who is responsible for my boyfriend coming into the world.

I cringe as Jasper bounces on his feet and Posey twirls around so her dress catches in the wind. Flashes of broken vases and toppled salad bowls zing through my mind.

My voice is low as we come to a stop in front of the black door. "Remember, don't touch anything, especially not anything breakable."

They roll their eyes in unison as they mutter, "We won't."

I love them to death, but I don't believe them for a second. At the first sight of a shiny knick-knack or any hockey memorabilia, they'll turn into grabby terrors.

I furrow my brow as Kam rings the doorbell. "You ring the doorbell at your own house?" Muffled barking accompanies the echo of the doorbell from inside. "And you have a dog?"

Ellie's mumbled words only enhance the anxiety coursing through my veins. "This stopped being our house when we turned eighteen and went to college."

The sound of barking draws closer as the rhythmic sound of thick nails clicking against hardwood reaches us from the other side of the door.

Kam scrunches his nose as he straightens to stand at his full height. "And *we* don't have a dog."

My heart pounds against my ribs as swift human footsteps mix with the barking.

Fleeting, blissful silence descends before the door is yanked open to reveal a little white dog clutched in the arms of Kam's mom. I can't help but notice her burgundy hair not only matches the mums on her porch, but is teased within an inch of its life. She looks down her nose at her children as the dog wiggles in her arms. "You're late."

My fingers find Posey's shoulder and dig into the fabric of her dress as she eyes the dog with interest.

Ellie's eye roll is legendary as she pushes past her mom without a second glance. "You told us to be here at noon. Well, it's noon." I can barely hear her next words as she disappears farther into the house. "I need a drink."

A fake smile pulls at their mom's lips as she turns her chocolate gaze toward her son. "I'm sure I said eleven-thirty. The caterers left almost fifteen minutes ago."

Kam breezes right past her complaints that I know for sure are unjustified. I saw the texts myself. "Mom, let me introduce you to some very important people." He uses our clasped hands to pull me closer to his side.

"This is Lila, my girlfriend." I don't know if I'll ever get used to him calling me that. "And this is her brother and sister, Jasper and Posey." His tight eyes turn to each of us. "Guys, this is my mom, Isobel."

Posey vibrates under my palm. "What's the puppy's name?"

Isobel clutches the tiny ball of fluff tighter to her chest as her eyes turn to the creature and soften. "This is Tilly." Despite the low growls coming from the tiny creature, Isobel runs her nose along the top of Tilly's head. "Don't let her growling fool you. She's harmless. Isn't that right, my little gem?"

A splitting smile stretches over Posey's face as she tries to keep her hands secured by her sides. "Can I pet her?"

The fake smile falls from Isobel's face as she eyes Posey with disdain. I tighten my hold on Posey as I pull her until her back touches my stomach. I plaster a smile to my face. "Not right now, Ladybug." I instantly regret not wiping my sweaty palm on my dress before offering it to Isobel for a handshake. "It's nice to meet you, Isobel. Thank you for having us for Thanksgiving."

Her fake smile returns to her face despite the crease that forms between her brows. Her hand is nearly limp in mine as her cool skin contacts my palm. "Ah, well, I wasn't expecting any guests today. I only ordered enough food for the three of us."

Kam clenches his jaw as I try not to fidget next to him. "I specifically told you Lila and her siblings were coming, Mom."

She rolls her eyes as she sets the dog down on its feet. "You said no such thing." The dog races after

Ellie's trail. My fingers dig further into Posey's shoulder as her body sways toward the tiny creature. "I would remember if you said you were bringing *strangers* into our home. I was so hoping to spend some alone time with you and your sister."

The irritation is clear in Kam's voice as his fingers tighten around mine. "They're not strangers, Mom."

She raises a brow. "They are to me." She turns on her heels to follow her daughter and the fluffy canine. "Come eat before the food gets cold."

I take a deep breath and follow her into the lion's den with clammy hands and a hell of a lot of apprehension.

CHAPTER 51
BEST FOR YOU

KAM

I grit my teeth as I focus on stacking the turkey on my plate instead of how much I want to strangle my mom.

Aluminum catering trays line the pristine counters of the kitchen that's never used. The smell of mashed potatoes and corn, that is usually so enticing, now seems dull compared to the intensity of the anger coursing through my veins.

How could she speak to them like that?

The room is silent, save for our footsteps and the clicking of Tilly's nails against the hardwood floor. I balance two plates in one hand as I fill my plate and Posey's with two very different things. An array of colors decorate my plate compared to the various shades of tan that fill hers.

Her light footsteps follow mine around the room as she silently points out the two slices of turkey, one scoop of mashed potatoes, and three rolls she wants.

I feel my mom's eyes digging into the back of my

head from where she sits at the dining table that we rarely use.

Ellie's worried eyes connect with mine as we take our usual seats. Her eyes flick from mine to the half empty wine glass sitting in front of her. The only time my sister touches alcohol is when we're in this house.

Forks scrape against ceramic plates as the silence grows thick.

Lila jumps in her seat next to me as my mom's voice breaks the silence. "I was talking with Camilla Hollingsworth last Monday while I was on my morning walk. She said Sebastian will be back in town over Christmas break. She was hoping you would join them for their New Year's party this year. I remember how much you enjoyed going to their get-togethers when you were in high school."

Those *get-togethers* were often a source of Ellie's tears.

Ellie hides her scoff behind her wine glass. "I'm sure Sebastian would love for me to show up at his house unannounced. Great idea, Mom."

Mom's beaming smile shows off her snow-white teeth. "Of course, dear. You could wear that red dress I've been begging you to wear since your freshman year. That would be perfect for a holiday party."

A full mouth of mashed potatoes muffles Ellie's reply. "Yeah, and I'll sprout some wings and fly through the faerie realm."

My mom raises a posh brow as Lila and I fight our laughter. "What was that, Ellie dear? You know it's not proper to talk with your mouth full."

Ellie swallows her bite as she bats her lashes at our mother. "Oh, nothing. It wasn't important."

My mom nods without looking up from her plate. "Lila, tell me about yourself."

Lila's fork clashes against her plate as her spine straightens in her seat next to me. "Uh, there's not much to tell. I, uh, work at The Penalty Box part-time while I'm taking classes."

"That's nice. Will you be visiting your parents this evening for Thanksgiving? I sure hope you gave them more notice than my dear son did. It's the courteous thing to do."

I cough as a bit of my water goes down the wrong way. Tears rim my eyes as I fight to control the spasms in my chest. "Uh, Mom, they lost their parents over the summer."

Her eyes actually lift from her plate as she looks at Lila with genuine sympathy. "Oh, I'm sorry. What a terrible loss. Who has taken custody of the children? They are so young to be without a mother and father."

Lila clears her throat as she tucks a strand of hair behind her ear. My hand finds her thigh under the table. "Thank you. It has been a difficult few months. I am actually their guardian."

My mom's brows raise as she steeples her hands in front of her. "I didn't know the court would give such a difficult responsibility to such a young person. Especially someone still in school like yourself."

Posey's eyes trace the path Tilly makes around the table as the twins stay oblivious to the tense conversation around them.

Ellie's voice holds a hard edge that wasn't present moments before. "Lila is an amazing guardian, Mom. She takes better care of the twins than some parents I know."

My mom waves away Ellie's harsh tone. "It's just an interesting decision, that's all." Her eyes blaze as they laser in on Posey. "I would have thought your parents would have taught you not to feed animals from the table." I turn in time to watch Tilly shrink away from the turkey in Posey's outstretched hand.

Lila jerks back like she's been slapped as Ellie straightens in her seat next to me. My voice is as hard as steel. "Mom, how could you say something like that?"

She just shrugs as she lifts her wineglass to her lips. "What? Is it not the truth?"

Ellie shakes her head in disgust next to me. "How could you be so insensitive?"

Posey's eyes shine with tears as an angry flush rises along Lila's neck. Jasper's eyes narrow on my mom like he might shoot lasers from them.

Mom moves the lettuce around her plate like she didn't just stab a knife through Lila's chest. "Have you heard from Richard this week, Kamden? He was hoping to go to lunch next week to discuss your contract." A smile pulls at her lips as she spears a cucumber slice. "He was so pleased with what he could offer you. He said it was the best offer he has seen in a long time."

I take a deep breath as I choose to move on with the conversation, so I don't say something I might regret. "I actually wanted to talk to you about that."

She sits up straighter in her seat and lays her fork on the edge of her plate. "You have some changes you want to make to the contract?"

I shake my head as Lila's fingers dig into my leg under the table. She'll never know how thankful I am for her silent show of support. "I actually wanted to let you know I won't be signing with Richard."

Mom's brows crease as much as her Botox will allow. "I don't understand. This is a great opportunity for you, Kamden." The crease between her brows flattens as the smile returns to her face. "Don't worry. Your dad got cold feet before he signed, too. You still have plenty of time to get everything worked out the way you want. You can't even sign until you graduate, anyway." Her languid laugh grates against my ears.

I shake my head as my voice slows. "You're not hearing me, Mom. I've already decided what I want to do. I won't be signing with Richard. The deal he's offering is pathetic, Mom. I would be a fool to sign with him."

Her eye twitches as she straightens the napkin in her lap. Her smile stays firmly secured on her face despite the hardness now visible in her eyes. "I know this is a lot for you to understand, Kamden. That's why your dad and I planned all this for you years ago. This is all your dad wanted for you. It would break his heart to see you turning your back on his wishes like this. We've just always wanted what's best for you. You saw what signing with the wrong agent did to him." I can practically see the memories floating behind her eyes. "His first agent practically destroyed this family. Richard was so good for him. That's all we ever wanted for you. Someone you can rely on."

My face heats as I fight to cool the rage bubbling within me. "This is *me* telling *you* what's best for me,

Mom. Richard might have been good for Dad, because he needed someone to rein him in. He needed someone that would take over and just tell him where to be, and what to do. That's not what I want for myself." I glance at Lila to find fire in her eyes, along with the courage I need to keep talking. "Who knows, maybe Lila will end up being my agent someday. She's better at reading contracts than any other agent I've ever talked to."

My mom's voice takes on a hard edge that sends a chill down my spine from the memories it brings to the surface. "I see what's really going on here. This girl shows up, and suddenly you're changing the plans that have been laid out for you since you first put a pair of skates on your feet. Don't force *me* to watch as *you* make unfixable mistakes, Kamden. I can't take watching you wither away like your father."

The warmth seeping from Lila's palm is as strong as the fire in her voice. "He's not forcing *you* to watch anything. *You're* the one who chooses to sit on the side-lines instead of actually taking a role in his life." A calmness settles in my chest with her words.

Lila's rage vibrates through me as my mom all but ignores her. With clenched fists, Mom looks down her nose like I'm still the small child cowering in front of her. "I prepared you for this world, so I wouldn't need to be at the center of yours."

I'm proud of the calm tone I keep in my voice. "Maybe instead of preparing me for the world, you should have been giving me a safe place to escape from it. Instead, you forced me out into a world that was just as cruel as the one I was born into." The tension relaxes from my shoulders as I uncurl my fist to find Lila's hand under the table. "So I went out and found my own safe place, Mom. I'm not about to give that up so I can walk in Dad's footsteps and be just as miserable as he was."

I can practically hear the grinding of her teeth. "So you don't want to play hockey at all? Is that what you're telling me?"

I shake my head. "No. That's not what I'm saying. I'm just going to do it my way."

She crosses her arms across her chest as she leans back in her seat. "Well, don't come crawling back to me when your *grand* idea doesn't work out."

I stand from my seat without a care for the food on my plate. "Don't worry, you wouldn't be the one I crawl back to, anyway." I look at my sister's shocked face, then at the wide eyes of the twins, only to settle on the beaming smile on Lila's face. "Are you guys ready to go? We have somewhere else we need to be."

Lila gives my hand a last squeeze before she helps the twins from their seats.

My eyes turn to my mom's to find utter shock on her face. Never one to forget my manners, I say, "Thank you for the lunch. We'll see you at Christmas."

I turn toward the front door, feeling lighter than I ever have before. I will never again carry the burden I left at that table.

I hear her scoff behind me. "I can't believe you're walking out of our Thanksgiving lunch because of a little quarrel. Ellie, dear, there's no reason to go along with your brother's tantrum. It was just as detrimental when you were a child, you know."

Ellie's eyes aren't nearly as silent as her voice. The

pain I see written all over her face takes me back to the nights she would cry herself to sleep. Our adjoining walls were thin enough to betray her quiet sobs she never wanted me to know existed.

Tilly's nails dig into my legs as she jumps around me, begging for attention. She abandons me in favor of my mom's call. I stalk through the front door without a backwards glance.

Lila's fingers find mine as the door clicks shut with an air of finality. "That was *the* sexiest thing I have ever seen, Trouble."

I stare into her crystal eyes as the autumn air flows over my skin. "It was time for me to free myself from a legacy of expectations. I just hate it took me this long to realize how monumental the weight truly was."

Ellie's voice reaches my ears for the first time in what seems like hours. "I'm proud of you, little brother."

Yeah, I'm pretty proud of myself, too.

CHAPTER 52
SMUT
LILA

Towering oak trees and pristine lawns blur by as we drive through my grandparents' neighborhood. I blow out a breath that feels like it deflates my chest. "Okay, I think we need a code word." My head rolls against the passenger seat headrest as I look at Kam. "You know, in case we need to enact an exit plan or something."

His hand flexes on the steering wheel as a smirk pulls at his lips. "Surely dinner can't go as badly as lunch."

Posey shifts in her booster seat behind me. "What's a code word?"

Jasper's handheld game closes with a click before he says, "Is it like a secret agent thing or something?"

"It's, um—" You never realize how difficult it is to explain something simple until you're faced with putting it into your own words. "It's just a word or phrase we can use to signal something to each other, without letting someone who doesn't know what the code word means in on the conversation."

I can practically hear the gears turning in Jasper's head as he says, "And it can be anything?"

Kam nods in my peripherals. "Yep! We can make it anything we want."

Silence fills the backseat before Posey blurts, "Unicorn!"

A quick glance at Kam shows my smile reflected on his face.

Genuine confusion shines through Jasper's voice. "Ah, come on! Why can't I pick the code word?"

The sound of Posey's dress ruffling reaches my ears. I would bet at least a hundred dollars she just crossed her arms. "Because I'm the most creative twin." Her last word is a mumbled, "Obviously."

Kam's eyes shine as he watches them in the rearview mirror. "Why don't we each pick a word to add to our code phrase, Tank? I've already got mine picked out." His eyes flash from the rearview mirror to me. "I think I'll go with Sunny."

I smile because of the ridiculousness. "Alright, so we've got Unicorn and Sunny, how about—" My stomach rumbles from our lack of lunch. "Tacos!"

Jasper's voice is so sudden and loud I almost flinch. "It can be a food word?"

I can hear the smile in Kam's voice. "It can be whatever you want it to be, Tank."

"I want my word to be Marshmallow, then!"

Kam bites on his lip as he raises his brows. "Sunny Marshmallow Unicorn Taco? Is that what we're going with?"

I nod as the twins say, "Yeah!"

Their words fade into a mumbled conversation in the backseat.

Kam's chest shakes with barely contained laughter. I raise my brows as my eyes trace his beaming smile. "What so funny, Trouble?"

Tears line his eyes when he glances over at me. "Make an acronym from the code words."

Sunny Marshmallow Unicorn Taco.

Oh shit.

SMUT.

Our code words spell *smut*.

I just inadvertently gave my eight-year-old siblings permission to say *smut* in front of our grandparents who are crucial to my custody arrangement. Great. Just great.

My eyes slide shut to shut out some of my embarrassment as Kam chuckles next to me. "Ah, come on, Sunshine. It could have been worse. We could have gone with Fluffy Ukulele Cupcake Kitten or Doodle Icicle Cat Kraken. It could always be worse."

I smile as I shake my head. "You're right, it could always be worse." My smile falls as their house comes into view. The mansion looms ahead of us like a mountain as we come to a stop in the driveway. "So, that means if any of us are uncomfortable and want to leave, we just have to say the code words." I twist back in my seat so I can see them. "Got it?"

They nod their heads as they look past me through the windshield.

The silence that blankets the Tahoe is only broken by the unfastening of seatbelts and the shuffle of shoes against the floorboards.

Posey's voice holds a tone of panic as she breaks the silence. "Oh no! My shoe!"

Her bare toes wiggle as she stands like a flamingo in the backseat. She searches the ground just outside her open door with frantic eyes.

"What happened, Ladybug?"

Her eyes well with tears, a reaction disproportionate to that of a dropped shoe. "My shoe fell out when I opened the door."

Kam's confused eyes flick to mine before he forces a smile to his face. "Hey, Rosie Posey, it's alright. We'll find your shoe in no time. I bet it just bounced under the car. Want to come help me look, Tank?"

Jasper's feet hit the ground with a thunk. "Yeah! I'll help!" His footfalls move around to my side of the door as my two guys drop to their knees and search the ground for my sister's fallen shoe.

They pay the occasional stray pebble and dirt no mind as they continue their search under the Tahoe.

Triumph rings clear through Jasper's voice as he emerges victorious with Posey's ballet-flat cliched proudly in his hand. "I found it!"

"Way to go, Tank! See, Posey, I told you we would find it. We just need to brush a little dirt off the side, and it'll be good as new."

Posey's bare foot disappears into her shoe as a smile graces her lips. "Thanks, Jas."

Kam effortlessly lifts Posey out of the car to stand her on her feet. "Now, what's really got you upset, Rosie Posey?"

Her gaze falls to her feet as a shrug lifts her shoulders. "I don't know."

"I don't believe that for a second. Are you going to tell me what it is, or am I going to have to tickle it out of you?" Kam's smile grows as his fingers dig into the most ticklish spot on her side.

Her musical laughter drifts along the breeze as she tries to dodge Kam's fingers." Okay! Okay!" Her breathing slows as Kam retracts his threat. "I don't want to have any more nightmares like I did last time we were here."

Kindness shines brightly in Kam's eyes as he pulls her into a crushing hug. "You won't have any more nightmares, Posey." His eyes flick to Jasper beside him. "Isn't that right, Tank?"

Jasper straightens to his full height, like he's standing before a general. "Kam's right, Posey. We're going to protect you from your bad dreams."

Tears rim my eyes as I realize Jasper won't be this little forever. He will grow into a man, go to college, get a job, get married, and have kids of his own someday. And if he wants to backpack around Europe and be single forever, that's alright, too.

I just hate that my mom and dad aren't here to see it.

If my dad can't be here to give Jasper and Posey an example of what a man should be, I can't imagine a better man for the job than Kamden Stryker.

CHAPTER 53
GAME FACE
LILA

The canopy of oak trees swallows Jasper and Posey's laughter as they skip up the driveway. Kam's warm eyes search my face as he straightens. "Everything alright?"

My finger's intertwine with his as I nod my head. "Yeah. I'm just really glad you're here, Trouble."

His smile shines brightly in the evening sun. "There's nowhere else I'd rather be."

The warmth of his palm seeps into mine like a calming balm on my soul as we follow the twins to the front door.

As Posey pushes the doorbell and the ding reverberates through the house, Kam's fingers tighten around mine. His voice is a gentle whisper that's easily lost in the autumn air. "Game faces, everyone. Just remember, we're a team. We always have each other's backs, no matter what."

The door swings open to reveal pursed lips and perfectly stenciled brows. Victoria doesn't say a word as she takes in our appearance. I'm sure our outfits wouldn't meet her standards, even if I was standing before her in a ball gown and Kam in a tux.

"Good evening. Our chef is almost ready for the first course." She steps to the side and waves a manicured hand. "If you'd join us in the parlor, we would like to have a few words before dinner."

I struggle to contain my eye roll at the mention of a chef. What exactly is Posey going to eat if they've hired a professional chef? And does no one have home-cooked meals for Thanksgiving anymore?

Our shoes click against the marble as we follow her into her museum of a home. Twenty-foot ceilings showcase the artwork adorning the walls of the grand entry. A spiral staircase leads to a second-floor balcony that's connected to two hallways leading in opposite directions.

The smell of fresh turkey and heavy spices lingers heavily in the air. I fight a sneeze that threatens to appear as we venture down a hallway that leads toward the back of the house.

Sunlight coming from the expansive windows illuminates the lack of movement of Victoria's hair in front of me as we make our way through the maze of hallways. The straw-like texture is styled into a stern bun that rests at the nape of her neck.

The twins are silent in front of me as Victoria disappears through a doorway at the end of the hall.

Massive windows framed by thick, sage curtains look out at the manicured backyard. Intricate molding lines the border of the ceiling and the pale green floral wallpaper.

Heavy furniture forms a seating area in the center of the room that is clearly meant for long discussions with business partners over drinks, instead of comfortably lounging around a fireplace with friends.

The evening sun silhouettes Maxwell as he overlooks the backyard from the central window. He doesn't bother turning to greet us as we file into the room.

Victoria sinks down onto the edge of a seat by the window. With her hands clasped in her lap, her eyes flick to her husband.

Maxwell's deep voice rumbles through the room as he finally turns. "Children, I'm glad you have finally arrived. We had a few details to discuss with the impending court date next week." He gestures to the seating area with a manicured hand. "Have a seat."

My brows furrow as my feet follow his command without my permission. The scratchy fabric of the couch is rough against my fingers, despite how much I'm sure it costs.

I nearly lose my balance as the cushions move with Kam's weight as he settles himself at the other end. The twins' feet dangle a few inches off the ground as they settle between us.

With a scrunch of his nose, Maxwell's fingers glide along the top of the fireplace.

I raise my brows as I clear my throat. "You had something you wanted to discuss?"

He wipes what I'm sure is minimal dust from the mantle on the handkerchief he pulls from his pocket. "Yes, well, I wanted to hear your plan for the twins." My brows furrow as he rests his hands on the back of the seat across from us. "I assume you have a plan in place?"

I shake my head as I rub the face of the watch on my wrist. "I'm not sure what you mean."

He raises his brows as he picks an imaginary piece of lint off his suit jacket. "So you're saying you don't have a plan for their college fund, summer programs, or extra-curricular activities?"

I swallow thickly as I straighten in my seat. "Well, Posey's ballet lessons are paid through the end of the year. Jasper plays hockey with his school team, so the cost for that so far has been minimal."

He nods slowly. "What do you plan to do after the prepaid ballet tuition has run out?"

My fingers twist in my lap as Kam shifts at the other end of the couch. I lift my head to keep my eyes from falling to my lap. "I've been taking more shifts at the restaurant. Tips have been pretty good recently, so I've got a few hundred saved for her tuition next year."

He raises his brows as I try not to cower in my seat. "A few hundred? Is that all? How do you expect to take care of two children when you take that long to save a few hundred dollars?"

"This is a temporary situation. After I graduate next year, I'll be able to work full time."

A smirk pulls at his lips that sends a chill down my spine. "Do you still plan on working at that restaurant after graduation?"

I shake my head. "Well, no, I—"

His voice cuts off my words at their roots. "We wanted to let the twins open their birthday present before dinner." My eyes scan the room, looking for a set of gift bags or boxes, but come up empty. The only unusual thing in the room is a file folder sitting in the middle of the coffee table. "With the court date for your custody hearing quickly approaching, we thought it was appropriate to make our final decision."

Final decision?

My muscles turn to stone as I clench my fists in my lap.

Victoria's sickly sweet smile churns my stomach. "Yes, what better day than Thanksgiving to bring the twins fully into our family?"

My eyes jerk to Kam as he grits his teeth. His voice holds a hard edge I've never heard before. "What do you mean, *exactly?*"

Maxwell tilts his head toward the folder on the table. "You will find copies of adoption papers in that folder. Our lawyer finalized them the day before their birthday. We were hoping to have this taken care of before the court date next week, but things haven't played out exactly as we planned." A slimy smile stretches his face. "If we get the paperwork signed before the court date, the transition will go much smoother."

Heat envelopes my face as my nails cut into my palms. "Do you really think I would sign away my rights to the twins?"

The twins sink further back into their couch next to me as I fight my natural instincts to cover them with my body.

Maxwell's smile grows as he moves closer to the folder on the table. "That's exactly what I think is going to happen. You just admitted to your lack of resources to look after them properly. Also, when the judge finds out you have had a stranger looking after the twins, a stranger whose father has a history of DUIs no less, she'll have no choice but to award custody to us."

Posey's fingers dig into my shirt as my voice vibrates with rage. "I will never sign away my rights. Why would you want guardianship, anyway? A nanny practically raised my mom."

Victoria's lips twist as she straightens even more in her seat. "Your mother was an ungrateful child who never understood the value of what she was born into. She chose to marry your father over the marriage we secured for her. We learned a lot from our time with your mother." I jerk at the mention of an arranged marriage. "We won't make the same mistakes again."

Sadness accompanies the rage flowing through my veins. "You tried to force her into an arranged marriage?"

Victoria narrows her eyes at me with a sneer on her face. "It was the least she could do after everything we gave her. She wanted for nothing. She had the world at her fingertips, and she threw it all away for some rat off the street. Your grandfather lost a very important business deal because of her lack of responsibility, and I'll never forgive her for it."

Rage vibrates through me as I stand. "My *dad* was not a rat off the street. He was a great husband and an even greater father."

Maxwell rolls his eyes as he sticks out his chest like a gorilla. "Please, his salary was pathetic. I'm surprised he could keep food on the table."

A calmness flows through me with the realization

that I don't need these people. I don't need them to take care of the twins. I've been doing just fine on my own these past few months, *despite* them. "There is more to life than the number in a bank account, Maxwell. Maybe try taking your head out of your ass for five seconds so you can see that your misery is your own making." I lock eyes with Kam's fury filled gaze from where he stands behind me. "Sunny Marshmallow Unicorn Taco." With a smile, I turn to the assholes in front of me. "That's our code words for wanting to get the hell out of here." My smile only grows. "The words spell out smut, by the way."

With my last words, I spin on my heels, grab Posey and Jasper by the hand, and walk out of the room with a sway to my hips.

I don't look over my shoulder as Kam's heavy foot-steps sound through the room to be followed by the sound of ripping paper. His voice shows the full magnitude of the fury I saw in his eyes. "If I were you, I wouldn't bother showing your faces at court next week."

My anger spikes at the sound of Maxwell's voice. "I do not take kindly to threats."

"Good thing I didn't threaten you, then."

Maxwell's scoff doesn't match the underlying fear he tries to hide from his voice. "We'll see you in court, Kamden."

I can hear the smirk in Kam's voice. "Yeah, I'm counting on it."

CHAPTER 54
US
LILA

The sun feels warmer on my face as I walk out the front door. Even the colors of the changing trees seem brighter as I tighten my hold on Posey's hand.

Her eyes hold a sadness that adds fuel to the fire burning within me. "Are they going to take us away, Lulu?"

I shake my head as I fall to my knees on the stone driveway. My fingers dig into her shoulders as I search her face. "No, Ladybug. I won't let them take you away from me."

She nods as some of the sadness fades from her eyes. Jasper's fingers intertwine with hers as a smile touches his lips. "Kam won't let them take us, Posey. They'd have to get through Kam, Dax, Wyatt, Mace, and Ellie first."

Kam's deep voice soothes my frayed nerves. "You've got that right, Tank. You guys are right where you belong." Some of the tension leaves his shoulders as his eyes meet mine. "Let's get out of here and get something to eat."

My knees groan as I stand. My fingers glide against the fabric of my dress as I smooth the wrinkles. "Sounds good to me!"

Jasper and Posey's footsteps mix with the wind and the gentle tumble of leaves as they race to the car. The air smells like relief and the wind feels like freedom as I walk to the car. The door even feels lighter on its hinges as I close it.

Blissful darkness descends around me as I close my eyes and lean my head against the headrest. The dark veil feels like a barrier to my problems instead of the illusion of solitude it really is.

As Kam's hand glides over my thigh, the warmth seeps through the fabric of my dress and into my skin.

My head rolls against the headrest as he takes the gentle curves through the neighborhood I hope to never visit again.

I open my eyes to watch cars pass by. As strangers, we travel along the same road without really knowing what's going on in each other's lives.

The day my parents died was the worst day of my life. Everyone else went about their day like my world wasn't falling apart.

Just like that day, these people drive by completely oblivious to the bomb that was just dropped by my feet. They drive by, unaware of the ticking clock above my head, counting down the seconds until the court date that will decide the fate of the rest of my life.

Two and a half months ago, my only worry was if I

was a good enough sister to take on this massive responsibility.

Now, someone threatens that responsibility. No, not a responsibility, but an honor. Because that's what this is. It's an honor to be trusted with something so special and monumental.

So, I'm going to fight like hell to keep it.

I just don't know if I'm strong enough to win the fight.

Relief flows through me as Kam's townhouse comes into view. The familiar cars piled in the driveway bring a smile to my face. Shades of pink and orange coat the front of the house as the sun sets.

Kam has barely put the car in park when I hear the twins' seatbelts click. Birdsong filters through their open doors before they slam them shut. Their heads bob over the rim of the hood as they disappear up the driveway without looking back. The Tahoe shakes as Kam's door closes behind him.

Pink light flows into the house as Ellie swings the door open before the twins have even gotten there. Her smiling face greets them as they almost knock her over, trying to get a hug.

I nearly jump out of my seat as my door swings open. Kam's outstretched hand brings a smile to my face. "You okay?" His fingers are warm against mine as he pulls me from the car.

A long breath throws my tension to the ground by my feet as Kam's fingers tighten in mine.

I shake my head as my eyes follow the twins from the car. "No. I just found out my grandparents tried to force my mom into a marriage she didn't want *and* they want to take the twins away from me. I'm not sure if I'll ever be okay again…" I take a deep breath to calm my anxiety. "What am I going to do, Kam? How am I supposed to fight someone like that? With all their resources?"

His thumb rubs a soothing pattern on the back of my hand as the leaves crunch under our feet. "You are the strongest person I know, Sunshine. And you don't have to fight them alone."

My laugh is humorless as the sun warms our backs. "I don't *feel* very strong right now." I pinch my fingers until there's barely a gap between them. "I feel like I'm this big."

He pushes a stray strand of hair out of my face with gentle fingers. "People like them are used to playing dirty and getting their way." The hair falls from his fingers as determination takes over his eyes. "So we need to think like them. Prepare for their dirty tactics and meet with evidence they can't dispute."

I swallow thickly as I clench my jaw. "How do we do that?"

A small smirk pulls at his lips. "Do you trust me?"

I speak without hesitation. "Yes." My eyes trace the curve of his lips. They follow the sharp angle of his jaw to his thick brows before landing on his chocolate eyes. His eyes pierce to the very center of my soul. "I trust you."

His smile is blinding as his fingers dig into my hip to pull me closer. "Can we just agree on one thing?" I nod my head for him to keep going. "Can it just be the four of us for Thanksgiving next year? I don't know how much more of this I can take." His eyes crinkle in the corners from the magnitude of his smile. "Why are you smiling like that?"

I slip my fingers in his belt loop to close the last few inches between us. "Cause, Trouble, that means you still expect there to be an 'us' this time next year."

His smile turns to a smirk. "Well, obviously. You say that like there's another option." Silence fills the space between us until the breeze is our only companion.

The wind carries Jasper's voice to us from where he stands on the porch. "Come on, you two! Mace says dinner is ready!"

That's exactly what I need. Dinner with my *chosen* family.

I was never a believer in the saying *blood is thicker than water*. As I walk through the doors to a home filled with love and laughter, I know that now more than ever, *family is a choice.*

LILA'S JOURNAL

    Hi, Mom

    Happy Thanksgiving.

    I'm sorry you felt like you couldn't tell me what they did to you. About how they tried to keep you and Dad apart.

    There's a part of me that's mad at you. I

know that's not fair, and I'm sorry. But how could you not tell me? I never would have sought them out had I known what type of people they were. I never would have brought them into Jasper and Posey's lives had I known they were monsters.

I thought I was doing the right thing, Mom. I really did.

Kam says he has a plan. That I need to trust him. And I do. I really do.

I just don't trust them. Why do they want custody? What could they possibly gain?

I wish you and Dad were here, Mom.

Love always.

Lila

CHAPTER 55
I NEED YOU
LILA

"What an asshole!" Shuffling accompanies Ellie's annoyance from her end of the phone call. "I can't believe he had the *audacity* to say that to you! If I get arrested for assault, will you bail me out? I'm pretty sure Kam would leave me there for a few days to teach me a lesson."

I laugh as I gather the last of the clean towels from the dryer. "Always, E. I wouldn't leave you there. That's not safe for the other inmates."

I can practically hear her eyes roll through my earbuds. "I grew up with a giant for a brother. Fighting dirty was a necessity. What do you people expect from me?"

The overloaded laundry basket digs into my arm as I close the dryer with my hip. "We love you just the way you are, and you know it."

"Yeah, yeah, yeah. I see how it is. Butter me up so I'll bring the good cookies to book club. I expected better from you, L."

I blow a stray strand of hair out of my face as I move through the living room with the basket tucked securely under my arm. "Speaking of book club, do you have a final head count? I need to know how many bookmarks to make."

Am I using our new book club to distract me from the impending court date? Yes. Yes, I am.

She blows out a deep breath that sounds like static on the phone. "I think it'll just be me, you, Valley, and her friend Jade for this first meeting. Everyone else went home for Thanksgiving and got stuck there from the snow."

I eye the banner Posey and I made last night. The colorful letters spelling out *Summit & Spines Book Club* contrasting against the white paper shine brightly in the morning sun. I'm thankful for the brief rays that will soon disappear behind another set of snow clouds. "Maybe that's for the best, since we have no idea what we're doing."

"It'll be great no matter how many people show up. You're going to *love* Valley. She is seriously the sweetest."

I raise my brows even though she can't see me. "What about her friend? Her name is Jade, right?"

The only sign of her shrug is a rustling of fabric. "Not sure. I've never met her. Hopefully, she's not a psycho or something."

Cold air seeps through the floorboards and up through my socks as I make my way down the hall. "I sure hope not! What time are you planning on coming over? You better not leave me alone in my house with two strangers. I—" My words stall in my mouth as wetness seeps through my sock. I close my eyes and take deep, calming breaths as I try not to freak out from the horrible sensation of cold liquid squishing between my toes. "You've *got* to be kidding me."

"What? What happened?"

"*Someone* must have spilled something in the hallway and not cleaned it up." Liquid drips from my drenched sock as I lift my foot from the ground. The stealthy puddle blends with the shadows of the hall, making it difficult to find a dry spot to sit my basket. I peel the soaked sock from my foot as I flip the light switch to the hall light. "What the hell?" A thin trail of water leads from the puddle by my feet into the hall bathroom.

"You're killing me here, L."

My damp foot leaves a trail of wet prints in my wake as I move into the bathroom the twins share. "It looks like it's coming from the bathroom." The chill of the cold tile seeps into my very soul as I flip the switch to illuminate the tiny room. My stomach sinks as I follow the wet grout line that leads right to the exterior wall. "I think I've got a problem here."

Her curiosity turns to concern on the other end of the call. "What do you mean? Did they spill something red? Oh! I bet Jasper dropped his popsicle again."

I shake my head even though she still can't see me. "Nope. It's worse than that. Much, much worse than that."

"Just spit it out, L."

My eyes trace the path of the water, hoping to find a different result. "I think I have a water leak. It looks like it's coming from the wall that connects to the backyard."

I can hear the cringe in her voice. "Shit."

I shake my head as the water on the floor turns to dollar signs. "Yeah, shit. How much is something like this going to cost to fix?"

"I don't know. What are you going to do?"

Call Kam.

Without hesitation, that's the first thought that pops into my head.

My feet move before I've truly thought through what I'm supposed to do. My wet feet slide against the hardwood floors as I move into the hall. "I'm going to get a shitload of towels to keep the water from ruining the wooden floors in the hall, and then I'm going to call your brother."

I hear more shuffling sounds coming from her end. "Great idea. I'll be right over." Her breathing turns labored, like she's moving quickly. "And L?"

I try to push the thought of how much this is going to cost from my mind as I pick up my discarded basket of clean towels and dump them on the floor. "Yeah?"

"Everything's going to be okay." When I say nothing, her voice softens. "I'll be right there. Call Kam as soon as I hang up. I'm going to call Wyatt. He'll know someone who can help. Okay?"

Water soaks through the white towels, turning them a light shade of grey. "Okay."

The line goes dead as I fight the tears threatening to spill down my cheeks. With trembling fingers, I dig my phone from my pocket and press dial on a number I now know by heart.

With every ring, a new tear falls down my face. A sob nearly breaks free when I hear the smile in his voice. "Hi, Sunshine. Do you need help setting up for book club?"

I'm not proud of the weakness I hear in my voice. "Kam?"

His voice turns to match the blades of ice hanging from my roof. "What's wrong?"

"I need you."

A door slams in the background as his thunderous footsteps pound down the stairs of his front porch. "I'm on my way."

CHAPTER 56
SUMMIT & SPINES BOOK CLUB
KAM

"Your pipes are definitely frozen." The plumber's knees pop like pop rocks as he stands. I'm just thankful Wyatt had a contact that could come out on a Friday, especially with the weather.

Lila wrings her hands next to me. "So, what do we do now?"

The plumber's fingers sound like they're moving over sandpaper as he scratches his beard. "Well, I won't be able to start on the repairs until Monday. This early in the season, many local nursing homes aren't prepared for this type of weather. I stopped by here on my way to my next job as a favor to Wyatt." With the panic rising in Lila's eyes, the plumber softens his voice. "I'm sorry, Miss Sullivan, but I can't turn the water back on to your house until I've made the repairs."

Lila's eyes turn distant as she nods her head. "Okay, so we won't have water until at least Monday, then?"

With kind eyes, the plumber nods his head. "I'm afraid so."

Lila's brows crease as she thumbs the screen of her watch. "Okay. Umm, is it safe for us to stay here in the meantime? And how much is this going to cost? Is there a way to set up a payment plan or something?"

I push off the doorway where I've been leaning for the past twenty minutes. "Alright, here's what's going to happen." Lila's eyes grow wide as I fully turn to her. "You're going to pack a bag with enough clothes for the three of you to last for the weekend. Grab everything you might need. Make sure you grab Posey's nightlight. I'm not sure we'll be able to get on the road after the next round of storms tonight." My gaze swivels to the plumber's wide eyes. "Get a payment plan set up for the minimum amount you'll accept. We can work out the details later."

The plumber's open mouth snaps shut as he nods. "Yes, sir. I'll get that sent over right away."

I give him a dip of my head. "Great. You have my number. Call me Monday." I don't wait for his nod before I grasp Lila's limp fingers and pull her through the door into the hall.

The clouds in her eyes are startling after going without them for so long. "What do you mean, *pack a bag*? Where are we supposed to go? I can't afford a hotel, Kam."

I tighten my hold on her hand like that alone might banish the clouds. "You're staying with me."

She shakes her head so adamantly I feel it through our joined hands. "I can't ask you for that, Kam. I don't want to be an imposition."

"You didn't ask, Sunshine. I'm telling you, that's what's going to happen." Her hair flies around her shoulders as I pull her closet door open with more force than necessary. "Now, pack a bag. We're leaving in five minutes."

Her fingers stall around the handle of a rolling suitcase. "But—But what about book club?"

I shake my head as I nudge her closer to her overflowing closet. "Don't worry about it. Everything's already being taken care of."

Her brows furrow. "What does that mean?"

The floorboards groan under me as I move toward the hall. "You'll see."

"Wait!" My feet halt their advance with her command. "Where are you going?"

I smirk over my shoulder, taking pride in the beautiful blush that creeps up her neck. "Someone has to help Jasper and Posey pack."

Lila's slacked jaw sends an overwhelming hit of satisfaction soaring through my veins as she looks around my living room. "You guys did all this?"

Mace's eyes sparkle as he looks around at their handiwork. "Sure did. We even dusted the ceiling fan."

Dax grins over his shoulder as he climbs the ladder to hang the banner I stole from Lila's house. "We couldn't let you have your first book club meeting in a dump, Sullivan."

Tears rim Lila's eyes as she looks around at my three best friends. "Thank you guys so much."

A rare smile flashes across Wyatt's face before disappearing. "You're part of the team now, Lila. We take care of our own."

Ellie's arm slides snugly over Lila's shoulders as her eyes roam around the room. "Color me impressed, boys. I didn't think you had it in you."

Dax rolls his eyes as he lands on his feet with a thunk at the bottom of the ladder. "Just cause we *choose* not to clean doesn't mean we don't know how, Ellie."

She rolls her eyes so hard I'm surprised they don't roll out of her head. "The fact you see nothing wrong with that statement just shows how far gone you really are, Declan."

Dax shivers like Ellie dumped cold water on his back. "Don't call me that, Ellie. You know how much I hate it."

The mischievous glint in Ellie's eyes only grows as she shrugs. "It's a perfectly good name, Dax. I'm not sure what your problem is with it."

A car door slamming out front silences Dax's argument. Instead, he rolls his eyes and pouts up the stairs. "Enjoy talking about the *porn* you're reading, Ellie. Make sure you talk aloud enough for Kam to hear. Every brother wants to hear their sister talking about their favorite sex positions, right?"

Ellie's face turns a frightening shade of red as she stares lasers into the back of Dax's head. Her fists vibrate at her side as she screams, "Don't knock it till you try it, *Declan!* You might learn a thing or two from my *porn* books!"

I roll my lips to keep my laugh firmly locked away. "Well, on that note—" I kiss Lila's smile as my voice falls to a whisper, "—have fun talking about your *porn* books."

Her smile turns into a full grin. "There's more to our books than sex, Trouble."

Ellie raises her brows as a knock sounds at the door. "Of course there is, but you have to admit that reading about it is pretty great."

I close my eyes as I let out a breath. "I'm going to pretend you didn't just say that."

Ellie's beaming smile greets me when I open my eyes. "What? Sex is a normal thing, little brother. And so is reading about it. Plus, sex actually only takes up like one percent of the book, if that."

I raise my brows. "Oh, I know. I just don't want to talk about it with my *sister*."

She shrugs as she unlocks the door. Her squeal reverberates through my bones as she opens the door and throws her arms around someone just out of view.

My smile returns as I look down at a grinning Lila. I plant a quick kiss on her nose that makes her smile turn even more radiant. "Have a good time."

Their voices fade behind me as I make my way to the hall leading to the kitchen. Jasper and Posey's red-stained smiles greet me from where they sit coloring at the kitchen counter.

I shake my head as my smile grows. "How can you guys eat popsicles when it's this cold out?"

Jasper looks at me like that's the stupidest question he's ever heard. "It's not cold in *here*, Kam. Plus, Matt said it's never too cold to eat a popsicle."

I raise a brow. "Matt, huh?"

He nods while licking a trail of syrup off his finger.

"Yeah. He's not so bad once you get to know him. He just needed a friend." Red food coloring tents his smile. "I made sure he knows he's not allowed to talk about Posey like that anymore, though. It doesn't matter if he's my friend. Sister trumps friend any day."

His hair is silky against my palm as I ruffle his hair. "You've got that right, Tank."

The sound of cabinet doors opening and closing fills the room as Mace looks through his stash. "What do you guys want for dinner tonight?"

"Guys!" Dax's booming voice and beaming smile pull everyone's attention. "I'm pretty sure I just met my future wife."

Even Wyatt's brows raise with Dax's declaration. "You just happened to meet your future wife on your way down the stairs?"

Dax rolls his eyes like Wyatt is the ridiculous one. "No. I met her in the living room."

Wyatt nods his head as he crosses his arms. "Oh, okay. Because that makes way more sense."

Dax nods as his smile grows. "It does, though! She's here for book club."

Mace crosses his arms as he abandons his search. "Oh yeah? What's her name?"

I can practically see the hearts in Dax's eyes as he leans against the counter. "I have no idea."

Posey bats her eyelashes as she swoons in her seat at the kitchen counter. "Aww! Dax is in love!"

Jasper wrinkles his brows as he takes another long lick of his popsicle. "Eww. I'm sorry, Dax. That sounds awful."

My palm connecting with Dax's shoulder sends a

loud clap through the kitchen. "Well, come on! I want to see your future wife."

Mace rubs his hands together. "Ah, yeah. This should be good."

Wyatt rolls his eyes, despite abandoning his seat to follow us to the doorway. The girls' voices grow from a distant murmur into recognizable words the closer we get.

Lila's laugh sends a bolt of lightning through my spine as a smile blooms on my face. "I loved that part! I can't believe he would just abduct her like that!"

I raise a brow as I whisper over my shoulder. "Well, which one is she?"

He grins as he strains to see around me. "The one in the pink shirt."

For the first time, I get a good look at the two strangers sitting on the couch across from my girlfriend and sister.

There's a girl in a black shirt with deep red hair. Her stern brows remind me of a female Wyatt as she sits back to observe the conversation happening around her.

The girl in the pink shirt, however, laughs quietly along with whatever Ellie just said. My sister's boisterous laugh almost drowns out her gentle voice.

Her stick straight, black hair is pulled back in a ponytail that sways behind her as she covers her mouth to laugh.

Her vaguely familiar brown eyes sparkle as she blushes from whatever Ellie just said.

Why does she look so familiar?

"Oh, shit." Wyatt's voice sends all four sets of eyes looking his way.

Dax elbows Wyatt in the ribs with more force than necessary. "What? What's wrong?"

Wyatt inclines his head to where the girls still sit, completely unaware of our observation. "That's Coach's daughter, man."

Dax's smile falls, and his face turns a sickly shade of white. "Coach's daughter? As in *our* coach's daughter?"

Of course. I must have seen her in the family photos Coach has lining his office.

Wyatt nods as he pats Dax's shoulder. "Sorry, man."

Mace's eyes fill with sympathy. "That's too bad, Dax." Mace wrinkles his nose as Dax glares at him. "There's more fish in the sea, though, right?"

Dax lets out a long breath as his eyes return to the girl who's captured his attention. "Yeah, I guess."

Dax's reluctant footsteps follow us into the kitchen, but his eyes never stop straying to the hall.

CHAPTER 57

IT WOULD BE MY HONOR

LILA

The snowstorm raging outside is no match for the storm raging in my chest as I stare at the empty bed.

I clear my throat as the click of Kam's bedroom door closing reverberates through the space like the caulk of a gun. "Thanks for getting the air mattresses set up for the twins. I, uh, I didn't know you had any."

Kam's laugh sends a thrill racing down my spine. "I didn't. I just bought them a few weeks ago." Fabric rustles behind me from his shrug. "I figured they might need to stay here at some point, and I wanted them to have their own places to sleep."

I twist my fingers in front of me as my eyes roam over the neatly made bed.

Kam's deep voice rumbles right through me. "There's no expectations. All we're going to do is sleep."

I take a deep breath before turning to face him. "What if I don't want to *just* sleep?"

His chocolate eyes darken as he clenches his jaw so

hard I'm shocked he doesn't crack a tooth. "You've been through hell these past few days. I'm not taking advantage of you, Lila." He shakes his head as fists form at his sides. *"I won't be that guy."*

A small smirk touches my lips as I inch toward him. "You're not *that* guy, Trouble. You're *my* guy. And you can't take advantage if I'm the one initiating. That's not how that works. This isn't a quick decision for me. I've been thinking about this for a while." I lift a brow as I continue my advance. "Now, if you're telling me this isn't what you want, I'll go into your bathroom, change into my pajamas, and we'll go to bed." The tendons in his neck flex as his eyes bore into mine. "But if this *is* what you want, I'm going to need you to take the lead here, cause I have no idea what I'm doing."

He swallows thickly as his eyes search my face. "I want you more than my next breath, Sunshine."

"And I *need* you more than mine."

With my words, his mouth collides with mine in a hungry kiss that feels like safety.

That feels like the type of love you only read about in books.

That feels like coming home.

I swallow his moan as his fingers weave through my hair to drag me as close as possible till only thin layers of clothing separate us.

Even so, it's not close enough. My words are so breathless I don't even recognize my own voice. "I need you closer, Kam."

He smiles against my lips as I twist my fingers in the back of his shirt. "Patience. I'm not going to rush this."

I'm not proud of the whimper that falls from my mouth. "But I *need* you."

"And you'll have me. Let me explore you first, Sunshine. Let me worship you." His smile turns wicked. "And then, after I've driven you to the brink of insanity, I'm going to make you mine in every way possible. That starts with me stripping you bare so I can see every inch of you. So I can explore every inch of this body that has been the star of my dreams for months. So I can etch my name on your very soul." A liquid inferno consumes his eyes. "Now, are you going to take your shirt off for me, or are you going to be a *good girl* and allow me the honor of doing it myself?"

A shiver trails down my spine that almost makes my knees buckle under my weight. "Are you sure you've never done this before? Those aren't the words of a virgin, Trouble."

"Just because I'm a virgin doesn't mean I don't know what you need. Trust me, I've had enough experience pleasing you in my dreams to know what I'm doing." His fingers tighten in my hair. "Before we get started, I need to know you want this." I open my mouth, but he's shaking his head before I have time to utter a single word. "I mean it, Lila. I'm going to lay you out on my bed and I'm going to fuck you unless you tell me otherwise. I need more than a nod of your head here. This isn't something we can take back once it's happened."

I nod anyway as my legs tremble. "Yes. I need you to strip me bare and explore my body. I need you to lay me on your bed and make me yours. I want to *give* my virginity to you, Kamden Stryker. And I want you to give yours to me in return."

His nostrils flare with my words. "If you want to stop, you say so. No judgement. No worries. We just stop. You got that?"

I nod my head again as my breathing grows as rapidly as my pulse. "Yes, Trouble. I've got it."

His nod is strained. "Good. Now lift your arms, Sunshine. I need to see you."

My arms tremble as I lift them from excitement instead of the nerves I thought I would feel when I imagined this situation. I expected awkward touches and self-conscious thoughts during my first time.

I never imagined I would be consumed with thoughts of love and a burning need for *more* instead.

Warm fingers graze the delicate skin of my stomach as he digs into the hem of my shirt. His hardness feels like a steel rod pressing against me.

My heart beats like a kick-drum in my chest as I say, "Wait!"

My heartbeat echoes in my ears as his movements halt, and his eyes flick to mine. "We don't have to do this. We can stop."

I shake my head as I grasp his fingers so tightly it has to hurt. "No, that's not why I wanted you to stop."

His brows furrow as his worried eyes search mine. "Then what's wrong?"

I can barely find my words for the butterflies taking flight in my stomach. "Nothing's wrong. I just want, no *need*, to say something first."

I hate the worry clouding his eyes as he nods. "Okay."

I take a deep breath as a splitting smile takes over my face. "I love you, Trouble." His eyes flare as my words register. "With everything going on, it's never felt like the right time to say it. I wanted this perfect, special moment to tell you what I've been feeling for a while now. But if I've learned anything these past few months, it's that nothing is guaranteed in life. There's no promise for tomorrow, Kam. And I couldn't waste another second of this life without you knowing how I feel." My finger over his lips stalls the words threatening to escape his mouth. "You don't have to say it back. I just needed you to know."

His smile grows under my finger. "Move your finger, Lila." My finger slides from his lip with a satisfying pop. Chills erupt across my skin as his warm fingers glide along my back, under my shirt. "I love you, too, Sunshine." He shakes his head as his smile grows. "You stubborn woman. If you would have given me a few minutes, I would have said it first."

Now it's my turn to sport furrowed brows. "You were going to say it first?" I poke him in the chest hard enough to bruise. "And I am *not* stubborn."

He nods as his smile shines brightly in his eyes. "I was really looking forward to saying it first, too." The warmth from his laugh flows through my body to settle between my legs. "And you are *definitely* stubborn. You might not be on Ellie's level, but you're still stubborn as hell. You would have to be in order to fight the way you have."

I shake my head as my gaze falls to our feet. "I'm not doing anything special. Anyone in my position would do the same."

His calloused fingers dig into my chin to force my eyes to meet his. "You couldn't be more wrong about that. Most people in your position would have run as far as they could. But not you. Not *my* Sunshine. No, you had to prove everyone wrong. You had to prove you can keep your kindness in the face of adversity. You had to prove that strength is found in the most unlikely places. And you look damn good while doing it." His eyes soften. "It's amazing to watch."

His face turns blurry from the tears brimming my eyes. "Take me to bed, Kam."

His soft eyes turn to molten lava in seconds. "It would be my *honor*."

CHAPTER 58
USE YOUR WORDS

KAM

My hands struggle to stay gentle as I dig my fingers into her waist and lift her. Her weight feels so right in my arms. *She* feels so right.

My lips greedily search for hers as I carry her the few feet separating us from my end goal. Her back conforms to my mattress as I gently lay her down, just as her soft lips fit perfectly against mine.

Her soft breaths flow over my mouth as I lean back to look at her. So I can take in this moment and sear it into my memory for the rest of my life. So I can take *her* in.

Her blonde waves fan around her on the comforter to create a halo fitting for an angel. A beautiful blush creeps over her cheeks as her chest rises and falls in a beat that mimics my own. "You are the most stunning sight I've ever seen." My cock grows with her blush. "Worthy of becoming art on my wall."

Her shy smile can't hide the heat in her eyes that threatens to consume me with a ferocity so foreign I can hardly breathe. "You make me feel beautiful, Kam."

My breath stutters as her words wash over me. "That's because you *are* beautiful. I just wish you didn't need my words to make you feel beautiful. Maybe one day you'll feel beautiful when you're standing alone in front of your mirror." Her sharp intake of breath sends another rush of blood between my legs. A smirk pulls at my lips as I run my nose along hers. "Until then, I'll tell you every day until you have no choice but to believe me."

She shakes her head as I settle my forearms on either side of her head. "It's not just your words, Kam." Her smile grows as I raise my brows. "It's the fire in your eyes. It's the care you make clear in your touches. It's the love you show in every word you say. So, no, it's not just your words. It's *everything*."

I shift so my hardness can settle on the apex of her legs. "Do you feel what you do to me?" She nods as her pupils dilate. "Do you feel how crazy you make me?"

Her eyes blaze molten lava and her fingers tighten in my shirt to the point I'm sure she'll rip the fabric. The tendons in her neck strain with coiling tension as a breathy whine leaves her kiss-swollen lips. "Kam."

My lips brush against hers with every word I speak. "I know what you need."

My calloused fingers feel unworthy of the goddess before me. That doesn't stop me from finding the seam between her shirt and leggings. It doesn't stop me from looking at my fill as I run a thumb over the scant inch of bare skin I yearn to trace with my tongue.

My fingers slide up the soft skin of her stomach to

push aside the fabric hiding her from me. With every inch of exposed skin, it becomes harder and harder to breathe. To even *think.*

Blood pumps through my veins like an overflowing river, begging for the dam to give and set it free. Begging for the release that waits just beyond the barrier. I struggle to swallow as black lace comes into view. My voice is unrecognizable as I struggle to take in a lungful of air. "I'm not going to last."

She shakes her head as desperate fingers slide under my shirt. "I don't care."

The contrast between her warm, smooth skin and the rough lace against the tips of my fingers has my cock twitching against the zipper of my pants. I trace the edge of the fabric with gentle fingers as I prepare myself to cross the barrier. To cross into the unknown world that lies beyond what strangers see at the beach or by the pool. To venture into a land of temptation like I've never known. "I'm going to make this good for you."

"Just being close to you will make it good for me."

I shake my head as the tip of my index finger disappears under the black fabric. "You misunderstand me." My smile grows with the furrow of her brow. "That just means you're going to have to be a *good girl* for me and come before I get inside you." My nostrils flare at just the thought of sinking into her. Of claiming her as mine. "Can you do that for me?" A soft moan escapes her lips as she nods. "Tell me, Lila. Use your words."

She tilts her head back to expose her gorgeous throat. "Yes."

My voice is a growl as the tip of my middle finger disappears under the fabric. "Yes, what?"

"Yes, I-I can be a—" her throat bobs as she struggles to find her words in the haze of my exploration, "—*good girl* and come before you get inside me."

Sweat beads on her brow as I grind my teeth.

Slowly, Kam. Take it slow.

Her hips lift involuntarily to seek the pressure and pleasure only I can give as I lift her shirt over her head. The swelling of her breasts rises and falls with every breath she takes.

Chills follow my finger as I trace the dip of her throat, down between her breasts, to reach her belly button. I hesitate for only a moment before continuing my path down to the hem of her leggings.

The pitiful excuse for a barrier gives easily under my determined fingers. The heat of her skin grows as I find purchase in the thin fabric and slowly start peeling it down her legs.

I don't take her trust for granted as she lays in the center of my bed with scraps of fabric covering her most intimate areas.

Her heated gaze follows every move I make as I neatly fold her clothes and place them on the end of the bed. Her voice is so quiet I almost can't hear her. "You don't have to do that."

I shake my head as I settle between her legs. "If I can't respect your things, how am I supposed to show you that I respect you?"

I grip the hem of my shirt with full intentions of ripping it over my head and slinging it to the floor. "Wait!" I raise my brows as she sits up. Her blush returns in full force. "Let me do it." My hands slowly lower to my sides. Her hair sways behind her as she settles on her knees in the middle of the bed. My knees nearly buckle under me as her eyes turn heated. She jerks her chin as her tiny fingers dig into the hem of my shirt. "Lift your arms, Trouble."

My immediate compliance earns me a breathtaking smile as she drags my shirt over my head. The muscles in my stomach flex and strain under her heated gaze as she carefully folds my shirt and places it over hers.

Shaky fingers grip my zipper as I fight to keep my hands still by my sides. The unintentional brush of her index finger over the bulge in my pants has a groan falling from my lips before I can contain it.

Her smile turns mischievous as she does it again, this time with much more deliberate movements.

"You're killing me, Sunshine."

Her answering smile distracts me for only a moment before she's pushing my pants down my legs. The cool air from the room is a welcome distraction against my overheated skin with every new inch of skin she reveals.

I allow her the symbolism of folding my pants and placing them on hers. As soon as her eyes lift from the neatly folded pile of clothes, my hand circles her ankle and pulls. The air rushes from her lungs as she lands on her back with a thunk. Her eyes flash with annoyance. "Hey! I wasn't done!"

The boxers still around my waist are the farthest thing from my mind. "I can't wait another second to see all of you."

My fingers are warm against her cool skin as I find

the clasp at her back. Our eyes connect and the world stills around us as I flick open the clasp. Her straps hang loosely on her shoulders for only a second before I'm pulling the fabric away.

My breath stalls in my chest as my eyes trace every inch of her. Her pink buds, the same color as the blush gracing her cheeks, stretch for me as the cool air hits them.

My fingers shake as I grasp the delicate fabric covering what's left of her and pull it down her legs. I don't allow myself to look at her before I get them all the way off. I'm not sure I'd be able to find the restraint to take care of them properly if I didn't.

As I finally look at her, at *all* of her, I can hardly breathe. To think someone so precious would want to give something so special to *me*.

Her fingers dig into the comforter under her as she watches me. I hate the worry I see in her eyes as she tries to gauge my reaction. To see if I *like* what I see. What a ridiculous thought.

I hope she can hear the awe, the *reverence*, in my voice. "I didn't think it was possible for you to be more beautiful." My hungry eyes trace every square inch of her body as I try to catch my breath. The juncture between her legs glistens in the dim light. "Where should I start? Should I start here?" I ghost the tip of my finger over the swell of her breast. Her quick intake of breath is fuel to my desire. With a featherlight touch, I trail my finger over her breast, down past her belly button, until I reach the soft patch of curls between her legs. "Or should I start here?"

The heat emanating from between her legs calls to a

primal part of me that has never been awakened before this moment. A part of my nature that feels like it was made for this woman before me.

Her mouth opens and closes as she searches for words that are just out of reach. I can't help but smile. I lower to my forearms to graze a quick kiss over her lips before descending to her chest.

Her mango scent drives me crazy as I trail my nose over every dip and curve until I find her nipple. The pink bud tastes like heaven as I run my warm tongue over her sensitive flesh. Her breath stutters in her chest as I suck the delectable treat into my mouth. I release the sensitive skin with a satisfying pop before giving its counterpart the same attention.

I leave a trail of featherlight kisses along her stomach on my way to where I truly wish to be. Her soft curls are silk against my nose as I glance up to find barely controlled *want* in her eyes.

I keep my eyes snared on hers as I finally get my first taste of her. Her plush skin molds to my tongue like this is the sole purpose of my existence. Her soft moan vibrates through me as I find the bundle of nerves that I know will bring her the most pleasure.

I suck the bundle into my mouth as I fight a smile. It takes a surprising amount of strength to hold her legs apart as I figure out the best way to swirl my tongue to bring her the most pleasure.

Sweat pools in the divot of her collar bones as I continue my assault. Her taste blooms over my tongue and threatens to hold me captive as she shakes.

Jumbled words fall from her mouth as I spread her with my fingers. She tries to quiet her words by putting her hand over her mouth. "Oh, shit! Kam! Oh, fuck!"

"Let me hear you, Sunshine. My bedroom walls are thick. No one can hear you but me." I groan as more of her wetness coats my tongue. I'm thankful for the added slickness that makes it easier to breach her walls with my fingers.

Another groan falls from my lips as I get to feel the texture of her for the first time against my finger. Her pussy grinds against my face as she chases the pleasure I'll gladly provide.

Her walls clamp down on my finger before waves of pleasure cascade through her body.

Her beautiful sounds wash over me as her face twists in bliss. I catch my breath as she comes down from the high I'm thrilled to have been the one to provide. "You're stunning when you come."

Her bottomless, blue eyes turn pleading as she reaches for me. "I need you now, Kam. Please don't make me wait."

How could I say no to that?

With shaking hands, I hook my fingers into my boxers and slowly slide them down my legs. Her eyes flare as I free my cock from its restraints. It pulses under her attention as it strains in her direction.

My erection is almost painful as I get a condom from my bedside drawer without taking my eyes off her. Her raised brow brings a smile to my face as I carefully tear open the foil. "I bought these two weeks ago. Don't look at me like that."

Her answering smile brightens the dim room. "Like what?"

"Like you're questioning my virgin status." My smile grows. "Again."

She rolls her eyes as she watches me roll the condom over my throbbing erection. "I wasn't questioning anything."

"Whatever you say." The air turns serious as the condom slides into place. "Are you sure you want to do this? We don't have to keep going."

A small smile touches her lips as she intertwines our fingers. "I've never been more sure of anything, Trouble."

CHAPTER 59
THE SHEETS BETWEEN US
LILA

A cloud of apprehension slides over his face as he looks down to where we will soon be joined. I clear my throat as I tighten my hold on his hand. "It's okay if you want to wait, Kam."

His eyes flare as his gaze connects with mine. "It's not that. It's just, um—" His eyes flick back down to my most intimate area as he struggles to swallow.

"It's okay. You can tell me whatever it is."

His worried eyes flick back up to mine. "It's just that I don't want to hurt you. I know that's silly because it's normal for it to hurt your first time, but I can't stand the thought of causing you pain."

I smile as I sit up so I can reach his lips. Some of the tension drains from his body when our lips meet. "It's alright, Trouble. It will probably hurt the first time. That's okay. I'm prepared for that."

He shakes his head as his words flow over my lips. "That doesn't make it easier."

My eyes gleam as I pull away. "I have an idea!"

His brows furrow as he searches my face. "That's sketchy."

I raise my brows as I move off the bed. "Me having an idea is sketchy?"

"When you have that look in your eye, it is." He cocks a brow. "Where are you going?"

I point to the spot I just vacated on the bed. "Lay down."

He complies despite the skepticism in his eyes. "How is this going to be any better?"

The bed dips under his weight as he settles on his bed. His cock juts to the ceiling and hardly moves as he puts his arms behind his head so he can look at me. "If I'm in control, it's like I'm hurting myself. You can't be the one hurting me if you're not the one moving."

The tension leaves his shoulders as he relaxes against the mattress. "I can live with that."

My knees struggle to find purchase on the mattress without me falling on top of him. That's the last thing I need during my first time. I can see the headlines now: *College hockey star's girlfriend breaks his penis during their first sexual encounter. It is unclear if he will continue to play hockey at this time.*

Kam raises a brow as his hands circle my waist, as I try to figure out the best way to straddle him from my position beside him on the bed. "What's so funny?"

I wave away his question as I realize for the first time just how large this man is. "Oh, nothing." I wave my hand in his general direction. "How am I supposed to do...*this?*"

He shrugs as his fingers dig into my waist. "As long as you don't hurt yourself, I don't really care. Just please, put me out of my misery and sit on my cock within the next thirty seconds. You look too damn good above me like this."

Heat envelopes my face as I put the palms of my hands on his chest for balance. Turns out that was totally unnecessary, because in the next breath, Kam lifts me completely off the bed and deposits me on his chest.

The wetness still present from the magic he worked with his fingers and mouth earlier drips onto his chest. I have never gotten myself to come like that, let alone that quickly.

Kam's eyes heat as they connect with where my pussy rests on his chest. "Fuck, Sunshine. Look how beautiful you look dripping all over me." The walls of my pussy clench around nothing as his words wash over me like a sweet summer rain. "Now sit on me, Lila. I need to feel your pussy wrapped around my cock."

He helps me lift off his chest enough to position his cock at my entrance. With the first brush of his shaft against my swollen lips, our eyes connect as our breaths stall in our chests.

And as I sink down on him, the pain is consumed by the thought that I can't imagine a better man to give this part of myself to. I can't imagine someone more worthy of this connection.

"Are you okay?" The worry never leaves his eyes as I take every inch of him.

A nod of my head will have to be good enough, because I seem to have forgotten how to speak.

Kam's jaw clenches and his eyes slide closed as I

bottom out. "You feel so good." His eyes are a blazing fire when they open. "Even *better* than I imagined." His fingers turn bruising as he tightens his grip on my waist. "You fit perfectly around my cock, Lila."

The pain fades to be replaced by an all-consuming stretch that feels so right. "I feel so full."

His eyes blaze even brighter at my words. The world tilts on its axis until I'm lying on my back and Kam's loving eyes shine above me. The shift of his cock against a bundle of nerves inside me almost takes my breath.

His eyes fall to where we're joined as a look of satisfaction takes over his face. "I never thought I would care if who I gave my virginity to was a virgin, but I have to say, knowing no other man has been here is thrilling. Knowing that you gave this part of yourself to me is an honor and a privilege I do not take for granted." His smirk is fully in place when he looks back up at me. "With that being said, I'm going to fuck you now, Sunshine."

I open my mouth, but don't have time to utter a word before the delicious drag of his cock against that bundle of nerves inside me strikes me mute. The feeling is so different compared to my clit that it steals my breath.

His eyes alternate between my face and my pussy as he finds a rhythm that has me gasping. With every thrust, I move farther up the bed until my hands against the headboard are a requirement.

I struggle to remember to breathe as Kam continues his relentless rhythm. The sound of skin on skin accompanies our labored breaths. Delicious warmth flows from his fingers as he explores my body like he alone has its map.

His clenched jaw turns to steel as he watches himself disappear into me. He seems unaware of his mumbled words. "How will I ever leave?" With every thrust, the pleasure at the base of my spine grows. His eyes leave where we're joined to flick to mine. "That's it. Come for me. I know you've got another one in you."

I open my mouth in a silent scream as the dam breaks and pleasure washes over me. My pussy grips onto his cock so tightly I'm surprised he can still move.

His thrusts turn choppy and a deep groan follows his release moments after mine fades into a dull pulsing between my legs.

Our labored breaths fill the room as the world comes back into focus. Kam smiles as his arms shake on either side of my head. "Holy fuck."

I nod my head as I try to catch my breath. "Yeah. Holy fuck."

The soft kiss he places on my lips is so different from the power he just used on my body.

He shifts to look down at where we're joined once again. "Are you sore? How badly did it hurt?"

I tighten my legs around his waist to pull him back down to me. "Don't ruin one of the best moments of my life, Trouble. The pain only lasted a few seconds."

He nods as he returns my smile. "Good! That's really good." His eyes return to where we're joined before a moan falls from his lips. "When can I have you again?"

My palm smacks against his chest as I playfully

shove him. "Is that all you're going to think about now?"

His smile turns into a full grin. "If by 'it' you mean the look on your face when you come? Then yes. Yes, it is." He doesn't miss the slight wince that falls from my lips as he pulls out of my body. "I knew it! You can't hide your pain from me."

My body feels like Jell-O as the warmth of his skin fades. His eyes never leave me as his bare feet land on the floor with a solid thunk.

"I'm fine! I swear!" His quick kiss on the forehead isn't nearly enough to satisfy my need for cuddles after such intense orgasms. "And where do you think you're going?"

I barely register his beaming smile over his shoulder as he walks to the connecting bathroom. I'm far too busy watching the dimple in his right butt cheek wink in and out of existence with every step he takes.

His laughter brings my attention back to his face. "Did you even hear a word I just said?"

With a sheepish smile, I shake my head. "Nope. Not a word."

The smile never leaves his face as he rolls his eyes. "I said I'm going to take care of the condom and get a warm, wet cloth for me to take care of my girl." His raised brow only accentuates his smirk. "That alright with you?"

I nod and smile at his retreating form as I settle farther into the comforter.

I don't take Kam's gentle touches for granted as he cleans me.

I don't take his loving kisses for granted as he tucks

me under his arm and pulls me close under the warm blankets.

And I don't take his words for granted as he whispers, "I love you, Sunshine."

Because at the end of an exhausting day filled with uncertainties, there's nowhere else I'd rather be.

So, with tired bodies and full hearts, we fall asleep with not even the sheets between us. "I love you, too, Trouble."

CHAPTER 60
ICE QUEEN
KAM

I wake from a dream only to discover that the dream is my new reality. That Lila's warmth really is radiating into me from her spot on my chest. That she gave herself to me last night with no reservations or hesitations. Her blonde curls standout against my dark sheets as her chest rises with every gentle breath.

Dim light cascades through the window over our untouched pile of clothes at the foot of the bed. The tidy sheets and dreamless night allude to the best night's sleep I think I've ever had.

Lila shifts in my arms and her mango scent washes over me like a tidal wave. Her soft exhale against my chest sends chills racing down my spine as memories of her making a very similar sound last night float to the surface of my mind.

A quick glance at the clock shows it's just after eight in the morning. I hesitantly run my fingers through the soft tendrils of her hair draped over my arm. "It's time to wake up, Sunshine."

Her soft groan brings a smile to my face. "What time is it?"

"It's just after eight. The twins will get up soon, if they aren't already."

Her nose is cold against my heated skin as she burrows farther into my chest. "Just five more minutes."

My gentle laugh vibrates against her smooth skin. "Is this why you were always late for our morning class? And here I pegged you as a morning person."

The usually warm depths of her blue eyes turn icy as she looks up at me with a frown on her pouty lips. "Why would you think that? I hate the mornings."

My shrug shifts her on my chest. "You're the brightest person I know. It would make sense for you to be a morning person." My voice turns to nearly a growl as I run my hands up her bare back. "I've learned a lot about you over the past twenty-four hours. You turn into an ice queen in the mornings, you kick in your sleep, and you make the sexiest noises when you come."

Her scoff makes my smile grow even more as her icy eyes meet mine once again. "I do *not* kick in my sleep!"

I nod my head. "How would you know? I bet I've got the bruises on my legs to prove it, too!"

She rolls her eyes as some of the ice melts from their depths. "You play hockey, Trouble. You *always* have bruises on your legs."

My arms tighten around her back. "Yeah, but these bruises would be from you."

She raises a brow. "You say that like it's a good thing."

"I'll wear them as a badge of honor if it means I get to have you in my bed every night, Sunshine."

A smile blooms on her face as more of the ice melts from her eyes. "Aww, you're so romantic in the mornings, Trouble."

The tips of my fingers dig into her sides. "In the mornings? What are you talking about? I'm always romantic."

I'm rewarded by her muscles tightening against my side and a squeal so loud it could wake the dead. Her voice turns breathless as I continue my tickle assault. "Fine! Fine! You're romantic all the time! Just spare me from your tickling, at least until I've had breakfast!"

My fingers soothe away her sensations left behind from my assault as I laugh. "So you're saying I can have my way with you after we eat breakfast?"

Her warm eyes shine as bright as her smile as she catches her breath. "No." Her smile turns mischievous as she says, "But you can have your way with me after we play in the snow."

My smile mimics hers. "It's a date, then."

I plant a quick kiss on her nose that pulls a laugh from her lips. "As much as I would like to stay and take advantage of your nose kisses, I can't ignore the screaming of my bladder."

My smile turns splitting. "You want to take advantage of me?"

Her eye roll can't hide the magnitude of the smile on her face. "You know what I mean. Now let me up before I pee myself!"

I reluctantly release my hold on her waist as she wiggles away from me. "Fine! We've got to get downstairs, anyway. I'm sure Mace already has breakfast—" My words stall in my mouth as the blanket falls away from her chest.

My elbows sink into the plush mattress as I sit up. Her laugh shakes the swell of her breasts as I lose all train of thought. "My eyes are up here, Trouble."

"I know where they are." My gaze doesn't move an inch. "These past few months, I've spent most of my time memorizing every shade of blue present in the depths of your eyes. Every fleck of gray and every thread of silver that only sparkles when you're in the sunshine. I've spent the last few months forcing myself to look at nothing *but* your eyes. So, yes, Sunshine, I know where your eyes are. I'm just choosing not to look at them right now."

She clears her throat as her legs squeeze together under the comforter. "Alright then, I'll just, um, go use the bathroom then."

I catalogue every new inch of skin that's exposed as she wiggles out of the blanket. I admire every tan line that's now visible in the dim morning light streaming through the sheer curtains.

I struggle to swallow as her feet land on my hard-wood floors, and her bare back comes fully into view. I struggle to breathe as her hips sway with every step she takes while she walks away. Relief only comes as the bathroom door closes, sealing her away from my view.

Only then can I catch my breath.

Only then can my thoughts clear enough to realize having Lila in my space is quickly becoming a requirement.

A necessity.

As important as breathing.

A chorus of voices and the metallic scrape of cutlery on ceramic transforms the kitchen into a living entity. The smell of bacon permeates the air like a beacon, calling all the residents of this house to a central location with the promise of a home-cooked meal.

Dax's voice booms through the space as his hand pauses halfway to his mouth with a fork full of scrambled eggs. "Nice of you to join us, Kila. If you would have waited much longer, the food would have been gone."

I raise a brow as Mace hands me a plate stacked high with pancakes. "Kila? Really, Dax?"

He shrugs as he talks around a mouth full of eggs. "What? All the cool people have a couples' name."

Jasper grins next to him as syrup runs down his chin. "Cool! What can my couples' name be?"

Posey rolls her eyes as she cuts up her pancake from her seat next to him. "You have to be in a *couple* before you can have a *couples'* name, dummy."

Lila's spine turns rigid as her eyes laser in on her sister. "We don't call people that, Posey. How would you feel if Jasper called *you* a dummy?"

Posey's face falls as she looks over at her brother's sad eyes. "Not very good."

Lila nods next to me. "Right. So what should you do?"

Posey lets out a deep breath as she wraps her tiny arms around her brother. His sweatshirt muffles her words. "Sorry, Jas."

His arms tighten around her as he smiles. "It's okay. You can make it up to me by helping me build a snowman later."

She nods as she pulls away from the hug with a smile. "Deal."

Mace's face holds a look of awe as he watches them. "If only the world's problems could all be solved by making snowmen."

The tension falls from Lila's shoulders, and a smile takes over her face as she looks down at the plate Mace just handed her. "Aww, Mace! Blueberry pancakes are my *favorite* breakfast food!"

The wink he sends her has my hackles raising before I remember he's my best friend. "I know." Lila's raised brows add to Mace's smile. "I asked you what your favorite breakfast food was the first night I met you at The Penalty Box. I figured that information would come in handy someday."

Lila's face flames as she stares at our friend with open mouthed shock. "You knew you'd be making me breakfast someday?"

His shrug shifts his apron around his shoulders. "I just had a feeling."

Dax shakes his head from his spot at the table. "You and your feelings, man."

Mace's arms fold across his chest, despite the spatula in his hand. "What? I can't help that I'm observant!"

I scoop a serving of scrambled eggs and bacon onto

mine and Lila's plates as I look around the kitchen in search of my third roommate. "Speaking of observant people, where's Ranger?"

Posey dabs the syrup from the corner of her mouth like the lady she is. "He went to get Ellie. She wants to come play in the snow with us."

He went to get her even though the roads are still covered in snow?

I don't let the worry show in my voice as I take my seat at the table. "Well, we better finish up so we can get outside! We've got to take full advantage of our snow day."

The twins' efforts double as they shovel food into their mouths. The tension doesn't fall from my shoulders until I hear the slamming of Wyatt's truck doors outside. Only then can I finally relax and enjoy breakfast with my family.

CHAPTER 61
NATURAL GLITTER
LILA

Tiny snowflakes drift along the backdrop of grey clouds that linger from last night's storm. Clouds that block the sun from burning away the field of white. Flakes fall and disappear into the blanket of wet snow that conceals a thin layer of ice just below its untouched surface.

The brisk winter wind that ushers the remaining clouds eastward blows my hair around my face as the back door clicks shut behind me.

I have always loved snow. It's a love I shared with my mom. She was always partial to watching the snow-fall at night. She would always talk about how it seems impossible that shimmering flecks of natural glitter can illuminate the night with only the reflection of the sun on the moon.

My favorite, however, has always been the morning after a winter storm. Almost unnatural stillness seems to consume the world as a few lingering soft flakes dance in the winter wind. The covering of white can make a dreary day such as this feel magical. Extraordinary, even.

As my boot breaks the untouched barrier and I take my first step into the yard, my crunchy footsteps take me back to my childhood. To a time in my life when it was just the three of us. To a time before the twins were born, and I had my parents' complete attention.

Some of my favorite memories were when my dad and I played astronaut the morning after a big snowstorm. I was obsessed with all things space when I was the twins' age. I once told my dad that the first steps out into the untouched snow was like taking the first steps on the moon.

My lone footprints in the snow were like leaving my mark on an untouched celestial being. In that moment, when my tiny boots would sink into the snow, I could be anything. I could *do* anything. As long as I had my dad right behind me, ready to catch me if I fell into the icy unknown.

Now, I stand alone in a frozen yard of a man who held me like I was something precious while I slept last night. While the snow fell and changed the landscape to make it almost unrecognizable, I slept soundly in the arms of the man I love.

A man my dad will never get to meet.

Bustling laughter and happy squeals spill from the door as my family emerges into the winter wonderland. I wipe a stray tear from the corner of my eye. Ellie's keen eye follows the movement as the twins run by in a blur of color and happiness.

Ellie raises a brow in a silent question that I answer

with a nod and a smile that says, *it's okay.* I can remember my parents and not fall into a pit of sadness. I can remember the wonderful memories and look forward to making new ones, even though they won't be in them.

My heart still hurts. I'm pretty sure it always will, but these people love me enough to add the extra cushion needed to keep it from bruising.

Dax's booming laugh follows the happy squeals of the twins farther into the yard, to where they're already covered in a layer of wet snow. He rubs his gloved hands together as he surveys the yard. "Alright! Gather 'round! If we're going to get all this done, we're going to have to be smart about it."

Wyatt and Mace roll their eyes, but follow their friend to the back of the lot anyway. Wyatt's mumbled words bring a smile to my face. "I told you he would do this."

Mace doesn't even try to hide his smile as they walk away. "Ah, come on, Ranger. Let the man build his snow fort."

I can hear the smile in Ellie's voice as she comes to a stop beside me. "How long before they give up and start throwing snowballs at each other?"

I tilt my head back and forth. "Um, I don't know. Maybe fifteen minutes?"

The back door clicks shut behind us as warm arms circle my waist. "I don't know, Sunshine. I think they'll last twenty at least."

I don't have to look at Ellie to know she just rolled her eyes. "You know *you* are included in the *they*, right, little brother?"

His laughter vibrates through me as he tightens his arms around my waist. "If I'm included, then I give us at least thirty!"

Dax's voice carries through the yard as he hands out snow shovels to all the willing participants. "Come on, Cap! We've got to get a move on if we want to be done by lunch!"

The kiss Kam plants on my forehead is far too quick. "I better go help before he sticks me with a sucky job like last year."

Dax's scoff makes my smile double. "It's not my fault you couldn't get your boots on quick enough, Cap." His eyes flick to Ellie and me as he puts his hands on his hips. "And don't think you two are getting out of putting in your fair share of work. I have it on good authority you're a work horse, Sullivan." His arms fall from his waist as he looks around his feet. "Did anyone bring the gardening shovels?"

A crease forms between Mace's brows as he stops shoveling the snow into a pile by Jasper's feet. "We have gardening shovels?"

Dax moves his toboggan around on his head to scratch his scalp. "Yeah. I found them in the upstairs hall closet when we moved in."

Ellie's fingers dig into my shoulder as she says, "L and I will go find them. You guys keep working." She pulls so hard on my shoulder that I almost fall on my ass as she turns to go back inside. "Come on."

I raise a brow as we dust the snow from our boots. "Do you even know where the shovels are?"

Her eyes twinkle as she takes her glove off to open the back door. "Hell no. I just don't want to get stuck shoveling snow. I plan on taking full advantage of the first snow day of the year. It's not like the snow will be here tomorrow."

Warm air hits my chilled cheeks as we step through the back door. The dampness from my boots coats my hands as I slip them from my feet. "I hope not. I don't want to reschedule our court date tomorrow." Careful steps are a requirement to keep my socks from the droplets of water my boots left behind. "I'm already worried about my final meeting with the social worker tonight. She said it shouldn't be a problem, though. Apparently, her husband is a snowplow driver."

She raises a brow as her snow pants crinkle with her movements. "Well, that's convenient. Did you ever talk to your lawyer about your last meeting with your grandparents?"

I nod my head as sweat beads on my brow from the warm air seeping through my snow jacket. "Yeah. He said not to worry about it. That he'll take care of everything."

She scrunches her nose as the stairs creak under us. "And you trust him?"

I shrug as she opens the hall closet door that sits tucked between Kam and Dax's rooms. The smell of dust and cardboard assaults my nose as the stale air washes over me. "Yeah, I do. He seemed pretty confident when I talked to him. I felt a lot better after he explained the schedule for tomorrow."

Boxes of hockey memorabilia and assorted blankets shift as we sort through the contents of the closet. "Let's hope for his sake everything goes smoothly tomorrow. I will gladly take those kids so far away from here, no one would ever find them." Her smile grows. "We only need to hide out until they turn eighteen. Then we can stage a miraculous rescue mission and bring them home. It'll be like nothing ever happened!"

It's my turn to scrunch my nose as my fingers come in contact with something crusty on the underside of a blanket that looks like it's seen better days. "Yeah, let's not do that if we can help it."

"Ah-ha! I found them!" Her brows furrow as she pulls the rusty shovels from the corner of the closet. Cobwebs fly behind the three rusted gardening tools like streamers. "What the hell happened to these things?"

I smile, thinking back to my mom's gardening basket she had in Chicago. "My mom once left an entire basket of tools outside while we were gone on vacation. It only took a week for her shovel to get rusted like this." I shake my head as my smile grows. "She was so disappointed. They were a birthday gift from my dad."

Ellie's face blurs as tears rim my eyes. Her gentle fingers squeeze my hand as I smile. "Hey, it's all going to be okay. You're not alone in this, L. We're going to fight like hell to keep those kids."

I use the back of my hand to wipe the tear that escapes since I don't want the mystery crusty stuff from the blanket anywhere near my face. "I hope you're right, E."

Her smile comes into view as my tears dry up. "I usually am."

Her smile falls as a shrill cry comes from the backyard. A bolt of dread zings down my spine as the cry truly registers.

I know that cry. I heard it every night for weeks when she would wake from her nightmares to burrow into my side. I heard it when she fell and busted her lip on her first day of preschool.

Posey.

CHAPTER 62
TIME TRAVEL
LILA

Hospitals have a certain smell. I'm not sure if it's the sharp smell of antiseptic or the lingering smell of old coffee that causes such a recognizable scent. Maybe it's the ever-present burn in your nose like you've just inhaled chlorine that makes the scent so easily distinguished.

Or maybe it's not a smell, but just a feeling. A feeling of all-consuming dread that seems to overtake anyone who walks through the sliding glass doors. For some, it's a feeling of déjà vu, like they're stepping back in time to revisit the worst day of their lives.

I used to not believe in time travel. There's no way that we mere humans could master such a complex theory. There's no way we could harness enough power and understanding to control something as intricate as time.

But as I walked through those sliding glass doors a few hours ago, I became a believer.

Time travel doesn't exist the way it does in movies and books, though.

It's not a futuristic car you can get in, push a few buttons, and speed off into a new era.

It's not a genetic disorder that causes you to spontaneously fade away into a different time.

It's not a blue police box that uses alien technology to travel anywhere in time and space.

No. It's the sound of a doorway made up of simple glass that squeaks as it opens.

It's the sharp smell of antiseptic and stale, cheap coffee.

It's a feeling that nothing will ever be okay again.

Because in reality, I'm sitting in a broken-down chair while I wait for a doctor to come and X-ray my sister's arm. My butt is numb, my stomach is growling, and I am exhausted. But, this isn't the worst day of my life.

My mind doesn't care about reality, though. No. My mind is stuck reliving that worst day over and over again.

My ears don't care that Posey is laughing at something Kam just said or that she doesn't need a heart monitor like the old lady in the next room. All my ears can hear are the mumbled words of the nurse, who couldn't keep the tears from her eyes as she said, *"I'm sorry, Miss Sullivan. There was nothing else we could do."*

My eyes don't care that Posey is smiling as she fidgets on the bed with the scratchy sheets. All my eyes can see are the bloodstains on the doctor's scrubs as he told me I was an orphan.

As he told me I'm *alone*.

"You alright, Sunshine?" Kam's worried eyes cause

a pit to open up in my stomach that threatens to swallow me whole.

The metal rings squeak against the curtain rod as the nurse pokes his head around the fabric divider. His sunken eyes and dark circles don't keep the smile from his face as he says, "Are you ready for that X-ray, Miss Posey?"

Posey's eyes gleam with anticipation as the nurse maneuvers the wheelchair into the room. "Do I get to ride in that?"

The nurse's smile never strays from his face as he pulls the lever to engage the brake on the chair. "You sure do! You get to take a ride to radiology, where we're going to take pictures of the inside of your arm."

Posey's eyes grow impossibly wide as she eyes the nurse like he's a magician. "Will I get to see the pictures?"

His eyes flick to mine as he raises a brow. "If it's alright with your mom."

I clear my throat as my face heats. "Oh, uh, sister, actually." I nod my head as his brows crease. "And yes, she can look at the X-rays." I turn to Posey with a smile on my face. "Jasper will be so jealous when we tell him you got to look at pictures of the inside of your arm. We'll have to keep him from slipping on the ice on purpose just so he'll be able to do the same."

She rolls her eyes as she shakes her head. "If he knew how bad it hurt, he wouldn't want to. It's not worth the cool pictures."

I can't help but smile at the scrunch of her nose. "Make sure you tell him that when we get home." My legs are reluctant to straighten as I stand from my chair to plant a kiss on the top of her head. "You be good for the nurses, Ladybug."

She rolls her eyes again. *Lord help us when she turns sixteen.* "I'm *always* good, Lulu."

Kam nods next to me as he ruffles the hair on the top of her head. "Of course you are, Rosie Posey. When we get home, you can pick the movie we watch tonight since you've been so brave."

Her eyes grow even wider as she vibrates in her seat. "Even a princess movie?"

Kam's smile grows as he laughs. "Even a princess movie."

Her eyes turn to the nurse, who's just as excited as the eight-year-old in front of him. She clammers from the bed without a care for her likely broken arm. "Let's go! Let's go!"

The nurse's face turns white as he tries to slow her movements. "Alright! We'll go as long as you promise to be more careful with your arm."

She sticks out her good hand for a handshake as she says, "Deal!"

His brows raise as he gently shakes her hand. "How old are you again?"

Her voice blends with the squeak of the wheelchair as they leave the room. "I just turned eight last month. How old are you?"

Kam's smile fades from his face as his full attention falls on me. "What's wrong?" He holds up a finger to stop the words threatening to spill from my mouth. "And don't tell me it's *nothing.* I know you better than that."

The smile I force onto my face only adds to the

worry in his eyes. "Just reliving some bad memories." I blow out a breath as I try to dispel some of the hospital smell that I can't seem to escape. "Hopefully, we can get out of here soon."

The warmth of his skin seeps into my palm as he intertwines our fingers. "It's okay to visit the memories, just don't get lost in them, Sunshine." His eyes dart to the clock on the wall before returning to mine. "You should probably call Evelyn to let her know you won't be able to make the final meeting tonight. Maybe she'll be able to talk you through everything over the phone instead?"

My hands turn clammy. "Evelyn has been amazing. I really couldn't have asked for a better social worker, but do you think she'll take it well when I call and tell her Posey broke her arm after I already had to move the meeting to your house after our pipes burst?" A crease forms between my brows as I tighten my hand around his. "That *has* to look bad, right?"

His nonchalant shrug doesn't match the worry I still see in his eyes. "I really don't know. I would like to say the injury won't matter. That kids get hurt all the time, and it's not a big deal."

I nod as I blow out another useless breath. "But you can't."

His sad smile causes an ache to form in the center of my chest. "But I can't." His fingers find mine to offer the strength I need. "Call her. You'll feel better after you get it over with."

This time, my deep breath has nothing to do with the smell in the air, and everything to do with the need for more oxygen. "You're right."

His usual smile sliding back into place makes the ache in my chest lessen. "I usually am."

I roll my eyes as my smile forms. "Sometimes I forget you and Ellie are twins. Then you say something like that, and it's like I'm looking right at her."

His nose scrunches as his smile falls. "That's disturbing."

I nod as I laugh. "You're telling me."

He raises a brow as he pries my phone from my clenched fingers. "Quit stalling."

I struggle to swallow as my clammy hand takes my phone from his outstretched hand. My reflection stares back at me from the black screen. "What if she says I've screwed everything up? What if she says I'm—"

Kam's familiar hand covering my reflection halts my words. His eyes are overflowing with love as I try to calm my racing heart. "Then *we* will deal with it."

"We?"

His smile never wavers as he nods. "We."

I nod along with him as I wipe the moisture from my hands onto my pants. "Okay." My fingers shake and leave spots of moisture on the glass screen as I find her contact and hit dial.

My pulse pounds through my temples as every ring feels like it lasts an eternity. "Hello?"

"Hi, Evelyn. It's Lila."

CHAPTER 63
SO I CAN CATCH YOU

LILA

The fabric of my dress feels like sandpaper against my skin. I knew I should have picked the blue dress instead of the green, like Ellie suggested.

A hiss of air escapes the cushion under me as I sit at the table in the front of the courtroom. My baby hairs dance around my face as the overhead vent blows cool air over my heated skin.

Unfamiliar voices merge with the familiarity of my friends' murmurs behind me. People move through the room like it's just a regular day at the office and not the most important day of my life.

I guess for the court reporter and the bailiff who are chatting like they're old friends, it is. It's just another Tuesday for them. Another name on the docket that they'll never think about again.

My heart falls through my chest as the doors open in the back of the room. Only when my lawyer's red face comes into view do my shoulders relax an inch. His hurried steps thump against the grey carpet as he descends the aisle. "So sorry for my tardiness, Miss Sullivan. I had a few last-minute details to iron out."

The smell of butterscotch and caramel candy washes over me as he sits. "It's okay. What can I do? Do I need to do anything else before we get started?"

He shakes his head as his briefcase flips open with a click. "No. You've done everything you can, Miss Sullivan. I saw the twins in the hall with your friend. I believe she said her name is Ellie?"

I nod as a small smile touches my lips. "Yes, Ellie is a good friend of mine. The twins are having a good day. Our friend made their favorite breakfast foods this morning."

His smile mimics my own as he shuffles papers around on the table in front of him. "They sound like good friends."

"Yeah." Kam's gaze warms the back of my neck as I try to loosen the tension from my muscles. "They really are."

Mr. Porter's eyes flick behind me as his smile grows. "Ah, Mr. Stryker. It's so nice to meet you in person, at last."

I raise my brows as my eyes volley between my lawyer and my boyfriend. "At last?"

Kam's usual smirk blooms as he accepts the offered handshake. "We've gotten to know each other pretty well this past week. Mr. Porter is an excellent researcher."

Mr. Porter's cheeks turn even redder under Kam's compliment. "Oh, I wouldn't say that, Mr. Stryker. You did most of the heavy lifting."

Kam's smile grows as Dax, Wyatt, and Mace try to

hide their smiles next to him. "And what did I say about calling me Mr. Stryker?"

Mr. Porter's eyes fall to his feet as a bashful smile takes over his face. "Yes. Right. Of course, Kam."

The doors in the back of the room open to draw everyone's attention as my heart takes residence on the floor by my feet.

A man who looks like he belongs in a New York penthouse with a glass of scotch in his hand emerges through the door first. His dull eyes match the grey of the carpet under his immaculate shoes that I'm sure cost more than I make in a month.

Maxwell's jet-black suit makes him look like the angel of death as he stalks down the aisle right behind him. Victoria's hunched shoulders and tiny steps are in such stark contrast to her usual self that I hardly recognize her as she follows her husband like the obedient wife she is.

None of them glance our way as they settle into their seats without a word.

The bailiff's deep voice resonates through my bones as he says, "All rise. The Court is now in session. The honorable Judge Alexandra Harris, presiding."

The shuffling of chairs and fabric can't drown out the beat of my heart as it echoes through my ears.

Judge Harris's black robe billows behind her as she comes from a door I hadn't noticed at the front of the room. "Good morning, everyone." Her glasses slide smoothly into place on the tip of her nose as she settles into her seat. Her eyes move quickly over the papers in front of her. "Am I understanding correctly that Mr. and

Mrs. Abernathy wish to petition this Court for full custody of Jasper and Posey Sullivan?"

Mr. New York clears his throat before he stands. "Yes, Your Honor. We have filed the paperwork within the allotted time and wish to address this matter swiftly."

A chilling smile pulls at Judge Harris' lips as she sits the neat stack of papers on the table in front of her. "I can see that, Mister...?" She raises a brow as she waits for him to provide his name.

"Mr. Thorne, Your Honor."

Her brows dip as she tilts her head like a mother does when deciding how best to punish a disobedient child. "Well, *Mr. Thorne,* I intend to handle this matter with the utmost respect it deserves, *no matter how long it may take.* Wouldn't you agree Jasper and Posey deserve that common courtesy?"

His answering smile is reminiscent of a crocodile. "Of course, Your Honor."

"Now that we have come to that agreement, I would like to proceed." Her eyes fall to the papers in front of her once again before flicking at me. "Miss Sullivan. I have Mrs. Evelyn Jones' final recommendations in front of me. Most of her assessment, however, was given under the assumption that you were the only candidate for full custody." She raises a brow as her eyes flick to the table opposite me. "That has since changed. There-fore, today's proceeding will not be as swift as I had previously hoped. Luckily, the case scheduled directly after yours has been postponed, so we can take as long as we need today."

A headache blooms as my teeth threaten to crack under the pressure from my clenched jaw.

I hear Kam's words from early this morning, like he's whispering them in my ear. *When you feel you're about to fall, look back at me so I can catch you.*

My eyes flick behind me to be snared by the warmth of chocolate and the safety of home. His mouthed *I love you* kickstarts my heart back into proper rhythm.

So, I do the only thing I can do. I turn back around and slide my game face into place so I can face my greatest adversary.

Because I *will* be victorious.

CHAPTER 64
YOUR HONOR

LILA

Judge Harris clasps her hands on the desk in front of her as she focuses her full attention on my grandparents. "I would like to start by hearing why you want full custody, Mr. and Mrs. Abernathy." Mr. Thorne opens his mouth, but Judge Harris' stern look halts his words. "I would like to hear the Abernathy's own words, Mr. Thorne. Not yours."

He tries and fails to hide the scrunch of his nose as Maxwell clears his throat. "We do not believe Miss Sullivan has the *capabilities* to raise two young children, Your Honor."

Judge Harris quirks a brow as her eyes flick to me before returning to Maxwell. "And what is your evidence of this?"

"She told us herself she has no plans for paying for Posey's dance lessons after the first of the year, Your Honor. How can she fully support their education if she can't even send the poor girl to dance class?"

I nearly jump out of my seat as Mr. Porter shuffles

the papers in front of him. "Your Honor, if I may, I would like to present you with the receipts showing Posey's ballet lessons have been paid in full through the end of next year."

What the hell?

I try to hide the shock from my face as the Judge inclines her head at the bailiff next to her. His heavy footsteps mimic the beating of my heart as it tries to escape my chest as he takes the paper and hands it to the judge.

I didn't pay for her classes. Who would have done that? Who would think to—

My hair sways around my shoulders as I look behind me to find a smiling Kam. His wink nearly sends me flying from my chair again.

Judge Harris' voice has me turning back around to find a smile on her face. "It seems that will no longer be an issue, Mr. Abernathy. What are your other concerns?"

Maxwell straightens his suit jacket as he says, "Miss Sullivan also admitted to the lack of a plan for the twins' college education."

The Judge's raised brow nearly sends a laugh flying from my mouth. "You mean their college education that won't happen for another ten years?"

His approving nod contrasts with the look on the Judge's face. "Yes, Your Honor."

"Are you purposefully trying to waste my time, Mr. Abernathy, or do you have any probable cause as to why Miss Sullivan shouldn't take full custody today?"

Maxwell's smile slips firmly from his face as he stares at her in open mouthed shock. "I assure you,

Your Honor, that we are what is best for the children. Miss Sullivan is but a *child* herself. Someone so young cannot *possibly* take on that level of responsibility." He finally composes his face. "She is not even staying in her own home, Your Honor. Her home is currently unfit for living, let alone for children." A smug smile slips through the iron bars he so carefully constructed. "In fact, she has all but moved in with her boyfriend of only a few months. A child himself who has, on multiple occasions, been *left alone* with the children who are supposed to be in her care. That's not to mention his family history of DUIs and addiction, Your Honor."

Even from his profile, I can see the underlying gleam of victory in his eyes that sends a ball of lead to the bottom of my stomach.

Mr. Porter once again clears his throat next to me. "Your Honor, if I may, I would like to present Mr. Stryker's latest drug test and his college transcripts to the Court."

The loud squeak of a chair fills the room as Mr. Thorne stands from his seat. "Objection! Relevance, Your Honor."

Judge Harris' eyes never stray from Mr. Jones. "Overruled."

Mr. Porter clears his throat before beginning again. "I think you will find ample evidence of the difference between Mr. Stryker and his late father. You will also find multiple character witness letters discussing the fact that not a single person has ever witnessed Mr. Stryker taking even a single sip of alcohol." His eyes stray to Maxwell before returning to the Judge. "You will also find a quote from a local plumber that lays out the plan to make Miss Sullivan's home livable after the unexpected weather that burst the pipes in her bathroom this past weekend."

Judge Harris doesn't bother fighting her smile as she inclines her head to the bailiff once again.

Silence consumes the room, only to be broken by the rustling of paper as she flicks through the stack the bailiff hands her. She settles the paper in a neat stack in front of her before returning her attention to Maxwell. "I don't think anyone should be held liable for the actions of their parents. Wouldn't you agree, Mr. Abernathy?"

A sneer pulls at his lip as he straightens in his seat. "Do you really want to trust the safety of those children to someone who makes such poor decisions, Your Honor? She's just like her mother! Jumping into bed with Mr. Stryker after knowing him for hardly a few months!"

Judge Harris also straightens in her seat. "I've yet to see ample evidence for any poor decision making on Miss Sullivan's part." She raises a brow as she tilts her head. "Unless you've yet to introduce all your findings to this Court?"

Mr. Thorne shuffles the papers in front of him as he says, "If I may, Your Honor, we would like to present character witnesses of our own."

I struggle to swallow as Maxwell's eyes connect with mine for the first time. What I see in them causes my hands to shake, and sweat to bead on my brow. Because what I'm looking at, as I stare into his eyes, is a man filled with pure desperation.

And sometimes, desperation is even more terrifying than determination.

The Judge inclines her head at the bailiff once again as I try to think of who they could have talked to. Her brows furrow as she flips through the papers he hands her. "When you said 'character witness', I assumed you meant someone who would validate *your* client's character, Mr. Thorne. All I see here are first-hand accounts of interactions with Miss Sullivan and Mr. Stryker."

My heart practically stops beating in my chest as the four men shift in their seats behind me.

Mr. Thorne dips his head in an apology I'm sure he doesn't mean as he says, "So sorry for my lack of explanation, Your Honor. Those detailed accounts clearly lay out a lack of maturity and decorum. Mr. Stryker clearly has a history of plotting against his peers. His schemes have resulted in physical injury, Your Honor. And Miss Sullivan clearly has a history of physical abandonment and altercations of her own."

Heat creeps up my neck as I struggle to catch my breath.

The breath Judge Harris lets out is full of exacerbation. "Do you know Colt Ramsey, Kim Adams, or Emma Johnson, Miss Sullivan?"

I wipe the accumulating moisture from my palms on the fabric of my dress as I struggle to find words. "Y-Yes, Your Honor." I swallow thickly. "Colt plays on the SSU hockey team with Kam. Kim is one of my co-workers, and Emma is Posey's ballet teacher."

Her eyes continue to scan the papers as she says, "What reason would Mr. Ramsey have for accusing Mr.

Stryker of assault, Miss Sullivan? It says here there was a show of unnecessary force that resulted in long-lasting injury." I open my mouth to say something, anything, but she continues before I get the chance. "*And* what reason would Miss Adams might have for accusing *you* of assault, Miss Sullivan? It says here there was an altercation that happened at your place of work. And why would Miss Johnson accuse you of neglect? She says the twins were often left in her care and in the care of her staffers outside of Posey's scheduled classes."

Am I going to lose this case?

I shake my head as her expectant eyes lift to me. "I, uh, I'm not sure, Your Honor." My tongue sticks to the roof of my mouth. "I've never assaulted anyone. It is not in my nature to be physically violent with someone. And I paid the receptionist at the ballet studio to watch Jasper while Posey was in class."

Her eyes fill with sympathy as she lays the papers on the desk. "Be that as it may, I have to take these accusations seriously, Miss Sullivan." Her accusatory eyes flick to Mr. Thorne. "Even though they are *not* signed affidavits. They are still very serious accusations."

I nod as my shoulders deflate. "I understand."

Soft murmurs accompany the sound of shifting bodies behind me as I try to keep my shit together. I've never been a violent person, but I know if I were to look over and see Maxwell's smug look, there's a very good chance I would punch the smugness right off his face.

Judge Harris adjusts her glasses as she says, "If there is no further evidence to be presented to this Court, I would like to invite Jasper and Posey to join us."

Mr. Thorne's chair creaks under him as he straightens. "Is that truly necessary, Your Honor? There's no need to bring those children in here for this. They're far too young to fully understand."

Her eyes turn cold as she levels Mr. Thorne with a glare I do not envy. "You will do well to realize the entire reason we are here is for *those* children, Mr. Thorne. Their opinions and wants mean more than anyone else's. After all, the decisions made in this room today will affect them for the rest of their lives. These decisions will shape their futures. That is not a responsibility I take lightly, Mr. Thorne. And neither should you." She inclines her head to the bailiff once again. "Bring them in."

CHAPTER 65
I PROMISE
LILA

The weight of my mom's watch on my wrist doubles with every step taken by Jasper and Posey down the aisle. Their frantic eyes flick between me, Kam, and our friends as Posey's neon pink cast shines brightly under the fluorescent lights. Ellie's hardened eyes stay locked on the back of Maxwell's head as she takes her seat next to her brother.

Whispered words from the other end of the room sends a chill down my spine before Mr. Thorne says, "Why were my clients not alerted to the fresh injury?"

Judge Harris' face flashes with annoyance as she says, "Miss Sullivan was under no legal requirement to report Posey's injury to your clients, Mr. Thorne."

His flawless skin turns a bright shade of red as he fumes in his seat. "It might not have been a legal requirement, but it is common courtesy, Your Honor. We need no further evidence of Miss Sullivan's lack of capabilities here, Your Honor. The children are obviously not safe in her care."

"Common courtesy holds no weight on our case today, Mr. Thorne. And since this is the first injury either child has suffered in the six months they have been in Miss Sullivan's care, it is not concerning." Softness takes over Judge Harris' face that's only fitting for someone who loves a child of her own. I'm not sure if she's a mother, an aunt, a bonus mom, or what, but she knows the love of a child. "I'm so happy you're here, Jasper and Posey." They settle into the two seats placed in the middle of the room, pointed toward the judge. I don't miss the irony of the placement. "I'm just going to ask you a few questions, then I'm going to ask if you have anything else you want to say. It is very important that you tell the truth here today, even if the truth might hurt someone's feelings. Does that sound good?" Posey's pigtails bounce as they nod. "First, I want to ask how your school year is going?"

Posey's voice shakes as she says, "It's been good. We like our teacher. She smells really nice." The waver in her voice falls away as Jasper clenches her hand in his. "Math has been really hard, but Dax helps with our homework."

Judge Harris' brows raise as her eyes flick to me before falling back on my brother and sister. "Oh? Who's Dax?"

Posey's smile beams in full force as she looks over her shoulder and points to where Dax sits behind me. "He's over there with my other friends." Her eyes move along the line of our friends behind me as she introduces them one by one. "That's Mace. He's a really good cook. And that's Wyatt, we love him even though he's grumpy sometimes. And Ellie is Kam's twin, just like I'm Jasper's twin." Her smile never falls as she looks back at the judge. "Dax likes to make people think he's not very smart, but I know it's not true. I want to be a teacher when I grow up. That's what Dax wants to be when he grows up, too."

Judge Harris nods along with Posey's words before turning to Jasper. "What about you, Jasper? What do you want to be when you grow up?"

It's his turn to look at our friends sitting behind me with a beaming smile on his face. "I want to play hockey like Kam." His eyes stay bright as he turns back to the judge. "But it's important to have a backup plan in case I get hurt or I don't like it anymore."

A small smile pulls at Judge Harris' lips. "And what is your backup plan?"

Jasper's shrug moves their clasped hands up and down. "I don't know yet. Kam said I don't have to know right now."

The judge's smile grows as she nods. "That's right. It's okay if you don't know." She tilts her head as she says, "If you could plan your perfect day, what would it look like?"

"Ummm." His eyes scrunch as he tilts his head in thought. "Mace would fix us breakfast. Probably scrambled eggs and chocolate pancakes. Then we would get to play outside on the swing set our friends got us for our birthday. We could build a sandcastle with Lulu and Ellie at the beach. Oh! Then we can go play in the water, but not alone. It's not safe for us to be alone in the water." He tilts his head even further to the side. "Do you know what a rip current is?"

Judge Harris nods as she laughs. "Yes, Jasper. I know what a rip current is."

His smile brightens as he straightens in his seat. "Good! They're dangerous. That's why you shouldn't swim alone."

Mr. Thorne's voice makes Posey jump as it booms through the space. "Objection, Your Honor! Narrative! The Court does not need to know about rip currents and playing on the beach!"

Jasper's hand tightens around Posey's as I fight to stay in my seat. His whispered words flow through the space as easily as if he yelled them. "It's okay, Posey. Lulu and Kam won't let them hurt us."

Judge Harris' eyes turn to steel as she levels a glare at Mr. Thorne. "Overruled. And do not use that tone in my courtroom again, Mr. Thorne." She leans forward with her elbows on the desk in front of her. "What else would you do during your perfect day?"

He tilts his head side to side. "Probably go home and watch a movie." He laughs as he shakes his head. "I would be the one to pick the movie instead of one of the girls. They always pick the sad movies." He raises a finger before he says, "We can only start the movie after Posey beats Dax at their racing game, though. And Mace will fix us dinner before we go home. He always fixes something extra for Posey to eat, since she's so picky. She's gotten a lot better about that, though. She even ate a pea yesterday! It was only one, but Lulu said it was a good start."

Judge Harris' attention falls on Posey. "What about you, Posey? What would be your perfect day?"

Posey's feet swing inches off the ground as she says,

"I wouldn't change anything that Jas said except the movie part. Kam let me pick the movie when I got pictures taken of the inside of my arm." Her beaming smile turns on her brother. "Everyone but *you* loved the princess movie. Even Wyatt teared up at the end."

Judge Harris inclines her head toward the neon pink cast on Posey's arm that I'm pretty sure could be seen from space. "What happened to your arm, Posey?"

I know the judge knows the answer. She has a copy of the hospital report on her desk.

Posey waves the cast around in front of her face. "Oh, I just fell on some ice yesterday. Kam told me not to run on it, and I didn't listen."

Judge Harris sits up farther in her seat to get a better view of the monstrosity. "What are all those markings on your cast?"

Posey bends her arm in unnatural positions as she examines the Sharpie marks. "All my friends wrote me notes so I would have them with me until I get the cast off in six weeks." Her brows crease as she reads the notes off. "Kam's note says, 'Get well soon, Rosie Posey.' And Dax's note says for me to get better soon so he can beat me at our racing game." Her eyes lift as she smiles. "It's funny he thinks he can beat me." Her eyes venture back down to the cast on her arm as she reads off the names and notes of all the people who love her.

Judge Harris' brows crease as Posey finishes. "Your grandparents didn't sign your cast?"

Mr. Thorne's mouth twists into a sneer as he says, "Objection, Your Honor! Relevance."

Posey shakes her head like she didn't even hear him

as she lays her injured arm in her lap. "No. Why would they?"

The judge's eyes flash with something I can't quite make out before she once turns to Mr. Throne. "Overruled, Mr. Thorne." Her eyes soften as they fall on the twins in front of her. "You both have done very well. Is there anything else I should know before you leave?"

Posey shakes her head, but shock flows through me as Jasper raises his hand like he's at school. "Can I say something?"

Surprise flashes across the judge's face before she can conceal it. "Yes, of course, Jasper."

He swallows thickly before looking down at his hand clasped tightly in his sister's. "I don't think I like Grandma and Grandpa."

Judge Harris' eyes flick to my grandparents, whose seats squeak with their sudden movements. She turns back to Jasper. "And why don't you like them, Jasper?"

His voice is timid as he says, "They say mean things about Lulu. They say she's not ready to be what we need. That she's not strong enough." A hard edge replaces the timidness in his voice. "That makes me mad. How can they know what we need when they don't even know what my favorite color is? How do they know what's best for us when they don't know how to calm Posey down after she has a nightmare? They don't even know that Posey doesn't like the crust on her PB&J." His eyes flash as he says, "They want me to take grandpa's place at his job when he retires, but I really want to play hockey. Kam said it's okay for me to say if I don't like someone, as long as I'm still nice to them." He sits up straighter in his seat. "I've never not been nice to them, *I promise.*"

They want me to take grandpa's place at his job when he retires.

My eyes flash to Maxwell in time to watch his jaw clench.

The judge grinds her teeth as she nods her head. "Thank you for being so brave. Kam is right. It's important to say when we don't like someone." Her eyes harden as they fall on the adults that act more like children. "But that doesn't give us permission to be mean to them or force them into something for the sake of legacy." The softness returns to her eyes as they land on me. "I've heard all I need to hear. I'm ready to make my decision."

CHAPTER 66
HOME
LILA

"I am awarding full custody of Posey and Jasper Sullivan to their sister, Lila Sullivan. Effective immediately." Her warm eyes flick to mine. "It looks like you found your village, Miss Sullivan."

My heart stalls in my chest as Maxwell's chair clatters against the floor. "You can't do this! We have ample evidence why that *child* should not have custody of those kids!"

Despite my heart being firmly lodged in my throat, my legs carry me swiftly to my wide-eyed siblings. Not even seconds later, a solid wall of muscle acts as a barrier between me and my grandparents. Ellie practically vibrates with rage next to me as she seethes under her breath. "Karma's a bitch, isn't it, old man?"

Mr. Thorne's face turns a ghostly shade of white as he backs away slowly from the scene developing in front of him like he's cornered by a wild animal instead of a grown ass man.

"Mr. Abernathy! You will exit this Court with

dignity before I find you in contempt." The judge's clenched teeth and stern palm halt the words threatening to spill from his mouth. "Yes, that's right. You think I didn't notice the slanderous letters regarding Mr. Stryker's and Miss Sullivan's character were not signed affidavits? I can't help but wonder why that is, Mr. Thorne." The bailiff's eyes flash with worry as he aligns himself between the judge and the table on the other side of the room. "The next time you find yourself in a courtroom, you would do well not to insult the judge's intelligence, Mr. Abernathy." A tilt of her head is all that's required to stop his coming words. "And yes, I believe there will be a next time, but not on this matter. You seem to be well acquainted with the Court of Law."

"But—But—"

How the judge doesn't roll her eyes, I'll never know. "Stammering is not befitting of a man of *your* stature, Mr. Abernathy." A smile touches the corner of her lips as she glances at me. "Court is adjourned."

"All rise."

Since I can't rise any more than I already am, I incline my head and return her smile as she disappears into her chambers.

Maxwell's face turns a bright shade of red as he backs away from the bailiff like a small child would his mother. "You can't do this to me! I have connections! Powerful connections!"

The placating tone of the bailiff's voice brings a smile to my face. "I'm sure you do, Mr. Abernathy. If you would please allow me to escort you to your car, we could all get on with our day."

Victoria's voice filters through the room for the first time as she lodges her handbag firmly on her shoulder. "Oh, for heaven's sake, Maxwell. Give it a rest already. I told you we didn't have a case. Can't you see you're only making a fool of yourself?"

Dax's shoulders shake from barely contained laughter in front of me as I watch through the gap of his arm and Kam's.

Maxwell's nostrils flare as he wags a finger in Victoria's face. "Do not talk back to *me*, woman!"

She rolls her eyes at her unhinged husband as she turns to leave. "I'll be in the car. Don't you *dare* make me late for my hair appointment, Maxwell. I won't have Alexander waiting for me. He's booked out for months." Her eyes flash to mine before she dips her head. "Goodbye, Lila."

The gap in the guy's arms closes, cutting off my view, as Maxwell's eyes blaze with a storm of fire. "Don't you walk away from me when I'm talking to you! *I* am the man of *this* house, and *you* will listen to *me*." His words fade as he storms after his wife, who is clearly unaffected by his behavior.

Dax whistles as he stuffs his hands in his pockets. "If they'll act like that in public, I'd hate to see how they act at home."

As the door slams closed behind Maxwell, the bailiff lets out an exhausted breath and drags his feet all the way to the door leading to the judge's chambers. He disappears without another word.

My dress bounces around my waist as Jasper pulls on the hem. "How'd we do, Lulu?"

I smile as I pull them both into a crushing hug. "You both did great! You were so brave."

His brows crease as he pulls away from my hug. "You're not mad?"

"Why would I be mad?"

He shrugs as he looks down at his feet. "I didn't want to tell you about the mean things they said. I knew it would make you sad."

My finger under his chin brings his eyes back to mine. "You did the right thing, Jas. I couldn't be more proud of you."

Mace saves me from having to explain the tears threatening to spill from my eyes as he says, "Who's ready for some homemade ice cream?"

A chorus of children and deep voices alike all say, "Me!"

Their laughter follows them all the way through the door as silent tears fall down my face. Warm, secure arms band around my waist as I cry. His deep voice, now as familiar as my own, rumbles through me as I lay my head back on his shoulder. "Are those happy tears?"

My smile is watery as I nod. "Yeah. They're happy tears."

I can feel his smile against the top of my head as his tender kiss melts into my very soul. "I figured. There aren't any clouds in your eyes."

His chocolate eyes snare mine as I look over my shoulder with a smile on my face. "When did you have time to pay for Posey's ballet and take that drug test?"

A blush creeps over his cheeks as he shrugs. "You make time for the people you love."

A fresh wave of tears threatens to spill down my cheeks. "Take me home, Trouble."

His smile mimics mine as he looks down at me with such love it takes my breath. "You are my home, Sunshine."

"And you are mine."

LILA'S JOURNAL

Hi, Mom
We're going to be okay.
Love always,
Lila

EPILOGUE

KAM

I hold up my pointer finger to start the countdown. Posey's eyes bulge as the hand over her mouth struggles to contain her laughter that's begging to burst free.

Jasper's sock covered feet bounce up and down on the hardwood floors as I hold up a second finger. He bites his lip to contain the smile that's threatening to take over his face.

I release my third finger, and we descend on the bed like a litter of kittens pouncing on a new toy.

Posey's giggles float through the room like bubbles in the summer wind. Her hair flies around her face as she bounces along the edge of the bed. "Wake up, Lulu! Wake up! We need to open our presents!"

Jasper's knees sink into the plush mattress as Lila's eyes fly open with a look of surprise I wish I could capture a picture of. Her soft yip of shock is lost beneath Jasper's laugh as he says, "Wake up! It's Christmas! It's time to open presents!"

I roll my lips to contain my smile as her ice queen

eyes flash to mine. The ice melts in record speed as a splitting smile takes over her face. "Just remember, you started it!"

Her arms appear out from under the blanket with a foam dart gun at the ready. Villainess laughter fills the room as she balances on the shaky mattress.

With her tousled curls barely missing the ceiling fan, she cocks the gun with a grin. "Run."

Limbs tangle together in an unrecognizable mass as the twins scramble from the bed like their lives depend on it. Their squeals and giggles chase them from the room as their socks struggle to find traction on the hardwood floors.

Lila's quirked brow brings an even bigger smile to my face. "Why aren't *you* running, Trouble?"

Her eyes flash as I reveal the matching weapon I've had stored behind my back since I walked into the room. "You've finally met your match, Sunshine."

Her smile turns sinister as the sound of my gun cocking ricochets through the room. "We'll see about that."

An assortment of torn wrapping paper and foam darts litter the ground around the small circle of four we've formed in the middle of the living room floor.

Posey's eyes brighten as she vibrates on the floor next to me. "Open mine next!"

The bright pink wrapping paper crinkles under my

calloused hands as I admire the package she hands me. "You got me a present, Rosie Posey?"

Her pigtails sway on her head as she nods. "Lulu let us each pick out a gift for you."

The lightweight box is surprising compared to its size. The contents of the nearly foot long square box feel solid and unmovable as I gently shake the gift.

Posey rolls her eyes as she watches me. "You're not going to guess what it is, so you might as well just open it."

From the corner of my eye, Lila rolls her lips with barely contained laughter as she sips her hot chocolate.

My heart hurts as I tear through the wrapping paper. The matching pink bow, however, goes straight in the pocket of my pajama pants. My brows furrow as the side of the box comes into view. The image of a golden crown with various gemstones sits proudly on the head of a little boy around the twins' age. I rotate the box in my hands until all the words come into view. The words, *Little Playhouse King Dress Up Crown*, sit proudly in the middle of the box in bright red script. I can't keep the wonder from my voice as I say, "You got me my own crown?"

She nods as she rocks on the balls of her feet. "I thought it was time for you to get your own crown for when you play with me."

Her soft strawberry scent surrounds me as I pull her into a hug. "Thank you, Rosie Posey. I love it."

"My turn!" Hockey sticks litter the wrapping paper of the small box Jasper forces into my hands. "You're going to love it!"

The object inside moves from side to side as I shake

the box. The inch thick box isn't any larger than a small envelope as I carefully tear through the paper, but not before I secured the black bow in my pocket where it belongs. Four slips of paper greet me as I open the box. I can't keep the awe from my voice as I look up at his smiling face. "You got me tickets to see The Penguins?"

His nod sends a few loose hairs down onto his forehead. "I wanted four tickets so we could all go. I knew you wouldn't want to go without us."

Tears line my eyes as I pull him into a hug. I see my own tears reflected in Lila's eyes as I make eye contact with her over Jasper's head. "Thank you, Tank."

The rattling of the doorknob steals his attention as our friends' bustling voices melt with the squeal of the front door.

I wipe a stray tear from the corner of my eye as Dax says, "Ahhh, you guys started opening presents without me?"

I can hear Ellie's eyes roll as their footsteps grow closer. "That's alright, Dax. We're the ones with all the food. We control who eats or not."

Mace's scoff brings a watery smile to my face. "There is no *we*, Ellie. *I'm* the one with the food."

Wyatt's exacerbated breath is almost lost as the sound of glass containers meeting the counter fills the space. "Don't bicker, *kids*. It's Christmas."

Our friends and the twins' voices fade as my eyes meet Lila's.

The sunshine in her eyes is in such contrast to the clouds I saw the day we first met, it nearly takes my breath. "Don't worry about the cost of the tickets. Wyatt knows a guy."

The worry fades from my face. "Of course he does."

Her soft voice flows over me like a warm summer breeze. "Are you ready for me to give you *my* gift?"

"I don't know how you could give me anything else. I already have everything I could ever want."

Her smile never wavers as she hands me a box neatly wrapped with a butter yellow paper. I raise my brows as I gently shake the impossibly lightweight gift. "No bow?"

Her answering shrug makes my smile grow as I carefully tear through the meticulously wrapped package. My heart stalls in my chest as a neatly tied white ribbon comes into view in the middle of the box. The strands of ribbon obscure the black ink on the paper just below it.

Her voice is shaky from the tears rimming her eyes as she says, "I wore that bow the first day we met."

My fingers caress the bow with reverence as a fresh tear falls down my cheek. "I've always had a thing for bows."

Her tears mix with mine as she laughs. "Yeah. I know." Her eyes fall to her feet as she shakes her head. "It's not anything expensive, or extravagant, but it felt right."

A blush creeps across her cheeks as I pull the lone paper from the bottom of the box. My eyebrows raise as I read through the printed email. "Sunshine…"

She bites her bottom lip as she fights her smile. "I've been keeping a secret." She swallows before the words spill from her like a geyser. "It's just an entry level position, and it doesn't pay the best right now." Her nose scrunches as she continues, "Especially since I don't have any clients of my own, but I'm really excited and terrified. I just hope I can—"

My lips against hers stop her words. I smile against her lips as her hurried breaths flow over my skin. "You already have a client." Her nose brushes mine as she shakes her head. "Yes. You do. I wouldn't have anyone else as my agent."

"But I'm not good yet. I still have so much to learn."

Her fingers feel so right against mine as I intertwine our fingers. "Sounds like the perfect setup, then."

The tension falls from her shoulders as she playfully rolls her eyes. "You shouldn't trust a newbie with your career."

"Who else would I trust?" I laugh as I use our intertwined hands to draw her to me. "I didn't have time to wrap your gift."

A smile touches her lips as she settles in my lap, right where she belongs. "You're changing the subject." She lists a brow. "And I thought my fuzzy socks were my gift?"

I shift her in my lap to gain better access to the pocket I've not been stuffing full of bows all morning. "Nah. That was your pre-gift." The small fabric bag is warm against my skin from how long it's been in my pocket. "I want you to wear this when you feel the clouds creeping back in."

Her eyes follow my movements as I pull on the drawstring and tip the bag so its contents spill out onto the palm of my hand. She sucks in a quick breath as the golden sun pendant comes fully into view.

Her quiet sniffling nearly brings me to my knees as she runs her index finger over the metal of the necklace.

"It's so beautiful." Her smile grows as she looks up at me with watery eyes. "Will you put it on me?"

I nod as I weave my fingers in the hair at the nape of her neck. The sparkling lights from the Christmas Tree beside us dance across her face as a single tear falls down her cheek.

I inhale her relieved breath as her lips mold to mine in a now-familiar dance. She breathes softly against my lips as she breaks the kiss to lean her forehead against mine. "I love you, Trouble."

"And I love you, Sunshine. Always."

ACKNOWLEDGMENTS

I never thought I would be here...writing the acknowledgements for my second novel. I released my debut, Bella Rosa, in March of 2022. I had every intention of continuing on with Julie's story and making Bella Rosa the first book in a series. I never counted on a years-long journey that ultimately lead to a fibromyalgia diagnosis.

Those were some of the hardest years of my life. Dealing with pain so severe I couldn't get up off the couch absolutely killed any and all creativity. I felt trapped and betrayed by my own body. I didn't mean for this to turn into a sob story, I swear. I just wanted to give a little hope to those of you reading this who find yourself in a similar situation, or to those of you who have a loved one dealing with a chronic illness.

Here comes the fun part! The part where the sadness fades away into a deep sense of fulfillment and pride in how far I've come. The part where I can say I've kicked fibromyalgia's ass! I still struggle everyday, don't get me wrong. Some days I don't know if I'll be able to walk down the stairs, but I can finally say—I did it. I wrote another book. I wrote a book I am so proud to call mine. A book that I wrote for no one but me. A book that I am—with tear filled eyes—giving to you. Take care of Kam and Lila for me.

A book that wouldn't have happened without my amazing husband who never gave up on my dream of writing a second book. Thank you, my love, for showing me the truest example of love. I hope each time you read Cloudless you find another hidden gem that tells our story.

A book that wouldn't have been what it is without the love and support of my parents. Thank you both for giving me the inspiration for Lila's parents. I hope you can feel the love I have for you through her.

A book that wouldn't be nearly as polished without my amazing friends and Beta readers. Thank you Lorissa (who is also my cover designer!) and January! I can always count on your unhinged comments and never-ending support.

And finally, thank *you* for reading! I hope you find as much comfort within these pages (digital or physical) as I do.

Love,
♡Katie

ABOUT THE AUTHOR

Katie B. Wright is a contemporary romance author who loves writing emotional, unique love stories. When she's not writing, she loves checking off books from her mile long TBR list, gaming, and spending time with her husband.

Visit KatieBWright.com to learn more about upcoming releases and to subscribe to Katie's newsletter! You can find Katie @KatieBWrightAuthor on her socials!